Caro Fraser was educated in Glasgow and the Isle of Man, before attending Watford School of Art and London University, King's College, where she studied law. She was called to the Bar of Middle Temple in 1979. After leaving Art School, Caro Fraser worked for three years as an advertising copywriter. She then studied law, and read for the Bar, after which she spent six months in pupillage. Before turning to writing, Caro Fraser worked as a shipping lawyer. She is married to a solicitor and has four children.

An Inheritance

CARO FRASER

PHŒNIX

A PHOENIX PAPERBACK

First published in Great Britain by Orion in 1996
This paperback edition published in 1997 by Phoenix,
a division of Orion Books Ltd,
Orion House, 5 Upper St Martin's Lane,
London WC2H 9EA

A CIP catalogue record for this book is available
from the British Library

ISBN: 1 85799 964 9

Typeset at The Spartan Press Ltd,
Lymington, Hants

Printed and bound in Great Britain by
The Guernsey Press Co. Ltd,
Guernsey, Channel Islands

Chapter One

Cicely Patrick sat at the polished oval table in the little dining room and stared at the yellow leaves drifting from the trees on to the lawn of Plumtree Villa. This letter really was the most difficult she had ever had to write. She sighed and looked back at the pad of Basildon Bond, lifted her pen and hesitated. Where did one start, for heaven's sake? He must know who Orlando was, she supposed – she hoped. One could hardly begin, *'Dear Sir Leonard, I am writing in connection with Orlando, your late son's illegitimate son, your grandson, whom you have never met, but whose existence I trust you recall.'* Then again, what if Sir Leonard D'Ewes were to open the letter, and have no idea who Cicely was talking about, or even who Cicely was, for that matter?

She put down her pen and sat back, staring again at the dull October sky. This letter, the necessity of turning to Orlando's grandparents for help after so many years, brought to her mind events which she had not dwelt on for a long time. She was forty-six now, but when her nephew Orlando was born, she had been just thirty-four, her sister Abigail thirty-one. Where had her life gone? At least Abigail had always had her teaching job. It struck Cicely that her own life had been an unfair series of stops and starts, of unfulfilled hopes. A progression of deaths and accidents seemed to have resigned her to a lifetime of looking after other people's children. And because of that, she had never had her own. Never had the chance. The chance was long gone, now.

It had started with her half-sisters, Melissa and Anne. Cicely and Abigail had been just children when their mother died, but when their father remarried and produced two more daughters, they had not minded. They liked their stepmother, and were fond of their baby half-sisters, who were a good fifteen years younger than they. But when their father and stepmother had died in an unfortunate road accident near the Potter's Bar interchange, leaving Melissa and Anne orphaned, life had changed dramatically. She had been twenty-three then, settling into a promising career in nursing, and Abigail had just finished teacher training college. She could not now remember how or why it had been decided that Abigail should carry on with her career, while Cicely should give up nursing to look after Melissa and Anne, but that had been the decision. Something to do with the awkwardness of nursing shifts. Anyway, someone had to do it. She had suddenly been burdened with all the responsibilities of mothering two budding adolescents, and that had put paid to the next ten years of her life.

They had been tiring, uninteresting years; a round of domestic chores, school fees, homework, exams, buying the girls clothes, arguing with them over boyfriends and bedtimes. She had spent her entire twenties preparing them for lives of their own, for freedom and possibilities which she herself had lost. But at least, when all that was over, when Melissa was off living in London and Anne was on the brink of going off to art school, she might still have had her chances. She had been planning to return to nursing, she remembered. At thirty-two, she had been confident of her own marriageability. There had been doctors – even consultants – out there, after all. It was easy to laugh at oneself now, she reflected, but it had been all she had ever wanted. The comfort and respectability of a home and husband of one's own.

She closed her eyes. From the kitchen she could hear Abigail clattering the cups and saucers. She would bring in tea in a moment. It had been a Sunday teatime, just like this one, when

Melissa had told them she was pregnant. Cicely opened her eyes and sighed. Poor Melissa. Poor lovely Melissa, with her long dark hair and her pretty face and her complete lack of brains. She had been so in love with Alec D'Ewes, had had such hopes of him. She had even dropped out of college to go and live with him in that commune in Chelsea, all those pathetic weirdos deluding themselves that they were artists, or musicians. Not that Cicely and Abigail had ever thought him anything but an idle layabout, albeit a wealthy and well-connected one. If he had lived, perhaps he would have married Melissa, and Orlando would have had parents, and Cicely's life would have been entirely different. But Alec had not lived. One summer's evening he had gone to a party, with Melissa on the pillion of his Harley Davidson, and at the party he had drunk a good deal and smoked – or partaken of – three joints of cannabis. So they learned later. Then he had had an argument with Melissa and stormed out of the house, leaving his crash helmet behind him, and had met his end on the M40. Thank you, Alec, for all that you left behind.

She looked up as Abigail came in with the tea tray, nudging the door open with her foot. She was wearing old trainers, Cicely noticed, a baggy denim skirt, and a maroon cardigan over a 'Save The Whale' T-shirt. The cardigan had a lump at the back where it had been hanging on a peg behind the kitchen door. Abigail was thin and angular, and someone had once told her that she looked like Vanessa Bell, so that she wore her untidy brown hair pinned up in a loose coil, which was forever shedding hairpins. Cicely, on the other hand, had a ripe fullness to her figure, and strong, comely features. Her hair, which was washed and set every Wednesday at the hairdresser's in Reigate, was dark and soft, if rather vigorously waved. While Cicely was attractive in an imposing way, Abigail affected a kind of defiant dowdiness, as if in deliberate opposition to her sister. Indeed, their lives seemed beset by a

3

kind of constant mutual friction, from which a balance of sorts had evolved. To Abigail, with the cares of her teaching job at a local girls' school, it seemed that Cicely led a cosy life of few real responsibilities. Cicely, on the other hand, envied her sister the dignity of being the breadwinner, in contrast to her own seemingly inferior domestic role. Each had become convinced, over the years, that the other had the best of the bargain, and they co-existed in a state of grudging antagonism, but mutual respect.

Abigail set down the tea tray on the table. 'Haven't you finished that thing yet?' she asked. 'You've been at it for over half an hour. How far have you got?'

'Nowhere,' sighed Cicely. 'I don't know where to begin. I don't even know how to address him. I mean, does one say, "Dear Lord D'Ewes", or "Dear Sir Leonard"?'

'How should I know?' said Abigail. 'I don't even see the point of writing to him. Why you should want to go cap in hand to that family after all these years is beyond me. Really it is.' She lifted the teapot in its hand-crocheted tea cosy and began to pour, using a little mesh tea strainer. Outside the grey sky was darkening and a spatter of chilly rain tapped at the windows.

'You know why,' replied Cicely, taking her cup and saucer from her sister and pushing the pad of writing paper aside. It irritated her that Abigail obtusely refused to acknowledge that a critical juncture had been reached in Orlando's career. Their slender resources, which consisted of the dwindling estate of their late father and Abigail's modest salary, had been stretched to pay for Orlando's prep school fees over the years, but now he was nearly twelve, and Cicely knew that, no matter what domestic sacrifices they might make, they could not afford the fees of Charterhouse or Winchester, and any inferior academic regime was, to Cicely's mind, unthinkable. She sipped thoughtfully at her tea, her mind running again over possible openings to her letter.

4

'Besides,' went on Abigail, taking a mouthful of scone and trying to wipe butter and crumbs from the edge of the copy of the *Radio Times* which she had picked up, 'the D'Ewes have never paid the slightest bit of attention to him, not from the day he was born. I don't see why you imagine they will now.'

'It was different then,' replied Cicely. 'If you remember, I suggested to Melissa when Orlando was born that Alec's family might want to take an interest in him, but she refused to have anything to do with them.'

'Well, no wonder, after the things that friend of Alec's told her that Sir Leonard D'Ewes had said – suggesting that Melissa would be coming after them for money, and that Orlando might not be Alec's son, and so on. Anyway, as I recall, the hostility was fairly mutual. They blamed Melissa for everything their silly son did, from dropping out of Oxford to getting himself killed on his motorbike. And they weren't exactly forthcoming with offers of help when Melissa died.'

'I often wonder,' said Cicely reflectively, setting down her cup and saucer, 'whether they knew about that at the time. I'm sure they would have done something. After all, their own grandson, an orphan . . .'

'Nonsense,' said Abigail briskly, getting up to draw the curtains. 'Melissa has been dead for four years now, and don't try to credit them with ignorance of the fact. That friend of Alec's came to the funeral, remember? Of course they knew. They just couldn't care less. Which is why it's a waste of time writing to them now. You'll only humiliate yourself.' She poured herself another cup of tea and settled back into a chair with her copy of the *Radio Times*.

'I have no intention of humiliating myself,' retorted Cicely. 'What we have to do is appeal to the man's better nature, if he has one. To his sense of decency.'

'Waste of time.'

Inspiration suddenly struck Cicely. 'I know – I won't write to Sir Leonard. I'll write to his wife instead. Suggest that she might like to see Orlando after all this time . . . Unless she's entirely flint-hearted, she'll want to do that. Alec was their only child, after all, and Orlando is his son.'

'If she wanted to see him, I imagine she'd have made the attempt by now. Do you want that last scone?'

'Oh, take it,' replied Cicely irritably. 'I really do think you might be a bit more positive about this. Orlando's future is at stake.'

'Just being realistic.'

'Anyway,' said Cicely, drawing the writing pad towards her and picking up her pen once more, 'that is what I shall do. A carefully worded letter . . . She's bound to show it to her husband. That's the best approach – nothing too obvious. It's worth a shot.'

'Then fire away, by all means,' said Abigail, and ate the remaining scone.

Stow Stocksley Hall, the ancestral seat of the D'Ewes family, lay in the leafy heart of Hampshire, some three miles from Winchester, set in several acres of parkland and surrounded by the farms, farmland and village forming the estate of Stow Stocksley. The Hall itself dated from Tudor times, with later handsome additions by Inigo Jones, and it was there, in the late nineteenth century, that the botanist Henry Trimen had established the famous Stow Stocksley hothouses. The D'Ewes family traced their ancestry back to the time of Henry VIII, through a long and illustrious line of county high sheriffs, clerks in chancery, and most notably the scholar and antiquarian, Sir Thomas D'Ewes, upon whom King Charles I conferred a baronetcy in 1644. This same Sir Thomas arranged a marriage for himself with a local lady of considerable estate, whose lands marched with his own, and the combined estates

6

had come down with the title over the centuries to the present day. The arms of the D'Ewes family, consisting of an argent ewe passant between three estoils, with the crest of a wolf's head couped in ermine issuing from a chaplet of oak leaves, were handsomely carved in the oak panelling above the great fireplace in Stow Stocksley Hall.

Sir Leonard D'Ewes, the eighth baronet, was the owner of Stow Stocksley Hall and its magnificent estate. He was a tall, dignified man in his late fifties, handsome in an uninspired fashion, and chilly and precise in his demeanour, though this masked an affectionate personality which his upbringing had taught him to conceal and control. The lands and farms of the estate of Stow Stocksley provided him with a healthy income, and the Hall itself was the repository of significant wealth in the form of art treasures, antiques, a noted botanical collection, and a magnificent and valuable library. Sir Leonard was thus left with ample leisure time to busy himself with genealogical pursuits, particularly the collation of the voluminous transcripts from cartularies, monastic registers and early wills compiled by his ancestor, Sir Thomas.

Sir Leonard and his wife, Lady Charlotte, herself the daughter of an earl, co-existed quietly in a state of polite amiability. The happiness of their marriage, which had not been one entirely of convenience, had been blighted by the death of their son, Alec, at the age of twenty-one. Undemonstrative people, both had sought to struggle privately with their grief, and the division which this had created between them had never entirely healed. Lady Charlotte, once an upright woman of strong personality and excellent humour, seemed almost perceptibly diminished in demeanour and spirit by her loss. Indeed, at the time it had astonished her to discover that, in spite of every instinct which told her that such black and insupportable unhappiness could not be outlasted, she somehow survived. She had carried on in spite of everything. The mundane tasks involved in managing the vast household of Stow Stocksley, the numerous charitable works with which she involved herself as the years passed by, all helped to alleviate her grief. Although not a day passed by when she did not think of Alec, she had grown to believe that she would never again experience the acute and violent misery of those early years.

That was, until the winter's morning when she received Cicely Patrick's letter.

She was standing by the fireplace in the morning room, the remains of breakfast on the table behind her. Sir Leonard was sitting reading his copy of *The Times*, his own pile of unopened mail next to his plate. She tore open the envelope, glancing at the unfamiliar, slanting handwriting, unfolded the two pages of notepaper and read the letter. As she did so, she felt a sudden tide of emotion wash up and over her, like a wave of fire. All the grief of Alec's death seemed suddenly sharply recalled, brought back by the contents of this letter. She put her hand to her chest and breathed in deeply, then went to sit back down at the breakfast table. She laid the letter on the tablecloth and poured herself a fresh cup of coffee. Her husband, absorbed in his newspaper, made some remark concerning the day's news without looking up at her, but Lady Charlotte did not hear it.

She drank her coffee and gazed out across the park at the line of trees, at the slow autumn rain dripping from their branches. Orlando. How often she had thought of her unseen grandson. She remembered how, when he was born, the very fact of his existence had seemed to temper her detestation of his mother, that girl. She had forgotten the mother's name now, but at the time of Alec's death she had hated her, had blamed her for taking their son, for having been instrumental in his destruction. She sighed and set down her cup. That had been absurd, of course. Whatever Alec had done, however much he had disappointed his parents by dropping out of Oxford, by going to live with that little middle-class nobody, by making the friends he did, doing the useless things he did, dying the way he had – all that had been of his own making. She knew that now. But, at the time, her hatred had seemed quite logical.

Orlando. She remembered how, when she had heard of his mother's death, she had longed to see him. Her rancour had been long spent by then, but she had felt it was too late to initiate any contact between the two families. Besides, Leonard would never have countenanced it. She had an idea that his animosity was more enduring than her own, and would be untouched by sentiment. Still, she remembered toying with the idea of writing a letter of condolence to those two aunts with whom Orlando lived. But, knowing her husband's views, recalling the determination which he had expressed at the time of Alec's death that they should have nothing to do with either mother or child, she had not wished to suggest anything which might incur his anger. And so she had done nothing, had tried to put the child from her mind.

Now she picked up the letter and unfolded the pages again. '. . . *Orlando is now eleven, and a delightful boy,'* she read, '*and it seems to us a great pity that he has never met his grandparents. He has been told about you, of course –* ' Here Lady Charlotte felt a distinct tightening of the throat '*– and I feel that you would find his interest and affection ample reward for time spent with him. He is a charming and intelligent child, and I earnestly hope that I can prevail upon you and your husband to take an interest in him . . .'*

The letter made no mention of money, was in no way coercive, and gave no hint that Orlando's material welfare was at stake. It was, as Lady Charlotte read it, simply a courteous and literate invitation to meet their own grandson.

She looked across at her husband, and felt determination

harden within her. 'Leonard,' she said, 'I have received this. It's a letter from Cicely Patrick.'

'From whom?' Sir Leonard flipped aside his paper and frowned.

Lady Charlotte hesitated. 'From Orlando's aunt.' There was a silence as she stretched her hand out above the coffee pot, holding out the letter. After a moment, Sir Leonard put down his paper, took the letter from her without a word, unfolded it and read it. As he did so, a car could be heard coming up the drive. Lady Charlotte glanced out.

'Here's Geraldine already,' she murmured. She turned back to her husband. 'I promised I would go into town with her.' She paused as Sir Leonard looked up from the letter, and her eyes met his. 'We can talk about it when I get back,' she added, 'but I want you to say yes. If you don't, I will see him on my own.' And she left the room.

After a few moments Sir Leonard rose, picked up the rest of his mail and Cicely's letter, and left the room. He crossed the stone-flagged hall and mounted the wide wooden staircase to his study. This study, which housed a small part of the Stow Stocksley library, was where Sir Leonard daily busied himself among his genealogies and manuscripts, with occasional estate business thrown in. It was a large room, with a Persian carpet covering the polished floorboards. At one end a handsome walnut desk stood beneath a window overlooking the park, and a fire which had been laid earlier burned in the grate opposite. The two other walls were lined with bookshelves from floor to ceiling. Against the dullness of the day Sir Leonard switched on the little gilded lamp which stood on his desk, and sat down, pondering the matter of Orlando. Despite the words which he had once uttered in anger, he knew in his heart that Orlando was in all probability Alec's child. Almost certainly so. He put the rest of his mail down on the desk, unfolded Cicely's letter once more, and re-read it.

In spite of his wife's belief to the contrary, Sir Leonard had thought increasingly of Orlando over the years. Time had reconciled him to many things, and among these was the knowledge that, whatever the tangle of misfortunes surrounding his birth, Orlando was not to blame for anything. It was not the child's fault that he was the offspring of a feckless young man who had been given too much money and too little purpose in life, and who had died before his time and without marrying his pregnant girlfriend. Sir Leonard rubbed his chin reflectively and looked out across the park. Had things been different, Alec might well have married Orlando's mother – although it was not a match of which he and Lady Charlotte would have approved – and Orlando would be his accepted grandson, and the prospective tenth baronet of Stow Stocksley. Instead, there he was being brought up by two maiden aunts in Reigate, while Sir Leonard's nephew, Roger Stafford-Roper, stood to inherit the estate instead.

At the thought of his nephew, Sir Leonard sighed involuntarily. It had suddenly come to his mind that Roger's parents, Barney and Alicia Stafford-Roper, Sir Leonard's sister, would be arriving in a couple of days to spend the weekend at Stow Stocksley. This visit, which occurred every six months, and which Sir Leonard dreaded, had been instituted by Lady Charlotte a few years after Alec's death, in view of the fact that Roger was now Sir Leonard's heir. While he had no particular enthusiasm for his sister, who had been an insipid but briefly beautiful deb in the fifties and who had turned into a whining, bored creature whose appetites could only be satisfied by wasteful shopping sprees and large amounts of useless travel, Sir Leonard actively detested his brother-in-law. He considered him effete and a vulgarian, albeit a rich one, and as he let out his sigh that morning, it was with the hope that Roger would not turn out to be of the same clay, and that sufficient of

11

the D'Ewes blood ran in his veins for him to be a creditable heir one day.

He thrust the thought of Barney from his mind and tried to concentrate on the matter of Orlando. What lay behind this letter of Cicely Patrick's? he wondered. He presumed the motive must be mercenary, although the letter gave no hint of that. Sir Leonard looked up and gazed out across the park, considering the possibilities. He supposed that it lay in his power simply to ignore the letter, to allow Orlando to continue as he had done until now, without any knowledge of his grandparents, and to prevent any disturbance to his own existence, and that of Lady Charlotte. After all, what good would it do for them to meet this child now? What was the point of it? Certainly, he had his own curiosity regarding the boy, but he must not allow sentiment to cloud his judgement. It could do all kinds of untold damage if they were to meet him. After all, it couldn't just end there. Charlotte wouldn't let it. The best thing to do would be to ignore the letter. But then he thought of his wife, and of what she had said. Whatever he decided to do, she was going to see the boy. He sighed. It might as well be faced – one way or another, this letter had brought Orlando into their lives.

But not today, he decided. The letter didn't demand an immediate reply. He would think about it, discuss it with his wife after he had recovered from the rigours of the impending weekend with his frightful brother-in-law. Sir Leonard folded up the letter, placed it in a drawer, and turned his attentions to the rest of the morning's mail.

That Saturday morning in Plumtree Villa, Abigail watched the look of disappointment settling on her sister's features as she scanned the letters which the postman had brought. So far, Cicely's letter to Lady Charlotte remained unanswered.

'I wouldn't keep your hopes up, if I were you,' remarked Abigail. 'They won't reply.'

Cicely said nothing. Oh, yes they will, she thought. She knew it. Her intuition told her. It was just a matter of time.

Chapter Two

That same Saturday evening, Sir Leonard and Lady Charlotte sat having pre-dinner drinks with Barney and Alicia Stafford-Roper in the downstairs drawing room at Stow Stocksley Hall. Sir Leonard regarded his brother-in-law gloomily over his whisky and soda and wondered if there was any way that Roger could possibly fail to be as great a disaster as his father. Barney Stafford-Roper, whose real name was Bernard, represented everything which Sir Leonard particularly disliked in a man. He had been a sixties playboy, handsome in a fleshy, blond way which had ultimately gone to seed, a darling of the gossip columns, famous for his liaisons with models and minor European royals. Now in his late forties, he still liked to think of himself as a jet-setter, having been something of a name in polo-playing circles and on the Cresta run, and after his marriage had continued to indulge in a number of ill-concealed affairs with a string of women, which Sir Leonard found particularly distasteful. Barney Stafford-Roper had never done a day's work in his life, but had been blessed with inherited wealth and a portfolio whose success was inspirational.

Sir Leonard had to acknowledge, however, that whatever his father's faults, Roger had succeeded in developing some spectacularly original ones of his own. The boy, whom Sir Leonard recalled as being a rather dandified but inoffensive adolescent, had come into a trust fund some ten months previously and, in a pattern of behaviour horribly reminiscent of Alec's, had immediately dropped out of university and

14

embarked upon a career of reckless ostentation. He bought expensive cars and crashed them, hired jets to take himself and his friends abroad, hosted extravagant parties in his house in Cadogan Square, became involved in numerous drunken escapades at expensive nightclubs, and was generally behaving like a rich, spoilt young idiot. His latest offence, which Alicia had done her best to conceal from her brother, was to have been fined, with a one-month suspended prison sentence, for possession of cocaine. Sir Leonard despaired at the thought of the heritage of centuries falling into such hands.

He sighed inwardly and listened as Barney trotted out his latest polo-playing gossip and a couple of seedy anecdotes which Sir Leonard thought he had heard before, and which made Lady Charlotte wince. He watched his sister toying with her gold bracelets, scarcely listening to her husband as she rearranged her hair and knocked back her third pink gin. Sir Leonard had once wondered why, in the light of her husband's catastrophic infidelities, his sister remained married to Bernard Stafford-Roper, but he had since realised that she was addicted to the shallow pleasures which his wealth could purchase, and too jaded to contemplate an alternative existence.

'. . . so he had the whole lot flattened and turned into polo fields. Bloody marvellous.' Barney took another sip of his whisky, and Sir Leonard wondered whether his brother-in-law would ever wake up to the fact that neither he nor Lady Charlotte had the faintest interest in polo. 'That's the kind of thing you could do with this place,' went on Barney. 'God knows you've got the space. Not that you're really much of a polo fan, are you, Leonard?' So the penny had dropped at last, thought Sir Leonard. Not that he supposed it would deflect Barney. 'Of course, the thing that really impressed Roger was the helicopter pad. I'll bet it's the first thing he'll

15

build here when you pop off, Leonard. Where that sunken garden is now – that's the place.'

Leonard stared at his brother-in-law coldly. 'You do realise,' he said, 'that that garden was designed by Capability Brown?'

'No – was it? Doubt if that's the kind of thing to appeal to Roger.'

Lady Charlotte coughed lightly, and then murmured, 'We haven't seen Roger for some time. I'd rather hoped he might come down with you this weekend.'

'I think he's in Italy with some chums,' said Alicia Stafford-Roper languidly, and ran her crimson nails once more through her hair. 'We don't actually seem to see that much of him, now that he has his own income.'

'Has he any thoughts as to his future – a career of sorts?' enquired Sir Leonard.

'Oh, good God, I don't know,' said Barney, setting down his whisky glass. 'Let him have a bloody good time, that's what I say. He's got his trust fund now, and good luck to him. Best thing for him is to learn how to spend serious money. Just the experience he needs for when he inherits this lot, eh?' Barney's wealth had been accumulated by his father through dubious arms dealings before the second world war, and, with the snobbery of the parvenu, he regarded the prospect of his son succeeding to a baronetcy with great satisfaction. 'Though frankly, I'm not sure what Roger is going to do with a museum and a few greenhouses.'

Sir Leonard gazed into his own whisky and soda, listening to his brother-in-law with a sinking heart. It suddenly occurred to him to wonder what kind of boy Orlando might be. Was he like Alec? Was he in danger of turning out to be someone as dreadful as Roger or his father? That was scarcely possible. Although he did not even know Orlando, it occurred to him that it was a pity that fate should have robbed the boy of his chance to become the heir to Stow Stocksley. Anything, he thought, as he finished his drink and rose to go in to dinner, would be better than Roger.

This train of thought continued over the weekend – the long, long weekend – and after the guests had departed on Sunday evening, Sir Leonard sat alone in his study and contemplated in detail an idea which he had begun to develop. What if there might be an alternative to Roger inheriting Stow Stocksley? The possibility was remote at first sight, admittedly, but it had occurred to Sir Leonard that it might be no bad idea to invite the child, Orlando, to Stow Stocksley, to see what sort of person he was. Quite where matters would progress from there, Sir Leonard was uncertain, but the visit would be something in the nature of a test for Orlando. Lady Charlotte seemed determined to acknowledge him, and if he acquitted himself well during his visit, she would wish to see more of him, to admit him into the family. Why not, then, bring him properly into things? If the boy was in any way suitable, might it not be possible, in time, to adopt him, make him the legal heir to Stow Stocksley? It was an enormous step to contemplate, certainly, and Sir Leonard was unclear as to the legalities of the matter, but he could not, in principle, see why such a thing should not be. The boy was his grandson, after all. He sat staring at the dying firelight in the darkened room, conscious of a faint excitement at the notion. Much, of course, would depend upon the kind of person Orlando turned out to be, and the thing would have to be taken gradually, but the first thing to do was to invite the child to spend a week here with him and Lady Charlotte.

Sir Leonard reached across the desk, switched on his lamp, and drew Cicely Patrick's letter from the drawer. He thought for a moment or two, then penned a brief, courteous reply. He read it over twice, then went to his wife to explain his idea to her, happily anticipating the pleasure it would give her.

*

Sir Leonard's letter arrived in the lunchtime post two days before Orlando was due to return home from prep school for half term. Cicely was conscious of a tremulous anticipation as she tore open the envelope and unfolded the stiff, ivory-coloured notepaper. She had known instantly that the letter was from the D'Ewes. As she read Sir Leonard's few short lines, she coloured with pleasure and relief. They had agreed to see him! She drew in a deep breath and hurried into the kitchen to put on the kettle. Then she stood reading the letter again, excited triumph in her heart. And Abigail had been so sceptical! This would show her. Admittedly it was only the first step, but it was also the biggest one. Sir Leonard said in the letter that he would ring in a day or two to arrange a time for Orlando to visit them. And here was half term! What better opportunity?

Abigail, when she came home from school later that afternoon, was grudgingly surprised at the contents of the letter which Cicely showed her. She slung a heap of fifth-form essays on to the kitchen table and read it as she sipped her mug of tea.

'Well, that's a start,' she remarked, and passed the letter back to her sister.

'It's more than that,' said Cicely. 'Don't you realise that we've cleared the biggest hurdle? They actually want to meet him! And how could anyone resist Orlando, once they've met him?'

'You haven't got any money yet,' Abigail reminded her sister.

'That, my dear, is merely a matter of time,' replied Cicely.

The irresistible Orlando climbed out of the train at Reigate station on Friday afternoon to be welcomed by his aunt Cicely. He was certainly a handsome boy, without any of the physical incongruities pertaining to ears and teeth which so often afflict boys of his age, with dark, straight hair flopping in a fringe over his forehead. His eyes were an indeterminate grey-green, like those of his mother, but his colouring was his father's. As she drove him home from the station, Cicely glanced at him, hardly listening as he chattered about school. She suddenly felt, in the recent triumph of her achievement and the impending glory of his visit to Stow Stocksley, a rush of devoted and sentimental affection towards him.

As they stopped at the traffic lights in the High Street, she turned to look at him again, thinking what a very good-looking boy he was, and remembered how beautiful he had been as a baby. He had quite eclipsed all the woeful presentiments she had had when Melissa had returned home after Alec's death, and announced the fact of her pregnancy. At that time there had been anxious confabulations between herself and Abigail. How could she look after a baby? Should she have an abortion? Melissa had been too tearful and hysterical to co-operate, to discuss anything. And then Orlando was born, and Cicely lost her heart to him. Six months later, when Melissa had recovered from the birth and from Alec's death, and had grown tired of the novelty of pushing Orlando round Reigate in his Silver Cross pram, she announced her intention of going back to London with Orlando, there to embark on a fine arts course. Cicely remembered her sense of panic at the announcement. The idea of losing Orlando was unthinkable. Where would they live, what would Melissa do with him while she studied? Melissa's vague notions of baby-minders appalled Cicely. But she gave no indication of her feelings. No, she congratulated herself now on handling that situation with tact and diplomacy. She merely suggested mildly to Melissa that it might be best if she were to leave Orlando in Reigate, where he could be properly cared for, while she went off to her studies in London. Then she could visit Orlando every weekend. Melissa accepted the suggestion with relief. Much as she loved Orlando, she was only twenty, and found the chores of motherhood irksome. She regularly delegated matters of bottle and nappy-changing to Cicely. And so Orlando became the charge of Cicely and Abigail, and Melissa was free to pursue an independent life in London. Cicely abandoned all ideas of returning to nursing. It suited everyone admirably. As for Orlando, so long as he was fed and watered, and had someone to coo and smile over him, he did not mind one way or the other.

Something Orlando was saying broke into her train of thought, as they drew up outside Plumtree Villa.

'. . . so could I have George over to tea next Wednesday, afterwards?'

'What?' Cicely put on the handbrake, and they got out of the car. 'Well, no, dear, I don't think so,' she said, taking his case from the boot and slamming it shut. Orlando pushed open the wrought-iron gate and walked up the leaf-strewn path ahead of her.

'Why not?' he asked.

'Well,' said Cicely, as she put her key in the latch, 'I have had some rather exciting news, and we have made other plans for you next week.' They went inside, and Orlando took off his overcoat and blazer, brushing his dark hair from his eyes.

'What news?' He followed his aunt through to the kitchen, flicking at the little lace doily on which the telephone stood on the hall table. 'What have you got planned? Why didn't you ask me?'

'Now, don't whine, Orlando. Tea, or a glass of milk?' She switched on the kettle.

'Tea, please. Have we got any chocolate biscuits?'

'In the tin. Well, now . . . this is really quite exciting news. You know that Abigail and I have talked from time to time about your grandparents?'

'What – the ones in Hampshire? The ones that live in the big house? That never send me a birthday card?'

Cicely hesitated as she set out the cups and saucers. 'Yes, that's right. Sir Leonard and Lady D'Ewes. Now, I'm sure that you must have been curious to meet them, and the lovely thing is, now they want to meet you!' She looked at Orlando with a smile of expectation, as though she had just handed him some wonderful gift.

He looked blankly back at her. 'Why?'

'Well, I wrote to them, you see, telling them all about you, what a splendid young man you are, and so forth, and I think they decided that it would be nice to meet you after all this time, and so they've very kindly invited you to stay with them at Stow Stocksley next week. I spoke to your grandfather about it just last night.' She poured milk into Orlando's tea, stirred in a spoonful of sugar, and handed it to him.

There was a long silence, during which Orlando ate three chocolate biscuits and drank a little of his tea, then asked for more milk. Just when Cicely was about to push him for a response, he asked, 'Why didn't they ever want to see me before now?'

Cicely thought for a moment, and then said candidly, 'I don't know.' She paused, wondering whether she should say this to him, but deciding to go ahead, anyway, and went on, 'But what I *do* know is that this could be quite important for you, Orlando. Your grandfather and grandmother may be in a position to help you, to do things for you that Abigail and I cannot. So I want you to behave as beautifully as I know you can on this visit, and to remember your manners. I will take you down on Sunday evening, and collect you at teatime on Friday.' He said nothing, and she added, 'I think you will like it there. It's a beautiful, big house, with some wonderful pictures, and lots of lovely countryside. You'll have fun, I'm sure.'

Orlando did not look convinced. 'Will there be any other boys there?'

21

'No, I hardly think so, dear.'

He sighed. 'All right. But I wish you'd asked me first.'

Two days later, Cicely drove Orlando to Stow Stocksley. Orlando spent the journey largely in silence. He had serious doubts about whether he was going to enjoy this visit. The prospect of being stuck in a big country house for a whole week with two old people whom he'd never met was not particularly alluring. As he stared out across the Surrey countryside, he found himself casting his mind back to his mother's death, which was something he hardly ever thought about. He had been eight and, although nobody had told him that his mother had lymphatic cancer, he had known, when she came back from London to live with them, that she was very ill. After a while she had been moved to the cottage hospital. He remembered sitting on a chintz sofa in the hospital between his aunts, with Anne sitting opposite, and he remembered, too, that Aunt Cicely had on a new pair of brogue shoes, whose intricate pattern he rather admired. He remembered being taken through to his mother's bedside, and looking at the delicate blue tracery of the veins on her eyelids and the dry, cracked flakiness of her lips. When the doctor had lifted her wrist to feel her pulse, it had reminded Orlando of the time he had found a dead bird in the shrubbery, and had lifted its leg up tentatively with the end of a stick. But more than that he could not recall. The recollection brought back no sense of grief, or loss. He hadn't seen his mother very often, really. It had always been his aunts who looked after him, helped him with his homework, played draughts with him, read to him, and kissed him goodnight. She had been an insubstantial presence, someone who came back to Reigate occasionally and took him out on treats. He had liked her, but he had not missed her. All that he had felt that day, when he left the cottage hospital with his

22

aunts, was relief that they would get home in time for *Dr Who*.

Cicely interrupted his thoughts. 'We're here,' she remarked. 'At any rate, this is the village. Your grandfather said to carry on straight through and the gates to the Hall are a few hundred yards on the other side. Keep your eyes peeled, Orlando.'

Orlando peered expectantly and obediently ahead, and after a bend in the road they came upon the unmistakably grand gates and driveway leading up to Stow Stocksley Hall. He had no idea what to expect, having only a hazy notion of what a large country house should look like from the time when Abigail had taken him to Hever Castle. Even so, he was astonished by the grandeur and size of the Hall as it came into view, and by the acres of carefully sculpted parkland which stretched away on either side.

Orlando suddenly felt acutely nervous at the thought of meeting the owners of this awesome and lovely place. He saw two figures come down the steps from the Hall as Cicely parked the Datsun, and was relieved, as they came closer, to see that they were just like any ordinary old man and lady. The man was quite tall, and looked a bit stern, but the lady was smiling and a little hesitant, and Orlando quite liked the look of her.

He could not remember, later, what was said when he first met Sir Leonard and Lady Charlotte, but he always remembered stepping into the large, stone-flagged hallway and gazing up at the minstrel's gallery, and the large oak staircase hung with portraits. The spirit of the place, of its long past, filled him instantly.

'Shall I show you your room, Orlando?' said his grandmother, observing his quiet absorption in his surroundings. 'Then perhaps Sir Leonard could show you around the Hall before tea.' Lady Charlotte turned to Cicely. 'Thank you so

23

much for bringing him. Perhaps I can offer you a cup of tea before you go?'

But Cicely said that she preferred to drive back before it got dark, and she handed Orlando his suitcase, kissed him, and left. She felt nervously elated as she drove back down towards the village, and hoped fervently that Orlando would acquit himself well over the coming week. It would have been a tough test of endurance for most eleven-year-olds, but she had faith in Orlando.

When he had unpacked his suitcase in his room, and spent some time leaning his elbows on the broad windowsill and gazing out across the park, Orlando went downstairs and found his grandmother organising tea things in the drawing room. As he glanced around the room, he saw on a side-table a silver-framed photograph of a young man. He went over to it slowly, and stood looking at it. It was his father. His mother had only had snapshots of him, not very good ones and nothing as big as this, but he recognised him instantly. He looked from the photograph to Lady Charlotte, and was struck for the first time by the realisation, the comprehension, that this old woman was his father's mother. It gave him an odd feeling, but the constraint which he had felt for the past few hours began to lessen slightly.

Over tea, Sir Leonard and Lady Charlotte mapped out for Orlando the various things they had planned for him during his visit, and he felt a certain relief that he would not be expected to amuse himself entirely. By the time he went to bed later that evening, after beating Sir Leonard twice at draughts, and being taught how to play clock patience by Lady Charlotte, Orlando felt more sanguine about this visit, and about his grandparents generally. They seemed pretty decent. His grandmother made quite funny jokes, and he could tell from the disgruntled expression on his grandfather's face when he had lost that last game that he wasn't one of those condescending adults who let children win things on purpose.

The next few days Orlando spent exploring and learning about his grandparents' home. His first problem was one of proportion. For someone who had been brought up in the confines of Plumtree Villa, it was difficult for him to imagine how two people could inhabit a place of such size, with such spacious rooms. His own room, overlooking the park, was quite snug compared to everywhere else, and even it was twice the size of his bedroom at home. And then there was so much of everything. He thought of the pieces of furniture in his aunts' house, the dining table and chairs, the sofas and armchairs, the piano that no one played, the hall table, the hat stand – each had possessed since his infancy an individual and familiar identity. How could anyone possibly get to know and love all the countless things in this great house? But, after a few days, he was surprised to discover how intimately both his grandparents seemed to know most of their possessions. It was something he liked. He began to see that it was possible properly to possess and live in a place such as this. His grandparents moved about it as a matter of course, sat on the lovely furniture, used the silver, and the beautiful plates and dishes (well, not all of them – most were locked up in vast glass cases), and walked in the vast stretches of parkland (well, the bit down to the lake, where Orlando threw sticks for his grandfather's gun-dog, Midas). He was taken from room to room by his grandmother, shown pictures and ornaments, and he listened patiently and asked questions frankly and ingenuously. Happily possessed of a greater aesthetic awareness and natural politeness than many eleven-year-olds, he did not betray any sense of boredom. For he was not bored. He was intrigued and fascinated to think that his father had grown up here, and that he actually belonged to the family that owned Stow Stocksley and all the lovely things in it, and the beautiful countryside surrounding it. He stood by the lake with his grandfather and surveyed the vista, Stow Stocksley Hall cresting the slope above them, thought of the neat rectangle of garden to the rear of Plumtree Villa, and marvelled.

All in all, the visit was a success. Orlando charmed Sir Leonard and Lady Charlotte with exactly the right blend of cheerful spirits and polite deference, and his dark good looks, which so resembled those of his late father, did much to assist. The likeness made Lady Charlotte's heart ache with tenderness towards him. It seemed absurd, she thought, as she sat watching him at tea on the last day of his visit, that they had let eleven long years slip by without once seeing him. Sir Leonard, too, felt this pang of regret as he observed the boy, but it was quickly eclipsed by the pleasure he took in him. Cautious though he would have to be – for who knew what kind of young man Orlando would turn into? – Sir Leonard was now beginning to nourish fresh hopes for the future of the D'Ewes lineage. He felt immensely grateful that Cicely had written to them when she had, and humbled by the realisation that his own pride had prevented him from initiating any contact with his own grandson.

When Cicely arrived to take Orlando home, she conversed briefly with Sir Leonard and it did credit to her powers of diplomacy that she managed to convey to him, without seeming to suggest that anything was expected of him, that there were certain financial difficulties where Orlando's immediate future was concerned. Sir Leonard digested this information, and after Orlando had departed, he poured out two large Scotches and sat discussing the matter with his wife. Both agreed that they should do something towards Orlando's education. When she went to bed that night, Lady Charlotte felt happier and closer to her husband than she had done for a long time.

*

When Orlando arrived back at Plumtree Villa, he discovered that Anne, the youngest of his aunts, had come to stay for the weekend. Orlando regarded Anne as distinctly glamorous. She was twenty-seven, and worked as a copywriter for a large London advertising agency, and Cicely and Abigail, whom she regarded as hopelessly boring and middle-class, were regularly given to understand that her job was immensely creative and important, and her social life exciting and enviable. Even Orlando recognised that much of what she said was to impress Cicely and Abigail, and to make them conscious of the inferior dreariness of their own lives. She was pretty and blonde, as his mother had been, and the relationship was such that Orlando regarded her more as a big sister than an aunt. When he heard that she was there, he rushed to look for her, eager to tell her of the new world that was now his. For he regarded Stow Stocksley and his wealthy grandparents as wonderful acquisitions, delightful new possessions. Abigail, however, stopped him on the stairs.

'Anne's having a little lie-down at the moment,' she said. 'You go and get your pyjamas on. It's getting late. You can have a talk with her tomorrow.'

Orlando went to his room, put on his pyjamas and his dressing gown, and unpacked his overnight case. He took out a shirt and carefully unrolled it, and drew out a small china figurine of a pierrot. He had admired it in the upstairs drawing room at Stow Stocksley, and had been astonished when Lady Charlotte, without any hesitation, had stretched out her hand, picked it up, and handed it to him. 'Here,' she had said, 'you may have him. As a memento of your visit to Stow Stocksley. I hope it may be the first of many. But look after him – he's quite valuable.' Orlando stood the figurine reverently on his chest of drawers and admired it. Then he unpacked the rest of his things and went downstairs. He had had tea three hours ago, and was hungry.

As he passed Anne's old room, he saw that the door was firmly shut. He thought about knocking, but decided he'd better not. There had been something in the tone of aunt Abigail's voice which warned him against it. Halfway downstairs he heard the sound of his aunts' voices coming clearly from the kitchen, where they were washing up. He stopped and crouched down, listening through the banisters. He heard Abigail say, '. . . well, I wouldn't expect her to confide in us, but it's perfectly obvious that he's ended it.'

There was the clink of cutlery being put into a drawer, and Cicely sighed and said, 'She does seem to get mixed up with some completely worthless types.'

The next bit was indistinct, but then he clearly heard Abigail say, 'I hate to say it, but I think she's one of those girls who's attracted to that kind of man . . .'

Cicely said something indistinct in reply to this, and then there was silence and the clatter of plates and closing of drawers. Tucking away these fragments of half-understood conversation for consideration later, Orlando thumped downstairs in ostentatious innocence, and asked if he could have some cheese sandwiches and watch the rest of *All Creatures Great and Small*.

The next morning when Orlando went down to breakfast, Anne was already up, sitting at the kitchen table, sipping black coffee and staring at the front page of Cicely's *Daily Mail*. Her normally vivacious, pretty face looked listless and slightly haggard, and her blonde hair was straggling and unwashed. Ever since Orlando could remember, there had been a mild antagonism between Anne and her two older half-sisters, presumably dating back to the days when Cicely had been responsible for looking after Anne as a teenager, and he was surprised that she should visit them now. She rarely returned to Plumtree Villa, unless from dire necessity.

With the exuberance of the egotist, however, Orlando did not stop to investigate the reason for her visit, but instead launched into an excited account of Stow Stocksley and its wonders. It was only after breakfast, when Abigail had gone into town and Cicely had disappeared on her household chores, that it occurred to him to ask why she was there.

'Oh, just a touch of flu, you know. I didn't feel like staying up in London on my own . . .' She glanced vaguely around, then looked back at Orlando and gave a sudden smile. How could she possibly tell an eleven-year-old that the only man she had ever loved (she was convinced that the other four had never been the real thing), and with whom she had gone to live only two months ago, had suddenly decided to end their relationship, and had asked her to move all her things out and find somewhere else to live as soon as possible? It had been bad enough having to come back to Cicely and Abigail, but it was the closest thing to home, and she badly needed the comfort of familiarity. Anyway, it was just for the weekend. Her best friend, Sarah, would be back from holiday next week, and she could move in with her until she got something sorted out.

'You don't look very well,' observed Orlando. He remembered what he had overheard his aunts saying the night before, wondered if it was because of some man that she was here. Anne had always had different boyfriends, ever since he could remember, and she had never really seemed particularly happy with any of them.

'Thanks,' said Anne, and gave him a wry glance. Then she suddenly added, 'Orlando, when you grow up, for God's sake treat women decently.' Then she went back to her newspaper.

Orlando gave this the briefest consideration. He saw no

reason why he should ever treat anyone badly. He finished his toast, and went back upstairs to have another look at his pierrot, leaving Anne alone with her coffee.

Chapter Three

Of course, Sir Leonard fully realised, from the exquisitely tactful hints dropped by Cicely at the end of Orlando's visit, that the Patricks' approach to the D'Ewes family had been made chiefly from mercenary considerations. But he was not disposed to let this rankle with him. Before meeting Orlando, he would certainly have been offended by such an approach, but now that he had met him, and felt such a liking for him, he felt he could disregard the motives of the Patrick sisters. In any event, everything coincided neatly with his own aspirations concerning the possible inheritance of Stow Stocksley. Orlando required a decent schooling, and since it lay in Sir Leonard's powers to assist, he would do what he could. It might ultimately be in the family interests, after all.

Orlando was invited to spend a few days at Stow Stocksley over Christmas, during which time he managed, quite effortlessly, to ingratiate himself further with his grandparents. Sir Leonard spent much time over the next two months pondering the choice of school for Orlando. He decided against Marlborough and Shrewsbury, neither of which seemed to have done Alec or Roger much good, and, after weighing up the pros and cons of the other major public schools, eventually came down in favour of Ampersand, being one of its alumni and therefore naturally prejudiced in its favour. It did not strike him that he was being in any way high-handed. If he was to pay for Orlando's schooling, then the choice should be his. He did not imagine that the Misses Patrick were likely to oppose his suggestions, and in this surmise he was correct.

During the Easter holidays Sir Leonard arranged to visit the Patrick sisters in Reigate to discuss the matter of Orlando's future with them. On the afternoon of his arrival, Cicely was busily laying out cups and saucers from the treasured Royal Doulton tea service, while Abigail marked exercise books at the kitchen table. Abigail glanced up, noticing that her sister was wearing her charm bracelet and new lambswool twin set especially for the occasion.

'He's not royalty, you know,' she remarked acerbically. 'The ordinary cups and saucers would have done.'

'I like things to be nice when we have guests,' replied Cicely, removing a madeira cake from its wrapping and slicing it carefully on to one of the gold-rimmed plates. 'And he is an important one, remember.'

'I'm aware of all that,' said Abigail, 'but it strikes me that he hasn't paid the sightest bit of attention to Orlando for eleven years, and now he thinks he can wade in and start dictating his future.'

Cicely sighed. Really, for all her intellectual pretensions, Abigail had absolutely no perspicacity, and even less foresight. 'That is the whole point of his visit. So long as he comes up with the money, you needn't worry about anything else. I will see to that.' She licked her thumb and dropped the cake wrapper in the bin. 'Anyway,' she added with a smile, 'I think you'll like him when you meet him. He's rather reserved – you know, proper – but very distinguished. Handsome, really.'

Abigail said nothing, but shot her sister a derisory glance and tugged her baggy sweater further around her as she continued with her marking.

Sir Leonard's visit went off smoothly, and to Cicely's relief Abigail did not do or say anything untoward, though she was perhaps a little frosty in her manner. He explained to them over tea his proposals regarding Orlando's schooling, with

32

the suggestion that Orlando should spend a part of each school holiday at Stow Stocksley, and found Cicely enthusiastic.

'It's meant to be a very good school, isn't it – Ampersand?' she remarked. 'I'm sure Orlando will love the thought of going there.'

Abigail, who felt that Sir Leonard might have consulted them beforehand, merely said, 'Perhaps it would be an idea to ask Orlando what he thinks.'

Cicely shot her sister a covert warning glance, then smiled at Sir Leonard. 'He's just upstairs. Why don't we call him down? I'm sure he'll be thrilled.'

Orlando, who was in his bedroom listening to 10cc, received the information with his customary equanimity, but in his heart he was delighted. He spent the rest of the summer term practising his cricket, dreaming of the day when he would make the Ampersand First XI.

It was inevitable that the Stafford-Ropers should come to learn of Sir Leonard's benevolence towards Orlando. The fact was, they had been altogether unaware of Orlando's existence until Lady Charlotte, in a moment of absent-mindedness, made reference to him in conversation during one of the Stafford-Roper's visits to Stow Stocksley. Although he had never intended any active concealment in the matter, Sir Leonard was rather irritated that they should know about Orlando so soon – it seemed to him that it might precipitate premature disputes and anxieties, and in this he was right.

'A grandson? What do you mean – a grandson? First I've heard of it.' The revelation had come during dinner, and Barney laid down his knife and fork and stared aggressively at his brother-in-law. Lady Charlotte realised that she should not have mentioned Orlando, and saw in the same instant that there was nothing she could do to rectify her mistake. She glanced at her husband.

After a moment's silence, Sir Leonard said, 'The fact of the matter is, the boy – Orlando – is Alec's child. His illegitimate child. He was born shortly after Alec died. The child lost his mother a few years ago, and we felt that we should give him some assistance.'

Barney leaned back and picked up his wine glass. 'For a moment I thought you were trying to do Roger out of his inheritance, digging up a male grandchild from nowhere. But being a bastard rather stops him in his tracks. Very kind of you to take an interest in him, Leonard. I hope you're quite sure he's Alec's.'

It would have given every satisfaction to Sir Leonard to point out to his brother-in-law that the question of succession was by no means clear, and that chickens should not necessarily be counted on Roger's behalf, but instinct told him to hold his tongue. He merely murmured a vague assent, and enquired as to how Roger's drug rehabilitation was going. Orlando's name was not mentioned again during the Stafford-Ropers' visit.

In the summer holidays Anne came for a brief visit to Plumtree Villa. She had recovered from her last ill-fated love affair and had now embarked on another, this time with a City solicitor. She listened idly as Cicely proudly informed her of the new connection established with the D'Ewes family, and of Sir Leonard's undertaking to finance Orlando's public school education.

'I don't know why you're so keen to send him off to one of those places,' she observed. 'He'll probably just come out queer. Most Englishmen who go to public school do.'

Cicely looked faintly appalled, but Abigail, who was busy mending the arm of her reading glasses with Scotch tape, dismissed this. She glanced appraisingly at her younger half-sister and replied, 'I would have thought you'd realise that that really is something of a cliché.'

'Besides,' said Cicely, over whose head this had passed, 'if there is to be any possibility of Orlando succeeding to the baronetcy when Sir Leonard dies, it's vital that he has the right kind of education and connections.'

'Where on earth do you get these notions about Orlando becoming a baronet?' asked Abigail in astonishment. 'Honestly – I sometimes think you read too much Georgette Heyer, Cicely, I really do. There has been no suggestion of anything of that kind.'

'Anyway,' observed Anne, 'I think all that kind of social manipulation is pathetic. I'm sure Orlando would still be just as wonderful if you sent him to the local comprehensive, like me – wouldn't you, wonder boy?'

'Wouldn't I what?' enquired Orlando, who had just come in from the garden through the open french windows.

'Be divine and supernaturally intelligent no matter what school they sent you to.'

Orlando frankly admitted that this was probably true.

At the end of the summer holidays, after he had been taken to Harrods by Cicely to purchase his new school uniform, Orlando went to Stow Stocksley to spend two weeks in the company of his grandparents. It was his third visit since the previous autumn, and there was growing in him a sense of the importance of Stow Stocksley Hall and the estate, and of the significance of his own position as Sir Leonard's grandson. He was already gaining a certain understanding of the history of the place, and the proud progression through the centuries of his grandfather's family. He liked to wander through the many rooms in the Hall, along the gallery, in and out of the heraldry room, where he would examine the coats of arms and old portraits, browsing through the nursery rooms at the top of the house, where relics of Sir Leonard's – and even his own father's – childhood were still stored. He would stand in the south window of the unused upstairs drawing room and look down across the lovely sweep of the park, enjoying the sense of inertia, of timelessness, that filled Stow Stocksley.

One day his grandfather came upon him, standing gazing up at the inscription, *Modice ac sapienter*, carved above the D'Ewes coat of arms over the fireplace in the great hall. He glanced up at his grandfather's approach and asked with candour, 'Why is my surname Patrick, and not D'Ewes?'

Sir Leonard hesitated for a moment; he did not know how much Orlando's mother, or his aunts, for that matter, had told him. Had he any idea, for instance, that he was illegitimate? He decided to adopt a cautious approach.

'Well . . . I think that because your mother brought you up, she thought you should have her name, you see.'

'Well,' said Orlando after a moment, letting out a sigh, 'I think it would be really nice to be called D'Ewes. It sounds much better.'

'Do you think so?' asked Sir Leonard, amused.

Orlando nodded and looked back at the coat of arms. 'Yes. Orlando D'Ewes. I think it sounds really brilliant.'

Sir Leonard smiled. 'Well, we shall see. But for the moment, I'm afraid that you will have to stay as you are.'

Sweet, that the child should wish to be called D'Ewes; Sir Leonard reminded himself that he really must speak to his lawyer about this whole matter, about adoption, and so forth. Still, he supposed, it would wait a while yet. These were early days, and Sir Leonard was all too aware that the promise of early youth did not always survive into adulthood. Or even adolescence, come to that. But it amused him to imagine the reaction of the presumptuous Barney if Roger were to be displaced as the heir to the baronetcy.

Orlando left Stow Stocksley at the end of August, promising his grandmother that he would write to them as soon as he had settled in at Ampersand. A week later, with the new leather-bound trunk from Barrow & Hepburn which Lady Charlotte had given him safely stowed in the boot of Cicely's Datsun, he left Plumtree Villa and set off for his new school.

By and large, Orlando was to enjoy the next seven years of his existence. At Ampersand he was fortunate enough not to be placed in a house where homosexuality was the accepted norm, thereby quietening Cicely's fears, and he survived the initial rigours of bullying and fagging reasonably well. He acquired a special friend in that first year, a boy called Daniel Coulthard, colloquially known as Big Dan, since he was enormous for a twelve-year-old, with a large, freckled face and a fringe of straw-coloured hair which stuck out over his forehead like overgrown thatch. He was the son of an Inverness-shire farmer, who hoped that an English public school education would endow his son with advantages which he himself lacked, and the bond which he and Orlando formed was so strong that it became part of the pattern of the year's calendar that Orlando spent every Easter and the occasional half-term holiday with Dan and his family in Scotland. Orlando was glad of this, for although he was grateful for the familiar and affectionate welcome of his aunts each time he returned to Plumtree Villa, he found that time hung heavy in their company and in the limited scope of his home town of Reigate. He secretly preferred those parts of the holidays which were spent at Stow Stocksley, where he had all the freedom of the estate, and Sir Leonard's dogs for company on his expeditions, and the spacious grandeur of the Hall to explore, a pastime of which he never tired. His grandfather made an effort to interest Orlando in the dusty mysteries of his genealogical pursuits, but Orlando did not find much romance in books and documents. He liked, however, to study the ancestral portraits which lined the walls of the great staircase; their soulful, dead gazes charmed him peculiarly, and it stirred him to think that where his shadow now fell on the creaking oak staircase, so their own shadows must once have fallen.

Sometimes Sir Leonard would take him on a tour of the estate, showing him how things were managed, the coppices, the coverts, the shoots, the tenant farms, and Orlando looked and learned. In his relationship with Lady Charlotte, too, he felt as though he were being prepared for some future event bound up with Stow Stocksley. She showed him around the rooms where precious china and silver were kept, and taught him small, rudimentary lessons in these matters, aware that the most valuable instruction was that received from habit and the everyday experience of being surrounded by lovely things. In a somewhat tutelary manner, she would take him on slow walks round the gardens, naming species of shrubs and flowers, aware that points of reference were all, that familiarity with excellence must show itself in the long run, casually, yet to the utmost effect. So, although the arthritis from which she had begun to suffer required her to use a stick, she undertook these excursions as a matter of duty. And, in fact, Orlando's company gave her immense pleasure.

One day in the summer holidays, when Orlando was thirteen, and when the bright, soft heat of the day made Lady Charlotte feel a little sprightlier than usual, they walked together all the way down to the lake.

'Siberian irises,' murmured his grandmother, indicating with her stick a mass of blue and white blooms that grew in profusion by the water's edge. 'You see how slender their leaves are? Quite beautiful – much more delicate than the evansia irises in the woods, though those are lovely, too.'

Orlando stood gazing out across the lightly ruffled waters of the lake, listening, unconsciously absorbing all these minute lessons. He liked to listen to his grandmother's gentle, rather distant voice as she talked about the things she knew and loved. Suddenly Lady Charlotte pointed across the water to an islet planted with trees and bushes, where the ducks nested.

'Your father swam all the way out to that island when he was seventeen,' she remarked. 'It was something he'd wanted to do since he was a small boy. I don't know why.'

'I do,' said Orlando. 'It looks mysterious. I'd like to do that one day.'

'I dare say,' said his grandmother, and smiled. She glanced at Orlando's handsome, serious face and strong, young body. She felt as though the very proximity of his youthfulness had some invigorating, health-giving property. 'Shall we walk back to the Hall and see what Mrs Cresswell has made us for lunch?' she said. 'Then I can show you that porcelain we were talking about this morning.'

It was all in very stark contrast to life at Plumtree Villa. Now that he was absent at school for so much of the year, Orlando had grown more critical and detached in his observations of his aunts and the life they led. A week after he had returned from Stow Stocksley, Orlando was idling on the sofa, watching the cricket on BBC2. He had drawn the curtains to improve the picture, and looked up in annoyance as Cicely came into the room and pushed them open again.

'What *are* you doing?' she demanded. 'It's perfectly ridiculous for a boy of your age to be loafing around watching television in the middle of a summer's day! Switch it off – and take your feet off that sofa! The cover's only just come back from the dry cleaners.'

Orlando glanced with distaste at the floral chintz sofa cover, and thought of the drawing room at Stow Stocksley. God, some of the things in this house were horrible. He glowered at his aunt. 'I don't ever get the chance to watch the cricket at school. And, anyway, there's nothing else to do round here.'

'Oh, is that a fact?' retorted his aunt. She stepped across and switched the television off. 'Well, I have a long list of shopping that you can fetch from the supermarket, and when you've done that, you can help me with the laundry. I'll find plenty to keep you busy, my boy.'

'Why do you always have to shout at me?' yelled Orlando, losing his temper. 'My grandmother never shouts at me! She never tells me what to do, or switches off the television when I'm watching it! She's civilised! God, I hate being here in the holidays sometimes!'

And Orlando stamped off to his room, only to be called down ten minutes later and sent to the supermarket with a list of groceries.

Although he loved his aunts, Orlando could not help comparing them unfavourably with his grandmother, whom he regarded with a degree of admiration, certainly not something which he felt for Cicely or Abigail. He did not realise, then, how much easier it was for Lady Charlotte to command both respect and love in the splendid setting of her husband's ancestral home, surrounded by the evidence of wealth and good breeding. She was naturally someone to be admired, freed from the petty domestic constraints which gave Cicely and Abigail permanent feet of clay. Whereas Lady Charlotte was able to pass pleasant hours with Orlando, showing him plants and pieces of porcelain, recounting family tales in her unhurried, languid fashion, his aunts were beset by financial worries, burdened with frustrations, and altogether set in a poor light compared to Lady Charlotte. All three women adored him, but poor Cicely and Abigail had so little to give, and Lady Charlotte so much.

Cut adrift from the female influences which had so far supplied all the warmth and affection in his young life, it was natural, within the masculine confines of his public school, that Orlando should be drawn to such vestiges of femininity and gentleness as existed there. The beginnings of his infatuation with Mrs Rees-Jones, his housemaster's wife, came in his fourteenth year, when he called one evening at their apartment within the school to collect an exercise book. Mrs Rees-Jones was young and pretty, with long, reddish hair, which she generally wore up, or in a plait. When she answered the door that evening in her dressing gown, her hair was loose and shining about her shoulders. She had recently had a baby, which Orlando found pleasantly mysterious in itself, and he could hear its faintly mewing cries in the background. Orlando had never seen her with her hair down before, nor had anyone in the school ever addressed him by his Christian name, as she did on that occasion, and when he returned to the prep room ten minutes later, Orlando carried away Mrs Rees-Jones' madonna-like image in his heart. That night, he dreamt of his mother for the first time in many years.

His capitulation was made complete a few weeks later, when he was struck on the head by a cricket ball during a match and confined to the sick bay. Matron had left him with two paracetamol and a cold compress, and he was lying alone in the antiseptic silence, reliving the humiliation of his fumbled catch, when the door opened and Mrs Rees-Jones came in. She soothed his head with the damp compress, and talked to him so kindly and sympathetically that Orlando was quite overwhelmed and burst into tears of self-pity. She put her arms round his shoulders and drew him to her, and he wept earnestly and softly for some minutes. She smelt warm and milky and wonderful, and when he had finished crying he felt a great relief. When she left him, she kissed him lightly on the forehead – something he was never to forget.

From then on, Orlando loved Mrs Rees-Jones reverently and at a distance. He sought her face out every Sunday in chapel, and was content to look at her from time to time between hymns. He dreamed up fantasies in which he was able to perform some great and spectacular service for her – the school caught fire and he was able to save her and her precious baby from the flaming ruins, or the baby suddenly contracted some dreadful illness in the night when her husband was away, and Orlando was fortuitously at hand, able to help. For the first time, his life was touched with romance.

Another summer drifted by, and the subtle changes taking place in Orlando began to coalesce. He was spared the torment of spending most of the summer holidays in Reigate and went on a school trip to Brittany with the rest of his friends. By the time he came back his voice had broken and his slender frame was beginning to develop a certain muscularity. Denied the contiguity which might have gentled the effect of Orlando's rapid metamorphosis from boy to young man, Cicely and Abigail found his physical presence in the confines of Plum-tree Villa most assertively and alarmingly masculine. Anne, who was making one of her rare visits to Plumtree Villa that August, was quite delighted by the change in Orlando.

'I'll have to keep my more rapacious friends well away from you in a couple of years' time,' she teased. 'And I don't just mean the female ones.' A remark which her half-sisters thought in remarkably poor taste.

Anne was using Reigate as a refuge while some unexpected hitch in the renovation of her new riverside flat was being carried out. She was as playful and loving as ever with Orlando, telling him over and over – until everyone, including Orlando, began to find it tiresome – how handsome he had become, but was disdainful and impatient with Cicely and Abigail. She used the telephone perpetually, and Orlando wondered if she had offered to pay Cicely and Abigail a share of the bill.

'I have to keep in touch with my office, you know,' he heard her retort to Abigail, in response to some mild deprecation.

42

'I thought you were meant to be on holiday?' replied Abigail. 'I doubt if your office will collapse without you.'

'Some holiday,' said Anne. 'Frankly, if I didn't have to be around to make sure this builder doesn't make a complete hash of things, I'd be spending these two weeks abroad, not here.' Then she turned to Orlando with her captivating smile and said, 'Let's go and find a country pub and have a lovely lunch. It'll give my ego a boost to be seen with a good-looking man.'

Anne loved driving fast around the Surrey lanes in her little red sports car, the top down and the wind blowing her hair, and so did Orlando. They found a pub with a garden, and Anne sat and told Orlando about her life in London, about the clubs she went to, the people she knew, minor social celebrities, and he listened entranced, unaware that Anne was inflating her own ego by using him as a naive and compliant audience. While Anne talked, Orlando amused himself by trapping wasps in his Coke bottle, but eventually she found even the topic of herself growing stale, and she turned her attention to Orlando.

'Haven't you got a girlfriend yet?' she asked, her eyes on his face.

Orlando laughed. 'You must be joking. We don't get to see any girls.'

'That sounds a bit iffy. You mean, there are no women at all in the place?'

'Well, there are the housemasters' wives, of course.' He blushed, feeling the faint, heart-stopping sensation that he always felt when he thought of Mrs Rees-Jones.

'Orlando, why are you going pink?' asked Anne in amusement. 'Have you got a crush on someone?'

He did not look up from beneath his dark fringe. He actually wished Anne wouldn't ask him questions like this. He felt exactly the same as he had when she had come into the

43

bathroom unexpectedly the other night, when he had been drying himself after his bath. She had thought it funny, but he had felt invaded, troubled.

'Of course not,' he said. 'Anyway – ' He suddenly took pity on the wasps and emptied them out in a small flurry of Coke drops on to the grass, where they staggered around before flying off ' – anyway, go on telling me about that friend of yours. He sounds like good fun.'

Anne sighed. 'Lord, he thinks he's fun. Bit of a drag, really. And never any money. What I really want, Orlando – ' She sat, head propped up on one hand, elbow resting on the wooden picnic table, gazing into the haze of the Surrey countryside ' – is a rich man. Not just – not just mildly or superficially rich, you know. Seriously rich. Deeply rich. So that I can live a wonderful, wonderful life, and never have to write crappy copy for soft drinks and frozen chickens and Parker Knoll recliners ever again.' She frowned. 'Sometimes I really feel like chucking my job in.'

'I thought you liked it,' said Orlando, relieved not to be the focus of her attention any more.

'Oh, well, maybe I do. It earns me a lot of money. But – ' She sighed ' – oh, I'd really like someone else's money to spend for a change. And somebody to love me, to absolutely adore me.' She looked at him slantingly. 'Don't you want that?'

Orlando looked blank. So far as he knew, he *was* loved and adored, and it didn't strike him as all that important. Probably it was different for girls.

She didn't wait for his answer. 'Well, *I* do. Somewhere out there – ' she flung her hand out in the general direction of Crawley ' – is the ideal man. Wealthy. Mature. Waiting. All I have to do is meet him.' She stared down into her empty glass, then said, 'Come on, let's go.' They stood up and sauntered over to her parked car. Anne put on her sunglasses and slid into the driver's seat. 'Only three more days till I go back to

London,' she observed. 'Oh, thank God.' She turned to Orlando. 'I wish you could come up with me and spend some time helping me get my new flat straight, but I don't suppose the deadly duo would let you.'

Orlando, too, wished that he could go, but knew that it would be another couple of years before he was allowed such licence. He sighed as he thought of Cicely and Abigail, then remembered that in a few days' time he was to go to Stow Stocksley, and that was, in a way, a kind of recompense.

Chapter Four

Orlando, now nearly sixteen, had not seen his grand-parents since the previous Christmas, and he found on this visit that Lady Charlotte's arthritis had now grown so bad that she had been forced to take to her bed. She had converted one of the large, first-floor drawing rooms in the Hall to her use, and her bed was installed in the bay of a mullioned window, so that she had a view over the park and the best of the afternoon sun and sunset each day. With this in mind, she had arranged for a curtain of butter muslin to be put up across one side of the window, held back with a cord near to hand, so that she could let the fine fabric act as a screen against the sun whenever she chose, without darken-ing the room. The room itself she had filled with her most precious possessions and, for Orlando, who spent much idle time there, it was a treasure trove. He would wander round the room, leaning here, sitting there, staring at this and that picture, talking or listening the while, drinking in all the accumulated pleasures of a lifetime – of many lifetimes. She lay in her bed, happy to direct his fancy, to talk to him about this or that piece, finding her delight in her hoard of objects doubled by his interest.

With his fingers Orlando would trace the lines of the art deco irises on the Purmerend dish which stood on the rosewood half-table near her bed, as he talked about his intentions to make the Second XV that winter.

'Omar Ramsden, my dear. My mother was very fond of his work. And of Sybil Dunlop's. She was quite a patroness, my mama. Almost the entire collection of art deco work at Stow Stocksley belonged to her.'

He liked to look at the few jewels which she kept by her, the rest banked long ago and rarely brought out. His favourites were earrings of sapphires and Ceylon diamonds. She would let him hold them up to the light and watch the late August sun turn them to crystal water, blue and white brilliance that flung prisms of light against the sun-softened muslin.

'Those belonged to your great-grandmama,' remarked Lady Charlotte. She smiled as he reached across to hold them up against her ears. 'Perhaps they will be yours to give to your wife someday. Would you like that?'

Orlando reflected with pleasure on this notion, then put the earrings back into their velvet-lined leather box, clasping the lid. Then Lady Charlotte glanced at her watch. 'Now, you see, it's nearly time for *Top of the Pops*. You'd have missed it, if I hadn't remembered. Would you mind, Orlando . . . ?'

He got up and switched on the television, catching the closing credits of *Tomorrow's World*. Apart from helping her with the *Telegraph* crossword and her intricate jigsaws, Orlando often kept his grandmother company while she watched the television which she had recently had installed in her room. Sir Leonard had a dislike of television, preferring to rely on newspapers and the radio, and only the most functional of small portables sat in the kitchen in Stow Stocksley Hall. But Lady Charlotte, with the tyranny of the invalid, had had her way about her own television, which was a very grand affair with a 24-inch screen. Her favourite programmes were *Crossroads* and *Coronation Street*, but she and Orlando regularly watched *Top of the Pops* every Thursday evening during his visits, a fact which would rather have surprised Sir Leonard, had he known of it. She took pleasure in letting Orlando guide her expertly through it; there was

47

something touching in his youthful kindness, imagining that he was helping her, interesting her.

'I think those Abba children are rather sweet,' she remarked. Orlando lounged across the foot of her bed, his chin cupped in his hands.

'No,' he advised her kindly. 'They're awful.'

'If you say so. That's a rather jolly song, though. "The winner takes it all . . ."' she hummed nicely, in her old lady's voice.

He shook his head, still watching the screen. 'They're naff as anything. Oh, great! This is David Bowie – now he's *really* good. You'll like this, Grandma . . .'

She gazed at him fondly. Sometimes, especially at times like this, when his head was half-turned from her, he looked so like Alec – the lean jawline, the high cheekbones. But it often seemed that Orlando was far closer to her than Alec had ever been. Alec had never lounged intimately, comfortably at the end of her bed when he was fifteen – but then, she reminded herself, she had not been ill and bedridden then. Still, there had been a difference . . .

When the programme was over, Lady Charlotte asked Orlando to switch the television off.

'Don't you want to see what's on next?' he asked. They rarely had the chance to watch television at school, and he would happily watch anything and everything in the holidays. She shook her head, feeling tired. He reached out and switched it off, then turned to smile at his grandmother. He looked at her in a leisurely way, quite without self-consciousness, liking her rather horsey, gentle face, the feathery peach skin that had never been spoilt by too much sunlight, or make-up, or drinking. She looked, he thought, exactly as one's grandmother should look, even to her white hair, which was still long, worn gently drawn back from her face and coiled up. She returned his smile, watched him watching her, raising her

48

chin slightly as she admired his features. The movement, sitting as she did against her pillows, head erect, hands folded one on top of the other, gave her a faintly regal air.

'You look like a queen,' observed Orlando. The compliment was perfectly delivered, with a blend of natural candour and masculine charm.

'Orlando,' relied his grandmother, 'you have a most winning way with women. That is a gift.'

Orlando rolled over on to his back, feet resting on the carpet. 'I like women,' he observed. And he did. Apart from his world of school, and his rather formal relationship with his grandfather, they were almost all that he knew.

After a moment's silence, Lady Charlotte said, 'Give me a kiss. Your grandfather will be up shortly. Go and get some supper.'

He kissed her gently on each cheek, as she had taught him to – not the snatched, messy embraces of his aunts, but dignified and affectionate exchanges. He lingered for a moment, enjoying the faint smell of parma violets and the thistledown touch of her cashmere bedjacket, his young, firm cheek against hers. And then he left her; she watched his graceful figure as the door closed, and lay back against the coolness of her pillow, marvelling at the boy's ability to leave her satisfied and contented, like a lover.

That autumn, Orlando went to spend half term with the Coulthards in Scotland. It was dismal and cold, and Dan went down with a cold and then flu, and was confined to his bed for several days. During that time, a friend of Mrs Coulthard's had been invited to lunch, bringing with her a sixteen-year-old niece, Hannah Lennox.

'I'm meant to be looking after her after lunch,' Orlando moaned to Dan, sitting on his bed and leafing through his copy of *Catcher In The Rye*. 'I really wish you were going to be there, too.'

'She's all right,' said Dan in blocked-up tones. 'You'll probably get on okay.'

Orlando was not at all sure about this, but when he met Hannah he was surprised. She was a slender, almost thin girl, as tall as he was and very pretty, with long, dark hair and bright, challenging blue eyes. Struck by her prettiness, Orlando gave her his best smile when they were introduced; she did not return it, but merely shook his hand and surveyed him expressionlessly. Matters did not improve much over lunch, for she seemed a touchy and faintly hostile creature, and Orlando's conversational gambits were not very successful. When lunch was over, Mrs Coulthard said to Orlando, 'Hannah's aunt and I have to go through some things I've put by for her sale, so maybe you and Hannah could find yourselves something to do in the playroom? Dan's having a nap, so I don't think you should disturb him.'

Mrs Coulthard, who was overly protective towards her only son, was accustomed to treating adolescents as though they were children. Although the playroom seemed an undignified proposition for a sixteen-year-old, Orlando could not think of anything else to do with this girl, who didn't seem to like him very much.

'D'you want a game of table tennis?' he asked her.

She shrugged indifferently. 'I don't mind.'

They made their way down to the playroom, so called because it housed a table tennis table, a rusting bagatelle, and a dartboard. The room was cold and dank, and smelled of paraffin heaters, and Hannah leaned against the windowsill, her face a mask of indifference, as Orlando hunted out a ball and two bats, the rubber flapping from one of them. He tossed the ball to Hannah and handed her the better of the two bats.

'You serve.'

They began to play, the friction at lunchtime making them competitive, and they did not speak between shots, except to

50

keep score. Orlando had begun by instinctively toning his game down for her, but she played with such fierce intensity that he was forced to step his play up. As the ball cracked backwards and forwards Hannah was panting with breathlessness; as she dived to retrieve the ball from a corner into which Orlando had struck it wildly, her hair began to come loose from its ribbon. She came back to the table, her eyes sparkling and her hair falling in wisps around her face and shoulders, and Orlando thought again how pretty she was, and how daunting. She stood ready to serve, pulling the ribbon from her hair and flinging it aside, wearing a look of stark determination.

When the score stood at 20–19 in Orlando's favour, he cracked a serve which barely skimmed the net and landed just on the corner's edge on Hannah's side. She only just managed to flip it back over the net, and it seemed to trickle off the side of the table, so that Orlando had to lunge down to return it. His return landed just on the other side of the net, but beyond Hannah's reach. As the ball dribbled towards her, Orlando straightened up with a grin of triumph.

'One game to me,' he said. 'Want another? Shall we make it the best out of three?'

She scooped the ball up in her hand and glared at him. 'You're joking!' she said. 'The ball bounced twice before you hit it! You didn't win that point!'

Orlando stared back at her, regaining his breath. 'You're the one who's joking,' he retorted. 'Do you think I wouldn't have said if it had bounced twice? Thanks very much.'

'I saw it bounce twice! *And* I heard it! If that's the way you play – '

'I don't cheat,' he interrupted calmly, holding out his hand towards her. 'Come on, if it's that important, we'll play the point again.'

'No,' she replied, clutching the ball to her. 'I don't feel like

51

playing with a cheat. You just couldn't bear to lose to a girl, could you?'

'I don't care what you are,' said Orlando in exasperation, 'but stop calling me a cheat. Come on, give me the ball.'

'No.'

He came round the table and she backed off slightly, watching him. She did not take her eyes from his as he grasped the wrist of the hand in which she held the ball. He tried to uncurl her fingers, then stopped, took her by the other wrist and, without thinking or hesitating, kissed her. He expected to encounter resistance, but he found her mouth quite soft and yielding, and they stood there in a tentative embrace, each sharply aware of the novel and faintly shocking scent of the other, touching skin and hair gently. Orlando suddenly experienced a rush of excitement of the most potent kind and, faintly embarrassed, brought the kiss to an end and stepped back.

She stared at him hard, her mouth soft and blurred, then she said huskily, 'I'm sorry I called you a cheat.'

'It doesn't matter,' he said. He looked at her, conscious only of wanting to kiss her again. 'Why are you so – I mean, why do you behave as though you don't really like me?'

'Because I do – really like you, I mean,' she said. He pulled her towards him and kissed her again for a long and wonderful space of time, until they were interrupted by the sound of Mrs Coulthard's voice at the top of the playroom stairs.

'Hannah? Your aunt is ready to go now, dear. Come and fetch your coat.'

Hannah picked her ribbon up from the floor and went to the door, tying her hair up as she did so.

'Can I meet you in town tomorrow?' he said suddenly. 'Dan's still not well enough to get up.'

She hesitated, then said, 'If you like. Do you know the Market Brae steps?'

He nodded. 'About two?'

'All right.'

They stared at one another for a moment. Then Hannah went upstairs to where her aunt was waiting. He followed and watched as she left the farm with her aunt, turning her coat collar up against the rain.

Over the days that followed, until Dan was up and about, Orlando saw her as often as possible. He discovered that she lived not far away, in an ancestral pile known as Capercailzie Castle. Orlando was intrigued, and wondered if it was anything like Stow Stocksley.

'You should come and see it one day,' said Hannah.

'I'd like to. What do your parents do?'

'My mother's dead. My father – well, he sort of runs the estate, and spends a lot of time taking people to court. I don't know . . . I think he's a bit mad, actually.'

He kissed her. 'Do you realise that I probably won't be able to see you again until Easter?' he said. 'I don't think I can stand it. But I'll write to you.'

'That would be nice,' she said. Her eyes searched his face. 'I really wish you didn't live in England.'

'You're not the only one,' replied Orlando, whose infatuation with Mrs Rees-Jones had been suddenly and entirely eclipsed.

He returned to Ampersand newly in love, and for some reason – possibly a supercharge of hormones – the rest of that winter term turned into something of a disaster for Orlando. A new apathy towards his school work overtook him, and he became aware of an antagonism towards authority in general, and schoolmasters in particular, which resulted in a vague desire for rebellion. He and Dan, who nursed artistic ambitions, formed an underground society called the Henri Rousseau Club, in memory of the painter whose work Dan revered. The society was dedicated largely to the music of The Jam and performance art involving the defacement of school notices – not merely as acts of vandalism, but with a degree of wit and black humour which Orlando hoped echoed the radical, anti-authoritarian practices of Joe Orton in relation to library books. But the school chaplain, a man called Wilson, whom they both detested, caught them in the act of defilement and they were duly punished for their outrages after public denouncement at assembly. When Orlando took his report home at the end of term, a sorrowful note was appended to it, detailing Dan and Orlando's crimes, and concluding that Orlando showed a regrettably rebellious attitude which could only impair his progress at Ampersand unless steps were taken to remedy his behaviour.

Orlando drank the cup of tea which Cicely had poured for him and watched her as she finished reading. He could almost feel the waves of reproach emanating from her, and tried to look duly contrite as he met her woeful gaze. Aunt Abigail took the letter from her sister, glanced at it, then threw it down on the table.

'Well, I suppose something of the sort has to be expected,' she remarked.

'I think it's a good deal more serious than that,' said Cicely. 'I can't imagine what Sir Leonard and Lady Charlotte will say. I don't think you realise how much may depend upon Sir Leonard's good opinion of you, Orlando. I don't think you quite realise that by paying for your schooling – '

Orlando groaned, and Abigail said brusquely to her sister, 'Enough.'

Cicely coloured. 'I was only saying – '

'Yes, well – it is Orlando's first day home, after all.' At that moment the telephone rang, and Abigail went to answer it. She came back and said to Orlando, 'It's for you. Some person called Hannah.'

Orlando smiled at his aunts and left the room.

After Christmas, Orlando went to stay at Stow Stocksley for a week. Aunt Cicely drove him down in the new Datsun. She had dressed carefully for the occasion, Orlando noticed, wearing a bottle green woollen dress with a matching scarf and low heels. As they turned in through the gates of Stow Stocksley Hall and up the long driveway, Orlando observed a slow smile of pleasure cross his aunt's face. Then she smiled and said enigmatically, 'You're such a lucky boy, Orlando.'

When they arrived, Orlando noticed that Cicely greeted Sir Leonard warmly. Relations between the two families were still fairly formal, but the reserve of earlier years had fallen away. Orlando noticed that his grandfather always treated Cicely with a rather reserved friendliness – it was not in his nature to be warmly cordial – and that this had the effect of bringing out a kind of buoyancy in her, an unaccustomed youthfulness in her movements and speech.

After he had taken his bag up to his room, Orlando came back downstairs and found his aunt seated by the blazing fire in the lower drawing room, her legs neatly crossed at the ankles, sipping a glass of sherry. She was leaning forward and gazing with bright interest at a volume of Bauer's *Illustrations of Orchidacheous Plants*, which Sir Leonard had brought out for her.

'. . . a strangely gothic beauty, I always think,' Orlando heard her remark as she surveyed a cross-section of a Blethia orchid stem. So far as he knew, his aunt was not remotely interested in plants, beyond the rather conventional contents of the garden at Plumtree Villa. 'Such wonderful illustrations,' she added, fingering the page before turning it over to gaze with apparently rapt interest at the next plate.

'Bauer, of course,' said Sir Leonard, pleased to be able to discuss one of his fields of expertise and fascination, 'was Kew's first official painter-in-residence – '

'Of course,' murmured Cicely, as if this were known to all,

her eye now wandering across a drawing of the sexual apparatus of a phragmipedium. Orlando slid into an armchair and watched her, smiling slightly.

'– and prepared several collections of microscopic studies. You see, from the late seventeenth century onwards, the microscope afforded a circular view, which was a novel perspective for artists at that time.'

'Naturally,' agreed Cicely, nodding.

'May I offer you another sherry?' asked Sir Leonard, smiling, pleased with himself. Lady Charlotte did not care for orchids, thought them vulgar and unnecessarily sexual, and he enjoyed the rare opportunity of sharing his enthusiasm. As Sir Leonard refilled her glass, Cicely remarked to Orlando, 'I was admiring the orchid prints hanging by the window, and your grandfather was kind enough to show me this.' She raised the large, vellum-bound volume slightly. 'Isn't it magnificent?'

'Lovely,' agreed Orlando. He looked up to see his grandfather advancing upon Cicely with her second sherry, preparing to regale her with more information concerning orchids, their habit and their history, and realised for the first time that it was possibly rather lonely for him at Stow Stocksley, with Lady Charlotte confined to her room, and only the estate manager, the housekeeper-and-gardener couple, and various local worthies to talk to. He mused on this, watching the pleasure his grandfather took in the friendly exchanges with his aunt, and wondered.

When Cicely had exhausted her store of non-specific observations regarding orchids, she said she had best be going before it got dark.

'I do hope that Lady Charlotte will soon be up and about,' said Cicely, drawing on her gloves. They were new, a Christmas present from Abigail, and they slipped taut and smooth on her plump fingers. Sir Leonard, looking for a moment a little grave, said that he thought, unfortunately, that this was unlikely in the foreseeable future, and Cicely made polite noises of concern and commiseration. 'I shall see you in a week,' she said, kissing Orlando, 'when Sir Leonard brings you back. Thank you *so* much for showing me that fascinating volume, Sir Leonard . . .' Just as she was searching in her bag for her car keys, she remembered Orlando's report and the headmaster's letter, and brought them out. 'On a rather less happy note,' she said, handing them to Sir Leonard, 'here is Orlando's school report. Not greatly to his credit, I'm sorry to say.' She gave Orlando a reproving look, and he merely smiled at her. 'However, perhaps it's best if Orlando explains it to you himself.' With that, she left, and Sir Leonard closed the door behind her.

'I had no idea your aunt was interested in orchids. Perhaps next time I should take her on a tour of the hothouses,' remarked Sir Leonard as he unfolded the report. Orlando stood, staring first at the carpet, then at the large windows which looked out across the wintry line of the park trees, while his grandfather sat down to read it. When he had read the letter, Sir Leonard subjected Orlando to a brief, dull lecture on the folly of his subversive behaviour. Just when Orlando thought he had finished, Sir Leonard rose from his armchair and paced slowly to the window, then turned back to Orlando.

'The reason I lecture you like this, Orlando, is that I have certain hopes invested in you.' He paused. 'I suppose now is as good a time as any to explain matters to you. You see, I have formed the intention, Orlando, of making you my heir, if possible. I think you should know this. You are aware, of course, that your mother and father did not marry before you were born. But you are my grandson, and I would wish – if it could be so – that you should one day inherit Stow Stocksley, and all that is in it. I imagine there will be legal formalities, certain procedures necessary to legitimise you – I don't know yet what these might be, and haven't spoken to my lawyer yet. I hope to do so soon. But you must understand, Orlando, that much depends upon you. Certain things in life must be earned. Your father – well, I cannot pretend that he was not a disappointment to me, but, had things been otherwise, this would have been his inheritance, for good or ill. But in your case, so far as it is within my power, I wish to make sure that if you are to inherit, it should be for good.' He fingered the folds of the report. 'Not for ill.' There was a silence, during which Orlando waited patiently. 'Your cousin, Roger, you see, seems to be turning into an entirely worthless specimen. You, on the other hand, have been a credit so far. But I cannot pin my hopes on someone who is prepared to indulge in nonsense of this kind, flout authority. Possibly all this sounds excessively pompous to you. But I think you understand what I am saying.' His eye met Orlando's for the first time. 'Don't disappoint me. Or your grandmother.' Orlando, after a brief silence, nodded. For a moment Sir Leonard surveyed his grandson's features and wondered what thoughts revolved behind that clear, candid gaze. But Orlando's face betrayed nothing. 'Now,' said Sir Leonard, 'go up and see her.'

Orlando rose and was about to leave, when Sir Leonard held out the report and the letter. 'Here, you had better show her these. You and I have said all we have to say on the subject.'

Orlando pocketed them and made his way up to his grandmother's room. He mounted the stairs slowly, awed by the prospect of possession, one day, of all the magnificence which surrounded him.

He found his grandmother propped up against her pillows, half-moon spectacles resting on the end of her nose, studying the Christmas double issue of the *Spectator*. She smiled a glad and peaceful smile at the sight of Orlando. He bent to kiss her, and she put the magazine aside, her movements tentative and frail, as he took his customary place at the end of her bed.

'This A.N. Wilson creature is such a dreary prig,' she remarked. 'Though I rather like the man Waugh. Some amusing thoughts, but obviously quite mad. And not so talented as his father, poor thing. His first wife, you know, was quite a friend of my elder sister, Maud. Her name was Evelyn, too.'

But Orlando was hardly listening. 'You've cut your hair, Grandma.' He was still young enough for the astonishment and dismay to show in his voice, and for a moment this made Lady Charlotte sad. She put up a thin hand and touched the back of her head.

'I'm afraid it was too much of a chore, having it washed, you know, Orlando. Such a sick old thing as I am. Really it was easier to have it all chopped off.' And she smiled sadly at the look of disappointment in his eyes.

Orlando regarded her. Without the soft waves of white-grey hair pulled back from her long face, she looked quite plain and like any ordinary old woman. There seemed to be nothing regal about her now. 'It looks very nice,' he said. 'I think it suits you.' But for once, his charm was unable to convince. He was too preoccupied in noticing the changes that seemed to have taken place in his grandmother since last summer. She seemed somewhat shrunken, stooped in the back, and the skin around her nose and on the backs of her hands had a shiny, tissuey quality, the bones near the surface. She must, he thought, be far more ill than he had imagined.

Still, he lounged on her bed and talked her through his term – he even told her about Hannah – and she lay and listened, sometimes closing her eyes, occasionally smiling.

'Oh, that reminds me – ' He dug in his pocket and produced his report and the letter. 'This is the bad news.'

He lay back on the lace counterpane, hands clasped behind his head, staring at the ceiling as she read.

'How wicked of you,' she murmured, then laughed. 'What exactly did you write on these notices?' Orlando told her, and Lady Charlotte laughed with the painful hilarity of the ill, and kissed Orlando. 'I suppose your grandfather was *very* displeased?'

'Somewhat,' said Orlando, smiling. 'So was Cicely.'

'I'm sure they were perfectly right to be . . .' She leaned back against her pillows. 'Oh, Orlando, I meant to tell you – *Star Wars* is on television tonight. I do rather like these holiday films. I watched *The Dirty Dozen* on Boxing Day, do you know? Hardly very festive, but then . . .'

So Orlando switched on the television and they watched *Star Wars* together until, at one point, Orlando turned to say something to his grandmother and found she was asleep, breathing gently. Switching off the television, he picked up his report from where it lay on her bedside table, crumpled it into a ball and flicked it neatly across the room into the fire, now burning low. Then he kissed his grandmother and went to his room.

Chapter Five

The following term, Orlando endeavoured to mend his ways and apply himself to his work, but chastisement seemed to have had a contrary effect upon Dan, who continued to rebel against authority, and regularly denounced the public school system as perpetuating bourgeois and non-egalitarian social values. Orlando, who shared a study with his friend, tried to treat him with tolerance, and beguiled his spare time by keeping up a tender correspondence with Hannah. By the time Easter came, when he was due to spend his customary fortnight's holiday with the Coulthards, he realised that, in spite of a fervent longing to see her, he had almost forgotten what she looked like.

But when he met her in Inverness, he could not imagine how such a potent image could ever have faded from his mind. They set off from the centre of town and wandered idly through the streets, talking and rediscovering one another, their awkwardness gradually falling away. They found a small park, and walked with heads bent beneath the spring trees, skirting the crocuses, talking, listening, absorbed in each other with grave delight, like children. They dawdled by the playground swings, sat on a bank beside the pond and tossed pebbles into the water, watched the gardeners bedding in new plants, and all the while talking, talking, unravelling the stuff of their young lives for one another. They were entirely self-absorbed, as though nothing else touched them. The park, the town, the trees, the sky, the world – everything was simply a backdrop for the drama of their own first love. When they kissed beneath the trees, Orlando did not think he would ever in his life feel as passionately for anyone as he did for Hannah.

At the end of the day they waited at the bus station for their respective buses, and Orlando said, 'I can't see you every day, I'm afraid.' He hesitated. 'But what about Thursday?'

Hannah nodded. 'Why don't you come out to Capercailzie? I could ask father if you could stay the night.'

He stared at her. 'Are you sure?' he asked, wondering how he could get this past Dan's mother.

She smiled. 'Of course I am.'

They arranged the time and place, and Orlando took the bus back to the farm, serenely happy. He returned to find an argument in full flight between Dan and his father. It seemed to Orlando that Dan and his father argued perpetually nowadays about everything – about school, about Dan's refusal to go to church on Sundays (the Coulthards were staunch Presbyterians and pillars of the local kirk), about the length of Dan's hair, and about what Mr Coulthard referred to as Dan's 'attitude'. Orlando took refuge in his room until it was over, and then the two of them went to the local pub for an illicit pint of beer and a few Benson & Hedges, and Orlando listened to Dan rail against his parents and the injustices of life. When Dan had mellowed slightly, Orlando set about enlisting his sympathy with regard to Hannah and Thursday night, and between them they managed to concoct a fairly satisfactory story involving a non-existent relative of Orlando's, which they hoped would keep Mrs Coulthard happy.

Three days later, as directed by Hannah, Orlando took the bus from Inverness to Kirkallan, a village which was little more than a cluster of houses, a shop, and a grim-looking hotel. He stood on the narrow, deserted pavement, with the wind from the hills beginning to drive in low, scudding clouds overhead. There was no sign of Hannah. The calm skies which had hung over the lochs and mountains for the past few days now suddenly gave way to sombre dullness and to chill, drenching rain. It began in a tentative, spitting way, then suddenly turned into a fierce downpour. Orlando was dressed only in his jeans and Barbour jacket, and the rain had already begun to soak his hair, dripping into the upturned collar of his coat. Swearing mildly, he was just about to head for shelter when he saw Hannah hurrying towards him, a large golfing umbrella held above her head.

'There you are!' she called. 'I thought maybe you'd missed the bus.' He kissed her, rain dripping over his face from his wet hair. 'Come on,' she said, and held the umbrella over his head. They set off through the village, the rain gusting unsteadily, the outlines of the surrounding hills almost invisible through the misty clouds which had descended. As they walked, a car approached them, an old Riley, its maroon bodywork glistening with rain, its windscreen wipers swishing gravely. It moved along the road towards them at a dignified trundle.

'Oh, thank heavens!' said Hannah suddenly. 'It's MacDermott.' The car slowed at the other side of the road, and Hannah took Orlando's hand and hurried towards it. The driver's window was cranked fitfully down, and a small, sour face looked out at them.

'I kent this was coming,' it remarked, nodding at the rain. 'I offered you a lift, but – oh, no, you wouldna have it,' he added in grumbling tones to Hannah, who was tugging at one of the rear doors and trying to put the umbrella down at the same time. The driver's window was wound up again. 'Who's he?' asked Orlando, as he took the dripping umbrella from Hannah.

'It's MacDermott. He's my father's man. He – he sort of housekeeps for us, helps with the estate,' she replied over her shoulder.

Orlando sank thankfully into the back seat of the car,

breathing in the smell of aged leather and watching with interest as the small figure in front, supported on two worn cushions, eased the car carefully into gear and set off through the rain.

'Thanks for coming to get us, MacDermott,' said Hannah in relief, tugging out her long hair from beneath her coat collar. Then she slid wet, secretive fingers into Orlando's. 'I really thought it would stay fine when I set out.'

'That's why ye took the umbrella, I suppose?' said MacDermott. He drove on a little. 'Wouldn't be told,' he added in grim satisfaction. Hannah flashed Orlando a quick smile, and he smiled uncertainly in return. They did not speak throughout the rest of the drive, which was a very slow one. MacDermott did not allow the car to go above twenty-five miles an hour, to the irritation of two drivers who got stuck behind the Riley, then sped past when MacDermott at last signalled left – Orlando noticed that the loud tick-tock of the indicator was accompanied by a yellow arrow snapping out of the side of the car. He had thought that such indicators were obsolete.

As MacDermott steered the car between the pillars of a stone gateway, Orlando gazed ahead at the broad sweep of driveway flanked by Douglas firs, and wondered if Capercailzie Castle was going to be the Scottish counterpart of Stow Stocksley Hall. But all thoughts of the well-tended, handsome approach to his grandfather's home faded as the Riley made its lumbering progress up the drive. The road had long ago fallen into disrepair, was now rutted and pocked with puddles, so that the car occasionally had to veer into the verge to avoid the deepest of these and, at one point, the shattered limb of a tree which partially blocked their path. The end of the curving driveway was marked by a dark tangle of overgrown rhododendrons which reared up on either side, glistening with rain.

Capercailzie Castle was a relic from a forgotten age. It looked larger than it was, with odd towers and false turrets at random intervals, but the effect was massive. It was a great, glowering building, its entrance a series of moulded Tudor arches, its windows thick and mullioned and scarcely visible in places through the dense veins of matted ivy which covered much of the walls. Broad steps led up to the entrance, flanked by grey stone balustrades, which were crumbling and broken in places, giving the place a decrepit air. Grounds spread away on either side of the castle, but these were misted into invisibility by the rain. No lights shone in any of the windows, despite the gloom. The whole place looked to Orlando like some Gothic folly gone to ruin.

The car drew to a halt and MacDermott pulled on the creaking handbrake. 'Oot ye get,' he said, and sighed as Orlando struggled and shoved at the door handle. They got out, and the Riley roared into life and chugged off round to the rear of the castle, as Orlando and Hannah headed through the rain to the front entrance. The large outer wooden doors stood ajar, and Orlando could tell from their warped outlines that they had stood in this position for many years. Hannah turned the handle of one of the inner doors and they passed through into the hallway.

Ahead of them was an enormous staircase, down the centre of which fell a cascade of very thin, worn tartan carpeting, pinned back with long brass stair-rods, some tarnished and bent, others missing altogether. Passages stretched away on either side of the staircase to the back of the house, and dark doors, firmly shut, led off the hallway into the main downstairs rooms. The air was cold and musty, like that of a museum, and when Hannah spoke, her voice echoed faintly.

'Have you brought a change of clothing?' she asked, glancing at Orlando's wet hair and the dark patches of damp on the knees of his jeans. Orlando, still taking in his surroundings, merely nodded. 'Perhaps you should go and change into some dry clothes, and I'll take your others down to the kitchen to dry. Come on, I'll show you your room.'

He followed Hannah up the broad staircase. At the top they turned right into a long corridor, with dark, panelled walls, occasionally relieved by arched, mullioned windows, set high up, which threw only a feeble light from the rainy afternoon outside. One or two ancestral portraits, grimy with age, hung on the walls, but the rest stood stacked at intervals along the floor of the corridor, back to back in uneven huddles, stiff, rusty hoops of wire sprouting from their heavy frames.

'This is some place,' murmured Orlando; again he thought of Stow Stocksley, of the light, elegant panelling of the corridor which led to his grandmother's room, of the fresh flowers, pretty antiques and carefully hung pictures.

'My room's right at the end,' said Hannah. 'This is yours.' They had stopped at a door halfway down the corridor. Hannah opened it and led Orlando in.

It was a big, square room, appreciably brighter than the rest of the house so far, with two large windows looking out across the driveway. In its centre stood a large bedstead, on which lay a lumpily stuffed mattress and two bolsters upholstered in threadbare satin. The bed had once been a four-poster, and four wooden posts sprouted from each corner, though the canopy had long since vanished. One of the curved poles stuck out askew, and Hannah wiggled it as she surveyed the bed and sighed.

'I thought MacDermott might have made it up. I'll have to get you some sheets and blankets.' She stood in the middle of the dark, uncarpeted floorboards and surveyed the room. 'It's a bit basic,' she said, 'but at least you've got a washbasin – the bathroom's absolutely miles away.' She hesitated. 'Well, I'll leave you to get changed. See you in a minute.' And she left him.

Orlando looked around. It was totally unlike anything he had expected. He dumped his rucksack down and walked over to the washbasin in the corner of the room, next to the window. It was the largest he had ever seen, a huge porcelain bath of a basin with brass and enamel taps and fittings, patterned all over with willow pattern and laced with a network of little cracks. Orlando turned on one of the taps and watched icy water sputter and splash into the basin. The plug consisted of a brass rod and plunger which reared up between the taps. He pushed it up and down experimentally a couple of times, then turned the tap off. He moved around the room, conscious of the chill in the air, that special, clammy coldness which belongs to unused, long shut-up rooms. In the corner opposite the washbasin stood a large mahogany wardrobe, leaning forward at a slight angle from the wall; he opened the door tentatively and stared into its dark, camphoric interior. Then he closed it, and stared at his reflection in the age-spotted oval glass of the door. He turned and surveyed the rest of the room. A wicker-seated chair stood next to the large marble fireplace, in which, he noted with pleasure, a fire had been carefully laid, with fresh paper spills, sticks and coal. He stared out of the window at the rain, which was easing off, then examined the grimy, but once-lovely wallpaper, the faded, moth-eaten brocade of the curtains that hung from tarnished rings on ivory rails, and wondered what his grand-mother would have made of it all. She would probably have loved it.

His curiosity satisfied, Orlando changed out of his damp jeans into the fresh pair of trousers which he had brought, combed his damp hair, and decided to go in search of Hannah. He went back down the corridor, descended the wide stair-case, and stood at the bottom, listening for sounds of household activity. He glanced at the two imposing double doorways to the right and left of the hall, but they did not look inviting. Following the hallway down the left-hand side of the staircase, he found himself in a dim passageway, lined with two more doors, leading to the top of a steep staircase. This apparently led to the lower regions of the house; there was a light from below, and he could hear the distant sound of voices. He set off down the curved stone stairway, and when he reached the bottom, found himself in a great empty, open room, stone-flagged, the walls yellow with old whitewash. There were cupboards, and a large stone trough of a sink in one corner, and a long, low window at the end of the room. Above the empty fireplace hung a board ranged with numbered bells; there were forty-eight of these, one, he presumed, for each room in the castle. Through the window he could see the rain splashing on the stones of a courtyard, and a flight of steps leading back up to ground level.

Suddenly he heard voices through the doorway on his left. He walked through, and there was Hannah, setting out glasses and plates on a large wooden table, while a very thin, tall man in extremely baggy tweeds stood at the middle of an old-fashioned kitchen range, stirring at a pot on the stove.

Hannah glanced up and smiled. 'You found your way all right. I was going to come and fetch you.' The thin man turned and glanced at Orlando, a swift, dark, intimidating look. He turned and stirred the pot once more, then stepped away from the range, wiping his long, narrow hands on his trousers. He stretched one out to Orlando.

'Patrick? Forfar Lennox.' Orlando shook his hand and murmured, 'How do you do?', a little startled by the forthright manner and absence of warmth in this greeting. Hannah's father went back to the range and glared down at the pot, and MacDermott bustled in with a basket of logs, then disappeared and came in again trailing two buckets of coal. He muttered to himself as he did so, but no one appeared to take any notice of him.

Hannah indicated a place at the table to Orlando, and he sat down next to Hannah, with MacDermott opposite him. Mr Lennox began to spoon broth out into bowls and set one in front of each person. The meal began in an uneasy silence, and then Forfar Lennox began to bark questions at Orlando about his school and family. Orlando felt that these were rather in the nature of a cross-examination than an attempt at conversation, but he answered as affably as he could, watching MacDermott tearing his bread into lumps and dropping them in his soup, then fishing them out again with his spoon and consuming them noisily. After the broth they had cold game pie, which Orlando was given to understand had been made by Mr Lennox himself – indeed, to the extent of having been reared and shot by him as well – and a salad.

When the meal was over and Hannah was clearing the plates away, Mr Lennox rose from the table and disappeared into a large pantry. Orlando could hear a light-pull being tugged ineffectually a few times and then, after clicks and curses, his host emerged clutching a dusty bottle of port and a tin of shortbread wrapped in cellophane. The ghost of a smile touched his lips as he sat down.

'Glasses, MacDermott,' he said, setting the bottle down and beginning to tear the cellophane from the tin. 'This,' he remarked to his daughter, 'is your Aunt Margaret's gift to me from last Christmas.' He glanced up at MacDermott as he placed three glasses on the table, and waved a long forefinger at him. 'Away and see to the fires and some bedding for Mr Patrick here.'

A little struck by the peremptory tone of this command, Orlando watched as MacDermott left, then turned his gaze back to the port which his host was carefully pouring into the glasses. There they sat, Hannah and her father and Orlando, sipping port and nibbling petticoat-tail shortbread as the night gathered outside.

Having by now the feeling that Hannah's father was not entirely antagonistic towards him, Orlando enquired tentatively how large his host's estate was. He presumed, from the nature of Capercailzie Castle, that a considerable amount of land must run with it.

'Some forty-five thousand acres,' replied Forfar Lennox with satisfaction, and poured himself another glass of port; the children were allowed only one. 'Some four hundred brace of grouse, forty stags, a hundred and twelve hinds. You shoot, Patrick?'

'Yes. Yes, I do,' replied Orlando, thinking of the Purdey which his grandfather had given him the Christmas before last.

'Well, maybe you can come up here next autumn and we'll take you out.' Mr Lennox stared ruminatively at his port and hardly seemed to hear when Orlando replied that he would very much like that. Orlando noticed Hannah motion with her eyes.

She turned towards her father and said, 'I think I'll take Orlando up and see if MacDermott has seen to his room. I'll be down in a bit to wash up.'

Mr Lennox looked up briefly, grunted 'goodnight' to Orlando, and helped himself to another triangle of shortbread.

The way upstairs was lit by gloomy electric lighting that appeared to date back to Edwardian times, but when he went into his room, Orlando discovered that it now looked rather cheerful, in an eccentric fashion. MacDermott had lit the fire, and drawn the heavy old curtains against the raw March night, and fresh linen had been put on the bed, together with blankets and a heavy old satin eiderdown which puffed duckdown when moved.

'There,' said Hannah. 'I hope you'll be comfortable enough.' She glanced around, her manner faintly remote, uneasy.

70

Orlando kicked the door closed, put his arms around her and kissed her. Her response was tentative, almost unwilling.

'I must taste of port,' she murmured.

'You taste wonderful,' said Orlando, then shivered. He drew her across the room, closer to the fire, where MacDermott had thoughtfully hung Orlando's Barbour over the back of the cane chair. 'I love you,' he murmured, kissing her again, conscious of the growing, enveloping warmth and feelings of desire as he pressed against her.

The thought of the bed behind them leapt into his mind, terrifying him with its possibilities. He had thought much about making love to Hannah, and the idea thrilled and frightened him all at once. But the notion of anything happening here, now, with her father sitting downstairs, was ludicrous. He drew away from Hannah, who opened her eyes and stood, lips parted, looking at him. That look, those wide blue eyes, dark and intense, seemed to Orlando unutterably lovely.

Then she sighed, slipped her arms from around him. 'I hope you don't find it all too strange here,' she said. 'Anyway, I'll let you get to bed. I'll show you around the place in the morning.'

'Okay. Goodnight.'

She closed the door and left him alone. Again he had that peculiar sensation, as if the castle, this room, were somehow suspended in a past era. In anyone else's house where one was a guest, there would be television to watch, or games of cards to play in brightly-lit rooms, conversation. At any rate, a sense of living in the present. He sat down on the bed, eerily aware of the silence in the rest of the castle, of the dark chill of the countless other uninhabited rooms surrounding his. There was nothing to do here but to go to bed, and so he did so. He lay there, watching the firelight flickering on the dark walls, distorting the shadows and enhancing the strangeness of the atmosphere, thinking of Stow Stocksley, of how its

71

well-nourished English heart still beat vigorously, while in this gloomy and decaying castle the pulse of life seemed barely to flicker.

Chapter Six

The next day Orlando opened his curtains to a blue, clear sky, all trace of the rain washed away. He took a brisk bath in the enormous tiled bathroom, where the pipes clanked and the hot water gushed and sputtered alternately, and after breakfast he and Hannah went outside in the light spring air to walk around the grounds. There was something in the imposing nature of the castle which, it seemed to Orlando, reduced himself and Hannah to the stature of children. He felt like a boy on holiday.

They started at the back, and Hannah showed Orlando the kitchen garden which had once supplied the whole household in the days when the castle had boasted two cooks and a butler, and a whole army of footmen, maids and chambermaids. Most of the garden was now wild and overgrown, expanses of docks and nettles stretching from the greenhouses to the old brick walls, where espaliered fruit trees, apple, peach, plum and pear, grew, wizened and long untended. But MacDermott still kept a sizeable corner close to the castle where he grew his own vegetables, and Hannah showed Orlando where gooseberry bushes and raspberry canes still flourished amid the tangle of undergrowth.

'How has everything become so neglected?' asked Orlando, as they waded through the weeds to the hothouses. As soon as he had said this, he hoped that he hadn't in some way offended her.

But she merely replied, 'Money. We haven't got any.'

They reached the hothouses, now cold and dilapidated,

with leaning wooden walls and floors overgrown with cushions of green moss. Fragments of glass lay scattered where loose panes had fallen from their rotted frames. They walked through the silent greenhouses filled with the mummified remains of former glories, beds of earth where vines had shrivelled and palms had withered, cold, grey networks of piping which had once hissed and steamed amid the roots of a Victorian hothouse jungle, great broken stacks of clay pots and rows of cloches, nets, pegs, canes – all neglected and untouched for years. In the last of the hothouses Orlando came upon a dead, vinelike plant which had twisted its way upwards towards the light and had broken through the glass. From the vine hung rows of little dried pods which seemed to be made of some dark, woven fibre, and which blew gently in the breeze through the broken pane.

'Loofahs,' said Hannah, setting the pods swaying with her finger. 'Little dead loofahs.'

'How long is it since all this – well, since it became disused?' asked Orlando, staring around.

'I don't know. Perhaps the thirties. Perhaps later. I can't ever remember it being different. My great-grandfather was the last person to have any real wealth. But he gambled a lot, lost most of it. Since then, we've just been poor.'

'But what about the estate?'

'Oh, that?' Hannah smiled and led him out past a smaller greenhouse, where tomato seedlings lay in neat rows in trays. 'I couldn't say anything in front of father, but most of the land went a year ago.' She paused. 'He's a darling, my father, but he's not – he's not very well, really. I mean, in his mind he's still the laird of Capercailzie, but in reality all that he's got is this castle, and he can't even afford to look after that.' They walked away from the greenhouses, through the stableyard and out on to the moors. 'Most of this – ' Hannah stretched out a hand across the expanse of moorland and craggy rock ' –

was bought by some English syndicate. They have shooting parties booked during the season. It all used to be ours.'

'Didn't that bring in a bit of money?'

'A lot. But it all went to pay off debts. Father likes to litigate, and lawyers are expensive. Especially if you lose all the time.' She glanced at Orlando. 'He won't leave Capercailzie, you see. It's just falling to pieces around us, and there's nothing we can do about it.'

'Doesn't that make you terribly sad?' asked Orlando, as they trekked across the springy, soft turf.

'Of course,' she replied. 'But I don't think about it. What can I do?'

They walked on for a mile or so, basking in the growing warmth of the air, laughing and wheeling around each other, until they reached the edge of a glen, fir trees skirting a rocky ascent, and the sound of water somewhere within.

'Come on,' said Hannah. 'I want to show you something.' She led him up through the dark firs, along a path which wound through a scatter of rocks and more firs to a rocky outcrop. Below them in a shallow gulley splashed a waterfall, its shining, foaming waters pouring down on to jagged rocks and crashing into a dark pool at the foot.

Orlando stretched himself and gazed down at the bright, tumbling torrent, fingering a pine cone which he had picked up from the ground beside him. Lightly he tossed it over and watched it disappear soundlessly into the waterfall.

'My mother used to bring me here on picnics,' said Hannah, kneeling down next to him.

'Maybe that's why we're such sympathetic souls,' said Orlando after a brief silence. 'Both having mothers who are dead.' He said it half-jokingly.

'Actually,' said Hannah after a moment, 'my mother ran off with an estate agent from Crieff years before she died. So I

75

probably don't feel quite the same way about her as you do about yours.'

'No,' he agreed, and reached out to stroke her neck as she leaned against him. 'We're too close to the edge of this thing,' he remarked, and shuffled backwards a little, bringing her with him. They lay down next to one another on the soft earth, carpeted with moss and pine needles. He kissed her for a long time, and when he slid his hand beneath her jumper, pushing her bra up to cup her breast, she did not stop him, only breathed a little faster and made a small moaning noise that was neither assent nor dissent, as his fingers travelled down across her body, unbuckling her belt clumsily and pulling her jeans open and down across her hips. Once he had touched her, realised that she wanted him and that there was no going back, he freed himself from his own trousers and, before either of them could think or speak, he thrust himself into her, gasping softly at the sensation, his mind lost and drowning in the sounds of the waterfall far below. After a moment or two, Orlando lay panting in something like astonishment and relief, and found her looking up at him with an expression of amusement.

'Oh, God!' he said. 'We shouldn't have . . .' He felt consumed with pleasure and guilt.

'Why not?'

He breathed deeply again. 'God, it was amazing . . . But it's just –we're meant to take precautions, you know.'

She wriggled away, pulling at her jeans. 'Don't worry,' she said. 'I wouldn't have let you if I didn't think it was all right.'

He thought she sounded fairly matter-of-fact about one of the most mind-blowing experiences ever. This isn't the way it's meant to be, thought Orlando. It has to be more romantic than this.

Hannah was sitting up and frowning, pulling bits of pine needle and dead leaf from her long hair, and zipping up her jeans. Feeling rather ungainly, Orlando hauled up his trousers and sat up, too.

'Hannah, Hannah,' he said, reaching out and taking both her hands. 'Slow down . . .' He kissed her. 'I love you. I've never done that with anyone before, and it was . . . I didn't hurt you, did I?'

She looked directly at him and smiled, then shook her head. He wondered if maybe it wasn't quite so good for girls. Then a doubt crossed his mind. 'That was the first time for you, too, wasn't it? I mean, you've never – '

She put a finger against his lips. 'No, I've never.'

'Don't worry. I love you. I'll look after you, whatever,' he added, bursting with the confidence of youth, his belief that all must turn out well for those in love, as he was in love. She said nothing, and he asked, 'Do you love me?'

'Yes,' she replied, her voice earnest and sure. He looked into her eyes and believed her, adored her, and was totally happy.

After a while they left the glen and started to walk back to the castle. As they walked, Orlando, a small glow of masculine triumph in his heart, thought that now it had happened, it was bound to happen again. And again. This sex thing was pretty good. He felt that some special milestone in his life had been passed.

When they got back to the castle, Forfar Lennox had gone to Inverness on business, and Hannah took Orlando through the countless rooms in the castle on a journey of exploration. In many of the rooms furniture stood draped in dustsheets, curtains closed against the fading ravages of sunlight. Orlando wondered how long ago they had been closed, by whose hand, and whether they would ever be opened again and the dustsheets laid aside. Some rooms stood entirely empty, and in others hung vast closets of clothes – hunting suits, tartans, tea dresses, smoking jackets, ballgowns,

77

tweeds. Hannah opened a closet in one room and ran her hands along the fold of the dresses hanging there.

'I used to come up to this room and play all the time when I was younger. Dressing up, making up stories. I was always the heroine. It was pretty lonely here, otherwise.' She stroked a fur cape, and little drifts of moth-eaten fur fell away in her fingers. 'It's just all rotting away here. And some of it's so lovely.' She pulled gently at a piece of braiding on a ballgown of ivory silk. It parted from the fabric with a liquid, gentle ripping sound, its delicate stitching worn to dust by time.

Orlando walked around the room, lifting the lids of trunks, marvelling at the heaps of linen, silk and cashmere which had lain there for two or three generations, undisturbed. He picked up and examined the length of a kid evening glove, with its little mother-of-pearl buttons and taper fingers.

He thought again of Stow Stocksley Hall, of all the well-loved treasures which his grandmother, and her mother before her, had collected so assiduously over the years, and the heritage which Sir Leonard's family had striven to keep alive over the centuries. Capercailzie and the Lennox family had drifted into this present state of decay, the folly of a single generation destroying the work of countless past lives, and the hopes of future ones. Was this what his grandfather feared for Stow Stocksley?

They went downstairs, and Hannah led him into the chill silence of one of the vast drawing rooms. She showed him a wind-up gramophone in a splendid cabinet of polished walnut, inlaid with tulipwood, and the store of pristine 78s, the little cardboard box of shining gramophone needles.

'I used to dance to all of these, or make up words to go with them. Really sad words for the waltzes.' She played a few of the records for him, and the dead air became bright with the forgotten melodies of foxtrots and waltzes, and the shades of lovely women and languid young men, their voices and laughter long still, seemed to Orlando to move among the untouched tables and chairs.

'Capercailzie was famous once, you know,' said Hannah, waltzing herself around. 'The Prince of Wales came here for the grouse shooting in my great-grandfather's day, and he brought Mrs Keppel once. So my father told me. Maybe she stayed in your room.' The languorous notes of an Ivor Novello melody filled the air, and she danced across to the window, the light falling on her face and shoulders.

After tea, Orlando had to leave. He said goodbye to Mr Lennox and thanked him, and set off to walk down to the village with Hannah. They stood on the pavement next to the Salutation Arms Hotel, her hand tucked anxiously into his.

'I want – I want things to be different, you know,' said Orlando, desperate with the realisation that school, home, time and distance would prevent him from seeing her for months. 'I want us to be able to be with each other, to sleep together – Hannah, I want you so much . . .' He could not find words to express the inadequacy of their situation. He kissed her, and then said, 'I love you,' thinking that he would never tire of saying this, wondering how he could ever once have thought it a banal and rather embarrassing sort of thing to say to anyone.

'I love you, too,' she said, and kissed him again. The sound of the bus could be heard coming up the road. 'I'll write to you, I promise.'

The bus drew up, and he picked up his rucksack and jumped aboard, preparing himself for the agonising emptiness that he would feel in leaving her.

Hannah watched the bus pull away, waved once, and then started to walk back to the castle. As she walked, she mused on the events of the morning. Certainly it had been wonderful, though he had been a bit too taken up with himself. Maybe she would have to teach him some of the things that Callum did, that lovely way he had of building everything up, so that she could hardly wait . . . She felt an unexpected surge of desire at the recollection of her encounters with Callum in the deserted stables at Capercailzie, before the sell-off of the land last year had meant that her father no longer really needed an estate manager. But Callum, for all his ways, his little teasing tricks of tenderness and excitement, had not loved her. And Orlando did. Orlando adored her, wanted her in a way that could not but entirely captivate her. And she loved him, she told herself, as she made her way up the dank, rutted driveway to the castle. She loved him with her heart and soul, and now with her body. And he need never know that she had lied.

Chapter Seven

That same Easter, Sir Leonard, at the behest of his wife, reluctantly rang his sister Alicia to invite her and Barney to spend a weekend at Stow Stocksley in a few weeks' time.

'I think it might be an idea if you were to bring Roger,' he added. 'The boy hasn't been near Stow Stocksley since he was twelve, and I'd like to see him take a bit more interest in the place. Besides, I am his godfather, and he could at least visit occasionally.'

'Oh, I'm afraid I don't think Roger will be able to come.' His sister's voice was worried and vague.

'Why not? Simply ask him!'

'Well, you see, he hasn't been very well recently – he's in hospital . . . well, a sort of hospital. It's frightfully good,' went on Alicia hurriedly. 'Some really top people have been there – they say they can do wonders . . .' Then she realised that she had said rather too much.

'Don't tell me,' said Sir Leonard in ominous tones, 'that this has to do with drugs.'

'Well, sort of – that is, you see, Roger just had the *teensiest* problem with heroin – nothing, really. Nothing he can't cope with, the psychiatrist thinks. But he thought it best if Roger went to a clinic for a while, just to help him. It really is only for a week or two, then he'll be as right as rain. I mean, it's supposed to be much better than the last place he went to. That was somewhere in America, and it cost Roger an absolute fortune – '

Sir Leonard interrupted her. 'How long,' he asked, 'has Roger been a heroin addict?'

'Oh, Leonard,' replied his sister, as though the question was too tiresome to bother with, 'I don't know. Two years – possibly three.' She sighed. 'It's all quite beyond my control. I mean, we've done everything, seen all the doctors . . . But I think Roger's really serious about giving it up this time. After all, he says he hasn't got very much of his trust fund left, so he has to be careful . . .'

At this Sir Leonard exploded. 'Alicia! Do you realise how much there was in that trust fund? Our father was misguided enough to assume that there would be more grandchildren than just this damn fool Roger, so there was a complete fortune! How on earth could anyone, even Roger, spend all that money in such a short space of time?'

'Well, he hasn't spent it *all*, Leonard. I do think that's a bit unfair. He still has the house in Cadogan Square . . . I'll admit he does have an extravagant lifestyle, but he spends so much on his friends. He really *is* dreadfully generous, and I think that's rather nice.'

Sir Leonard could stand no more of this. 'Alicia, I do not care to think what kind of friends Roger has. I must say I am appalled by what you tell me. I shall have to think matters over very seriously indeed.'

'I can't think what there is to think over,' replied his sister petulantly. 'Anyway, I shall find out if Barney is free that weekend. We should love to come to see you and Charlotte. It's just a shame about Roger.'

Sir Leonard put the phone down with a heavy heart. That it was a shame about Roger was putting it mildly. It was time, he realised, to put an end to all this. If Orlando could be made legitimate, and Roger put out of the picture for good, then it must be done now. Clearly Roger had been leading, and continued to lead, a life of extraordinary dissipation, one in which he had managed to squander a complete fortune. Sir Leonard was resolved to do his utmost to prevent him from doing the same to Stow Stocksley and its riches. After sitting pondering the matter for a further ten minutes, he telephoned young Mr Baskerville of Baskerville & Beeston, New Square, Lincoln's Inn, and arranged to see him the following morning.

Later that day he gave Lady Charlotte an account of his conversation with Alicia, and told her that he intended to set in train the procedure for legitimising Orlando.

'Don't you think you should tell Bernard and Alicia first?' said Lady Charlotte. 'I mean, we have invited them down for the weekend in a fortnight's time, and I should feel as though we were having them here under false pretences, if all the time you were trying to disinherit Roger. It wouldn't really do.'

'No,' said Sir Leonard thoughtfully. 'I suppose it might be seen as somewhat underhand. Well, in that case I will call Bernard this afternoon. I can't say I look forward to hearing his reaction.'

Sir Leonard's apprehensions were well-founded.

'What in God's name are you talking about?' demanded Barney, as Sir Leonard tried tactfully to explain his position. 'You can't just go around substituting heirs! Roger is due to inherit that pile, and that's all there is to it!'

'I'm afraid,' said Sir Leonard levelly, 'that the manner in which Roger is presently conducting himself leads me to fear for the future of Stow Stocksley. I believe there is another avenue open to me, and I intend to pursue it, and ensure that Orlando inherits Stow Stocksley, if possible. He is my grandson, when all is said and done. I simply felt that I must let you know of my intentions.'

'Well, all is not said and done, not by a long chalk!' fulminated Barney. 'For a start, I don't believe you can do any of this, and if you try, I shall personally drag you backwards through the Chancery courts! I'll be speaking to my lawyers!'

83

And he banged the receiver down. Sir Leonard went to tell Lady Charlotte that he did not think she need expect Barney and Alicia in a fortnight's time.

The next day Sir Leonard travelled up to London and took a taxi to the offices of Baskerville and Beeston.

Sir Leonard still thought of Henry Baskerville as the young Mr Baskerville, although he had succeeded to the position of senior partner on the death of his father some fifteen years before. Admittedly Henry Baskerville, now in his fifties like Sir Leonard, seemed to inhabit a kind of perpetually youthful middle age; his face was pink and plump, and his hair still brown and thick, and the grave manner which he assumed when dealing with legal matters seemed almost playful. He was, however, a lawyer of exceptional capability, a man who prided himself on being able to give a ready and expert response to any question which a client might put to him. Even so, he was momentarily thrown by Sir Leonard's out-of-the-way query.

Sir Leonard approached the matter succinctly. 'I wish to know, Mr Baskerville, what the procedure might be for the adoption of one's grandson.' Young Mr Baskerville looked startled, but he smiled steadily at his client, waiting for elucidation. 'Orlando – my grandson, you see – is my late son's child.' Henry Baskerville nodded. 'But my son and Orlando's mother were not married. Alec, my son, died when he was only twenty, and Orlando was born a few months after his death. His mother then died a few years later. I now wish to adopt the boy. To make him my legal heir.'

Henry Baskerville was struck by two conflicting desires. The first was to answer Sir Leonard's enquiry swiftly and with certitude; the second was to facilitate his client's wishes. But in this case the two desires were incompatible and, although a man of tact, he could not fudge this. He made swift, neat notes and then regarded Sir Leonard thoughtfully.

'Well,' he said slowly, 'there are, as I see it, two issues here. One is the adoption. That in itself is not a problem, provided the boy's present guardians are agreeable.' Sir Leonard hesitated at this then nodded. 'The second is the title, the property, and the manner in which that devolves...' Henry Baskerville's voice took on a vague, brooding note. 'This is where we encounter our difficulties.'

'Really?' said Sir Leonard in surprise.

The lawyer sighed and leaned back. 'Well, you see, Sir Leonard, provided all the proper formalities are observed, there is no bar to your adoption of – it was Orlando, wasn't it? Yes, well. Adoption and so forth – not a problem. But you say that you wish to make Orlando your heir as well...'

'Does not one automatically follow the other?'

Henry Baskerville gazed at Sir Leonard's grim, handsome features and wished there were some way in which he could grant his client's wishes, for he was a benevolently disposed man and preferred to gratify rather than to disappoint.

'I'm afraid not. You see, adoption does not affect the descent of any peerage or title of honour. In this case I refer, of course, to the baronetcy of Stow Stocksley. That must pass, on your death, to the next male heir.'

Sir Leonard sat impassively for a moment, then stood up and moved restlessly round the room. 'But the boy is my grandson! He is my son's son! If I adopt him, how can it possibly be that he does not become my heir?'

'I'm afraid that is the legal position, Sir Leonard,' said the lawyer. 'Orlando may be your grandson, but the fact remains that he is illegitimate. And adoption cannot change that fact. Therefore, he cannot inherit the title which you presently hold. As I have explained.'

Sir Leonard sat down again. 'Then there is nothing I can do to alter his status – to remedy his illegitimacy?'

'Well,' replied Henry Baskerville, drawing in his breath, 'legitimisation can always be effected by a subsequent marriage by the parents, or by parental recognition.' There was a silence. 'But, in this case, given that Orlando's parents have both predeceased him, those are not options open to us. From what you say, there can have been no presumption of marriage – your son and the boy's mother did not live together as man and wife for a number of years, for instance? No . . . In that case, I do not believe there is anything which could alter his status in the eyes of the law.'

A silence fell.

'If that is the case,' said Sir Leonard at length, 'then Stow Stocksley Hall and the estate will pass with the title to the next heir. It is not even in my power to leave any of that to my grandson?'

'As the estate is entailed, Sir Leonard – no. Adoption, just as it does not affect descent of the title, cannot affect the devolution of any property which is limited to devolve along with it.'

There was a long pause. Then Sir Leonard said, 'I had particular reasons for wishing my grandson to become my heir, instead of my nephew . . .'

Henry Baskerville, thinking that he had heard stranger things in this room before, picked up his pen again and fiddled with it, capping and uncapping it. 'Of course, Sir Leonard, not all the property which you possess is entailed. I need not tell you that. If it is a question of benefiting your grandson, or securing his future, there are ample assets available to ensure that. If that is your aim, then I would suggest that a revision of your will, or the establishment of a trust fund, would be a timely act.'

'That was not my principal concern. However . . .' Sir Leonard folded his gloves neatly together and looked up at the lawyer '... it is certainly something to think about.' He hesitated. 'You are quite sure? I mean, there is no question ... ?'

Baskerville shook his head slowly. 'I shall undertake some more research, of course, and will be writing to you, but I'm afraid that, on the face of it, your grandson cannot become your heir. As to the adoption, however ... ?' The question hung in the air.

Sir Leonard nodded. 'I wish that to go ahead, in any event. I shall discuss it with you again. There is no hurry.'

Sir Leonard's journey back to Stow Stocksley was a melancholy one. He had not anticipated difficulties, had merely presumed that by adopting Orlando, he would solve the problem of his birth outside wedlock. The stark word which Henry Baskerville had used – illegitimate – had served to jolt Sir Leonard. He had grown attached to Orlando, and so accustomed to thinking of him as his natural heir that it pained him to be so forcefully reminded of the boy's true status. They could say what they liked, he thought ruefully, as he emerged from the train at Stow Stocksley; to be born a bastard in the enlightened latter half of the twentieth century might not carry with it the superficial stigma which it had done decades before, but the penalties exacted by the law and by society were still severe.

Sir Leonard collected his Bentley from the newly-installed park-and-ride car park, and trundled back to the Hall through the moist April afternoon. When he reached home he changed into corduroys and a battered windcheater, and cap and wellingtons, and walked the length of the park down to the lake with Midas. Thinking had been troublesome to him on the train. The carriage was claustrophobic and depressing, and he had not been able to follow a coherent line of thought. Here, beneath the grey, soft sky, the wind brisk and bracing, fields and woods around him, he felt he could think more clearly, deliberate properly upon the ramifications of Baskerville's advice.

One thing was crystal clear, he realised, as he reached the edge of the lake, and that was that Roger must inevitably inherit the title and the estate. It was an appalling prospect. He had a vivid notion of the havoc which Roger could wreak, even if God granted him a limited lifespan as a result of his miserable addiction, on the estate and its treasures. He sighed, picked up and snapped a fallen branch and flung it for Midas, who plunged into the cold waters of the lake to retrieve it. A flurry of ducks rose from the reed bed. Sir Leonard stared at the new green of the willow leaves feathering the water's cold surface, then turned to make his way back across the park to the Hall, Midas at his heels, weighing this new sorrow in his heart.

It was his custom to take tea with Lady Charlotte in the late afternoon, to discuss the affairs of the day, and he did so that day. Their relationship had softened gradually since the onset of Lady Charlotte's illness – her physical isolation had lent her a kind of pivotal force within the establishment. All the energies of domestic organisation which had once been scattered over time and place were now concentrated, and Sir Leonard found that he came to her room each day as to a sanctuary, where all his troubles could be brought together and addressed in her company. He was aware now of his former lack of appreciation of her talents for preserving harmony and order in Stow Stocksley, and was sorry for it. He knew, too, that Orlando was responsible for mending many fences between them which had been broken at the time of Alec's death. He felt a kind of melancholy at the prospect of relating what Henry Baskerville had told him earlier that day. Like him, Lady Charlotte had assumed that their adoption of Orlando would act as a corrective to all the mistakes of the past.

He found her listening to the radio, propped up in her bed, the tea tray already set out on the high, spindle-legged table next to it.

'I saw you down at the lake with Midas,' she said, leaning forward to pour his tea; he knew this would be difficult for her and intercepted the teapot.

'Let me do that,' he said.

She went on, 'I had hoped you would come straight in and tell me how things went with Baskerville.'

'I thought you might be napping,' lied Sir Leonard.

'Well?' said Lady Charlotte. Sir Leonard poured milk into his tea, and then helped himself to a sandwich.

'I'm afraid that things will not be quite as we had hoped.' Five years before he would have said 'I' instead of 'we'. 'Cannot be,' he added.

'Why not?'

He sipped his tea and glanced at his wife; the strain of her illness had brought about a loss of weight over the past few months, and anxiety at his tone and expression heightened her gauntness.

'It seems that there are insurmountable legal obstacles. Not to Orlando's adoption, but in other respects.' And he told her all that Henry Baskerville had said.

Lady Charlotte leaned back against her pillows and pulled her cashmere bed jacket closer about her. After a silence she looked up at her husband and said, 'But Roger is not fit to take responsibility for – ' she stretched her arm out around her, then let it fall back on the counterpane ' – for all of this. He is not even fit to look after himself!' Another silence fell between them. 'Cannot *something* be done? The idea that Roger should . . .' Her voice trailed away, and she turned her gaze across the park, where the late afternoon light was beginning to fade. 'And Orlando is Alec's son! The thing cannot be right.'

'I know,' agreed Sir Leonard. 'But whatever Roger's vices, he is not the first and will not be the last wastrel to come into an inheritance.' And he sighed and poured himself another cup of tea.

Later that evening, Sir Leonard was not surprised to receive a phone call from Barney, who had, as Sir Leonard had imagined he would, been consulting lawyers of his own. When he was not crowing with triumph at the stillbirth of Sir Leonard's plan, Barney was blasting his brother-in-law for having the temerity to attempt to rob his son of what he saw as his birthright. Sir Leonard listened to as much of this as he could stand and, suppressing a desire to point out to Barney that if Roger were the Prince of Wales, bills would be passed through parliament to prevent his accession, he put the phone down. If he felt any regret at having told his brother-in-law of his intentions before taking legal advice, he was consoled by the fact that the resultant altercation had effectively severed relations between them, and for that he gave heartfelt thanks.

At the outset, that summer term at Ampersand seemed full of promise to Orlando. He had made the First XI, the weather was warm and tranquil, his existence in the lower sixth was not blighted by anything more serious than mock A-levels, and he was in love. This fact was a ceaseless, thrilling delight to him. But when he encountered Mrs Rees-Jones in school, Orlando could not help feeling guilty of some minor treachery. She never failed to smile at him, or single him out for a few words of conversation, and once he even felt, with a shock, that her glance had held his just a fraction too long in chapel. For the rest, however, he did not think about her. He merely counted the days to half term, when he had contrived to be invited to the Coulthards and would be able to see Hannah once more.

He managed to meet her in Inverness, and they took refuge in the woods on the outskirts of town.

'God, it's awful,' muttered Orlando, lying next to her on top of his jacket, still breathing hard from the force of his spent passion. 'I miss you so much, and then when I see you, I – I can't seem to control myself. Sorry.'

She smiled, and thought moodily of Callum for a brief, disloyal instant. 'It doesn't matter,' she murmured.

'But it does!' said Orlando. 'It does! If only I saw you more often, had more time with you . . . I can't stand not seeing you for months on end. Do you realise – ' he propped himself up on one elbow ' – that I might not see you till next October? I mean, it's mad!' She looked up at him, stroking his dark hair from his forehead and said nothing. 'Well, it's not going to be like that,' he said after a silence. 'I just want us to be able to go off together somewhere. But since we can't . . .'

'Well?'

'I'll just have to come up to see you during the summer holidays.' He stared up into the dark ceiling of pine branches.

'It's a long way.'

'I don't care.'

'I don't know that my father would be very keen on you staying. I mean, he likes you, and so on, and he didn't mind you staying that one night, but – well, he can be a bit funny.'

'I'll find somewhere. Don't worry. I get a bit of money from my grandparents, and there are always bed-and-breakfast places.'

Hannah had started to unbutton her blouse. She had noticed that the innocent Orlando, unlike Callum, never bothered much with preliminaries. It was something she would have to teach him. As he talked, she deftly unhooked her bra and slid it off. Taking Orlando's hand, she stroked his fingers across her breast, shivering at the sensation. Orlando stopped talking and looked down at her. Who cared about

Callum? she thought, as he bent his head to kiss her. She had Orlando, and that was more than enough.

The initial happiness of that term was eclipsed by an incident shortly after half term which led to Dan's expulsion from Ampersand. It had started trivially enough, with Wilson, the school chaplain, taking Dan to task for failing to get his hair cut over half term. It ended with Dan punching the chaplain and knocking him to the floor. The offence was too serious to warrant anything less than Dan's expulsion. He had a track record of insubordination, and in his interview with the headmaster he did and said nothing to mitigate his position. On the evening before Dan's father was due to arrive and take Dan away, Orlando sat in the study commiserating with his big friend. But Dan just shook his head.

'To tell you the truth, Paddy, I can't wait to get out of this place. It's not so bad for you. You like all this shit – the rugby and cricket and everything. And you'll do all right in your exams. But I hate all this team stuff, this "spirit of the school" crap. It's a joke.'

'Your old man's not going to be too pleased,' said Orlando.

'That's tough. I'm not going to let them send me to another school, or to some crammer to finish my A-levels. I've thought about it. I'm going to London to stay with my cousin, Stephen. He's got a house down there. And I'll try to get into art school. There's no point in staying in Scotland. I hate the place.'

'Well, look, write to me,' said Orlando. 'I mean, if you do go to London, we can get together, and stuff. Write and tell me where you're staying.'

'Yeah, I'll do that, Paddy.'

When the summer holidays came, Orlando returned to Reigate without enthusiasm. Each time he came back to Plumtree Villa, it seemed more cramped and claustrophobic than the last. He loved his aunts, and was conscious of the fuss they made, and the trouble they took when he came home, getting in his favourite food, trying to suggest interesting things for him to do, and generally treating him like a young god, but he knew that days in their company would drag interminably. It was a pleasant surprise, therefore, to find that Anne was already in residence at Plumtree Villa, and would be staying for a few days.

It didn't take Orlando long to detect the altered atmosphere between his aunts. The faint superiority with which Cicely had always treated Anne, being so much the elder, seemed to have disappeared, and there was something uneasy in the manner in which she now spoke to her. Abigail, too, seemed vaguely deferential. On the Saturday after his return, when both Cicely and Abigail had gone to do the weekly shopping, Orlando decided to take it up with Anne. He wandered out to the patio where she sat in a deckchair, reading. Best to be direct, he thought.

'So, tell me what's going on between you three,' he said, his manner curious and friendly.

'What?' Anne looked up at him through her dark glasses, then pushed them up on to her blonde hair. She laughed. 'Well, you are a knowing young man, aren't you. What makes you think there's anything "going on"?'

Orlando smiled and sat down on the warm flagstones. 'Come off it. Cicely's going around treating you like you might bite her any minute, and Abigail is being unbelievably polite. What have you done to make them so terrified of you?'

Anne lowered her glasses again. 'I wouldn't put it that strongly.' Her attention seemed to have shifted back to her book, but after a few seconds she looked up again and said, 'It's simply money, my dear. What all things boil down to in the end – money.'

'How do you mean?' asked Orlando.

There was another pause, and then Anne said, 'I don't know

whether Cicely and Abigail would want me to tell you this –
in fact, I'm sure they wouldn't, but I think perhaps it's about
time you understood how the land lies ... You see, lately
Cicely and Abigail have been having a hard time of it
financially. They incurred quite a few debts when you were
younger, and recently they discovered that a lot of the shares
which they inherited from our father are completely worthless. The companies have crashed, and they're valueless. But
you know what those two are like – they haven't got a clue
what's going on financially. If I'd known what they were
holding I could have told them ages ago to sell up, but they're
so used to treating me like some infant, it would have been
beneath them to discuss it with me.' She chuckled. 'Well, it's
not beneath them any more. They've got themselves in a
complete financial muddle, and I have kindly agreed to bail
them out.'

'How?' asked Orlando wonderingly.

'I've agreed to make them a loan – quite a substantial one – in
exchange for a charge on the property. Plumtree Villa, that is.
After all, I've got money sitting in the bank from the profit I
made on selling my last place, so it seemed the decent thing to
do. That's why they're treating me pleasantly for a change. I
don't need to ask them for anything any more. They have to
come to me.'

Orlando absorbed this in silence. He remembered when
Anne had been a student, how she had been dependent on her
half-sisters, how money had always been an issue. He recalled
the regular arguments, Anne's sullen truculence and Cicely's
tight-lipped anger. How Anne must have hated asking them
for anything. No wonder she spoke now of these altered
circumstances with such satisfaction.

'Why didn't you just lend them the money – or even give it
to them?' asked Orlando.

Anne smiled and looked at him; her eyes were hidden

behind her dark glasses, and he could not read her expression properly. 'Because that's not the way things work, darling Orlando. Things have to be done in a businesslike manner, so everybody knows exactly where they stand.'

'But they're your family.'

She paused, smiled again. 'Exactly.'

They said no more on the subject, but Orlando spent the rest of the day pondering these new developments, and the way in which the balance of power could shift between people. He had always thought of Anne, since she was so much younger than his other two aunts, as less effective, not quite as formidable as they. Now he saw that this was not so. Looking at Anne in this new light, he realised that there was something quite ruthless about her. Later that afternoon, as he watched Cicely and Abigail unloading shopping from the car and struggling up the path with it to the door of their beloved villa, which they no longer completely owned, he felt sorry for them for the first time in his life.

A few days later, after Anne had returned to London, it began to seem to Orlando that the information which Anne had imparted regarding his aunts' affairs somehow had the effect of diminishing their authority over him. They were not so powerful, after all. He was nearly grown up, and capable of making his own decisions. If he were to decide to do something, they could not necessarily stop him.

This realisation came to him one day when he was lying sunbathing in the back garden, while Cicely weeded the borders of petunias and busy lizzies. He had been thinking, as usual, of Hannah, of how much he wanted to see her, and how long the summer holidays would drag on.

'Orlando, why can't you find something to *do*?' asked his aunt in exasperation, straightening up and glancing at Orlando's muscular and scantily-clad young body lying sprawled on the lawn.

'There's nothing *to* do,' replied Orlando. He turned over on to his back, flapping a copy of *Catch 22* at a wasp.

'Don't you think you should put a top on – and something a little more substantial than those shorts? It can't be very pleasant for the old ladies in the home to have to look at you lying around half-naked.'

Orlando squinted up at the windows of the old people's home which overlooked the garden. 'I should think it's the best fun they've had all week,' he replied. Lying there, he suddenly came to a decision, and said, 'By the way, I'm going away tomorrow.'

His aunt turned to look at him. 'Where? Who with?'

'Scotland. On my own.'

'Well, I don't know ... I think I had better speak to Abigail –'

'Aunt Cicely!' said Orlando. 'I'm seventeen! I've got some money saved up, and I want to go up to see my girl-friend.'

Cicely sighed and picked up her garden fork again. 'Well, I don't suppose we can stop you – we had rather hoped that you'd like to come to Ireland with us for a fortnight, before you go to Stow Stocksley.'

'That's a nice idea,' said Orlando, 'but no thanks.' And he closed his eyes and put his book over his face.

That evening, elated by his spur-of-the-moment decision, he tried to ring Hannah, but got only an unobtainable tone. The same thing half an hour later. He wondered if he should put off his trip until he could speak to her. No – now that he had made his mind up, he badly wanted to go. Anyway, he could just set off and ring her when he changed trains at Glasgow. He checked the times of trains from Euston, and set about packing a rucksack with basic items of clothing, a copy of *Rabbit Redux*, and a packet of condoms.

The next morning he set off early for London, had breakfast at Euston, and bought six Mars Bars and a bag of apples to sustain him till he reached Inverness. During the journey he kept thinking, between chapters of John Updike, of how pleased Hannah would be to see him, of the time they would be able to spend together – a rich expanse of time such as they'd never shared before. At Glasgow he tried to ring Capercailzie again, but still the phone was out of order. He would just have to surprise her.

By the time he caught the bus from Inverness to Kirkallan, it was half past five, and as he got on board a sudden cold thought clutched at him – what if she was away on holiday? God, perhaps he'd been mad to set off without checking first. Then he thought of Mr Lennox, of the castle, and his fears quietened. It seemed unlikely that Hannah and her father should do anything as normal and civilised as going on holiday.

He got off the bus at Kirkallan and set off on the half-mile walk to the castle. All was soft summer quiet around him. The air was filled with the honeyed scent of the heather and myrtle which stretched out on either side of the road, and the late sun touched the mountains with a majestic light. Orlando turned as he heard the sound of an engine behind him on the little road, and saw a Range Rover coming towards him, a man in a tweed cap at the wheel. For a moment Orlando thought of hitching a lift as far as the castle gates, but he was enjoying the walk and the sweet sensation of anticipation, and let the Range Rover speed past him and into the distance.

At last he turned through the dilapidated gateway and into the shadow of the fir trees that lined the driveway up to Capercailzie. In the evening sunlight the castle looked less gloomy and forbidding than on his last visit, but also rather more decrepit. A hole seemed to have appeared in the roof – not a large one, but one which he was sure hadn't been there before – and the grass which had grown throughout the spring and summer now lapped at the crumbling stone balustrades of the house, giving it a wild, neglected look.

He went up to the front door and pulled at the great wire bell-pull; he knew that its chime must have sounded deep in the bowels of the house, but, although he waited for a few moments, no answer came. He went down the steps and round to the back of the castle, down the area steps to the back door, but there was no one in the kitchen. He came back up and walked uncertainly into the stable yard. Then he saw the Range Rover parked up by the estate office. He did not associate it with the one he had seen earlier on the road, but it did bring to his mind the idea that Hannah might be in the office, doing some work for her father. He set his rucksack down on the cobbles, walked across and pushed the door open.

The picture that met his eyes was to remain vividly in his mind for the next several hours, despite his attempts to obliterate it. The back of the man was what he saw first, a checked shirt, olive-coloured corduroys, and roughly-cut, dark blond hair. Then the man turned, and he saw Hannah – Hannah with her shirt unbuttoned to the waist, the curve of one milky breast visible, her jeans unzipped and around her hips. He saw the look on her face, astonished and disbelieving, the way her hair fell loose around her shoulders, and the blood seemed to sing in his ears, impinging on the sides of his vision, momentarily darkening it. It was a stark, ridiculous, frozen tableau. Orlando looked from Hannah's face to the man's, and was instantly struck by how old he looked. He must have been in his late twenties. He had a leathery, not unpleasant face, and he was tall. He seemed initially surprised at the sight of Orlando, but then smiled sardonically.

'It would be an idea to knock before entering,' he remarked

mildly; his accent was a gentle Highland drawl, the kind Orlando had always liked before. Now it sounded odiously patronising. The man was buckling his belt, and Hannah was pulling her shirt together with one hand, fumbling at the zip of her jeans with the other. Orlando could think of nothing to say. He didn't know who this man was, but the fact that she had been like this with him, was clearly going to allow him to have her, here in this shabby little office, up against a battered old filing cabinet, struck him like a hard, horrible blow. He had come all this way to find her doing this – and how many other times, on other days, in other months? This man – this man whose look and voice made Orlando feel like the schoolboy he was – was obviously local. It must have been going on for a while – for all the time that he, Orlando, had been in love with her, and had believed that she loved him, too. So he was not the first, and she had lied to him. She had lied all along.

As these thoughts ticked through his brain, Orlando suddenly realised, from the man's expression, how foolish he must look standing there in the doorway. The man clearly found it amusing, for he scratched his head, and turned to Hannah and said, 'Bit crowded in here for me. I'll best be getting back.' There was, too, a note of irritation in his casual tone. His afternoon's dalliance had been interrupted, and he was not pleased. He pushed past Orlando and out of the estate office.

Orlando stood staring at Hannah for a long moment. She tried to say something, but he simply turned and walked out. Callum was standing in the stableyard lighting a roll-up, one hand cupping the match against the evening breeze; Orlando noticed the thin, crinkled paper and caught the sudden waft of woody tobacco smoke. All his senses seemed alert, heightened by the shock he had just had. Dazedly he picked up his rucksack, then felt Hannah's hand on his arm. He pulled it away and turned to look at her.

'Orlando, I didn't know you were coming – ' she began.

'Obviously,' he retorted. He waited for whatever she had to say, astonished that she should try to say anything at all.

'It's not the way it looks – really.' Her voice was a sad whimper.

'You're joking, aren't you?' Orlando almost laughed at her through his anger and humiliation. 'You were practically undressed in there! He had his hands halfway down your jeans!' He shook his head. 'Forget it, Hannah. Just forget the whole thing.' As he turned away, he was aware that Callum was watching them from some way off. Again she put her hand upon his arm, her voice low and desperately insistent.

'Orlando, I'm sorry. I'm sorry. I'm really sorry . . .'

He couldn't listen any more. His beautiful, bright love lay shattered, wrecked, and he hated her for it. He walked away, hearing her voice behind him, the tears rising in it, pleading with him, but he ignored it, trying to drown it with the sound of his own feet on the cobblestones. After a moment he couldn't hear it any more, and just kept walking, walking away from the castle down the grassy verge of the driveway, ducking the low fir branches, kicking at scattered cones, hauling his rucksack on his back, no thoughts, only pain and rage and the recurring image of what he had just seen filling his mind. Then he heard the sound of the Range Rover bumping down the rutted drive; it slowed, and he heard the man's voice say, 'Need a lift?' He said nothing, did not even look round; this was the last, unbearable humiliation. He was a joke, a joke to everybody. He marched on, heard the sound of the engine revving up before the Range Rover roared past him once again, and the man flicked the butt of his roll-up out of the open window. It smouldered on the grass as Orlando strode past it, walking back the way he had come just fifteen minutes before.

Chapter Eight

T here was nothing to do but take the next bus back into Inverness, and Orlando sat waiting for forty minutes outside the Salutation Arms, murder and misery in his heart. Occasionally he would glance back along the road, half-expecting Hannah to have followed him, but no one appeared. Eventually the bus came, and he boarded it.

Back in Inverness he consoled himself in a cafe with a fry-up and two cups of sweet tea, then tramped around looking for a likely bed-and-breakfast. But the tourist season was at its height, and everywhere seemed crammed with its quota of hikers, cyclists and European backpackers. At last he managed to find a bed at a large, seedy establishment on the edge of town, which announced itself as specialising in group bookings.

'However,' said the manager, a grizzled youth of sixty or so, who wore his grey hair in a ponytail and sported an Iron Maiden '82 UK Tour T-shirt, 'there's a spare bed in wan o' the big rooms. That dae ye?'

Orlando said it would do him, thinking that it would have to, and the manager showed him to one of the large first-floor back rooms of what had once been a very grand house. Now it was no more than a battered hostel, echoing to the shouts of half a dozen different languages and reeking of fried bacon and porridge. The five other occupants of the room – who, the manager informed him, were Swedish – were apparently out, but their belongings were strewn over five of the six beds which occupied the room, together with two wardrobes and an MFI dressing table, circa 1964, on which there were a lace doily and a vase with a plastic rose in it, and a copy of the fire regulations.

Thankful that he had the place to himself, and that most of the residents of the bed-and-breakfast appeared to be out enjoying the limited pleasures of Inverness, he took a shower, put on the clean set of underclothes which he had rolled up, together with a fresh shirt and jeans, in his rucksack, and crept beneath the thin covers of his bed and slept.

A few hours later Orlando was acknowledging his good fortune in two respects – one, that he had gone to bed early enough to have had at least three hours of uninterrupted sleep, and two, that life at an English public school was an excellent preparation for the business of sharing a poorly-ventilated bedroom with five large and noisy Swedes. He lay in the semi-darkness, listening to their subdued conversation and laughter, counting the long, long moments until they had all at last rolled into bed and were more or less quiet. These were the crucial fifteen minutes, he knew – if he didn't get back to sleep now, before someone started snoring, then he never would. One of the Swedes farted gently and, sighing, Orlando turned over and tried to sleep, pushing the image of Hannah and her lover from his mind. The next morning, sick at heart, he set out to hitchhike to Glasgow and catch the first train back to London.

While his grandson was trying his luck with the lorries on the A9, at Stow Stocksley Sir Leonard was deciding that, despite what Baskerville had told him, he would go ahead with his plan of adopting Orlando. He foresaw that the idea might come as something of a surprise to the Misses Patrick, to say the least, and that it would need to be canvassed in a tactful and circumspect manner. He rang Cicely to arrange a meeting with both sisters. Cicely promptly invited Sir Leonard to lunch the following day, since the schools had broken up and Abigail would be at home, but Sir Leonard said that unfortunately he had business which would take him through lunchtime, and suggested tea instead. Mildly disappointed at being denied the opportunity to impress Sir Leonard with her chicken Marengo, Cicely said that they would look forward to seeing him then.

The next day carried on the unbroken spell of summer heat which had hung over southern England for two weeks. Cicely decided that it was an occasion to wear her new maroon sleeveless sundress, and possibly those sandals with the rather high heels which she had bought in an impetuous moment last summer and had yet to wear.

Abigail, who was sitting in the garden in a deck chair, wearing her late father's panama hat and reading a copy of the *Times Literary Supplement*, looked up in surprise at her sister when she came down after lunch in her new red sundress.

'I hope you don't expect me to get all dolled-up for this visit,' she remarked.

Cicely replied with acerbity, 'It is merely in the nature of a courtesy to our visitor that I should change into something smart.' She regarded Abigail's faded T-shirt and crumpled cotton skirt with distaste. 'I hope you remembered to take that cream sponge out of the freezer,' she added.

Sir Leonard, too, was struck by Cicely's appearance when he arrived at Plumtree Villa, and was all too well aware that it was for his benefit. He was not unaccustomed to receiving the same kind of flattering demonstrations from certain ladies in the Stow Stocksley area, and recognised this one accordingly. On the other hand, he could not help thinking, as he glanced fleetingly at Cicely's modestly displayed cleavage, that she was a handsome woman in her way, if a little unsophisticated for his taste.

They had tea on the little patio at the rear of the villa, and Abigail helped everyone to slices of cream sponge, which still had a slightly frozen consistency in the middle. Sir Leonard decided secretly that he rather liked this, and determined that he should buy a couple of these things and put them in the freezer at home. The cake reminded him, for some indefinable reason, of sweet, synthetic cakes bought by his nursemaid in his boyhood, and he experienced a pleasurable little gust of nostalgia with each mouthful.

'Earl Grey, Sir Leonard,' said Cicely with an arch smile, handing him his cup. 'I recall it as being your favourite – is that right?'

Sir Leonard murmured agreeably that it was, and noticed that Cicely was wearing lipstick of the same red as her dress. Lady Charlotte rarely wore lipstick.

'Now,' said Sir Leonard, setting his cup and saucer down on the little round metalwork table and shifting in his folding canvas chair, 'I shall tell you what it is I have come to discuss with you both.' He said this with an air of quiet authority which Cicely found faintly thrilling, and she folded her hands and looked with what she hoped was an intelligent, quiescent expression at Sir Leonard. Abigail merely gave her sister a derisive glance and dug a piece of garden soil from beneath one fingernail with another.

'Lady Charlotte and I both feel that Orlando has been very lucky to have been brought up by people who care as much for him as both of you do. But perhaps you share our feeling that Orlando has, by the accident of his birth, always laboured beneath a handicap – that is to say, the fact of his illegitimacy.' For some reason, Sir Leonard felt almost indelicate using this word. But the expression of neither sister flickered; they merely looked at him, waiting. 'It is something which my wife and I are anxious to remedy, and that is why I have come to see you today.'

'How can you remedy it?' asked Abigail. 'He's illegitimate. That's that.'

'Well, yes,' said Sir Leonard, 'that is so. Nothing can alter that. But Lady Charlotte and I thought that it might be in Orlando's best interests – might help him in his future life, that is – if he were able to bear his family name. We propose, if you are both agreeable, to adopt Orlando.'

'Adopt him? But he doesn't need adopting!' said Abigail in astonishment.

Cicely wished that Abigail would think before making these rather terse utterances. She felt she could see exactly where this was leading.

'Oh, certainly I have no wish to detract from your standing in any way, Miss Patrick. That was not my intention. It is just that it might be – well, if he were to bear the name of D'Ewes – '

'You mean,' interrupted Cicely quietly, 'that should he come to inherit Stow Stocksley, it would be only natural that he should carry the family name?' Cicely felt that she had perspicaciously touched on the nub of the matter.

There was a pause, during which Sir Leonard pressed a few stray cake crumbs against the table top with his thumb.

'That had originally been in my mind, Miss Patrick – ' began Sir Leonard. 'Oh, please – Cicely,' murmured Cicely. ' – but,' he continued, 'I find from my lawyers that Orlando can never inherit Stow Stocksley, nor the title, since you mention the matter. It is the fact of his illegitimacy, you see. That, apparently, is an insurmountable obstacle.'

'But I thought you said that, by adopting Orlando, you would be remedying that?' said Cicely faintly, her bright dreams of Orlando's titled future evaporating in the bright summer sunshine.

'Unfortunately, as a remedy, it would not extend so far as to make Orlando my heir.'

'Even though he is your grandson?'

'Even though he is my grandson.' Sir Leonard nodded. 'It would allow him to be recognised – properly recognised – as a member of the family and he could bear his father's name, but it does not go beyond that.'

'Then where's the point of adopting him?' asked Abigail, eyebrows raised. Really, she thought, this was all so much palaver over nothing. If he wasn't to become the next baronet, then why could not Orlando stay just as he was?

Abigail's peremptory enquiry left the beginnings of an uncomfortable silence in the air, but Cicely broke it by rallying and saying pacifically, 'I can see, Abigail, that this is not just a question of any inheritance, but a matter touching upon – well, family pride, shall we say?' It had occurred to her that there was still the matter of money –Orlando might do very well out of being a D'Ewes, in the long run. 'Orlando is a D'Ewes, after all – '

'Every bit as much a Patrick,' retorted Abigail, who had kicked off one of her canvas loafers and was scratching vigorously at a calloused big toe.

'– and I can see that it would be much better for him to be recognised as such. In the eyes of the world.'

'I am glad you understand my motives so perfectly – Cicely,' said Sir Leonard. Cicely gave a modest smile.

'Who is going to inherit Stow Stocksley, then?' asked Abigail, replacing her threadbare loafer.

Sir Leonard turned to her with a small, frosty smile. 'My nephew, Roger Stafford-Roper.' He said nothing more for a moment or two. Then, just as Cicely was going to suggest a fresh pot of tea, he added, 'The matter of Orlando not becoming my heir is as much a disappointment for me as it is, perhaps, for you.' The two women said nothing. 'Which is why I intend, at some time subsequent to the adoption, to settle a sum of money on Orlando, in trust. A substantial sum, something which will allow him to lead his life without undue financial worries.'

'Well, as you have already done so much for him, Sir

Leonard, I can only say that we regard that as very generous. Don't we, Abigail? Abigail and I have, as you can imagine, rather slender resources on which to draw where Orlando's future is concerned. What you say is most reassuring.'

'I propose to continue to fund Orlando's education,' said Sir Leonard, 'but the trust settlement will be subject to demonstrations by Orlando that he intends to conduct his life sensibly. I imagine – I hope that he will continue to be a great credit to both our families.' Sir Leonard thought that this rather neatly marked out the Patrick family as standing in equal importance to the D'Ewes. 'Has Orlando given you any indication as to how he sees his future after he leaves Ampersand?'

'No,' said Cicely doubtfully. 'I don't think he has settled on any particular career as yet.'

'No – well, he has another year yet,' said Sir Leonard. He tapped his knees lightly with the tips of his fingers. 'Where is he, by the way? I had thought I might see him today.'

Cicely hesitated, and then said, 'He's in Scotland, actually – he went there for a few days to see a friend.'

'Oh,' said Sir Leonard, looking faintly surprised.

'But I know he's looking forward tremendously to his visit to you in August. Is he – ' Cicely's voice was tentative ' – is he aware of how things stand? With the inheritance, I mean?'

This question troubled Sir Leonard. He remembered all that he had said to Orlando that Christmas, after the trouble at school. He realised now what a mistake it had been to raise the boy's expectations. And yet, had they not always been there? He and Lady Charlotte had probably always given him the impression, over the years, that his future was somehow bound up with Stow Stocksley.

'No,' he replied. 'I must tell him, of course, when he comes to visit. But I hope he is the kind of young man for whom such a thing will not be a great disappointment.' He did not, however, feel convinced of this.

There was a silence, during which Abigail fiddled with her untidy plait of straw-coloured hair and Cicely stirred the leafy dregs of her tea.

'Well,' said Sir Leonard, in a tone of slightly relieved finality, 'may I take it that you do not oppose my project? That I have your permission to go ahead?'

Cicely and Abigail glanced at one another. Abigail shrugged and looked away, and Cicely smiled at Sir Leonard.

'I'm sure that if you think it is in Orlando's best interests, then we have no objection to the plan.'

'Very good,' said Sir Leonard. 'And now I'm afraid that I shall have to be making my way back to Stow Stocksley. Thank you both for your hospitality, and for your understanding.'

He rose and was about to shake hands before going, when Abigail suddenly looked up, squinting against the afternoon sunshine, and said roughly, 'It won't make any difference, will it, this adoption business? I mean, this will still be his home?'

'Of course. It is really largely a legal formality to enable me to bring Orlando properly into our family and make provision for him in the future. We wish to make no greater claim on him than that, rest assured.'

Abigail said nothing, but looked away across the garden. Cicely showed Sir Leonard out, watching his tall figure as he made his way to his car, fluttering her fingers at him as he drove away.

She went back into the garden, where Abigail was throwing the dregs from the teapot into a flower bed.

'I notice you didn't mention Orlando's girlfriend,' she observed dryly. 'Skirted round that one.'

'Well, I thought it best just to keep the thing general, you know,' said her sister lightly. She sat down in her folding chair, her movements a trifle heavier than when she was in Sir

Leonard's company. She sighed. 'Pity about the baronetcy, and so forth.' She licked her finger and picked up some cake crumbs, then licked it again thoughtfully. 'Anyway, I hope he's having a nice time in Scotland.'

On the way back down to London in the train, Orlando debated what to do when he got there. He couldn't just go straight home to Reigate. His aunts would speculate on his sudden return, and he would have to nurse his guessed-at misery in public. He had two other options – either to go and see Anne, or to get in touch with Dan. There was something comforting in the thought of Anne. She would look after him, feed him, and he might even have enough of a good time to stop thinking about Hannah for a while. But on the other hand, she would guess that something was up, would want to know everything, and he didn't feel like talking to anyone about what had happened. He didn't think he ever would. It was by far and away the worst thing that had ever happened to him.

What about Dan, then? He didn't know what Dan's cousin, Stephen, was like, how big the place was, or even if he'd be welcome, but somehow the idea of just taking things as they came, sleeping on Dan's floor if he had to, letting the days drift painfully by, seemed starkly appropriate to his mood.

It was after seven when Orlando's train pulled into Euston. He rang Dan from the station and, without elaborating on his traumatic experiences in Inverness, explained that he was in London and needed a bed for the night.

'Sure,' said Dan, pleased at the prospect of Orlando's company. Although he had begun to put a portfolio together and was applying to various art schools, time had been hanging rather heavy. His cousin was ten years older than he, and although Stephen and his friends were kind enough, inviting him along to the pub to play darts with them, he felt very young in their company. He suspected himself of homesickness, occasionally, and was conscious that his new existence made him feel rather lonely, after the enforced intimacy of school and family life. He very much wanted to see Orlando. 'Where are you?' he asked.

'I'm at Euston. How do I get to yours?'

Dan explained it to him. 'There's a pub opposite the tube station – I've forgotten what it's called, but you can't miss it. I'll meet you there.'

'Okay,' said Orlando, feeling suddenly better for talking to someone familiar after the desolation of the past day or so. 'I'll see you soon.' And he set off for the underground, his spirits rising with his sense of purpose and the thought of Dan waiting for him at the other end.

Dan was startled by Orlando's appearance when he saw him threading his way between the pub tables. He looked older, his face tense and tired – or maybe it was just the effect of two-day stubble.

'Man, you look rough,' said Dan as Orlando set down his rucksack and sat down. 'What'll you have? A half?'

'No,' said Orlando flatly, fishing in his pocket for the money which he had intended to spend in Scotland. 'A large Scotch, and one for yourself.'

'You sure?' said Dan with a grin.

'I need it,' said Orlando. He had, in fact, only drunk whisky once before, at his grandfather's, but right at this moment that didn't seem to matter. This was now, a different world, a different context, and he was a different person. The kind who ordered large Scotches.

Dan brought the drinks back to the table, and after a couple of swallows, Orlando decided that this had been entirely the right thing to do. Everything was beginning to seem better. He took another large mouthful and felt it go down, burning, filling the ends of his fingers with a delicious kind of fire.

Dan asked Orlando how he came to be here, and Orlando explained how he had planned to go to Inverness to see Hannah, how he had found her – he told him everything. Dan commiserated, but Orlando just shook his head. 'She's history. Forget it.' Then he added, 'Do you fancy another?' He felt light-headed and reckless. Hannah didn't matter. None of it mattered. He would never, ever allow himself to be taken in by any female in that way again. Not ever. He had a new view of the world now. In a way, he was glad that it had happened, glad that he had had his eyes opened.

So, with Orlando's money to spend, they had another large Scotch each, then set off into the night to Dan's cousin's place, both fairly drunk. They passed a fish and chip shop, and Orlando, who had eaten nothing that day except a roll and an apple, said that he was hungry. So they ordered cod and chips twice, and, when they passed an off-licence further on, Orlando thought it would be a good idea to buy a bottle of whisky to wash it down.

Dan's cousin's place was a terraced house in a quiet Camberwell street. When they got there, Stephen was out for the evening, so they sat in the kitchen, talking and eating their fish and chips, and recklessly drinking Bell's whisky.

The hours which ensued for Orlando after the consumption of the fish and chips grew murkier and murkier. Dan put on some music in the living room – Spandau Ballet, then Genesis – and as the whisky bottle grew steadily emptier, Orlando raved squalidly and unhappily about Hannah and about love.

That much he was able to recall the following morning, when he awoke on the sofa, partially covered by Dan's sleeping bag, and with a pain in his head so severe that he could scarcely move it without feeling sick. But he had already been sick the night before, copiously, on Stephen's bathroom floor. And in Stephen's hallway. As he moved his shivering, feeble frame into a sitting position, Dan came into the room.

'Do you feel as bad as I do?' asked Orlando, removing his head from between his hands and staring up at his friend. Dan was wearing only a grubby towelling bathrobe, and his eyes were bloodshot and pouchy. He nodded. 'Christ . . .' Orlando put his head between his hands again and stared at the carpet.

'The thing is,' said Dan uneasily, 'Stephen's not exactly keen on you staying here – after last night, and everything . . .' His tone was apologetic.

'I don't blame him,' muttered Orlando. The taste in his mouth was foul. 'Don't worry,' he added. 'I'll be going. I'm sorry.'

'My fault as much as yours,' said Dan. 'I suppose I'm lucky Stephen's not kicking me out as well.'

Out of the goodness of his heart, Stephen allowed Orlando an hour or so to regain some kind of normality, and Orlando spent that time at the kitchen table, barely able to think or speak, with a mug of tea growing cold before him. At noon he went into Dan's room to say goodbye. Dan had gone back to bed and was still lying beneath the duvet, curtains drawn.

'Can I borrow a razor?' asked Orlando. 'I left mine at the bed-and-breakfast, and I can't go back to my aunts looking like this.'

Dan obligingly hauled himself from his bed of pain and fetched Orlando a razor. As he shaved with a shaking hand, horribly aware of the smell of his own scrubbed-away vomit in the air, Orlando felt sick, ashamed and depressed. He went back into the living room to put his things together. As he did so, he caught sight of the empty bottle of Bell's standing on the floor by the grate, and almost retched at the recollection of the previous night.

113

He opened the front door of the house to a day which was electrifyingly sunny and hot. The alcohol that still coursed sluggishly round his system made the colours seem limpid and surreal as he walked to the nearest main road, and his head ached blindingly beneath the July sun. He badly needed some paracetamol – earlier this morning he would have been incapable of taking anything, would just have thrown it straight up again – but the long line of shops past which he walked revealed no chemist. He stood aimlessly at a bus stop, waiting for a bus, any bus, which would take him into central London and the beginning of his long trek home to Plumtree Villa.

It was five o'clock by the time he walked up the path to his aunts' house, and the day behind him had been long and nightmarish, punctuated with spells of raging thirst and extreme nausea. His headache had grown so bad that it seemed to encase his head in a shell of pure pain. His limbs ached. His lower back ached. Orlando did not think he had ever felt so unwell in his whole life. It seemed to him little short of a miracle that he had managed, on some kind of autopilot, to navigate his way from Camberwell to Reigate. Now, as he put his key in the front door, he prayed that his aunts might be out. Sounds from the kitchen made him aware that they were not, but perhaps if he could just make his way upstairs unheard, and wash and change and drink a couple of glasses of water, then he might be able to make himself vaguely presentable. But as he put his foot on the bottom step, some sixth sense caused Cicely to step back from the cooker, where she was preparing the evening meal, and glance out into the hallway.

'Orlando!' she said, and put down the skillet she was holding. She came along the little narrow hallway, and Orlando grew horribly conscious of his red eyes, his badly-shaven chin, his lank, uncombed hair, and his faintly malodorous body in clothes which he had been wearing for two days and a night. His aunt looked at him mournfully, which was not exactly the expression he had expected to see on her face. Surprise, perhaps – even distaste. But she simply looked – well, miserable.

'Oh, Orlando, I hadn't expected you back so soon. I'm afraid there is some rather bad news . . .'

A strong smell of frying onions drifted up the hallway with the gust of air produced as Abigail came in through the back door. Orlando felt as though he were going to be sick, and put a hand on the banister to steady himself. Cicely turned to Abigail, who came up beside her sister.

'Does he . . . ?'

'No, no, I haven't told him.'

'What?' Orlando almost shouted. 'What is it?'

'I'm afraid that your grandmother died yesterday evening, Orlando,' said Abigail quietly. Orlando stared at her. 'It was something called an embolism – a sort of blood clot, your grandfather says. Like a stroke.'

'I'm sure it was very quick and painless,' added Cicely. 'She would know nothing about it.'

Orlando suddenly pictured his grandmother lying in her bed, surrounded by her lovely treasures, the afternoon sun grazing the butter muslin hooked up against the window. He realised that his aunts were looking at him anxiously, expectantly, that some reaction was required.

'I see,' he said, then became horribly aware that the drink of water which he had had at the station was threatening to well up from his stomach, surge into his throat. He felt dizzy and ill, almost incapable of speech. 'I'm going upstairs,' he muttered. 'I'll be down in a bit.'

He went quickly upstairs, closed the bathroom door, and was sick as quietly as possible into the lavatory. Then, his heart thudding like a drum, his mouth tasting rank, he went and lay down on his bed, wondering why his life, which had been so splendid, so golden only days before, suddenly seemed to have descended precipitately into hell.

Chapter Nine

The funeral of Lady Charlotte took place three days after Orlando's return from Scotland. The death of his grandmother, coming as it did on the heels of Hannah's betrayal, affected him badly. He felt as though she had deserted him, and that her death had robbed him of all the most vital of the ties binding him to Stow Stocksley. His contact with it would now, he assumed, be only formal and impersonal, rather like his relationship with his grandfather. It was Lady Charlotte who had provided all the warmth and sense of companionship during his visits to Stow Stocksley; Sir Leonard had taught him much about the place, certainly, but Orlando and his grandfather had never been more than cordially polite to one another, and certainly never intimate. He contemplated his impending visit to Stow Stocksley, and wondered how he and his grandfather would cope now that she was gone.

Sir Leonard had already begun to find out. In the two weeks between the funeral and Orlando's visit, he discovered a depth of loneliness and emptiness in his great house such as he had not experienced since the death of Alec seventeen years before. Orlando was all his family now. Alicia and Barney, who had attended the funeral – mercifully without Roger, who, his sister assured him, was currently receiving psychiatric treatment and doing well – scarcely counted any more. But he, too, was aware that relations between himself and his grandson were bereft of warmth, despite all the affection which he felt for the boy. He had no idea how to remedy this. He took some comfort in the notion of Orlando's adoption, and although he felt a certain diffidence about the matter, now that Orlando was more or less grown up, he eventually broached the subject one morning at breakfast. Orlando, busy digging into the remains of the Cooper's Vintage Oxford, listened as his grandfather explained. When Sir Leonard had finished, Orlando chewed his toast and regarded his grandfather with his open gaze.

'Become a D'Ewes?'

'Yes – well, to all intents and purposes, you are one. You are my grandson, after all. This would merely be a formality to change your surname, bring you officially into our family.' Orlando sat back, staring at the tablecloth, and Sir Leonard suddenly recalled his words of a few months ago, when he had told Orlando that he hoped, one day, to make him his heir. He realised that Orlando might, at this moment, be assuming that the adoption would legitimise him, as everyone had once expected, and he hurried to dispel any such illusions. But he was a little late in doing so, for in those seconds Orlando had already begun to revolve in his mind the prospect of becoming the future owner of Stow Stocksley and its magnificence. 'I must tell you, though,' added his grandfather quickly, 'that adoption cannot remedy the – well, the unfortunate circumstances of your birth. It cannot legitimise you, so the lawyers tell me.'

Orlando let out a breath. 'What do you mean?'

'I mean that, even if I adopt you, I cannot, as I had very much hoped, make you my heir. Roger will still inherit everything.' His grandfather, gazing at him, wondered what the boy was thinking, and realised he had no insights, that he lacked the familiarity which might have permitted him to ask. He hesitated, and then said, 'I don't wish you to imagine, however, that the adoption would be an entirely empty gesture. It would mean a great deal to me. And would have, I know, to your grandmother. I think you might find, too, that

118

the name may be of assistance to you in the future. We live in a world which cares about such things, you know.'

Orlando forced a smile. 'I suppose so. Yes – I like the idea very much. Thank you.'

Orlando left his grandfather to pour himself another cup of coffee and to peruse his morning mail, and made his way down to the lake, Midas, now fat and wheezing, at his heels. He flung a few desultory sticks and watched as Midas lumbered, splashing, into the cold water to retrieve them. He felt in his heart a cold anger which he had not been able to express to his grandfather. It seemed as though this was the culmination of a lifetime of expectations and disappointments. He thought about the loss of his mother, a loss which he had only recently begun to appreciate, about Hannah and her destruction of his faith and affection; he thought of his grandmother, and how she had brought him to an understanding of so many things, and had then simply left him, robbing his relationship with his grandfather's home of its sense and beauty. At least there had still been Stow Stocksley. Until now. Orlando, thinking of everything his grandfather had just told him, felt as though a precious and deeply personal treasure had suddenly been put into his hands, and then snatched away from him. To be the possessor of Stow Stocksley had been his dream, a half-secret hope which he had grown up with, and he had not fully acknowledged the depth of his longing until a moment ago, when it had suddenly seemed a possibility. Now he thought of the time when his grandfather must die, and the estate pass into someone else's hands, the time when he would no longer be able to come here, to live here, and felt it like a physical pain. He stood by the lake and wished for a moment that his grandparents had never come into his life, brought him here, raised his expectations, educated him to believe that all this would some day be his. It was a moment of transition from

119

childhood, and all its pleasant pretences, into the cold reality of adulthood.

The events of the summer, if they had matured him, also produced in Orlando a new sense of bitterness. When he came back from Stow Stocksley he realised that he felt too wretched to spend the remaining last few days of the holidays in the company of Abigail and Cicely. He would be going back to school at the end of next week, and he needed to be able to talk to someone about all the horrible things that had been happening to him, to unburden his feelings. Cicely and Abigail, who had once been everything to him, seemed to him the last people in whom he could confide. On impulse he rang Anne and asked if he could come up to stay with her for the weekend. She might be able to understand what was happening to him. Of course he could, if he wanted, she said. Orlando went upstairs to pack a few bits of clothing and consult his train timetable. When he came down, he looked in on Abigail, who was busy at the dining table with the new term's schedules.

'When you see Cicely, tell her I've gone up to town to stay with Anne for the weekend. I'll see you both on Monday,' he said, and then left without saying anything further. When Cicely returned, Abigail gave her Orlando's message.

'Is that what he said?' asked Cicely, slowly taking off her jacket. 'I mean, he just said, "Tell Cicely"? Not Aunt Cicely?'

'That's what he said,' replied Abigail with a shrug, glancing at her sister. Cicely said nothing, but went into the kitchen to prepare the vegetables for their evening meal, telling herself that it was ridiculous to be bothered by such a thing, but conscious of a certain sadness of heart.

That evening at Anne's, Orlando drank too much wine and unburdened his soul. He told Anne about Hannah, and about the confusion of his feelings.

'I want, you know, to hate her . . . I mean I *do*! I do really hate her. But . . . God, I don't know . . .'

'It's not exactly a new thing, Orlando,' replied Anne. She sat opposite him, curled up in an armchair. Night had almost fallen, and the room was lit only by the glow of the lights from the river. Orlando could scarcely make out her features. 'I mean, you still love her. All that stuff about love being close to hate. You know.' Orlando took another mouthful of wine, even though he knew he didn't want to drink it, that he had drunk too much already. 'Anyway,' sighed Anne, throwing back her head and closing her eyes momentarily, 'it's a sad little lesson you're learning. We all have to learn it sometime. The business of being hurt by people we trusted.'

There was silence for a moment, then Orlando said, 'I remember once, just after I'd been to Stow Stocksley that first time, when I came home you were there. You were shut up in your room and I wasn't allowed to go and see you. Cicely said you weren't well, but it was something to do with some man, wasn't it? I mean, you were a real mess,' added Orlando, with the pitilessness of the candid young drunk.

Anne stretched her legs out thoughtfully. 'I remember that. But do you know what?' She looked up, and Orlando could just make out a smile. 'I can't even remember his name now. I mean, I remember he was called David, but that's all. At the time I thought my world had come to an end. Which just shows you. Anyway,' she shrugged, 'the lesson I learned, the one you've got to learn, is that you must use people before they use you. It all comes down to that in the end. You asked me why I didn't just give Cicely and Abigail the money they needed. That's why. I'm not going to be used again. Not by anybody.'

Orlando digested this. She was right, he told himself. People just used other people. His grandfather had used him, brought him into his life to serve some purpose of his own,

121

without caring or thinking how it would be for him, Orlando, if things did not go his way. Hannah had, too. He would never let anyone use him again. But he did not think he could ever forget Hannah's second name, nor anything about her, ever.

'What about love?' he asked. 'Don't you believe in that?'

'Oh, yes. I still have this idea that a wonderful, wonderful man, someone kind and intelligent and funny and all the things we've been taught to imagine possible, is waiting for me. Hmm.' She laughed and stared into her glass. 'But the more men I meet, the more unlikely it begins to seem. Still, no matter how many disappointments, we never give up hope.'

'Here's to hope,' said Orlando, raising his almost empty glass. Then he yawned, closed his eyes, and fell asleep without meaning to.

When he returned to school that autumn, his new-found cynicism had begun to develop, the thinnest of shells. It seemed to him as though much in his life had been mere delusion – the future that Lady Charlotte had painted for him, which he had imagined, the love which he had felt for Hannah and which he had thought was returned – and so he was scarcely surprised when, in his last term at Ampersand, another of his illusions was destroyed.

It came about at the end of the house cricket finals in June, on a sweltering day, when Orlando was captaining his own house team. The entire school had turned out to watch, together with a large number of parents, and a marquee had been erected at the far end of the pitch to serve a tea of strawberries and cream and wine cup afterwards. The Minister for Sport and Drought, himself an Old Ampersonian, had been prevailed upon to present the trophy.

Orlando, as he stood in the outfield at the end of the afternoon, watching philosophically as his team bowled its way to ultimate victory, thought the day as perfect as any day could be, just the kind of day he would want to remember when he looked back on his time at school. When he went up to collect the house shield on behalf of his team, he did so with engaging modesty and to the ragged cheers of many enthusiastic boys, to whom Orlando was a hero.

Mrs Rees-Jones stood at one end of the semicircle of adult onlookers, one eye on her four-year-old son, who was jumping over the marquee's guy ropes, and the other on Orlando. She reflected on the special godlike charm which Orlando possessed in this moment, and which she had seen in other upper sixth formers. It always passed away, of course. She had seen so many, heroes of the past, returning to the school on open days, or visiting younger brothers, and had seen the wistfulness in their eyes as they gazed around at the scenes of their forgotten triumphs, of former adulation. She clapped her gloved hands as Orlando received his trophy, and when his glance caught hers, she smiled at him.

Only the members of the cricket teams and the adult spectators were to be permitted the delights of the marquee, and the rest of the school was herded, grumbling, back to hall for tea as usual. Orlando ate a couple of ham croquettes, two chicken legs and a dish of strawberries, and decided the wine cup was pretty repulsive. He talked politely to the Minister for Sport and Drought, and with studied, artificial casualness to some members of staff, and wished he could get away for a shower. It had been a long day, the sun relentless, and despite the exhilaration of captaining the winning team, he felt he had the beginnings of a headache. He saw the headmaster approach him, his long, yellow teeth bared in a smile of congratulation. He pumped Orlando's hand in one of his acts of demonstrative physicality, and congratulated him.

'Splendid performance! A most enjoyable day's cricket.' He indicated the house shield which stood on the table at Orlando's elbow. Orlando had been carrying it around with him in a self-conscious fashion since being presented with it, and was rather at a loss as to what to do with it. 'We mustn't leave that thing lying around. In fact, if you don't mind, it might as well go back in the display cupboard now.' The headmaster dug out a bunch of keys, slipped a small one from it, and handed it to Orlando. 'There you are. You know where it lives. We can have it engraved over the summer. I can trust you to lock everything up safely, then bring the key back to me.'

Dutifully Orlando took the key and the shield and headed back towards the school, glad to be on his own, strolling in the bright, quiet air, away from the genteel clamour of the marquee. He went through the wide door next to the library, and along the corridor to the display case beneath the honours board. The air in the corridor was cool, wax-scented, and he could hear from a distance the murmurous rumble of the voices of the boys at tea in the hall. He stood in the quiet for a moment, staring at the trophies, then unlocked the cabinet with the little key and placed the shield inside. Then he shut the creaking glass door, locked it, and pocketed the key.

He walked back past the library, and just before he reached the door he heard someone call his name. He turned in surprise, for people at Ampersand rarely used Christian names. 'Orlando,' the woman's voice said again. It was Mrs Rees-Jones, standing in the doorway of one of the boot rooms, where the boys chucked their dirty rugby and cricket gear for the fags to clean later.

'Hello,' he said uncertainly, stopping. She came out of the doorway a little way.

'I just came in here to sponge down my skirt. Alexander decided it would look better with strawberry all over it,' she said, glancing down and rubbing at a stain on the front of her dress with a damp cloth. 'Little horror. Hold on while I switch

124

the tap off.' She went back into the boot room and Orlando stood in the doorway, watching her at the basin. She was still rubbing at the stain as she spoke to him over her shoulder. 'You did well in the cricket today. I was very proud that our house won the trophy.'

Orlando came properly into the room to catch her words. 'I think it was on the cards from the beginning,' he said immodestly, but truthfully.

'Mmm.' She straightened up, put the cloth on the lip of the basin, and turned the tap off. 'There now.' She pushed her reddish hair back from her face and leaned against the basin. 'So,' she said, 'what will you be doing when you leave us, Orlando?'

Orlando wondered whether he shouldn't be getting back, but it seemed impolite not to respond to her small talk.

'Well, I hope to get a place at Trinity, but it all depends, you know . . .'

'Oh, yes,' she said, and smiled. She paused just a little longer than necessary, her eyes on his. 'James did mention it.' Orlando hesitated, wondering what was coming next. He was aware, in the dimness of the room, of a shaft of sunlight from the high window, which lit up dancing dust motes in the air and fell on one side of Mrs Rees-Jones' red, curling hair, burnishing it with gold. Then she said, 'Do you remember the cricket match four years ago, when you missed that catch and got hit on the head?'

Orlando smiled, then swallowed, recollecting the cool silence of the sick room, and how Mrs Rees-Jones had come in to him when he was lying there alone, and had held him and comforted him. 'Yes,' he said, and smiled again, suddenly nervous at the memory.

She simply stood there, looking at him, and he felt a faint blush rising to his face as he rememberd how, for a long time after that day, he had worshipped her ardently and happily, remembered, too, his little fantasies of performing wonderful deeds for her, winning her admiration.

'And here we are,' she said softly. 'Another cricket match.' He said nothing, and she moved towards him, coming so close that she could place her hands on his upper arms. Then he felt her breath against his cheek as she said, 'I gave you a kiss that day.' Orlando did not move, and before he knew quite what was happening, she pressed her mouth very gently against his, and then her body. He was amazed at the delicacy of her movements, and in his astonishment that she should kiss him like this, he put his arms around her and kissed her back. He felt the warm cushion of her breasts against him, and touched her, thinking how different this was from Hannah, how unresisting and pillowy she was. And astonishingly exciting. But it was when she pulled open the top buttons of her dress and placed his hand urgently against her bare skin, that he was suddenly struck by the absurdity of the situation. He moved away.

'Look, I'm sorry – ' he began, feeling that he had committed some dreadful faux pas.

'What for?' she asked, her voice husky, her breathing rapid. She did not release him, but was tugging at the buttons of his cricket trousers.

'Hold on a minute – ' began Orlando again, but she put her mouth against his and pushed him back against the door, which slammed gently shut. She seemed so aroused by now, so intent on not letting him go, that it occurred to Orlando, who was happily helping her tug off his trousers, that it would be rude to go now, just when she seemed to be enjoying herself so much. And so he slid to the floor with her among the jumble of boots, bats and pads, and embarked upon a fifteen-minute episode which he was, in later years, to regard as one of the most erotic of his life.

That was not quite how he looked at it later that night,

126

however, as he lay in bed, wide awake, appalled at what he had done. She was Mrs Rees-Jones, his housemaster's wife, and he had had sex with her on the floor of the boot room. Twice. Good God. He spoke the words aloud. Worst of all, when it was over, all she had said, after buttoning up her dress and straightening her hair, was, 'Goodbye, Orlando.' And he had just sat there on the floor, trying to get his trousers on, wondering why and how it had all happened. Were all women like this, he wondered – predatory, destructive?

He turned over in the dark, remembering how he had loved her when he was fourteen, would have done anything for her. His infatuation had been utterly pure, filled with such chaste little fantasies. He remembered, too, once telling his grandmother that he liked women. He had been a child then, and had known nothing about them. Now he knew, and he no longer felt that he liked or trusted any of them.

Thus Orlando's schooldays came to a close, and he returned to Reigate with his trunk and trophies and newly hardened heart, and announced to his aunts that he was going up to London for a few weeks to stay with Anne.

'Your aunt Abigail is going on a painting holiday in the Dordogne,' said Cicely, with faint derision in her tone, 'so that leaves me all alone here in Reigate, I suppose.'

But Orlando was not going to rise to this emotional bait. He could not face the prospect of staying at Plumtree Villa with just Cicely. 'Why don't you go on a painting holiday as well?' he asked. She looked at him. 'Or something. Anyway, after Anne's, Dan and I are going to Greece for a couple of weeks before I go to Grandfather's.'

'Greece?' echoed his aunt. 'How are you going to afford that?'

'With some of the money that Grandma left me.'

'I thought you were saving that.'

'Well, this is one of the things I've been saving it for. Anyway, I haven't really had a proper holiday in a long time, except for school trips.'

'We took you to Rhyl three years ago. And Walberswick the year before that. And we did invite you to come to Ireland with us last year.'

Orlando sighed. 'I know. But I want to do something on my own.'

'Well, I hope you know what you're doing,' said Cicely. It was one of the things she said a lot recently, and Orlando was never quite sure what it meant, exactly.

A few days after both Orlando and Abigail had gone, Cicely began to realise how empty and depressing life could be on one's own at Plumtree Villa; she had never been alone there for more than a weekend before. Now the summer days seemed long and heavy. In truth, Abigail's decision to go on this painting holiday in France had caused her more than a little consternation. The sisters had always gone on holiday together in the past, and the fact that Abigail was going with a male friend – an ineffectual, spindly, bearded creature called Michael, whom Abigail had met at her evening art class – had set Cicely in a mild state of panic, from which she could not recover. She had seen enough of Michael to know that he was probably a truly confirmed bachelor, who would doubtless be terrified at the prospect of marrying anyone, but what if the unthinkable should happen? What if, at her time of life, she should suddenly be left here alone, while Orlando and Abigail carved out new and fulfilling lives for themselves? The thought gnawed at her during those first few days, as she gardened, shopped, cooked and ate alone. The idea that she – she who had always been regarded as the attractive one, the one most likely to find a husband – might be left on the shelf at fifty-two was galling. True, she had the WI, her bridge club, her friends . . . but how tolerable would all that be if Abigail were to marry and set up home triumphantly elsewhere?

It was while she was thumbing through some brochures for the summer flower shows that the idea came to her. Sir Leonard. There he was, stuck away all on his own in that great big house at Stow Stocksley, and she in the villa at Reigate. What could be more sensible and pleasant than that they should spend some time together? Once the idea had come to her, Cicely was quite excited by it. She remembered the letter which Sir Leonard had sent after Lady Charlotte's funeral, thanking her and her sister for the flowers, and hoping that he might see them at Stow Stocksley some time. True, the letter had referred to 'you both', but Cicely interpreted this as diplomacy on Sir Leonard's part – of course, he had meant her, Cicely, for she felt that he was aware, as she was, of the little bonds of understanding which had sprung up between them on the afternoon of her last visit to Stow Stocksley. Their conversation about the orchids, his attentiveness, plying her with sherry, insisting on showing her those botanical plates ... True, that had been three years ago, but still ... She sat back in her garden chair and sighed, the brochures in her lap. How lonely he must be. It would be nothing short of an act of kindness to go and visit, and then to arrange some outings for them both, perhaps to the flower show at Hampton Court, or Linden Castle. But how to contrive the thing? It would look a little direct, if she were just to show up with the brochures. But might she not make it look like a fleeting visit, as though she had just happened to be in the neighbourhood and thought of dropping by? Yes, that was it. She recalled mentioning to him once before that she was a friend of the chairwoman of the Kings Worthy WI, not far from Stow Stocksley. That would be her pretext. More than a little thrilled, Cicely forgot the loneliness of the past few days and went upstairs to examine the contents of her wardrobe and map out a plan of campaign.

Three days later, just as he was finishing an afternoon's dalliance with Crispin's *Vita Herluini*, Sir Leonard went to answer the chime at his front door and was surprised to discover the plump figure of Cicely Patrick standing there. Cicely, in turn, was surprised to see Sir Leonard, for she had a vague idea that some servant or other would answer.

'Sir Leonard, I was in the area on some WI business and thought I would just drop by. I do hope I'm not disturbing you?'

'Do come in,' said Sir Leonard politely, and ushered her into the hall.

Cicely, uncertain whether she was entitled to proceed from the hallway into the drawing room, whose door stood open, or whether this would be in the nature of an impertinence, paused on the stone flags; Sir Leonard paused, too, and they both stood looking uncertainly at one another.

'I suppose you must be wondering what on earth brings me here,' burst out Cicely, then laughed girlishly. 'But the fact is, I was visiting the chairwoman of the WI in Kings Worthy, and thought I would drop in. You see, I have something I thought might interest you.'

'Please,' said Sir Leonard, gesturing towards the drawing room, 'come in. I was just about to have a drink before dinner.' Then he added, following Cicely through, 'I suppose you'll think me rather an old maid, having my meal so early, but I find that I really don't enjoy eating late in the evening these days.'

'Oh, I do so agree,' said Cicely. 'My sister and I usually have supper by seven, at the latest.' As soon as she had said this, Cicely wondered whether she should have said 'dinner' instead of 'supper', and was consumed briefly by anxiety.

It quickly passed away, however, in the geniality of Sir Leonard's welcome. He was genuinely rather pleased to have

130

company, for he saw few people these days. He had become conscious, during the past year, of the acuteness of his solitude at Stow Stocksley. He still entertained, but only occasionally, and it was hardly the same as in the years before Lady Charlotte's ill-health. Their circle of friends had, in their turn, grown older, and entertained less frequently. Most evenings found Sir Leonard alone, seated at the end of the long mahogany table, with a glass of wine and a solitary meal, prepared by Mrs Cresswell, one half of his invaluable couple. It had been thus in the days before Lady Charlotte's death, of course, but he had not felt so alone then as he did now. Cicely's visit was a welcome diversion from his stale routine of a drink with the six o'clock news, then dinner alone. He was not afraid to acknowledge this, as he poured her out a generous glass of sherry.

'There is plenty to keep me occupied during the day, but the hours between late afternoon and bedtime sometimes seem very long,' he said. Cicely took her sherry and sipped at it carefully, watching Sir Leonard as he sat down in an armchair opposite, crossing his long legs and hitching the knee of his trousers slightly. How very handsome he is, thought Cicely for the hundredth time. Such breeding, such self-possession. 'I have been thinking recently, in fact, that it might do me some good to get up to London more often. I haven't been near my club for months. I had even thought of taking a flat in town,' he mused.

Cicely watched him with her large, brown eyes, gratified at being the recipient of such unexpected confidences.

'I think it is important, when one is alone, to have outside interests,' she said.

'You're right, of course. I'm afraid that all my recreations are rather solitary ones.'

'Well, not necessarily so,' said Cicely, preparing to play her card. 'Especially not if there are others who share your

131

interests. In fact, that is just why I thought you might be interested to see this.' She set down her glass and produced from her handbag a folded pamphlet, which she handed to Sir Leonard. He took it with interest. 'There is to be a special exhibition of tropical plants at Kingsmead, and I thought, since you are so fond of orchids, that the Cymbidium section might be of particular interest. I generally try to get to one or two of the more important horticultural exhibitions during the year,' she lied, 'and, of course, the flower shows.'

'I should very much like to see this,' said Sir Leonard, scanning the brochure. 'Very much indeed.' There was a small silence, during which Cicely sipped nervously at her sherry and Sir Leonard kept his eyes fastened to the brochure, his mind rapidly calculating the possible ways in which she could misinterpret any suggestion that they should go to the exhibition together. It would seem impolite to express an intention to go without including her. He looked up. 'Why don't we go together? I see that it is on from – let's see . . . July the fifteenth until mid-August. We could go next week, perhaps.'

'What a very nice idea!' exclaimed Cicely. She took a large gulp of sherry.

'Perhaps I could telephone you and make arrangements,' said Sir Leonard. Cicely nodded, containing her excitement. 'Thank you for showing me this,' he added.

'Do please keep it,' said Cicely. 'I have another at home.' She finished her sherry. 'Well,' she said, 'I suppose I should be getting back . . .' And she stood up, smoothing down the front of the silk dress she had put on especially for this occasion. It was smart, but not too smart, and she knew that its low, scooping neckline and short sleeves showed off her handsome bust and plump, smooth arms. As Sir Leonard looked at her, he realised that she was rather attractive, in a bosomy way. Then he recalled that he had thought so before.

And there was something about her open, rather naive face which he found touching. She was not a sophisticated woman, but she thought she was, and he liked this.

He stood up and said impulsively, 'Won't you have another drink?' And then, before he could help himself, he added, 'Perhaps you would even care to stay to dinner? Unless your sister is expecting you?'

Entranced, but anxious to retain her composure, Cicely replied, 'Oh, my sister is abroad at present. I'm rather in the same boat as you –all alone in a great big house.' She realised that this sounded absurd as soon as she had said it, but covered it with a light laugh, and then added, 'No, I should be delighted to have dinner with you.' Oh, how intimate it sounded. It was like something out of that film with Deborah Kerr and Cary Grant.

'Excellent,' said Sir Leonard, who was already having faint misgivings. Still, he wanted to hear all about Orlando, and she would be company. 'I'll just go and tell Mrs Cresswell,' he said.

Alone, Cicely sat back down and stared around her. In Sir Leonard's company she could do little more than shoot covert glances at the splendour which surrounded her. Now she took it all in. She sat back in her armchair and smoothed a hand over the surface of the little rosewood table next to her. Orlando had told her that the furniture in this room was eighteenth century, and she swiftly scrutinised a satinwood secretaire, a figured mahogany sideboard beneath an oil painting of a harbour scene, and the scattering of Hepplewhite sofas and armchairs upholstered in ivory damask, wondering if she could risk any intelligent observations on these. Perhaps not. Though she decided that she might venture a remark along the lines of, 'What a charming eighteenth-century table . . .' and hope that Sir Leonard might just pick it up and run with it, so to speak. That was what had happened with the orchids. She began to rehearse the little exclamatory remark in her head, the manner in which she would say it, the voice in which she would deliver it.

Then Sir Leonard returned. 'Here, let me pour you another drink,' he said.

'Thank you,' said Cicely, taking the glass from him with what she thought of as her voluptuous smile, involving a flirtatious upward glance. Then she said, indicating the little tea table, 'I have just been admiring this charming eighteenth-century table.'

'It is rather lovely, isn't it?' replied Sir Leonard, pleased, but deciding that it would be rude to tell her that it was, in fact, nineteenth century. 'It's attributed to John McLean, actually.' Cicely nodded intelligently. 'You see this brass reeding . . . ? One of my favourite pieces in this room. Are you interested in furniture, Miss Patrick?'

'Please – Cicely,' she insisted with a light laugh. 'Well, I do enjoy visiting stately homes. One sees such lovely pieces. But I can't claim to be a connoisseur.' She thought that this suggested a certain amount of knowledge cloaked with modesty.

'In that case, I must show you some of the Stow Stocksley furniture,' said Sir Leonard, and, having refreshed his own drink, he sat down opposite her and began to tell her about some of the more important pieces. Cicely settled comfortably back in her seat, feeling that she had done well thus far, and that Sir Leonard's own loquacious enthusiasm, with a little guidance from her, could be guaranteed to see them safely through dinner.

A week later they went together to Kingsmead to see the tropical plant exhibition, and when Abigail came home from a disappointingly dull holiday, in which she had painted the same hillside twice and suffered a bout of diarrhoea, Cicely was able to regale her sister with details of her day out with Sir

Leonard. She managed to hint at a subtle intimacy (which had by no means developed, but which it pleased Cicely to imagine) between herself and Sir Leonard. Abigail was unpleasantly sceptical about the whole thing, but was forced into outright astonishment when, a week later, Cicely returned triumphantly from taking a telephone call, and announced that Sir Leonard had invited her to accompany him to the Royal Horticultural Society's Flower Show at Wisley two weeks hence.

'What makes him think you know anything about plants?' asked Abigail, to whom Michael had been less than attentive since their return from the Dordogne. In fact, she was convinced that he had actively avoided her by dashing into Superdrug in the High Street the other day.

'I might remind you that it is I who do the gardening, not you,' replied Cicely. 'Besides, perhaps he happens to enjoy my company.' And she glowed at the prospect of another outing with Sir Leonard, happily building all kinds of new and beautiful castles in this intoxicating air. Stow Stocksley might be denied to Orlando, but what if . . . ? She dared to take the thought no further. The thing must be managed step by step, she told herself. One had to walk before one could run.

Chapter Ten

While his aunt Cicely was thus engaged in weaving her romantic fancies, Orlando was tasting the delights of eighteen-year-old freedom in London. Anne liked having him in the flat – it amused her to have a handsome young man around whom she could introduce to her friends as her nephew, alternately flirting with him and showing him off. At thirty-two, the joke still had an appeal for her which might be lost in a few more years. He, in turn, was enjoying his temporary residence in her flat, which was a fashionable loft conversion on the fringes of Chelsea, a series of long, large-windowed rooms overlooking the river, with floors of stripped and polished pine, black minimalist furniture, large, spotlit modern paintings on the whitewashed brick walls, and discreetly positioned photographer's lamps for lighting. It was beyond the bounds of good taste, redolent of '80s West End chic, and Orlando loved it.

Anne had a CD player, in the days when these were new and wondrous things, and a sound system that took Orlando's breath away. He slept on a futon, had yoghurt with honey and freshly-squeezed orange juice for breakfast, instead of cornflakes and sweet tea, and could do exactly as he liked, when he liked, without having to obey lesson bells or answer Aunt Cicely's shrill summons at mealtimes. It was a million miles away from the unambitious, suburban atmosphere of Plumtree Villa, or the clamorous impersonality of school – or even the quiet grandeur of Stow Stocksley.

On the Friday night of his last weekend there, Anne took

136

Orlando to dinner with some friends, and then to a fashionable night club. It was the kind of club Orlando had never been to before, and he found the experience both exhilarating and intimidating. He felt very young amongst the crowd of sophisticated and glamorous twenty-somethings, and wished he had enough money to dress in silk shirts and Armani suits, and take out the kind of girls he saw all around him. They were sleek and lovely and seemed to be made for the sole purpose of being both desirable and untouchable. One or two of these enchanting creatures came up to their table, which was large and noisy, to chat to friends, and Orlando lived half in fear and half in hope that one of them might speak to him. What could he possibly have to say?

While he was thus musing on his inadequacies, Anne got up to dance. Orlando watched her as she made her way on to the floor, and as he did so, he caught sight of a girl making her way through the dancers in the general direction of their table. She was pretty, blonde, her hair raggedly piled up on her head and falling in wisps around her ears and neck, and she stood out from the rest of the girls in the club because of the expression on her face. She was not wearing the requisite cool, knowing smile, nor affecting sidelong glances and elegantly self-conscious movements; she looked anxious, her glance skittering from side to side. She reached a pillar near their table and stood there for a few seconds, glancing into the crowd behind her. When she looked back in his direction, Orlando saw that her face was now panic-stricken. He was fascinated. At that moment, his gaze collided with hers and, to his astonishment, she suddenly smiled and gave a little wave, then started to move round the table towards him. She sat down in Anne's empty chair, the skimpy skirt of her black halter-neck dress riding up her thighs, put her arms around his neck and kissed him affectionately. Then, still smiling, she drew her face a few inches away from his, her slender arms still around his neck, and said, 'Please, please, just sit there and pretend you know me.'

'Why?' he asked, glancing at the dance floor.

'Because – oh, just do it!'

He looked back at her. Her teeth were gritted, and he could feel her hands locked tight with nervousness behind his neck. She was very pretty, with a small, neat face and a kind of pushed-up, nice nose and a wide, if somewhat fixed smile. Her eyes were a light, almost golden, brown, and she had freckles, very faint ones, all over her forehead, nose and cheekbones, which he rather liked. They reminded him of Mrs Rees-Jones and, thinking of Mrs Rees-Jones, he realised that one should never look a gift horse in the mouth, certainly not twice. He decided to capitalise on the situation and kiss her, and as he was doing so he suddenly became aware of a large figure standing next to him, and then another. He looked up and saw two thick-set, unsmiling men, apparently of Middle-Eastern extraction, staring down at the girl.

'Mr Afiq wishes you to come back now,' said one of the men. His voice was quiet and cold.

'I'm sorry – I don't know who these people are,' said the blonde girl to Orlando.

'Please don't bother the young lady,' said Orlando as he disengaged her arms from his neck. He sounded more confident than he felt. He was aware that talk at the table was dying away, and people were looking at the two men, and at him.

'Mr Afiq wishes you to come back,' repeated the man. The other man clamped a hamlike hand around the girl's upper arm, and she tried to pull away. The grip was like a vice. The man who had spoken put a hand gently but firmly against Orlando's chest to prevent him rising. Orlando was now wishing that this girl had picked anyone else in the room but him. Then one of Anne's friends, a tall, dark individual in his thirties, leaned across and said to the man, 'If you don't let go of that young lady, I shall call the management. They are close personal friends, I can assure you.'

Both men looked frozenly at him, and then a reassuring little posse of bouncers materialised from among the dancers and made their way swiftly to the table. Anne had come back by now and stood glaring from the men to Orlando.

'What the hell's going on?' she demanded. Then she turned to the bouncers. 'I think these men are troubling my guests,' she said, but the bouncers were already descending upon the men who, sizing up the situation and the odds, released the girl and Orlando and moved back a little.

'No trouble,' said one of them, holding up a fat, placatory hand, heavy with gold jewellery. 'No trouble. But this young lady is thief.' He pointed to the girl in Anne's chair.

'Come on, squire,' said one of the bouncers coldly. 'You don't sort out your troubles in here. On your way.' The little phalanx of bouncers hustled the men towards the door; people in the vicinity had fallen quiet and were looking over. The man who had grabbed the girl's arm turned and glared threateningly at her as he reached the door, and she looked away. The hubbub died down, and the atmosphere returned to normal.

'Well,' said Anne, standing behind the seated girl, 'I'm afraid I don't think you belong to our party, do you?' Her tone was not unpleasant, but her meaning clear. The girl rose, tucking back a strand of hair behind one ear.

'Thanks,' she said to Orlando, and started to move away.

'Hold on,' said Orlando, getting to his feet.

'Don't worry,' murmured the girl, shrugging away from Orlando's hand and moving off through the crowd.

Orlando followed her. 'Come on,' he said as he caught up with her. 'Come and have a drink.' She hesitated, shrugged, and went with him to a quiet table near the bar. She laid her handbag flat on the table, and Orlando noticed that her fingers were still trembling a little.

'What was all that about?' he asked. She said nothing. 'I want to know.'

'No – I don't think you do, actually,' replied the girl, and gave him a lopsided smile, her glance wandering off in the direction of the bar. She rummaged in her bag for some cigarettes, lit one, and looked at Orlando. Blowing out some smoke, she added, 'Look, thanks for helping me out. But you don't get any medals. You haven't earned my undying trust and affection, or anything like that.' Then she said impatiently, 'Oh, if you're going to sit there, at least buy me a drink.'

Orlando went to the bar and brought back two Cokes. She sipped hers and eyed Orlando.

'How old are you?' she asked.

'How old do you think I am?' replied Orlando.

'Oh,' she said musingly, drawing in a deep lungful of smoke, 'about nineteen. Too young for this place.'

He nodded. 'Nearly,' he said, then smiled. She smiled back. 'But I'd really like to know what that was all about,' he added.

'What's your name?' she asked.

'Orlando.'

She half shut her eyes, rolled her cigarette between index and middle fingers. 'Orlando,' she repeated. 'Beautiful.' She spoke with a kind of relish.

'What's yours?'

'Jo,' she replied; her mouth stayed in an 'o' shape for a few seconds as she stubbed out her cigarette.

'Well – Jo.' He paused. 'Aren't you going to tell me who those men were, and why you needed me to help you out?'

She sighed and looked at him. 'They are a couple of pretty nasty gentlemen who wanted to take me outside and slap me about a bit, and I knew that if I managed to – to attach myself to a bunch of people like the ones you were with, then that would make it difficult for them. And there you were, looking straight at me, with an empty chair next to you. So.'

Orlando sipped his Coke and sat back. He was aware that here was a different world, something far removed from his safe existence. 'Why would they want to do that? What had you done?'

'Orlando,' she said in a resigned fashion, 'I am a call girl. This evening I had a booking with a Mr Afiq, who is some kind of Arab businessman, or something. I don't know. But he's as rich as stink and as big as Cyril Smith. He picked me up in this big stretch limo, about as long as that bar, with those two nutters up front, one driving and the other picking his nose.' She spoke rapidly, conversationally. 'So I'm sitting there in this limo, and there's a little drinks cabinet, crystal glasses, you name it, a TV, a fax, a phone – and this Mr Afiq taking up half the width of the seat, with a bum like a bean bag and a face to match. Would you fancy making it with something like that? No. Well, he's sitting there with a glass of Scotch in one fat hand, and the other on my crotch, and he leans forward to knock on the glass to one of his minders, and I see this bill-fold lying between me and him on the seat. He's so fat it's popped right out on to the seat. So there it is, a nice handful of fifties, and there am I. He's babbling away to his heavies, I don't feel like sticking around but I feel I should be paid for my trouble, and the lights are red, so I pick up the money, and I'm out of the car and on to the pavement so fast it would make your head swim.'

'Then what?' Orlando was both disgusted and amused.

She smiled her crooked smile. 'I'm a fashion victim, that's what.' She pointed down at the spindly heels of her black sandals. 'It's difficult legging it up the road in a pair of these. You want to try it. So his minders are out the car and coming after me, and Mr Fattie Afiq's standing on the pavement shouting his head off, and I make for here. I've got a head start, a few seconds to catch my breath and smile at the doorman, and I'm inside.' She lit another cigarette. 'The rest you know.'

'You stole his money?'

'He's so rich he won't miss it. It was probably what he was going to pay me, anyway. Look, I have to go. Thanks for the drink.' She rose to leave.

Orlando stood up. 'Hold on,' he said, 'I'll come with you. They might still be outside.'

She laughed. 'You're something else, aren't you? My young Sir Galahad.'

They went out through the smoked glass doors and into the street. There was no sign of Mr Afiq or his minders.

'Listen, off you go, back to your friends,' she said. 'I'm going to find a cab. I'll be all right, you know.'

Orlando thrust his hands into his trouser pockets. 'I don't really want to go back. I've had enough for one night. I'd rather talk to you.'

She gave him a curious look, then sighed. Oh, well, the evening was shot to hell, and she still hadn't had any dinner. He'd be company. He was good-looking, a bit of a toff, but he was all right. She hoped he didn't think he was on for a quick one, something to tell his friends, this hooker he met in a night club.

When she said as much to him, he simply turned and glanced at her.

'No – don't worry,' he said calmly, and she was momentarily taken aback by the tone of his voice. After the merest pause, he smiled and said, 'Shall we go and have a drink somewhere?'

She hesitated for a moment, suddenly feeling less in control. Then she shrugged. 'I'd rather have something to eat.'

'Okay,' said Orlando. 'Let's find a cab. You say where you want to go.'

She took him to the Up All Night Restaurant in the King's Road, and they sat talking over hamburgers and beer. He told her about his aunts, and his grandfather, and about Stow Stocksley and school, aware that she was listening to it all with a faintly derisory amusement. He didn't mind. He enjoyed watching her smile her streetwise smile, liked her pretty, even teeth and her rude, smoky laugh. And those freckles. Really pretty, all over the top of her face, right up into her blonde hair. He couldn't help wondering, as he wondered about most women between sixteen and thirty, what she would be like to go to bed with. He found the idea that she was a call girl simultaneously exciting and repulsive. But, nice though she had been to kiss, he decided that one could hardly be interested in a prostitute.

'So,' asked Orlando, when he felt she had heard enough about him, 'how did you come to be doing what you do for a living?'

She lit one of her endless Virginia Slims and sat fiddling with her lighter, wondering why it was she suddenly wished that she'd never told him that about herself. She sighed.

'You mean, what's a nice girl like me doing something like that, when I could be behind the make-up counter at Boot's, or stacking shelves?' She laughed. 'Well, the money's better, for a start.'

Orlando nodded and ate some more of his hamburger. 'Is it fun, though? Do you like it?'

She stared at him. His candid gaze, which gave nothing away, somehow unsettled her. She could not tell if the question was naive or prurient.

'No, of course I don't *like* it,' she said. 'It's just a job. But it pays for a much better flat, and nicer clothes, and – oh, thousands of things I couldn't have if I had an ordinary job.'

143

She blew out some smoke. 'A nice job. Like a dental receptionist.' She laughed. 'Actually, I was a trainee beautician once. I left school when I was sixteen and I had this job working in a beauty salon – you know, answering the phone, slapping on the odd face pack. I had this idea that I'd get trained up, doing manicures and facials and all that stuff, and that I'd meet some nice bloke, someone with a bit of money, and I'd get married, and then have my own salon . . .' She rested her chin on one hand and looked at Orlando with her yellowy-brown eyes. Cat's eyes, thought Orlando. 'That's what sixteen-year-old girls dream about, see? Well, a certain type do. Anyway, I was one of those.'

'So what happened?'

'Oh, I got into debt, spending far more than I could afford, and I took a loan out from this bloke – I finished up in a complete hole, financially. Anyway, there was this one woman who used to come into the salon, came in every other week for a manicure and a facial. Big redhead, she was. I forget her name. One day when I was putting some gunk on her face I found myself telling her about the mess I was in, and she began talking about this agency a friend of hers ran, and how you could earn up to a hundred a night, and stuff. She said, all that happened was these men would ring up the agency – you know, businessmen who were in London and were a bit lonely, wanted some company – and the agency would sort of give them details of the girls who were on their books – escorts, we were called – and they'd pick one out and take her out for the evening. And the man would pay the agency, and the agency would take some of the money and you'd get the rest. It sounded dead easy. I mean, all that money just for going and having a bit of dinner with some bloke.'

'Didn't you realise that there had to be more to it than that?' asked Orlando.

'You don't know what I was like. Seventeen, didn't know my arse from my elbow. I really didn't catch on. Anyway, I got the name of this agency, and rang them up and mentioned the woman's name – the woman from the salon, I mean – and they told me to come along. And so I went to these offices in Kensington. They seemed really pukka, everything expensive, the woman who saw me was all beautifully made-up, nice suit, all that stuff. She asked me a load of questions, had I done this kind of work before . . . Well, I thought it might blow it for me if I said I hadn't, so I said yes, I had. And I lied about my age. And that was that. Anyway, I suppose I was unlucky, really. The first punter that took me out was – well, he was really quite nice. He was dead old, forty-something, but he was quite nice-looking. I didn't fancy him or anything, but when it came to – well, when he asked me back to his hotel and I realised what he expected me to do – well, it wasn't as bad as it could have been. And I just kept thinking about the money, how badly I needed it.'

'What do you mean, then – you were unlucky?'

'Well, if it had been someone like Mr Afiq, I'd probably have run a mile, gone back to the salon and got on with my respectable little life, sorted things out somehow. As it was – ' she sighed and reached for another cigarette ' – I realised it wasn't that difficult, sleeping with someone for money. And so that's how it went on. What happens, you see, is you get used to earning two or three hundred a night – I mean, that's really serious money. And you start buying good clothes, going to nice clubs and restaurants, you get yourself a nice flat . . . And by the time that happens, you look around and realise you can't go back.'

'So, how long are you going to carry on doing it?' he asked.

'I don't know. You don't think ahead, really.' She sat back, pushing her wispy blonde fringe out of her eyes, lifting her chin as she smoked. 'I've got a lot of friends in this racket, and they all make different excuses for their life. But they're all just after the same thing.' She smiled. 'It's the same thing all women want, whether they're tarts or not.'

'And what's that?' asked Orlando, watching her face.

'Security, that's what. A rich bloke. Men have this idea that women are romantic, that they'll do anything for love. Maybe some women are like that. But most of them are just looking out for number one. They'll do anything for money and security.'

Somehow, this did not surprise Orlando. 'What about you?' he asked.

She laughed and shrugged. 'Well, I'm no different, am I? But I want a bit of independence first. I'm just saving up enough to get out of this racket. What I want to be is a photographer. I bought this really nice Pentax, got a friend who does it professionally to show me all about lighting and stuff . . .' Her gaze became distant. 'That's what I'll be doing in ten years' time. I just need to sell a few pictures, get established. What I want is enough money to put a dark room in my flat. Then I can live a nice, clean, respectable life – just like anybody else.' Orlando, sipping at the remains of his beer, contemplated her, musing on the morality that allowed her to steal money, and prostitute herself, and still imagine that she could discard it all and assume a new guise of decency in a few years' time. Jo glanced at him, and added, 'Anyway, I don't know why you want to know all this. It's not exactly part of the world you live in, is it? Not Planet Respectable.'

'I suppose not,' said Orlando.

Jo stubbed out her cigarette, then lifted her eyes to look at Orlando for a long moment. He was nice, no question. 'Do you fancy coming back to my place?' she asked quietly.

He put his chin on one hand and considered this. 'I don't think so,' he said politely. 'It's not that I don't like you – I just don't think it's a terribly good idea.'

'What – because I'm a hooker?'

He said nothing, but signalled to the waitress for the bill. She sat there, trying to work out why his blend of eighteen-year-old charm and arrogance should be so fascinating and attractive. As he scribbled on the bill, he surprised her by saying suddenly, 'I've had a really good time tonight. I'd like to keep in touch. Why don't you give me your phone number?' He held out his pen. Jo, since she had just been summarily rejected by him, felt like telling him to drop dead, but when he smiled at her, she found she couldn't. She tore the top off her cigarette packet and scribbled her number down, watching as he tucked it carelessly into his pocket. No doubt he would lose it, or forget it.

They left the restaurant and walked down the King's Road as far as Smith Street, where Jo lived, and stopped on the corner. Orlando smiled and said, 'I'll give you a call some-time.'

'Sure,' said Jo. 'Anyway, thanks for the favour.' She watched as he walked away, and thought, if ever he did keep in touch, she wasn't going to let that one get away in a hurry.

Anne's flat was in darkness when he returned, and he assumed she must be asleep, but she came padding out in her nightshirt while he was getting a drink of orange juice.

'At last,' she said. 'I was worried about you.'

'I'm sorry. I should have told you I was leaving. I took that girl for something to eat.'

Anne leaned against the door frame. 'You know what she is, don't you?'

'Yes,' replied Orlando. He closed the fridge door. 'Well, she told me.' Then he looked in faint surprise at Anne. 'How did you know?'

'That she was a tart? Oh, Orlando, by the time you reach my age there are some things you know instinctively. Which is why I wasn't too keen on you hanging around her.'

147

'She's rather interesting, actually,' said Orlando, and drank his juice.

'Don't tell me you fancy her?' asked Anne in alarm.

'No, I don't,' replied Orlando. 'Stop bringing everything down to basics. I just liked her, and we had an interesting talk.'

'It's just that at your age, with all that testosterone charging around your body, or whatever . . .' She yawned. 'Put the light off before you come to bed. I'm going to lock up.' And she padded off.

That was the end of the harmonious phase of Orlando's stay at Anne's. The weekend brought a storm of phone calls and sudden disappearances on Anne's part, and on Sunday evening she came home late, looking tired and drawn.

'Are you all right?' asked Orlando, looking up from the sofa where he lay reading the Sunday papers.

'Oh, don't ask,' replied Anne, and went to pour herself a drink. Then she went to her bedroom and did not reappear.

The next morning she had left for work before Orlando got up. It was his last day in London, and he took a bus to the V&A and spent the morning there, then went across to Dan's for the rest of the day. When he got home late in the evening, he went into the living room and found Anne standing at the windows overlooking the river, fiddling with the micro blind. A man was lounging on the long, white leather sofa, a glass in one hand, his other arm stretched out across the back of the sofa. They both looked round as Orlando came in.

Anne came forward. She was not smiling, looked worn out. 'Hi, Orlando.' She turned listlessly to the man on the sofa. 'Raymond, this is Orlando, my nephew.'

The man did not rise, but stretched out a languid hand to Orlando and smiled. 'Hello. I understand you're staying for a few weeks?' He made easy, polite conversation with Orlando for a moment or two, asking him about his A-levels and

Cambridge. Orlando gave his stock answers, but was aware that this smoothly-delivered small talk was an attempt to mask an unpleasant atmosphere. He studied the man as they talked. Fifty, at least, but quite attractive, Orlando supposed; tall, expensively dressed, very assured and almost offhand in his manner. Orlando was aware that Anne was standing watching them intently, as though waiting for them to finish.

'Well,' said Orlando at an appropriate juncture, 'I'd better get off to bed.' He glanced at the man. 'Nice to meet you.' Raymond stretched his mouth in a smile and nodded, then drained his glass.

'I'd better be making tracks, too,' he said, and rose. Anne glanced at him quickly, her mouth tight. Then she smiled, trying visibly to relax.

'Can't you stay a little longer?' she asked, her voice nervous and light.

'Afraid not,' replied Raymond, shrugging his arms in his jacket shoulders as though to ease a slight stiffness. His tone was light but very final. Sensing the tension in the atmosphere, Orlando murmured 'goodnight' and left quickly.

From his room he could hear their voices in the living room, Anne's tense and urgent at first, then growing subdued. The man's was low and even throughout. Then the voices stopped, and he heard the door of the apartment close. Orlando sat on the edge of the bed for a few moments, then went through to the living room. Anne was standing with her back to him, one hand over her face. He could tell that she was crying.

'Are you okay? Can I get you something?' he asked.

She shook her head and took her hand away, sniffing. 'No, I'm all right.'

'Who is he?'

'He's – he's just someone I've been seeing for a while.' She moved away and sat down on the sofa, pressing her hands together between her knees. She looked down at the floor, her

149

blonde hair falling like a curtain over the side of her face. 'He's been away for a while. Abroad. And I'd been so looking forward to seeing him again . . .' She wiped a finger against her nose, sniffed again. 'When he came back on Saturday I went to meet him and he told me – well, he just told me that we should stop seeing each other. Tonight was my last pathetic attempt to keep him.' She laughed, and it turned into fresh weeping. Orlando sat down beside her. He had never seen her lose her self-possession before.

'Come on,' he said soothingly, and put a tentative arm around her.

'You see, he's married,' she went on. 'He says he doesn't love her, that it went wrong ages ago – and when we first started he said he was going to leave her. But – ' She sighed, looked up, wiped her eyes with the back of her hand ' – months went by and nothing happened. He would make excuses – she was ill, he couldn't do it to the boys – they're in their twenties, for God's sake! So I said, either you leave her by this summer, or it's over.'

'And he didn't leave her?'

'No, he didn't.' She shook her head. 'I don't think he ever intended to.'

'So you're the one who ended it,' said Orlando, thinking that at least she could salvage this scrap of pride.

'That's the pathetic part. I couldn't even stick to my own ultimatum. When he told me on Saturday that he wasn't going to leave her, and that he supposed, in the light of what I'd said, that it had come to an end between us, d'you know what I said?' Her voice trembled with faint hysteria between laughter and tears. 'I actually said that I didn't care. That he could stay with her, just as long as he went on seeing me. God, how I demeaned myself . . .' She bit her lip, staring straight ahead. 'And then he said that he didn't want it to go on in any event. That he thought there was nothing left.'

150

'Forget him,' said Orlando. 'I didn't like him, anyway. Far too old for you. Old enough to be your father.'

'I suppose that's one of the things I liked about him,' replied Anne sadly. 'God, I need a tissue.' She got up and went in search of one, and Orlando sat reflecting on what she had just told him. Anne came and sat back down, blowing her nose. 'I really thought, in the beginning, that he wanted to marry me, that he would look after me.'

'Is that what you want?' he asked, slightly surprised. She had always seemed so independent, unafraid of life.

'Oh, Orlando,' she answered, 'that's all any woman wants. Security.' She looked at him. 'And love.'

Orlando stared out across the river at the lights on the far bank, thinking about what Jo had said. That was the one thing she hadn't mentioned.

Chapter Eleven

Orlando did keep in touch with Jo. He rang her during the Christmas holidays after his first term at Cambridge, and they met for lunch in Notting Hill. Thereafter, they established a pattern, always meeting at the same restaurant during the holdiays. They developed an odd, intimate relationship, but one in which the boundaries which had been established at their first meeting were never transgressed. Jo might find Orlando attractive, but she regarded him as unattainable, his background too far removed from her own. For his part, although he thought Jo remarkably pretty, and theoretically desirable, Jo's profession led Orlando to regard her almost as an asexual being. Their relationship thrived on the differences between them, and Orlando enjoyed Jo's lurid tales from her alien world, just as she liked to hear about his life at Cambridge, and about Stow Stocksley. They confided in one another about their various romances, although most of Orlando's were short-lived. He had learned too well from his encounter with Hannah not to give too much of himself. He sometimes thought that, apart from his aunts, Jo was the only woman he was really fond of.

In the summer after Orlando graduated, he came up to London to stay with Anne, and arranged to meet Jo at their usual restaurant. He had not seen her since the previous winter, and it struck him, when she arrived, that she was looking remarkably well, after her own particular fashion – suntanned, her blonde hair cropped short, and wearing the tightest of denim jeans and a blouse tied below her midriff. He was aware of men glancing surreptitiously in her direction as she made her way to their table.

He could tell as soon as she sat down that she was bursting with some important piece of personal news, and she waited only until their first glass of wine to deliver it. She had met someone, a journalist called Paul, he was divine, she was in love, and they were going overland to Africa together. She had given up the call-girl business, she told Orlando, and she intended to live her life now as though that part of it had never happened. Orlando listened as she told him about her new love.

'I met him at some film thing at the ICA – I mean, I'd never normally go there, all black coffee and subtitles, but I went as a favour to a friend. It was just an instant thing between me and Paul. And this Africa thing is going to be fantastic. He's got a Land Rover, the lot, and I'm selling the flat and putting up half the money for the trip. I'm going to take pictures while I'm out there, and maybe I can get started as a photographer. Everything's going to be different from now on.' She looked at him. 'Aren't you pleased for me?'

Orlando sat back. 'Of course,' he said shortly, wondering why everything she had just told him faintly annoyed him. Their relationship was purely platonic, and yet he was aware of a certain jealousy, a dislike of this unknown journalist.

'So,' she went on, smiling her crooked smile at him, 'What about you, Orlando? What happens now you've finished university? Off to see the wide world? You want to go out to India, travel a bit. My friend Kes did that. He said it was completely mind-blowing, you really become a different person. And he brought back some really good dope,' she added.

Orlando, who liked to think that he had developed a certain maturity and polish during his time at university, thought of the carefully planned interviews which, with the assistance of his grandfather and college tutor, had been lined up for him, designed to secure a promising City job. 'No,' he replied. 'I don't think that's really me, somehow. I plan to go into finance, banking, something like that.' He raised his eyes to look at her, and noticed for the first time that she had freckles on her smooth, golden shoulders, and a little spattering of them disappearing into her cleavage.

'Listen to you,' she said. 'You've got it all set up, haven't you? Talk about a privileged background. I'll bet you always get everything you want.' She said this musingly, without rancour.

For some reason, Orlando suddenly thought of Stow Stocksley. 'Possibly not,' he said. He glanced at the empty bottle of wine. 'Come on,' he said. 'Let's go for a walk.'

They dawdled out into the sunshine and into the local park. All the time she talked and talked about her journalist, until Orlando didn't think he could take much more. He sat down beneath a tree, while Jo stretched out on the grass and closed her eyes, still talking.

To stem her panegyric waffle about Paul, he suddenly asked, 'How long are you going to Africa for?' He began idly to pick daisies, splitting their sappy stems and threading them through one another.

'Oh, I dunno. Six months. A year. All depends . . .' Jo opened her eyes and shaded them with one hand, looking up at Orlando. 'You are pleased I'm off the game, aren't you?'

'Why should it matter to me one way or the other?' replied Orlando. Then he added, 'Yes, of course I am,' and wove another daisy into the chain. She closed her eyes again and was silent for a while. He looked across at her, and it struck him that he was irritated that she was going away just when he would be moving to London. Not that he could exactly include her in his social circle, but he had been looking forward to seeing more of her.

'Have you got anyone at the moment?' Jo asked suddenly.

'No, not right now,' replied Orlando. 'Anyway, you know I always tell you about whoever it is, if there is anyone.'

'I sometimes think,' she said, 'that it's a real shame, you being what you are, and me what I am . . . or was. We'd've got on all right, wouldn't we?'

He sat looking at her, saying nothing, and then set the little circlet of daisies like a crown on her short, soft hair.

It had been four years since the silent formalities of Orlando's adoption, and there was no doubt that to be Sir Leonard's grandson, and to bear the same illustrious surname, brought advantages in life. The family name, together with the influence and backing of Colin Crichton, who was an old friend of Sir Leonard's and who was to be Orlando's introductory mentor in the City, seemed to assure him a ready entrée into its magical world. Orlando had interviews with three financial institutions – a firm of stockbrokers, a merchant bank, and the London branch of a large American West Coast banking corporation.

'Obviously it's best to cast the net wide,' Crichton told Orlando over a working breakfast at Crichton's club, 'but I rather think that your best bet is with the Americans. Amerco is a very good institution, and Pfeiffer is a personal friend, obviously, so I think the job's as good as yours. If you want something that's not too much on the dull side, as you say you do, I think foreign exchange dealing is probably as good a start as any. Throws you in at the deep end. Just the thing if you're young and sharp. Mind you, although buying and selling currency sounds simple enough, you have to have the right temperament. Have to be able to keep your nerve.' Crichton helped himself to more marmalade. 'You're dealing in very large sums of money most of the time, which can be a bit unnerving for some chaps. Just a question of staying cool under pressure. And being quick off the mark – you've got to be able to mentally calculate your currency position at all times, keep in your head how much you've bought and sold, try to anticipate what's going to happen in the market. Dealers have to react in a split second, you know. Tough stuff.' He took a bite of his toast and poured Orlando more coffee.

Orlando sat back, considering this. He had enough belief in his own powers to assume he could handle a job like that. 'It sounds fairly demanding,' he observed.

'Well, it is,' replied Crichton. 'Which is why the rewards are considerable. You could be looking at forty thousand a year, plus bonuses. Possibly twice as much again in a good year.'

Even to Orlando, who received a generous allowance from his grandfather and had become used, at Cambridge, to leading a relatively carefree financial existence compared to many other students, this sounded an enormous amount of money. It occurred to him that there was possibly something inherently unfair in a system which rewarded background and excellent connections as much as it did talent and industry, and which would allow him the chance to earn large sums of money, while the same opportunities were denied to others less socially advantaged than he was. But the thought did not trouble him for long. He could hardly rid himself of his advantages, after all, or manufacture obstacles for himself. He was who he was.

Certainly, when it came to the interviews, Orlando felt a preference for the American bank. It seemed to him to be devoid of the self-satisfied air of the merchant bank and the excessive seriousness of the stockbroking firm, and the atmosphere was sharp and friendly. He liked Mr Pfeiffer, the chief financial executive, who was an easy-going, jovial American of the Phil Silvers variety, with a kind, bloodhound face, and sharp, intelligent eyes behind large spectacles. He spent three-quarters of an hour talking to Orlando, whom he found personable, charming, and, when thrown a variety of searching questions regarding the world of finance, well-informed and mentally agile.

'Come on,' he said, rising to his feet at the end of the interview, 'I'll show you around.'

He took Orlando on a brief tour of the building, and finished up in the dealing room, which was vast, with circular banks of dealing desks set out concentrically. Orlando knew he should be trying to concentrate on what Mr Pfeiffer was saying to him about Teledate and Reuters, but he was too busy absorbing the electrifying atmosphere of the place. The drama and urgency of the room, with shirt-sleeved dealers rising and falling, gesticulating and shouting constantly, touched his sense of romance. He wanted to do this, be one of these young men, spinning the wheels of the money markets.

'Does it take long to pick it up?' he asked, turning to Mr Pfeiffer.

'No time at all,' said Mr Pfeiffer confidently. 'Provided you have an aptitude for the thing. Of course, every new dealer goes on probation for a year. We assign you to someone experienced, see how you do, and you pick it up gradually. I should say you'd catch on pretty fast.'

And so, at the end of that summer, after a hard-earned holiday in Italy with three Cambridge friends, a newly mature and sophisticated twenty-two-year-old Orlando was to start work as a currency dealer with Amerco West, under the wing of Barry Henson, a portly, astute East Ender who was one of the bank's most successful dealers. Barry was sharp and crude, and more than a little sceptical of the accent and manner of his new recruit, and he and Orlando disliked one another on sight. But Orlando, who knew his grandfather would have preferred him to be working for a merchant bank, was determined to succeed in his new profession and to convince everyone of his abilities. Barry simply added to the challenge.

Sir Leonard, content that at least Orlando had settled on a career of some kind, offered, as an advance birthday present, to put down a deposit on a flat in London for his grandson, on which Orlando could pay the mortgage once he started his new job in September. He thought that this might bring Orlando to a healthy appreciation of life's responsibilities. Orlando, who, after years of enforced sharing of accommodation with others was initially quite keen on the idea of a place of his own, duly found himself a modest second-floor flat in an eccentric backwater between Kensington Church Street and Notting Hill Gate, with two bedrooms, a bathroom, a kitchen and a sitting room, with shared use of the garden. While he was waiting, in early September, for the conveyance of this desirable residence to be completed, Orlando stayed with Anne in Chelsea.

Anne was now in her mid-thirties, and creative group head at her agency, still leading, so far as Orlando could see, a glamorous and expensive life at a relentless pace. He lay on her white leather sofa on Friday evening and listened to her make and take several phone calls, heard the constant stream of media gossip, the bright laughter, the arrangements and assignations, and marvelled at the sheer energy which characterised even her leisure time.

'Do you know,' he said to her as she emerged later from the shower, 'over the past three years, on every occasion I've stayed here, you've gone out practically every night. Don't you ever just stay in and do nothing?'

She swept her wet, blonde hair up into a towel, tucking in the ends to make a turban, then padded across the carpet to pour herself a drink.

'No. Hardly ever.' She went into the kitchen and Orlando heard the clink and splash of ice cubes in her glass. 'Do you want something?' she called.

'No, thanks.'

She came back through, smiling, stirring her drink with her finger. 'The fact is, I'm not very fond of my own company. I find I brood. And that's unhealthy.'

'What do you brood about? Work?'

'God, no.' She took a sip and sank into the sofa next to him. 'My biological time clock.' Orlando looked at her, at the tiny lines which had appeared round her eyes in the last year or so, the slight thickening of the veins on the backs of her hands. Still lovely, he thought, but unmistakably in her thirties. 'And,' she went on, leaning her head back, 'about all the rich, marriageable men in the world, wondering where they are. Certainly not around here, that's for sure.'

'Does he really have to be rich?'

'Certainly,' replied Anne, and set her drink down on the floor as she loosened the turban and began to towel her hair dry.

'God, women are mercenary,' murmured Orlando. 'So that's why there's all this relentless socialising every night – looking for rich Mr Right?'

'I told you – it's not just that. Only partly. It's also to stop me becoming mournful and introverted.'

The phone rang, and Anne reached over to answer it. 'For you,' she said, handing it to Orlando, and then went off to dry her hair and get dressed.

'How come she – whoever she was – knew you were staying here?' asked Anne when she re-emerged.

Orlando sat running his fingers through his dark hair, looking thoughtful. 'I always tell her when I'm going to be here.' There was a pause. The phone call, which had been from Jo, saying goodbye before she went away, had baffled and annoyed him. Suddenly he felt like talking about her. 'Do you remember that time you took me to a night club two or three years ago?' he asked, turning to Anne.

She was staring intently into the mirror as she applied her

159

lipstick. 'Which club? When?' she asked indistinctly.

'When I was eighteen, staying here. You took me to a club and a girl came and sat with me, then these heavies moved in – remember?'

'Oh, yes,' murmured Anne, recapping her lipstick and making a mouth at her reflection. 'The hooker.' She paused, then turned to Orlando. 'You haven't been seeing her, have you? Not for three years?'

He smiled faintly. 'Well, yes. Not in the way you mean, though. I've just kept in touch. God knows why. We meet up every time I'm in London.'

'If you take my advice, nephew, that is not the kind of company you should keep if you want to make social headway in this city. It's not what beautiful young Trinity graduates should be doing. What you want is something dewy-fresh from Queen Charlotte's Ball.'

'I've told you – she's just a friend. Anyway, she's going to Africa with some journalist.'

'Good. I hope she gets eaten.'

'She wants to become a photographer. She's given up being a call girl.'

'I don't care if she's the next Eve Arnold. Any tart, even an ex-one, is bad news.' She slipped on her coat. 'Now, there's some lasagne in the freezer. Don't wait up.'

Orlando sighed and settled back on the sofa, stretching his feet out, and began to think about the job he was to start in three days' time.

By the end of the month, Orlando felt that he was making creditable headway in his new job, if not in his relationship with Barry. After initial uncertainties, he was enjoying the work in the dealing room. He had, too, the novel pleasure of his flat. For the first few weeks it was a relief to have a place of his own to come home to in the evenings. In Cambridge he had shared a variety of flats and houses with other students, with the incidental arguments over whose was what in the fridge, whose turn it was to clean the bath, and who had made the most phone calls that month. Now he had his own space and silence, and never had to come home to a kitchen which someone else was using, or a television programme which he didn't want to watch, or a bathroom which was permanently occupied.

As the autumn nights drew in, however, and he grew accustomed to his new life, he became conscious, when he came home to the empty flat, that it might be pleasant to have someone else to share supper with, or go out to the pub with. He wondered if he didn't now regret turning down the offers of flatshares from other Cambridge friends now in London, in favour of his grandfather's present. One of these might have been more convivial. He saw his friends at weekends, but most of them worked hard from Monday to Friday and weren't inclined to go out on weekday evenings. Those evenings alone began to drag.

He and Dan had taken to meeting once a week in a pub in Covent Garden, near to the small design studio where Dan worked. Dan had spent three years at St Martin's School of Art, living very frugally at Stephen's on a local authority grant, and wasn't earning much at his job as a layout artist. Orlando was always conscious, when they met, of the smartness of his own Savoy Tailors Guild suits and Liberty ties, in contrast to Dan's unvarying uniform of jeans, Doc Marten's, and a paint-smeared denim jacket worn over an old jumper. Dan now wore his unkempt, sandy hair to his shoulders, and had grown a beard, which was reddish and made him look surprisingly fierce.

It was as they sat there one evening in October, Orlando listening while Dan joked about his workmates, that Orlando was suddenly struck by how much he enjoyed Dan's

161

company, how much he made him laugh, and how he always looked forward to the evenings when they met. He realised that he wasn't really looking forward to going back to his empty flat after they had finished their drinks and parted for the evening.

He waited for a pause in the conversation, and then suddenly said to Dan, 'How would you feel about moving in with me?'

'You serious?' asked Dan.

'Of course. It gets a bit boring living there on my own. It would be good to have you sharing.'

Dan scratched his beard and stared reflectively at his pint. 'Funny you should ask, actually. Stephen's got this girlfriend – well, woman – and I think he wants her to move in with him. I mean, he'd never kick me out, but she and I don't exactly hit it off, and I'm beginning to feel – what's the word?'

'De trop?'

'Right, one too many. Anyway, I'd been thinking that I'd stayed there long enough.' Dan pondered the proposal for a minute or two, then said, 'Yeah, okay.' And he smiled slowly, boyishly. 'I won't be able to pay you much by way of rent,' he added.

'Don't worry. We'll sort something out. It'll help with the mortgage.'

'Mortgage,' murmured Dan, eyeing Orlando. 'You live in a whole, grown-up world, don't you? I mean, job in the City, mortgage . . . It'll be a car next.'

'Actually,' said Orlando, 'I've been looking at a new Golf GTI. They're pretty fantastic. Don't know if I can run to a soft-top, though.'

Dan shook his head, then thought for a moment. 'Paddy, maybe it's not such a good idea, you and me sharing. I mean, I doubt if I'd get on with any of your City friends. I lead a pretty basic life, just doing paste-up, hardly any money . . . And I'm

162

probably a bit too much of a socialist for your tastes. I mean, you being one of Thatcher's children, and all.'

They both laughed, and Orlando aimed a fake punch at Dan's head; Dan put up his hands and pretended to fend it off.

'Thanks,' said Orlando. Then he added, 'Look, we'll have a brilliant time. It'll be like school again, only better.'

And so it was agreed that Dan should move into Orlando's flat that weekend, paying a nominal rent, sharing the bills for heating, electricity, the phone and groceries, and such adversities or pleasures as fate might bring.

Chapter Twelve

L ife in the flat was harmonious at first, but after a while there began to be occasional moments of friction between Orlando and Dan, usually involving money. They had agreed to split the bills, but it sometimes seemed to Orlando that he was buying most of the groceries and paying more than his fair share of the phone bill. He knew Dan was hard up, but it still annoyed him. On the other hand, when Dan's lack of money stood in the way of something Orlando wanted to do, he would grow exasperated by Dan's refusal to let Orlando lend him money.

One Friday evening in December, Orlando came home from the dealing room exhausted and irritable. He badly wanted to go out and relax over a few beers in the pub, but Dan wasn't home yet. Orlando made himself a bacon sandwich to while away the time until Dan came in, and reflected on the progress he was making in his job. There were times when he wondered whether he'd really chosen the right career. Barry seemed to be getting at him all the time, showing him up, making him feel he wasn't up to the job. Orlando tried to convince himself that it was because Barry resented him, mistrusted his accent and his background, but there were days – days like the one he had just had – when he felt he did not have the mettle for the work in the dealing room. He was impatient for his probationary year to end, and longed to find some way of proving himself.

His thoughts were interrupted by the sound of Dan's key in the front door. 'God, I'm glad you're back,' said Orlando, as

Dan unwound his scarf and chucked his canvas satchel on to the kitchen table. 'I've had a rotten day, and I badly need to go and drown my sorrows. Fancy coming down to the Salisbury?'

'Sorry, Paddy,' sighed Dan. 'Can't do it. I'm broke, and my pay cheque won't clear till Tuesday.'

'Oh, come on, I'll pay for you.'

'No – I can't let you do that.' Dan plugged in the kettle. 'I can't let you pay for every round of drinks for a whole evening.'

'Well, let me lend you a few quid till Tuesday, then,' said Orlando. He didn't relish the prospect of staying in all evening.

'No – if we start that, it'll just go on and on, and I don't want to be in debt to you.'

'Oh, stop being so bloody principled!' said Orlando. 'It's just a few drinks!'

'I haven't got the money, and I'm not going,' said Dan patiently, and took a mug from the cupboard.

'I don't know why you stay with that left-wing outfit you work for. They pay you peanuts. You could easily get a better paid job. Why don't you get a job in advertising? Anne should be able to get you into an agency somewhere. She practically runs a whole studio. Then at least you'd earn some decent money and have some fun.'

'You know what I think about advertising,' said Dan. 'It's crap.'

'That's what you say about most things that bring in any money. You don't have to go round being a martyr all the time you know. Get a life.' Orlando picked up his coat and banged out of the flat. He walked moodily down Kensington Church Street, past the pub. He hated drinking in pubs on his own, and, anyway, he was still dressed in his City suit. Then he noticed across the road the lights of the new wine bar which had opened recently. He might as well go in and see what it

165

was like. He could just have one drink and then go back and make it up with Dan.

He stopped off at the newsagent's to buy an *Evening Standard*, then went into the wine bar. The scent of newly varnished wood hung in the air, and the place still lacked atmosphere, but there was quite a crowd of customers. Orlando bought a glass of wine and took it over to a small table near the window. He sipped his wine, looking out through the wooden slats of the blinds at the evening traffic, and then opened his paper. As he did so, he noticed a girl standing at the bar. She was quite tall, wearing a cream-coloured suit, and she had smooth, dark hair falling to her shoulders. She glanced over her shoulder as Orlando looked up, and he was struck by the loveliness of her face. She had dark, almond-shaped eyes and a curving mouth. For a moment he thought she was smiling at him, until he saw her turn back and laugh at something the girl behind the bar had said. Evidently they knew one another. After scanning his paper abstractedly, Orlando looked up again. She was sipping her wine, still chatting to the barmaid. Evidently she was waiting for someone. A man, Orlando supposed. Any girl who looked like that had to be. He sighed. Chatting up strange girls in wine bars wasn't his thing, anyway. He had nearly finished his drink, and had decided to pick up a pizza for himself and Dan on the way back. Dan could hardly argue with that.

He drained his glass and was folding up his paper when he looked up and saw, to his surprise, that the girl was walking over to his table. She was smiling – a very cool, secretive kind of smile, he thought – and when she sat down in the chair opposite his, he wondered fleetingly if she was a high-class version of Jo.

'Hi,' she said, 'I just came over to see what you think of the wine bar. My brother opened the place last week, and we like to welcome new customers.'

'Ah,' said Orlando. 'I see. Well . . .' He glanced around. 'It's very nice. I mean, I've only had one glass of wine, and I was just stopping by for a few minutes . . .'

'Do you live locally?' she asked. She was gazing at him, chin on hand, smiling her faint, enigmatic smile.

'Yes, yes, I do, actually. Just a few streets away.' She was even prettier close up, he thought, and wondered how on earth he could get round to asking her out. But, as he saw the expression in her eyes, he realised that he wasn't going to have to. He felt the familiar flicker of interest and desire that he always experienced when some girl was about to make her move.

She glanced at his empty glass and smiled. 'Why don't you stay and have another glass of wine? On the house, of course.'

He met her gaze and nodded, returning her smile. 'That sounds like a very good idea. My name's Orlando.'

'Louisa,' said the girl. And after that, Orlando thought no more about Dan, or pizzas, or going back to the flat.

He spent the rest of the evening in the wine bar, and by the time he wandered back to the flat that night, Orlando was completely infatuated. He had arranged to see her again the following evening, and by the end of the week they had embarked on a love affair of unexpected intensity. Orlando had not felt so passionately about anyone since Hannah, and for the first month he existed in a state of sexual and romantic intoxication.

Eventually, inevitably, their mutual ardour began to cool slightly, and they grew careless and familiar in one another's company. After a few weeks Orlando began to discover that Louisa's cool, calm gaze, and the smile which he found so wonderfully enigmatic, were extremely deceptive. She was a volatile creature, and began to go through spells of moody discontent, during which she and Orlando would frequently argue violently. Orlando came to the conclusion that she enjoyed provoking arguments, since most of them ended up in tearful remorse and passionate lovemaking, which was very much Louisa's speciality. Much as he enjoyed sex with Louisa, however, Orlando now found himself cast into an emotional vortex in which animosity seemed to play almost as great a part as love and desire. It was not the kind of relationship he had ever experienced before, and it did not make for a life of quiet happiness.

Perhaps the thing which he began to find most tiresome was her jealousy, which seemed to him extreme and quite irrational, even though she herself was not beyond flirting provocatively with wine bar customers when Orlando was there, just to goad him. After a couple of months, when the novelty of her inventive sexuality was beginning to wear off, he began to long for a life without the constant friction of stormy arguments, recrimination, jealousy and remorseful lovemaking. Things came to a head one evening in February, when, after a long and stressful day at work, Orlando went to pick up Louisa from her flat to take her to a dinner dance. As soon as she opened the door and turned away, stalking into the living room with her long dress swishing angrily, Orlando knew that a row was about to ensue. He leaned against the door frame for a few seconds, wondering whether he was up to it, and wondering whether he even cared what imagined slight or vexation had brought it about. He sighed and went in, closing the door behind him.

Louisa's bad temper had been provoked, it seemed, by the fact that Orlando had been seen by a mutual friend lunching alone with some attractive girl in the City earlier in the week. That the girl was the daughter of a visiting American colleague of Mr Pfeiffer's, and that Orlando had merely been asked to look after her for the day and show her around, was of no interest to Louisa. The row which developed lasted fifteen minutes, and was brought to an abrupt halt when Louisa slapped Orlando hard across the face. It was something she had never done before.

'Christ, Louisa!' exclaimed Orlando, and grabbed her by the wrist. Then he realised that his pulse was racing, that every nerve in his body was taut, and that the tension of the argument had made him feel almost physically sick. And for what? What exactly were they arguing about? Suddenly Orlando knew that he could go on like this no longer. He dropped her wrist and sat down in a chair, resting his elbows on his knees and running his fingers through his dark hair. Then he looked up at her.

'This is no good, you know,' he said in level tones. Something in his voice must have alarmed her, for she dropped to her knees and put her arms around him.

'Oh, God! I'm sorry! I'm sorry!' she said, easy tears welling up. She reached up to touch his face where she had slapped him, but he moved away. 'I can't help it,' she said, as though agonised. 'I love you so much . . . too much.'

He looked at her. 'We don't love each other,' he said. 'If we did, we wouldn't do this to one another. It's just . . . never-ending.' He pushed her gently away and rose. 'I'm sorry. I'm not going on with this.'

He had every intention of leaving there and then, of ending the affair completely. But Louisa could not bear such a thing to happen. If a relationship had to end, it had to end with her in the ascendant. She caught up with him as he reached the front door and laid her hand on his arm.

'You're right,' she said with quiet contrition. 'I know you're right. Don't you think I feel the same?' She put up a hand and turned his face towards her, so that he had to look at her. 'Please, let's try to be different. Let's be kinder to one another.' She moved her body against his, and he felt an instant sense of arousal. He knew that she only had to look across a room at him sometimes, as she had that first night in the wine bar, and

169

he would want her. He let her kiss him, felt his resolve melting away, hating himself for his weakness. She drew her mouth away; he stood still for a few seconds, lips parted, eyes closed, feeling unutterably weary and filled with a loathing of all this melodrama.

'Look,' she said, smiling, 'I'll go and fix my face a bit, then we'll go to the party. Forget about this evening. Start all over again. Yes?' Her voice was gentle and faintly pleading. He had heard it all before. But he nodded and said, 'Yes. Okay. Go on.'

The dinner dance was a charity event in Knightsbridge, and Orlando had been to one or two similar events with Louisa before. This one was a noisy, mainly young affair, with plenty of champagne beforehand, and by the time he and the four other couples at their table sat down to dinner, Orlando was feeling a little drunk and fairly depressed. He watched his friend Lionel fold his place-card into a paper aeroplane and launch it at Louisa, and realised that he was not in the mood for hilarity or horseplay. The meal began, and Orlando tried to make sensible conversation with the Australian girl on his left, who giggled a lot and spilled her wine. Bored, he glanced round the table and found himself once again looking at the man sitting almost opposite him. He was a casual acquaint-ance of Lionel's, tall and blond, with a wasted look about his attractive face, and snatches of his conversation which Orlando had managed to catch earlier seemed to consist of an amusing blend of arrogance and self-deprecation. He studied the man, wondering why, though they had never met before, his face seemed vaguely familiar. Orlando guessed he must be in his mid-thirties, or thereabouts. The man, in the act of lighting a cigarette, caught his eye. He clicked his lighter shut, smiled and, raising his voice slightly, said, 'We haven't been introduced, have we? Roger Stafford-Roper.'

Orlando stretched his hand across. 'Orlando D'Ewes.'

The blond man stared at him for a moment, then threw back his head and laughed. 'Christ, it's my cousin!'

Orlando stared back at him. So this was the dreadful Roger, he thought, and looked at him with interest. He did not in the least resemble the depraved, shambolic figure which his grandfather's remarks had always conjured up. Orlando had for the past few years imagined some pathetic, abject figure living in a squat, malnourished and constantly stoned. Roger, however, was handsome and elegant, his clothes well-cut, and the languorous, amused pose which he now struck complemented the rather raffish expression of his eyes, which were faintly rimmed with red. Orlando noticed a slight tremor in his cousin's hand as he reached for his wine glass.

'Tell me, how is my dear uncle Leonard?' asked Roger, sipping his wine and looking at Orlando over the rim of his glass.

'Fine,' replied Orlando coolly. 'I haven't seen him since Christmas. But he's fine.'

Roger smiled and tapped the ash from his cigarette. 'Talk about me a lot, does he? No? I suppose not.' Roger turned to the girl on his left, a beautiful, bored-looking blonde. 'Sweetie, this is my cousin, Orlando.' The blonde looked at Orlando and murmured something, her smile not reaching her eyes. Roger looked back at Orlando. 'He's the darling little baa-lamb of the family. I'm the black sheep.' He lowered his eyelids slightly, and then added, 'We must get together later, have a little family reunion all of our own.' Then he ceased to take any further interest whatsoever in Orlando, and turned to continue his conversation with his neighbour.

Orlando looked away, feeling somehow a little foolish. Louisa touched his arm and said, 'Is he really your cousin?'

'I suppose he must be,' replied Orlando, 'if he's who he says he is.'

'He's very beautiful. Quite decadent.'

171

'Quite,' said Orlando, and glanced at Roger again.

After dinner was over, Louisa went to dance with Lionel, and Orlando sat alone, wondering how soon he could leave and go home to bed. He noticed Roger's girlfriend returning to the table, which she had left earlier. Roger was lounging back in his chair and exchanging desultory conversation with the Australian girl, who had moved round the table to be nearer to him. He glanced up as his girlfriend sat down next to him, then leaned forward to murmur something to her. Orlando saw her open her evening bag, take something from it, then slide it discreetly beneath the table to Roger, who, with a practised smile to the Australian girl, rose, put out his cigarette and left the table.

Orlando glanced behind him to see where Roger was going, and it was then that he noticed the girl in the white dress. She was standing with her back to him, talking to someone, and her dark, shining hair fell in curls over her bare shoulders. Orlando knew instantly who it was, even before Hannah turned, her face in profile, glancing across the room. She turned and said something else to the woman to whom she had been speaking, then looked round again, this time taking in the entire room. Her eyes met Orlando's, and he felt as though a great space had opened up beneath his heart. She stared at him, and then smiled very slowly; he realised he had no idea of the expression on his own face. He watched her come towards him, the folds of her white dress foaming out as she walked, looking exactly as he had always remembered, though more graceful now, more poised.

He stood up as she came close. He did not quite know what he felt – whether it was pleasure or pain.

'Hello,' she said. Her voice was quiet, her smile tentative.

'Hello.' For want of something better to say, he added, 'This is – this is quite extraordinary.'

'Isn't it?' she agreed. There was a silence, during which she glanced at the floor in mild embarrassment, and he wondered what on earth to say next.

'You look very well.' That was the best he could do, but at least it was sincere. 'Tremendously well.'

'Thank you.' She accepted the compliment gracefully; he suddenly remembered how much she used to hate it if ever he paid her a compliment, would frown and say, 'God, no, I look awful.' Then she said hesitantly, as though with slight difficulty, 'I had wondered if I would ever see you again. A couple of times I nearly wrote to you . . .'

He could not cope with that – with the sudden gesture towards intimacy. He still had not forgotten how she had looked the last time he ever saw her, nor how he had felt then, and for a long time after. With a slight brusqueness he deflected her line of conversation, and asked, 'What brings you to London?'

'I'm living here, for the present,' she replied. 'I work for Rowena, the committee chairman of the appeal fund.' She indicated the woman to whom she had been talking. 'I was working for the Edinburgh branch of the charity, and she offered me the job down here.'

'I see . . . And your father – Capercailzie – all well?' He wondered how long he could keep up this fatuous small talk.

'My father died three years ago.'

'Oh. Oh, I'm sorry.'

'As for Capercailzie – ' She fingered the thin gold choker at her neck. ' – I sold it, and what was left of the land, before I came down here.'

'You sold it?' Orlando was surprised. 'I thought you were very attached to the place.'

'Chained to it, more like.' He enjoyed hearing the pleasant burr of her accent; it took him back in time in a way he rather liked. 'Besides, I needed the money. I couldn't afford to keep

173

the repairs up, or pay all the debts my father left. So Callum helped me to find a buyer.'

'Callum?'

She flushed suddenly, a beautiful, burning tinge that covered her throat and face, and then faded as rapidly as it had come. He had a sudden impulse to reach out and touch the soft skin of her neck. Then he realised that she must have been referring to the man she had been with in the estate office that day. Her lover.

'He was my father's estate manager,' she said. Her glance wandered for a moment, then returned to Orlando's face. 'He helped me sell it to a development company. They're turning it into a hotel, with a conference centre, a health resort, a golf course, fly fishing, shooting . . . You know the kind of thing. They paid me much more than I ever thought I'd get.'

Orlando had a vision of interior decorators and builders ripping out the mouldering gothic heart from Capercailzie Castle and putting in its place modern, boxlike rooms with en suite bathrooms and trouser presses, of tractors and land-scapers carving up the wild, wonderful moorland and plan-ing it into smooth greens and rolling fairways dotted with bunkers and unlikely clumps of trees. He felt a pang of sadness as he recalled the castle's magnificent melancholy, and suddenly remembered the drawing room in which Hannah had played waltzes on the wind-up gramophone, the sunlight spilling across the shrouded furniture.

'And what about you?' she asked. 'What are you doing these days, Orlando?'

'I work in a bank – as a foreign exchange dealer. You know, buying and selling currency. I might give it up and have a shot at merchant banking, though. I'm not sure.' He felt awkward now, and oddly unhappy. There was no going back, and seeing her like this only brought the past closer, painfully, needlessly so. He half-wished that she could have

174

vanished from his life altogether, as he once imagined she had.

Suddenly she said, 'Would you like to dance?'

Orlando hesitated, then said, 'If you like.' His diffidence masked a strong desire to touch her again.

They danced together, Orlando letting the silly, sentimental music of 'Lady in Red' wash over him and wondering if there was the smallest, remotest chance that she still cared for him. That she was here, that she had suddenly reappeared in his life, looking as she did, was agonising, but perfectly touched every romantic chord in his heart. He looked down at her, and suddenly wanted to bury his face in the soft, dark cloud of her hair, kiss the white skin of her neck. He wanted it to be as it had been the first time he ever saw her, all those years ago. On impulse, he brushed her neck with his lips. She drew away, but slowly, and smiled as the music stopped, then turned her head. Orlando looked up and saw a tall, dark-haired man with glasses approaching them.

'Orlando, this is my fiancé, Max,' said Hannah. She took the dark-haired man's hand. 'Max, this is Orlando, an old friend from – from Scotland.'

Max smiled faintly and extended his hand, and Orlando shook it. It was the worst of clichés, thought Orlando. He felt like Humphrey Bogart. With the sensation of having been badly winded twice in one evening, he said, 'Look, really nice to meet you – and to see you again, Hannah – but I'm afraid I have to be . . .'

'Oh, wait,' said Hannah. 'Give me your telephone number, and perhaps we can have lunch together. Max, have you a pen?'

Orlando glanced at Max's face, which was expressionless, then scribbled down his work and home phone numbers with the pen Max handed to him. Then he said goodnight and made his way back to the table, feeling dazed by the events of the last ten minutes. It was as though his life had suddenly been rocked on its axis, all the hopes and feelings of six years ago rising to the surface. As he reached the table, Lionel, looking harassed, stopped him.

'Orlando, you'd better come – look, I don't know what to do – ' His voice was agitated, almost incoherent.

'What?' asked Orlando, staring at him. 'What?'

'Your cousin – that chap at our table – oh, come on, before someone else finds him!' He hustled Orlando out of the ballroom towards the lavatories. They went in through the door of the gents and into the tiled interior of the washroom. 'He's in that cubicle there,' said Lionel, pointing to a half-open door. 'The door was ajar, and I didn't realise there was anyone in there. Anyway – oh, Christ, you take a look.'

Cautiously Orlando pushed open the cubicle door. It was blocked by some object, so he stepped and looked round.

'Oh, God,' he breathed, as he looked at the figure of Roger slumped on the floor, one arm flung across the toilet bowl, the other hanging down by his side, his sleeve rolled up to the elbow. A syringe was sticking out of his arm, which Orlando saw was blackened and scarred from repeated injections. Roger's face was bluish-white, the edges of his nostrils waxen.

Orlando knelt down next to him, gritted his teeth, and plucked the syringe from Roger's arm. Pulling his handkerchief from his pocket, he wrapped the syringe carefully in it and slid it into Roger's pocket.

'Shouldn't we call a doctor?' asked Lionel.

Orlando said nothing. Trying to remember all the first aid he had ever learnt at school in the CCF – and it hadn't included resuscitating junkies – he put his mouth over Roger's, pinching his nose and breathing into him. At the same time he slipped his hand inside Roger's dress shirt and massaged the area around his heart. Just as he was beginning to think that Lionel might be right about the doctor, Roger groaned and moved.

'Come on,' said Orlando. 'Help me get him up.' And together they hauled Roger up and sat him on the lavatory seat. Orlando crouched there, staring at his cousin, watching as the eyelids flickered and Roger began to mumble. He didn't know much about these things, but Orlando reckoned that Roger might prefer it if there were no doctors, no one to see what had happened.

'Roger, are you all right?' he asked, slapping Roger's cheek lightly. Roger lifted his chin and leaned his head back against the lavatory walls. He began to breathe in deep, slow breaths.

'I don't think he's dying, at any rate,' said Orlando. He slapped Roger again, and the eyes flickered open once more. 'I'd better get him home. Christ, what an evening.' He stood up, putting a hand on the wall. Then he realised that the tiles were spattered with a fine spray of Roger's blood. 'Can you hold on here a minute?' he asked Lionel. 'I'm going to find that girlfriend of his.'

She was sitting at the table, her back to Orlando, smoking and watching the dancers. As he bent down to speak to her, he realised he didn't even know her name. She glanced up at him, smiling, her eyes deep, vacant pools, her smile like the smile of a ghost, emphasising the hollows around her eyes and cheekbones, her face stretched and dead.

'Look,' said Orlando, keeping his voice low, 'Roger is in the gents, stoned out of his mind. He collapsed, but I think he's coming round. Can you get him home as quickly as possible, do you think?'

The smile faded, and she took another drag of her cigarette and looked back towards the dance floor. 'Roger can go fuck himself, for all I care,' said the girl. 'I'm not looking after him. Anyway – ' she turned back to Orlando ' – you're his cousin. You take care of him.' Orlando realised she was so stoned that she wouldn't have been much help, even if she'd wanted to be.

'Can you at least tell me where he lives?' demanded Orlando. The girl told him, and Orlando headed back to the gents, repeating the address under his breath.

Louisa stepped up to him just as he reached the door. 'You haven't danced once with me all evening – and who was that girl you were talking to before?'

'Look,' said Orlando impatiently, 'I've got a bit of a problem at the moment – '

'I don't care!' she snapped. 'I'm bored, and I want to go!' She looked drunk and sulky. He could already foresee the row that she would manufacture later, and felt suddenly weary.

'Louisa,' he said, 'I have better things to do right now than take you home. Find someone else to do it.' Seeing that she was about to flare up in indignation, he added, 'Now, I am going to say something, and this time I mean it. We are finished. I don't want this to go on. I don't like the rows, I don't like the scenes and, frankly, I don't think I like you. So, don't ring me, don't come round – and I'll return the favour. Goodbye.'

He turned and walked away before she could say anything. Lionel was still standing outside the cubicle.

'I've been getting some bloody funny looks, standing guard here.'

'You've been great,' said Orlando. 'Give me a hand to get him outside to the front door. The worst thing he'll look is pissed. I shouldn't have a problem getting a taxi.'

Roger was leaning forward on the toilet seat now, his head in his hands. He managed to get to his feet, though he still needed Lionel and Orlando to help him out of the washroom and to the entrance steps. A cab came in seconds, and they manoeuvred Roger inside. Orlando got in next to him and gave the driver the address in Ladbroke Grove. The driver nodded, glancing in the mirror at Roger.

'Had one too many, your friend? Just make sure he doesn't

178

throw up all over the back of my cab. Otherwise you pay for the cleaning.'

'Don't worry,' said Orlando, 'I think he's past all that.' He glanced at Roger, who had raised his head and was staring out of the window with blank, lost eyes.

By the time he had managed to get Roger into his ground-floor flat, Roger had sunk into a stupor again. Orlando snapped on the light, sat Roger down, and went in search of a kettle and coffee. He made the coffee as strong as he thought Roger could bear it, and managed to make him drink a cup. Then Orlando took off his jacket, took off Roger's, got him to his feet, and started walking him round and round the room. He did this for an hour or so, back and forth, back and forth, until his shoulder ached. Occasionally he would sit Roger back down on the sofa and try to feed him more coffee, but Roger refused it. Orlando didn't blame him. Then the walking would resume. He wasn't quite sure why he was doing this, but he'd read about it somewhere; keep him moving. At last Roger seemed to be entirely awake, if still spaced-out. He was talking, at any rate, and seemed to know where he was and who Orlando was.

'What a sweetheart cousin you are . . .' he murmured.

'Come on,' urged Orlando, 'keep going.'

'Darling, I want to sit down now, I think,' said Roger in a faded voice. Orlando let him down on to the sofa and Roger sat back heavily. He lay there for a long time, staring into space, blinking occasionally.

Orlando made himself a coffee in the cramped kitchen and came back into the living room. 'How do you feel now?' he asked.

'Never better,' murmured Roger. 'Dear God, just a little too, too much this evening, I think.'

'I found you in a lavatory with a needle sticking out of your arm,' said Orlando pointedly.

179

'Did you? How very unpleasant for you,' murmured Roger. He coughed. 'Pass me my jacket, there's a dear cousin. I need a cigarette.' Orlando watched as Roger lit a cigarette and leaned back again. The face, though still haggard, was regaining its handsome composure.

'Do you have to do this? Take drugs, I mean,' asked Orlando, sitting down opposite him and glancing round the tatty, badly-lit room. The sofa on which Roger was sitting was deep and high-backed, upholstered in dark green velvet with gold braiding; once beautiful, it was now stained and battered, the braiding grimy and coming away from the cushions.

Roger laughed. 'Well, now ... What a question.' He mused for a moment, smoking. 'Yes – yes, I really do have to do it. I have been doing it for ten years, after all. I'm rather good at it now. Well, apart from instances like this evening. Where's Chrissie?' He frowned suddenly, remembering his companion.

'She didn't seem particularly interested in your predicament,' said Orlando.

'Bitch,' said Roger. He sighed. 'Oh, God, help yourself to a drink.' He waved in the direction of a shabby sideboard, on which stood a half-empty bottle of Black Label.

Orlando ignored this. 'But how can you live like this?' he persisted. 'Look at yourself – and this place.'

'Oh, please – that's one of the reasons I take drugs. Which reminds me ...' Roger stood up and left the room. After a moment or two, Orlando got up and followed him. He found Roger in the bathroom, cutting up lines of coke. Roger glanced at him, took a ten-pound note from his pocket, rolled it up, and swiftly snorted up the four lines.

'Are you really sure you should be doing that – after that stuff this evening?' Orlando enquired, watching as Roger took a drink of water from a tooth mug.

'That's precisely why I *am* doing it, dear thing.' He shook his head, swept back his blond hair from his face and sniffed. 'God, that's better.' He licked his finger, pressed it against the few grains of coke which still lay there, and then rubbed his finger across his gums. 'Waste not, want not.' He smiled at Orlando, then went back through to the living room. 'Now, what we need is some music.' He went over to a stack of records in the corner of the room and crouched down, a fresh cigarette between his lips, eyes narrowed against the drift of smoke. Orlando glanced down at the records and was mildy astonished. It seemed that Roger possessed every Andy Williams album ever recorded – *Born Free, Getting Over You, Andy Williams' Christmas Album, Home Loving Man, Music to Watch Girls By, Andy Williams' Greatest Hits, The Way We Were, Get Together with Andy Williams* ... the singer's smiling, leathery face, frozen in countless poses, beamed out from a dozen tattered covers as Roger flicked through the albums. He finally selected an LP entitled *Most Requested Songs* and laid it gently on the turntable, switched it on, and watched as the stylus lifted and settled. The yearning sounds of 'Moon River' drifted across the room, and Roger, smiling, stood up and went back to the sofa, where he settled back and closed his eyes.

Orlando gazed at his cousin. How could he just sit there, calmly listening to this ridiculous music, when only a few hours ago death had brushed him with its wings?

'Christ, Roger!' he exclaimed. 'You could have died this evening, you know!'

'Ah, but you were there to save me, weren't you?' replied Roger, opening his eyes. 'I'm most awfully grateful.' He looked at Orlando for a few seconds. 'Truly.' He closed his eyes again. Then he added, 'Do help yourself to a drink – and pour me one, if you would.' Orlando, feeling that he needed a drink after the various shocks of the evening, fetched two glasses from the kitchen and poured an inch or so of Scotch into each.

'So,' said Roger, raising his glass to Orlando, 'I no sooner meet my long-lost little cousin, than he saves my life. Cheers.' He drank, then added, 'I do hope I didn't spoil your evening, by the way. Did you have to desert your rather lovely brunette friend?'

Orlando winced as he recalled what he had said to Louisa. Then he sighed and glanced at his watch. Quarter to one. He knew that he should be getting home if he was to make it through the next demanding day in the dealing room. But for some reason he felt compelled to stay. He was curious about his cousin, wanted to know how someone with an upbringing and education not so very different from his own, could finish up like this, spending his life scoring, shooting up, and living in this dreadful flat. It was rather like confronting the worst possibilities in himself, wondering if he, too, given different circumstances, could become like this. And he felt he should stay because, in spite of Roger's pose of amused indifference, he sensed a certain frailty in the man, and did not think he should leave him alone just yet.

They talked for an hour or so, Roger changing the records every so often, buoyant with cocaine.

'So what happened after you dropped out of university?' asked Orlando, declining Roger's offer of another Scotch. Roger was on his tenth cigarette and his third drink.

'Well, that was the late seventies – post-Vietnam. I went to New York – the trust fund was still very fat and new then, you know. Oh, I did it all. Hung out at Studio 54, saw Bianca Jagger ride in on a white horse on her thirtieth birthday, met Andy Warhol ... Then Sag Harbour, LA, Mexico – you know, Puerto Vallarta, full of rich trustafarians.' Roger laughed, narrowed his eyes. 'We used to buy eightballs of coke and freebase, drink tequila till it was coming out of our ears ... stayed up all night, slept all day. I think that was when I got married – or was it? Anyway, some minor Spanish royal, long gone.'

'Did you divorce?' Orlando didn't recall his grandfather mentioning that Roger was married.

'She died, darling. OD'd.' Roger put out his cigarette. 'Mexico was wonderful. You can buy speed over the counter there. That was when I had my first taste of heroin. Oh . . .' He drew in a deep breath. 'What a moment! Nothing like it – takes you far, far away, helps you forget absolutely everything. Coke for parties, heroin for oblivion. My absolute favourite, though, is smack in one arm, coke in the other. Called a snowball. Heaven. Like being crucified.'

Orlando listened in appalled fascination, then glanced around at the tatty furnishings, the threadbare brown curtains, the handful of tattered paperbacks and the vast stack of LPs. 'How do you afford it?' he asked.

'How indeed? Well, the trust fund ran out about a year ago. I remember blowing about fifty thousand of it in the first nine months. I must have worked my way through quite a bit over the years . . . Anyway, then I started to sell things – trinkets, my collection of snuff boxes.' He sighed. 'All gone now. Last month I got rid of two Seagos at Sotheby's – Great-uncle Simon left me those. That was a bit of a boost to funds. Pity, really, because I did like those pictures. You familiar with East Anglia, Orlando? Incredible bleakness about the coastline – marvellous. So I'm still rubbing along on that. Of course, mothers being what they are, dear mama makes sure I don't starve. So it's just a question of hanging in there until Uncle Leonard pops it.'

'That could be another twenty years, do you realise? He's only sixty-two,' said Orlando, then yawned hugely before he could help himself.

'There is that worry,' said Roger. 'But look, cousin, you're whacked. My fault for keeping you up so late.'

'You're right. God, look at the time . . . I have to go. Got to be up at seven.' Orlando rose.

As he passed the sofa on the way to the door, Roger put out a slender, detaining hand. 'Look, would you do me a favour?' His voice was casual, but held a note of urgency. 'Would you – I mean, you'll think it rather weak, but then I am weak – '

'What?' Orlando looked down at him. While he might hate the fact that Roger was one day to inherit all that he himself loved and knew, he couldn't help liking his cousin. For all his pathetic futility, there was an irresistible, faded charm about him.

'Would you mind staying here? I can get a bit – well . . . spooked, as Dame Edna would say. There's a spare bed. Would you mind?'

'No – no, that's all right,' he replied. 'I'll stay.'

'Thank you,' said Roger, and rose. 'I'll show you the way . . .' He paused in the doorway and looked at Orlando. 'Do you resent me?' he asked.

'Resent you? How?'

'I mean, if it hadn't been for old Alec failing to marry your mother, Uncle Leonard's pile would all be yours some day.'

'It's not important,' said Orlando. He thought briefly of Stow Stocksley, and wondered how long it would take Roger to work his way through the entire inheritance. God, he realised, it might be worthwhile trying to help Roger to sort himself out, if only to ensure that all that beauty and magnificence didn't finish up going into Roger's arm, or up his nose. He remembered what Hannah had told him this evening about Capercailzie Castle, its ignoble end, and realised that one day Stow Stocksley could suffer an even worse fate.

Roger smiled at Orlando, that fine smile which transformed his gaunt tired features entirely. 'Just wondered,' he said.

Orlando lay in the narrow bed in Roger's spare room, thinking about Hannah. He had a very clear picture of her coming towards him in that white dress, like some lovely pre-Raphaelite. What was the use of time, what was the use of experience, if the mere sight of her could still affect him so profoundly? He wished he had never seen her again . . . No, he didn't. He wished instead that that bloody man, Max, did not exist. But if not Max, then someone else. There would always be someone else, just as it seemed there always had been. What had his name been? Callum. Forget about her, he told himself. But he fell asleep with the vision of her still in his mind.

Chapter Thirteen

A few weeks later when Anne and Orlando met for lunch, she passed on to him a postcard from Abidjan, sent by Jo.

'I take it that's the girl from the nightclub?' asked Anne. He nodded as he read the card. 'Orlando,' she said, 'I don't wish to pry into your social life, but it really isn't a very good idea to go around having affairs with prostitutes.'

'I am *not* having an affair with a prostitute,' replied Orlando in exasperation. 'Or with anyone, for that matter.' He thought of the phone calls from Louisa, which had eventually died away after a week of Dan's staunch hedging and evasion. No, he didn't regret the termination of that relationship, although he did often think about her warm, wonderfully enthusiastic body.

'Anyway,' said Anne, 'tell me what you've been doing with yourself recently. Every time I call you at home, you seem to be out.'

'As a matter of fact –' Orlando hesitated. 'Well, you know I've mentioned this cousin, Roger, the one who's going to inherit Stow Stocksley?'

Anne nodded and prodded at her salad. 'I've met him, actually.'

'When?' asked Orlando in surprise. 'You didn't tell me.'

'Why should I? It was years ago – well, five years ago, at some wedding. Quite a memorable young man, as I recall. But high as a kite.'

'He's a junkie,' said Orlando shortly. 'He's awful. He lives in a squalid flat in Ladbroke Grove and all he thinks about is heroin. His entire life revolves around it – getting it, injecting it, and being out of it. He's got something like four good suits, a handful of junkie society friends, and he's funding his habit by selling off paintings that his uncle left him. When that runs out . . . well, I don't know. I really don't know. Anyway, I've been spending a lot of time with him.'

'What on earth for?' asked Anne. 'Sounds foul.'

'Do you really want to know why? Because I can't stand the idea of what Roger might do with Stow Stocksley when my grandfather dies. If he stays the way he is, he'll just blow it all, and ruin himself. I know that my grandfather can't bear the prospect of Roger squandering everything. In fact, that's why he adopted me – did you know that?' Anne shook her head. 'He'd hoped that, since I was his grandson, a sort of direct heir, that it might legitimise me, that he could replace Roger with me.'

'And I take it it doesn't work that way?'

'No – once a bastard, always a bastard. In my case, at any rate. Anyway, going back to Roger, I had this idea that if I could help Roger to clean up his act, kick his habit altogether, then he might not be quite the appalling prospect as an heir which he presently is. I don't want to see Stow Stocksley go the way of Roger's trust fund. He managed to work his way through an absolute fortune in just nine years.'

Anne chewed thoughtfully, then said, 'But haven't people tried to help Roger before? I mean, his family must have done something.'

'Oh, they've done everything. He's been to clinics, there was more than one psychiatrist – his mother even had him sectioned once, put in a general hospital ward for loonies. But they've given up on him, and I can't say I blame them. I just thought it might be different if I tried to help him. Maybe when his money runs out and it's not so easy to score, that he'll be more prepared to find treatment.'

187

'I don't think it works that way,' said Anne. 'He'll just find other ways of raising money. I had a friend whose sister's husband was a junkie. He'd pocket the silver every time he came round to dinner, if he got half a chance. And leave needles in the bathroom.'

Orlando sighed. 'Yes, well, don't think I'm doing this because I like it. Although – ' he paused thoughtfully, ' – believe it or not, Roger does sort of grow on you. I mean, beneath all the drugs stuff, he's actually a very intelligent, funny man.'

'Who's killing himself.' Anne glanced up at Orlando. 'Maybe it wouldn't be such a bad thing if he did.' Orlando said nothing, just looked at Anne with his impenetrable gaze. It had already occurred to him that if Roger's self-destruction meant that he, Orlando, were to inherit, then he would not lift a finger to help him. Still, if Anne cared to think him altruistic, let her. It was Stow Stocksley that mattered to Orlando, not Roger. After a moment, Anne said, 'Let's talk about something else. Tell me all about the big, wide, wonderful world of finance . . .'

A week later, during one of her rare visits to her half-sisters in Reigate, Anne mentioned that she had had lunch with Orlando.

'How very lucky you are,' remarked Cicely moodily. 'We rarely see him these days.' Now that she no longer had even the university holidays in which to coddle her beloved nephew, Cicely felt that her purpose in life was somehow diminished. There was no certainty about when he would come to see them, the calendar held none of the fixed points of school holidays and half terms by which, it seemed, she had lived her entire life. 'Empty nest syndrome,' Abigail had told her curtly, when Cicely had confided her woes. Abigail, whose life seemed to Cicely to grow ever fuller and busier. She was the acting deputy headmistress of her girls' school now, with the possibility of the appointment becoming permanent, and she was involved with a group of people setting up a crafts centre in the town, with a vegetarian snack bar and a small art gallery. Running Plumtree Villa for the benefit of her working sister, with her busy social life, seemed to Cicely to be a poor excuse for existence. But she still had hopes of Sir Leonard. The distance between Stow Stocksley and Reigate didn't help, but they went on outings together, visited horticultural exhibitions, and attended lectures in Vincent Square. These London outings gave Cicely her highest, sweetest hopes. It seemed to her that they possessed a special kind of intimacy. He would meet her at Victoria Station, they would lunch together (he always paid, despite her attempts to insist on the bill being divided – such delightful altercations), and then they would walk round to the Royal Horticultural Society's Halls. There was a sense of ritual to all this which Cicely felt betokened something. And yet, and yet . . . Over three years had passed, and although their relationship was of the most cordial kind, it never seemed to progress as she had imagined it might. She had no idea how to give it impetus, had no experience in the arts of flirtation and seduction. As a consolation she had, without intending to, become something of an expert on the subject of orchids, and found her innocent little deception had transformed itself into a genuine, if marginal interest. But what was the point in being able to tell the difference between Cephalanthera and Spiranthes, if that was to be the sum total of her relationship with Sir Leonard? Still, she told herself, he was a man of breeding and sensitivity, and these things could take time. But that time, without Orlando on whom to bestow her affections, often seemed to Cicely to stretch out interminably.

'I hope he's well, and happy in his job,' she added. 'I know that Leonard would have preferred him to take up merchant banking instead of this whatever-it-is dealing that he's doing.' She knew it irritated Abigail to hear her dispense with the 'Sir' in front of Sir Leonard's name, which was why she did it. And she wanted Anne to be able to infer the existence of intimacy between herself and Orlando's grandfather.

'Oh, he's well enough,' said Anne, 'but did you know that he's struck up a friendship with this cousin of his, Roger, the one who's going to inherit Stow Stocksley and everything else?' Relieved, for a change, to have something of interest to discuss with her half-sisters, Anne threw them this morsel and watched their reactions with amusement.

'But that man is a drug addict!'

'Leonard has always made him out to be the most corrupt creature! What *can* Orlando be thinking of?'

'Apparently he's on a mission to save Roger from himself. Or rather, Stow Stocksley from Roger. Since Sir Leonard is reputedly in the depths of despair about what Roger will do with the property once he inherits it, Orlando's solution is to reform Roger, turn him into a worthwhile citizen.'

Abigail went out to the kitchen to refresh the pot of tea, and Cicely tapped the polished surface of the table with worried fingers. 'Well, of course, I might have known that Orlando would act only from the very best of motives, but I really do think that it's very dangerous for him to associate with such a person. He is still young and impressionable, after all.'

Anne, thinking of the faint hardness in her nephew's eyes of late, did not entirely agree with this assessment of him. But she merely said idly, 'It seems to be something of a hobby with him these days, mixing with the underworld. He's even taken up with some streetwalker, apparently.' She regretted this almost as soon as it was uttered, and hastened to repair the damage. Cicely's plump face was scandalised, 'No, that's really a sort of a joke, Cicely. It's just some friend of his who has a bit of a dubious background, that's all. Forget I said it.'

Cicely took another ginger cream from the plate and bit into

190

it, her face preoccupied and concerned. Then she shook her head.

'I always thought it was a mistake when he let that schoolfriend move in with him, the one who was expelled, the Coulthard boy. Orlando told me that he goes on demonstrations and marches.'

'Well, so do I,' remarked Abigail, coming back through from the kitchen.

'CND is different,' retorted Cicely. 'Apparently he espouses extreme left-wing causes, helps put up posters saying things like "smash capitalism". And he lectures Orlando, tells him that his job is iniquitous and exploits the workers.'

'What? Buying and selling dollars?' Anne laughed.

'Oh, I don't think it bothers Orlando,' said Abigail. 'He finds it quite amusing, I imagine.'

'Nonetheless, I can't help feeling that he's falling in with the wrong kind of people. I'm sure that Leonard would be most concerned to learn of all this, particularly about his association with his cousin, Roger.'

'You're not going to mention it to Sir Leonard, are you?' said Anne, who had only just noticed her half-sister's use of the familiar appellation in reference to Orlando's grandfather. 'I don't know if that's a good idea.'

Cicely seized upon this opportunity to hint significantly at the intimacy of her relationship with Sir Leonard. 'I am lunching with Leonard at Stow Stocksley on Thursday. I don't really see how I can, in all conscience, keep from him the fact that Orlando has struck up a friendship with Roger. I think he is entitled to know.'

'Why?'

Cicely hesitated, then said, 'Well, the fact is, he told us some time ago that he intends to set up a trust fund for Orlando. But he has indicated that he wants to be sure first that Orlando is conducting himself responsibly, and that the money will not be frittered or put to bad use.'

'Oh, surely you're not going to put a spanner in the works, are you?' asked Anne. She wished now that she'd never opened her mouth. She knew how self-righteous Cicely could be.

'I hardly look at it in that light,' replied Cicely. 'I am merely telling you why I think Orlando's grandfather is entitled to know of the friendships which Orlando is forming.'

There was an uncomfortable silence among the three women. Then Anne put down her cup. 'Look, thank you both for lunch. It's been a nice afternoon.' It hadn't been, but she felt that it was a duty and a kindness to visit them both occasionally. 'I think I'd best be heading back before it gets dark.'

She hoped, as she made her way out to her car, calling goodbye to Cicely and Abigail, that she hadn't made any mischief for Orlando. She certainly hadn't meant to.

Cicely had known all along that she would tell Sir Leonard everything that Anne had said. To resist would have been an impossibility. In her hearts of hearts, she acknowledged that she could not pass up the opportunity to unite herself even more closely with him by sharing a matter of importance. She felt that it enhanced her status to be the bearer of such significant information. The evident concern expressed by Sir Leonard at her news was gratifying.

'I find this hard to believe,' he said, laying down his knife and fork. 'Orlando associating with Roger? Good God.' He was silent for a moment. 'I cannot conceive of two more dissimilar characters. A creature like Roger is the last person I would wish to see anywhere near Orlando.'

Cicely was aware of an internal flutter of excitement. 'I did feel it important that you should know . . .'

Sir Leonard looked up. 'What possible attraction could there be for Orlando in the society of someone like Roger? I dread to think . . .'.

'From what Anne tells me, this is not the only questionable friendship which he may have formed. She also mentioned that he was friendly with a – a prostitute.'

Sir Leonard stared at her. 'Has the boy gone stark, raving mad? What kind of people is he getting to know in London, for heaven's sake?'

It occurred to Cicely that the alleged altruism with which Anne credited Orlando in the formation of his friendship with Roger could be left for Sir Leonard to discover for himself. If it were the case. The companionability of this mutual concern for Orlando's moral well-being was too delightful to disturb with the mention of any mitigating circumstances. She returned Sir Leonard's anxious gaze with a look of appropriate gravity.

'It is mere hearsay, of course,' she murmured, 'but Anne sees Orlando quite often, and she has more knowledge of his doings than any of us.'

'Thank you for telling me this,' said Sir Leonard. 'I feel it certainly requires my intervention. I don't think I will tax Orlando directly with the matter, though. Not at first. He is an adult, after all, and might resent my interference.' He paused. 'I think I should speak to – was it Anne? I think I should speak to her first, and find out exactly what she knows. Would she mind, do you think?'

Cicely swallowed nervously. It was perhaps a little late now to mention Orlando's possibly noble motive in befriending Roger. 'Of course, I'm sure she would be only too glad to help.' She was far from sure, and she gave Sir Leonard Anne's address and phone number with a twinge of apprehension.

After four days Sir Leonard was growing tired of leaving messages on Anne Patrick's answerphone. There was nothing for it but to go and see the woman. He must find out what was going on with Orlando. He sat at his desk, the fire casting flickering shadows against the low shadows of his study, and turned over the pages of his diary. If he went up to town the day after tomorrow, he could stay at his club and call on her in the evening. Even if she went out every night, as she appeared to, there was a likelihood that she would come home first. He would try to catch her around seven, before she went out. It would be a good opportunity, too, to make enquiries about the flat in town which he had long intended to look for. Really, he should have done it a few years ago. He found the journeys up to London, whether on business or with Cicely to various shows and lectures, very tiring these days. And it was a source of constant annoyance to him to read of concerts at the Wigmore Hall or the Barbican which he would have liked to attend, had distance been less of a problem. There was his club, but he could only tolerate that occasionally. No, it was high time he took a place of his own. This would be an ideal opportunity, a way of killing two birds with one stone.

Every evening for the past four days Anne had returned to find a message from Sir Leonard D'Ewes on her answering machine, asking if she would be so kind as to contact him when she had a moment, the number was ... etc, etc. Twice he had called when she was actually in, but she made a point in the evenings of keeping the answerphone on. She didn't wish to speak to Orlando's grandfather. Obviously Cicely must have repeated everything which she had been told about Orlando and Roger – why else should Sir Leonard, whom Anne had never met in her life, be bombarding her with phone calls? Well, she didn't feel like talking to him, certainly not about Orlando. She had a nasty feeling that she might have caused trouble for him through her indiscretion.

On Thursday evening Anne came home from an exhausting day, one which she and her creative team had spent trying to come up with a new and exciting angle in pitching for a large washing-powder account. There was nothing new in the world to say about washing powder, she realised. Was this really the life she wanted to go on living? she wondered, as she closed the door of her flat and kicked off her shoes in the hallway. At least she wasn't going out tonight – she could just laze around, watch some television, and try not to think about how close her thirty-sixth birthday was.

She had just mixed herself a large vodka and tonic and was about to run a bath, when the buzzer of the downstairs front door sounded. She wasn't expecting any visitors – it was probably one of the friends of that Italian on the floor below. They seemed congenitally incapable of pressing the right buzzer. Irritated, she snapped on the intercom.

'Yes?'

There was a pause, and then a voice said, 'Miss Patrick?' It was a man's voice, refined, and with a note of stiffness in it.

'Yes?' she replied.

'Ah – this is Sir Leonard D'Ewes, Miss Patrick. I wondered if I might have a word with you?'

Downstairs at the entrance to the riverside apartment block, Sir Leonard felt rather asinine, speaking into a little box. Possibly this was not a good idea. He waited for a reply. After a few seconds, the young woman's voice said, 'Yes. Yes, all right. Push the door when the buzzer goes.' She did not sound very enthusiastic.

Anne pushed the buzzer to open the front door downstairs, sighed, and went to slip her shoes on. She had to give Orlando's grandfather marks for persistence. After a few minutes the doorbell sounded, and she opened the door to Sir Leonard.

Anne had not thought much about what Orlando's grandfather might look like. Old, she supposed, probably fat and boring. Instead she found herself looking at a most attractive

195

man, no more than sixty, she guessed, tall, grey-haired, wearing a rather elegant, old-fashioned tweed suit. His features were aquiline and slightly brooding, but the smile he gave her was charming and boyish. Rather like Orlando, she thought. She smiled back in spite of herself and said, 'Come in.'

He stepped into the hallway, his manner somewhat nervous and hesitant. 'I do hope that this isn't an inconvenient time to call . . . I had left messages on the – ah – on your machine, but perhaps you were away.'

Anne did not know what to say for a second. He must have thought her very rude for not calling back. 'Oh – oh, it's just that I've been very busy . . .'

She led him through and he stopped in the doorway, looking round admiringly at the cool, bright interior of the large living room. The crooning murmur of a Billie Holiday tape which Anne had put on earlier floated out across the air, and through the big windows the lovely light of the early spring evening gilded the river and the city skyline.

'What a very fine view!' exclaimed Sir Leonard. 'I had no idea that people were taking the time and trouble to renovate these old dockland buildings. Aren't they splendid? Extremely spacious. You are very fortunate.'

'I was just about to have a drink,' said Anne. 'Can I offer you something?'

Sir Leonard glanced at her, his hesitancy returning. She really was much more attractive than he had imagined she would be, having half-expected a slightly younger version of Cicely or Abigail. But this woman was quite different altogether, self-possessed and rather lovely, with blonde hair and a pretty figure, somewhere in her thirties, he guessed.

'Oh, well . . . that is very kind. Do you have any Scotch and soda?'

Anne glanced at her tray of drinks. 'Just out, I'm afraid.'

196

'In that case, I'll have whatever you are having.'

She went through to the kitchen, returning with a glass stacked high with ice and a slice of lime, and poured vodka and tonic into it. She handed him his drink and took her own over to the sofa. 'Please – do sit down,' she said.

He looked around and then sat down opposite her in an armchair, and sipped at his drink. He did not feel relaxed. Then he realised that she was waiting for him to speak.

'I don't know if you have any idea why I wished to speak to you, Miss Patrick –' he began, leaning forward and nursing his drink between his hands.

'Call me Anne, please.'

'– but I saw your sister, Cicely, last week, and she told me certain things which rather disturbed me.'

'About Orlando?'

'About Orlando, yes.'

'What did she say?'

'Well, that Orlando is spending a lot of time in the company of his cousin, Roger.' He paused. 'I don't know if you know much about Roger, Miss Patrick – Anne – but he is a drug addict. He has manipulated and deceived all those who love him most, and who have tried hard to help him, and he has worked his way through a small fortune in a matter of just a few years. He inhabits, I assume, a world of utter squalor, and I have no wish for Orlando to number him among his companions.'

'Is that all Cicely told you?'

'She mentioned something equally distressing, something about a prostitute with whom Orlando associates – naturally, one begins to wonder what kind of life the boy is leading in London. I felt you might be able to enlighten me.'

Anne smiled. 'Well, I don't think you need worry too much.'

Sir Leonard took another swallow of his drink, and realised

197

that it was stronger than he had thought. 'But I'm afraid I do. Orlando is only twenty-two – '

'Orlando is an adult,' interrupted Anne gently. She leaned forward as she spoke, her gaze candid. What very nice blue eyes, thought Sir Leonard. 'And I don't think that Cicely has been entirely fair. She doesn't seem to have told you the reason why Orlando has been spending time with Roger.'

Sir Leonard shook his head. 'I wish I could think of one that did not confirm my worst fears.'

Anne sat back. 'Orlando thinks he might be able to help Roger. Get him to come off his drugs, help him to become a bit more responsible. And by doing so, he thinks he can spare you all your anxieties concerning your estate, or whatever it is. He knows you're worried about what Roger might do with it, and this is his way of helping. Rather noble, don't you think?'

Sir Leonard pondered this surprising news for a moment. 'What – what an odd boy he can be,' he murmured, staring past Anne at the window.

'I don't think so,' replied Anne. 'Maybe you misjudge him.'

He met her gaze, and the tension which Sir Leonard had felt until now began suddenly to ease. He let his shoulders droop slightly and sighed, though his sad, handsome face remained impassive. 'As you know,' said Sir Leonard at last, speaking as though with slight difficulty, 'I neglected Orlando for the first eight years of his life. I foolishly blamed his mother for the loss of my son. It sounds absurd now, I know, but I never even thought of Orlando – if I thought of him at all – as my own flesh and blood. It was my wife who persuaded me eventually to see him, to meet him . . . I realise now that if I denied myself anything in refusing to see him for all that time, I denied her even more.' He shook his head. Then he looked back at Anne, surprised that he should say so much to a stranger. Well, perhaps not a stranger – she was part of Orlando's family as

198

well. She had known Orlando through all the years that he had missed. 'Which is why I am so anxious that he should be safe and happy. That I shouldn't have failed him as I may have failed Alec, his father.'

'How did you fail Alec?' asked Anne quietly, aware that this was not a man who confided easily.

'I was very remote, I suppose. I thought that if all his material needs were satisfied, that if he had enough money and went to the right schools, well ... I thought that was enough.'

'What more have you done for Orlando?'

Sir Leonard looked up quickly. 'I have given him my time. My attention. Things I rarely gave Alec. Poor Alec – things must have been confusing for his generation. I think he grew up expecting to fight a war, just as his father and his grandfather had done. Only there was no war to fight. Not of that kind.' He sighed. 'I just hope that in all the time he has spent at Stow Stocksley, Orlando has never doubted that he is cared for, listened to, thought about. I have been anxious not to make the same mistake twice.' He paused, and then said, 'Do you think he has any chance of succeeding with Roger, where everyone else has failed?'

'No,' replied Anne. 'I shouldn't think so.' She rose and took Sir Leonard's glass from his hand. 'Let me top this up,' she said. As she refilled his glass, she suddenly turned to him and asked, 'Have you ever tried to help Roger?'

'I?' Sir Leonard considered this question with some surprise. 'I? No – no, well, not directly ... He has his parents, of course. I was never really in a position to ...' He felt he was floundering, and accepted his fresh drink gratefully. Anne stood looking down at him.

'Perhaps you should have made an effort. Perhaps it would have been worthwhile. Orlando thinks it worthwhile.'

Sir Leonard felt mildly abashed. He looked up at her and

smiled, faintly amused and thrilled at being reproved by a lovely young woman almost half his age.

Anne saw him smile and realised that when he smiled, it made her want to smile as well. 'What are you laughing at?' she asked.

'Oh, I wasn't laughing,' said Sir Leonard, still smiling. He took a sip of his drink and watched her as she went back to the sofa. This time she kicked off her shoes quite unselfconsciously, and tucked her legs up beneath her. Sir Leonard found the casual gesture mildly exciting, he realised, and began to wonder exactly what effect this young woman was having on him. Perhaps it was just this drink. Whatever it was, he felt easier, more relaxed now.

'As for the prostitute thing,' said Anne, breaking his train of thought, 'I don't think she is anything to worry about either. She's certainly not his lover.' She glanced up and met Sir Leonard's eyes as she said this, and Sir Leonard looked away, momentarily confused. 'I think she's just a curiosity – a friend.'

Sir Leonard sighed. 'Nonetheless, when I think of what Roger actually does – there is a rather dangerous criminal element involved. I worry about Orlando from that point of view. It could so easily wreck his life, if he were accidentally to get mixed up in that. I don't think he realises.'

'I would be as worried as you, I promise, if I thought he was in any danger. But I don't honestly think he is. He looks after his own interests, believe me.'

'Perhaps I've been unduly concerned . . . You obviously have Orlando's welfare very much at heart.'

'Well, that's something we have in common.'

For some reason, this remark caused an instant's coincidence of thought, charging the atmosphere momentarily. They exchanged glances, and then there was an embarrassed pause.

'Well,' said Sir Leonard, rising and taking a final drink before setting his glass down, 'I can't say that I'm happy that Orlando is friendly with Roger, but if you think no harm can come of it . . .' He broke off, frowning, then looked at her. He really is quite extraordinarily handsome, in an over-dignified way, thought Anne. Probably has no idea of the effect of that devastating smile on poor old Cicely. She smiled involuntarily at the thought, and he caught this.

'Now it's my turn to ask why you are laughing,' he said.

She laughed aloud now. 'Well, I was thinking of Cicely, as a matter of fact.'

'Oh. Ah. Yes. Cicely.' He frowned slightly again. 'She does seem to have made rather a mountain out of a molehill. I suppose I had better try to set her fears at rest . . .' Suddenly he realised that he did not wish to think of Cicely. He glanced up at Anne again and became conscious of his pulse quickening. 'I'm sorry to have disturbed your evening,' he said. 'I hope I haven't delayed you – I mean, your plans . . .'

'Oh, I didn't have any,' replied Anne, untucking her feet and setting her glass down.

He felt his heart beating very fast now. She might think him a dreadful fool, but he felt he could not let the moment pass. Instinct told him that a chance like this might never come again. 'I wonder . . . I wonder, in that case, if you would care to have dinner with me?'

He could hardly believe he had said it. She looked up at him in complete surprise, astonished at the idea – and then realised it was one she quite liked. Yes, why not?

'Why, thank you – yes, I should like to.' There was a brief, uncertain silence. 'Perhaps I should change,' said Anne doubtfully, glancing down at her dress.

'Oh, no – please. You look very nice as you are,' said Sir Leonard quickly. 'Very nice.' He was still somewhat astonished at his own temerity. 'Perhaps somewhere

201

local . . .? I'm afraid I don't know the area, so I must be guided by you.'

Anne fetched her bag and they left the building, each silently bewildered by the events of the past half hour, tentative in the other's company. Anne took Sir Leonard to a local Thai restaurant, small and expensive, tucked away in a back street. The food was a novelty to Sir Leonard, but he liked it very much. It amused him to be introduced to something new, and he found Anne good company. She had a casual, mischievous air, which he found refreshing; it was some time since he had enjoyed the individual company of a woman of her age.

They talked much of Orlando first, naturally, but gradually the conversation turned to Stow Stocksley, and Anne listened as Sir Leonard described his life there, his daily routine. Then he asked her about her work, and she told him, described the kind of day she had just spent.

'It sounds most exciting, the world of advertising,' said Sir Leonard, and sipped his wine. 'I rather like that one you see on television occasionally – the one with the little men and the teabags, you know.'

'That's the opposition,' said Anne, smiling.

'Oh!' said Sir Leonard, and nodded and laughed. How well he felt, sitting in this charming little place, his jacket off, legs crossed, chatting with this pretty young woman. He had not felt so relaxed in years.

'I think I'd swap advertising for your life any day,' said Anne, resting her chin on her hand.

'It's a rather lonely one, I'm afraid,' murmured Sir Leonard. At that moment the waitress brought their bill. Sir Leonard picked it up, and Anne watched as he searched in his jacket pocket for his fountain pen, admired the long, capable fingers as he scribbled his name swiftly on the slip. He looked up and smiled at her. 'Shall we go?'

They sauntered back through the streets together, talking idly about the river, and as he watched her mouth as she spoke, and the way she brushed her hair from her face with her fingers, Sir Leonard realised that he was experiencing thoughts and desires such as he had not felt in a long, long time.

They stopped in the doorway of her apartment block.

'Thank you for a lovely evening,' said Anne, smiling up at him.

'It was a charming and unexpected pleasure,' replied Sir Leonard. I am too old for this, he told himself, but he did not care. He put one hand on her shoulder, bent his head, and kissed her lightly. Before either of them could think about it, he found himself drawing her close against him and kissing her as thoroughly and passionately as if he were twenty. In that moment he did not feel too old for anything. And Anne, overwhelmed by the intensity of the attraction she felt for him, the pleasure she took in being kissed by him, told herself that life, just when you thought it had grown stale, was always capable of astonishing you.

Chapter Fourteen

Four weeks later, Abigail and Cicely were standing together in the doorway of the smallest bedroom in Plumtree Villa, surveying its contents. Cardboard boxes, folders and files, old clothes and shoes and items of discarded, but not entirely useless, furniture and household appliances littered most of the available space.

'Well, we shall certainly have to clear out this junk to make room for it,' said Abigail. 'That knitting machine of yours can go in the attic, for a start.'

'But what if I want to use it?' said Cicely, fingering her imitation pearls and looking doubtfully at the machine, which she had once bought in a fit of creative enthusiasm with the idea that she might start a little business from home, making Fair Isle sweaters. It had been used to produce one Fair Isle tank top which Orlando had never worn, a cherry-coloured woollen suit which was baggy in all the wrong places and ended up in a jumble sale, and a matinee jacket for a friend's baby which would have taken Cicely one-fifth of the time with a conventional pair of needles and a ball of wool.

'Then if the urge takes you, you can always get it back down again,' said Abigail firmly, standing with her hands planted on her bony hips. 'I have to have somewhere to put my computer.'

'Computer!' muttered Cicely. 'I think it's pretentious non-sense, if you want to know. What possible use can you have for a computer? Nothing that you couldn't do with a type-writer, I'll bet.'

'Cicely,' replied Abigail, 'I imagine that the mysteries of information technology will always remain so to you. Some of us, however, live in the real world. It will be useful for a number of things, not least of all the timetabling I have to do, collating reports and running the crafts centre. Anyway, like it or not, the thing is coming, and I need a room in which to keep it.' She moved into the room a little way, her ankles knocking against the edges of boxes, and pointed to a potty-like object. 'That foot spa can go in the attic, too. Ridiculous thing. You shouldn't be allowed near a mail-order catalogue, really you shouldn't. I still haven't forgotten that microwaveable hot water bottle, or the vibrating neck massager.'

'Half the things in here are yours,' retorted Cicely. 'These files, for a start.'

'I will clear my share into the attic, and you can clear yours.'

'I shouldn't think there's room in the attic,' grumbled Cicely. 'Nobody's sorted it out in years.'

'Well, it's about time someone started.'

'When is this contraption of yours arriving?'

'Well . . . I haven't exactly got it yet.'

'Oh!'

'There is a great deal on the market, Cicely. It's important to make sure one gets exactly the right system. Compatibility, that's the whole point. Michael has a friend who knows all about computers, and he is coming round one evening next week with some brochures, so that we can work out exactly what it is that I want.'

'Right. Well, let me know when you've actually got it, and I might make a start on this room. In the meantime, I have other things to attend to.' Cicely stalked off triumphantly, just as the phone began to ring downstairs. She trotted quickly down, slippers soundless on the dove grey Wilton, hoping against hope that it might be Sir Leonard.

It was Orlando. Cicely had never in her life thought that she would be disappointed to hear his voice, and she felt a little guilty. But the thought of Leonard, the idea of seeing him, had recently become quite obsessive with her. It was an inclination she had always kept in check before – oddly enough, seeing him at regular intervals made that easier – but as she had not seen him now for over two months, the thing was growing into a fixation.

'Oh, Orlando, how lovely! How are you? We do miss you so. It's not the same now that there aren't the holidays . . . no . . . Well, of course, I know how busy it keeps you . . . yes. Are you? Well, that would be lovely . . . This weekend. I'll get a joint of beef. Yes . . . lovely. And we'll hear all of your news. I'll just go and tell Abigail . . . yes . . . see you then, dear.'

She replaced the receiver. 'That was Orlando,' she called up to her sister. 'He's coming down this weekend.' Cicely stood in the hallway for a moment or two, smiling to herself. Then her smile faded. She glanced at the telephone, hesitating. Should she call Stow Stocksley? She had tried once a week for the past three weeks, and each time Mrs Cresswell had answered, telling her that Sir Leonard was away, and that it was not known when he was expected back. Over the years Cicely had adopted a variety of different demeanours in her encounters with Mrs Cresswell – gracious superiority, cheerful familiarity, cold indifference – but she never felt that she had the measure of the woman. Mrs Cresswell's manner was polite but proprietorial where Sir Leonard was concerned, as though she had divined Cicely's ambitions and was resolved to give her no encouragement. Cicely's most recent tack with Mrs Cresswell had been one of deferential sweetness, but still Mrs Cresswell stood firm, giving not one hint of Sir Leonard's whereabouts or movements.

'Is he staying with friends in London, do you know?' Cicely had asked on the last occasion she had rung. 'Because if he is, I

206

could always get in touch with him there.' Cicely had no such intention, but her obsession meant that she had to know where he was, what he was doing. She tormented herself with the idea that Sir Leonard had become involved with some wealthy widow, a London socialite, that he had succumbed to her charms and was lost for ever.

But Mrs Cresswell had countered the question firmly. She had no idea with whom Sir Leonard might be staying, and she couldn't possibly give out private telephone numbers. The memory of that rebuff made Cicely wince. Her hand, which had been hovering over the telephone, fell to her side. She would not ring Stow Stocksley this week. She would just have to contain herself patiently until he called again, which he would, she knew. He always did.

Two days later Orlando arrived at Plumtree Villa, parking his red Metro on the gravel next to Cicely and Abigail's Datsun Cherry.

'Quite the city slicker,' remarked Abigail, looking up from her Sunday task of peeling the vegetables, and watching Orlando as he got out of his car.

Cicely joined her sister and craned to get a glimpse out of the kitchen window. She watched as Orlando took off his sunglasses and placed them on the dashboard, then closed the car door.

'I think he's grown a little taller,' she remarked admiringly.

Orlando glanced towards the house and smiled involuntarily at the sight of his aunts' heads peeping out together at the window, one mousy and dishevelled, the other dark and carefully permed. He waved.

He liked going back to Plumtree Villa, though each time he returned, it was as though to a place locked in time. It seemed that while his own life moved fluidly on, the home of his childhood stood rooted in the past. Nothing changed; the meals were the same, the clock in the living room ticked its same industrious little tick, the hallway still smelled of polish and raincoats, and the books on the bookshelf were always Reader's Digest abridgements or Book Club choices.

Even the gossip was the same. Orlando ate his lunch of roast beef and cabbage and mashed potato and listened to Cicely's account of the unfortunate double-booking last weekend of the Church hall by both the Scouts and the WI, and her altercation with the Scout leader, who had refused to let his bring-and-buy give way to the WI cake sale, until the vicar had intervened and told the Scouts they would have to re-schedule till next Saturday, otherwise the cakes would go stale, whereas jumble wouldn't. He listened to Abigail's complex tales of woe regarding the reorganisation of syllabuses, exam marking, and the iniquities of the national curriculum, to the scandalous details of behind-hand attempts to sneak through plans for the building of a new Tesco's on the spare land behind the railway, and to his aunts' conflicting views on the sexual orientation of the new deacon. When they had exhausted these topics, they quizzed him about his life in London. Even as he spoke of his doings in the dealing room, of some new furniture which he bought for his kitchen, he knew the topic which they were waiting to spring on him. Cicely broached it casually during a pause in which Orlando was helping himself to more gravy.

'I understand that you've been seeing something of your cousin, Roger?' she remarked, with studied casualness.

'Yes. Actually, I see him every few days.' It depressed him to talk of Roger, just as it depressed him to see him. He hoped they weren't going to linger over the subject, and was determined to be as curt as possible without being rude.

'Anne mentioned it last time she came to see us,' Cicely paused. 'I had thought your grandfather might have spoken to you about it. I know he was very concerned to hear that you had struck up this friendship.'

'Who told him? You, I suppose?' said Orlando, staring at his aunt.

'I felt he should be told, yes,' replied Cicely.

Orlando shrugged his shoulders and carried on eating. Then, thinking of what Cicely had said a moment ago, he added, 'Well, he hasn't spoken to me about it, so he can't be that concerned.'

'Didn't he say he was going to talk to Anne about it first?' said Abigail. 'I think this horseradish sauce is past its best, Cicely . . . Good grief, yes – look at that. May '86!'

'Anne? But he doesn't even know Anne,' said Orlando. 'Anyway, why should he want to talk to her?'

'I scarcely know,' replied Cicely. 'But I still don't think it's a very good idea for you to be friendly with that man.'

'Look,' said Orlando, 'it's not a thing I have a choice about any more. I befriended him because I am concerned about Stow Stocksley.' Not for the first time, Orlando wished that Stow Stocksley had never become known to him, that he had never been educated to imagine that it might eventually be his. There was a bitterness about all of this which threatened to choke him. 'I thought I might be able to help him,' he added wearily.

'And are you helping him?' asked Abigail.

'I don't know. I doubt it. But it's got to the point now where he needs me. Out of all the people he knows, I'm not part of his drugs scene. I don't want anything from him, and there's nothing he can take from me.'

'There's money,' said Abigail shortly.

Orlando said nothing. Abigail had voiced a fear which had been with him for a few weeks now. Although Roger received money regularly from his mother, it was not much, and the money he had made from selling the last of his trinkets and the paintings was running out. How long before Roger turned to Orlando, and tried to bleed him? The silence at the table lasted for an uncomfortable thirty seconds, and Abigail, to ease the atmosphere, remarked, 'Anne looked very well the last time we saw her. Have you seen much of her?'

Relieved at the change of topic, Orlando replied, 'Yes, I saw her last week, as a matter of fact. She's got some new man in tow, but she wouldn't tell me much about him She just spent the evening glowing, in a sort of secretive way.'

'Glowing? What colourful language,' said Cicely, who always affected ironic amusement where Anne's men friends were concerned.

Orlando smiled. 'She seems very happy, actually. I just hope this one lasts.'

'Quite.'

'Anyway, look, I thought after tea that I'd drive over to Stow Stocksley and see grandfather. I'll set off about five, if you don't mind.'

'But you'll never get back to London in time for work tomorrow,' said Abigail.

'Oh, I'm taking the day off. I'm due some time. I thought I'd sleep at Stow Stocksley, spend some time with grandfather tomorrow. I feel rather bad that I haven't been to see him for so long.'

'Well,' remarked Cicely, starting to clear the plates away, 'you'll be lucky if you find him there. I'd ring first if I were you. He's been away these past three weeks.'

'How do you know?' asked Abigail, glancing enquiringly at her sister.

Flushing slightly, Cicely said nothing and went into the kitchen with the dishes.

Orlando rang Stow Stocksley after lunch and found that Cicely had been right, and that his grandfather was still away. Mrs Cresswell was considerably more forthcoming with Orlando than she had been with his aunt.

'I do believe he's spending some time up in London looking

for a flat to buy,' she said. 'If you want him, you'll probably find him at his club.'

Orlando drove back to London that night, wondering now how he would fill in time on his day off.

The next morning he slept until ten, then went through to the kitchen and the debris of Dan's hurried breakfast. As he clattered dishes into the sink and emptied coffee dregs, Orlando saw an envelope addressed to him lying next to the kettle. He recognised Anne's handwriting and ripped it open. Inside was a postcard, a picture of the changing of the guard at Buckingham Palace. He turned it over.

'Cheers!' he read. '*I've been back a month now, sorry I haven't been in touch. Working in Cuff's wine bar in Ebury Street. Pop in and see me some time. Luv, Jo.*'

He turned the card back over, smiling, and stared at the picture of the guardsmen, conscious of a sharp sense of pleasure at the thought that she was back. For some obscure reason he had wanted her around over the past few months, even though he knew she could never be properly a part of his social life. He felt a certain possessiveness about her, and had taken it as something of a betrayal that she should have gone abroad just when he moved to London for good. On impulse he picked up the phone, rang the wine bar, and asked to speak to her.

'Orlando! Did you get my card?'

'Eventually,' he replied. 'My aunt forwarded it here. I've got my own flat now. Look, what time do you get off work? I've got the day off, so I can pick you up.'

'Three.'

'I'll see you then.'

When he arrived at the empty wine bar, Jo was finishing clearing up. She hugged him, and said, 'God, you're a sight for sore eyes.'

'You too,' said Orlando, looking her over. She was still

211

tanned, her blonde hair longer now. 'You look really well. More freckles than ever.'

'Tell me about it,' she said, rubbing the bridge of her nose. 'Hold on, I'll just get my things.'

They walked out and along Ebury Street.

'Where shall we go?' asked Jo.

'Wherever you like,' said Orlando. 'In fact, why don't you come back and see my new flat?'

So they went back to Kensington, where Orlando made tea for them both, and listened to Jo's accounts of her travels through Mali to the Ivory Coast. She had lost her camera and all her film to military police at an armed checkpoint in Agadez, but didn't seem particularly bothered about it. Orlando suspected that the passion for photography had run its course. He wondered whether this was also true of Paul, the journalist. He asked about him.

'Oh, him.' Jo's voice was cold. 'As soon as we got back to France I dumped him. We had rows the whole time. By the time we got to Algeria, I was ready to kill him.'

Orlando found himself unaccountably pleased by this news.

'So, how come you're not back with the agency? Why the wine bar?'

'Oh, you know . . . been there, done that. Anyway, I told you – all that's history.'

'I'm glad,' he said. 'For you, I mean. You'll probably be happier.'

'And poorer. Anyway, now I've bored you to death with Africa, tell me what you've been doing.'

He told her about his job, about Barry, about Dan, and about Louisa. But he did not mention Hannah, about seeing her again. He did not think he ever wished to tell Jo about Hannah. So he told her about Roger instead.

'I had this idea that I might have some influence over him,

help him to give up his habit. But lately,' sighed Orlando, 'I've begun to think that I'm wasting my time.'

Jo brooded on this. 'If he's been hooked for ten years, he's probably past help. It's not easy to come off. Half the girls on the game were smoking heroin – not injecting, because punters don't like track marks. I even did a bit of coke for a while, but I don't like wasting my money. But it's very hard to get anyone to kick their habit unless they really want to do it themselves.'

'When it started off,' said Orlando suddenly, in an uncharacteristic burst of candour, 'I was more interested in preserving Stow Stocksley than Roger. But it's got to the point where I actually want to help him – he's rather a sweet man, actually. Well-educated, urbane ... just on auto-destruct.' Orlando paused, then smiled to himself. 'He's very much into Andy Williams.'

'Andy Williams? Call that urbane?' Jo laughed. 'I'd like to meet this bloke.'

'I'm going round to see him this evening,' said Orlando. 'Monday night is one of my nights for looking in and seeing if he's okay. If he's functioning properly, we sometimes go out together.' He glanced at Jo. 'You can come with me if you want. If he's on form he's really rather amusing.' She was, he realised, the only girl he knew who wouldn't shudder with distaste at the thought of visiting a Ladbroke Grove junkie.

'Okay.' Jo paused, then said, 'You haven't noticed anything different about me, have you?'

Orlando gazed at her, the pretty, pugnacious face, the blonde hair, her freckled shoulders and slender arms, her hands with their multitudes of silver rings, all the way down to her ankles and the slightly chipped coral varnish on her toenails. He had never looked at her that way, she realised, and she liked it.

'No, everything seems in order to me.'

213

'I've stopped smoking. Gave it up in Africa when we ran out and couldn't get decent fags any more. Seemed like the ideal opportunity.'

'Well, well. Your image is certainly undergoing serious reconstruction.' He glanced at his watch. 'Come on, let's go and get something to eat and then go round to see my dear cousin.'

It was nearly seven when they left the restaurant in Kensington Church Street and walked up towards Notting Hill Gate. They found the front door of Roger's block of flats wedged open with a milk crate, and Orlando led the way into the grimy hallway. A dusty sheaf of mail and circulars for some long-gone tenant lay, as it had lain for months, on the linoleum.

When he knocked on the door of Roger's flat there was no reply. Orlando knocked again. 'He must be in. I can hear his stereo.' Orlando tried the handle, and found the door was open.

They went in and stood tentatively in the narrow hallway. Then Orlando pushed open the door to the living room and froze, Jo behind him. Roger was sitting on a chair next to the table, on which were spread his works, a small, zip-up toilet bag, a litter of tinfoil, a cooking spoon, half a dozen disposable syringes, his little platinum lighter. He had an Old Salopian tie twisted and wrapped tight around the top of his left arm, his elbow pressing into the scratchy, cheap wood of the table top as he stared down at his arm, his face white and tense, muttering, 'Come on . . . come on . . .' But the arm at which he was staring, searching frantically for a place to hit, was wrecked, a festering network of black lines with a purplish swelling inside the elbow joint. The right hand with which Roger held the syringe, a drop of clear liquid at its tip, began to tremble violently, so that the liquid flew off the end of the syringe and Roger all but dropped it. Orlando and Jo could do no more than stare as Roger, swearing, flipped his arm over and began to clench and unclench his fist, jerking and flapping his arm, looking for a vein on the back of his hand.

As Andy Williams' smoky tenor climbed to the top notes of 'Can't Get Used To Losing You', Roger found his vein, hit his mark. A slender column of blood backed up inside the syringe, delicate as a flower stem, and then Roger pushed the plunger, his head swooning forward as the heroin's stunning effect spread through his limbs. Then, slowly as a dancer, he threw back his head on its long, supple neck, smiling, his right hand dropping the syringe and reaching up to untwist the tie. He shook his arm and glanced vacantly up at Orlando and Jo, who still stood in the doorway. The whole episode had lasted no more than thirty seconds.

Orlando came forward as Roger began to roll down the sleeves of his faded Eagle Club sweatshirt, which was spattered at the bottom with cigarette burns. Orlando recognised the sweatshirt, realised that there must have been a time when this emaciated, ruined creature had been young and athletic, and had skied every January in Gstaad.

'Sorry you caught me powdering my nose, darling,' murmured Roger to Orlando, his dark eyes incandescent, fathomless. 'Didn't realise the front door was open.' Then his jaw clenched and he began to shake uncontrollably, hunching over to contain spasms.

'Christ,' said Orlando, 'are you all right?'

Jo stepped forward and placed her hand on Roger's forehead. 'He's burning up,' she said. 'He must have some kind of infection. Did you see the state of his arm?'

'Yes,' replied Orlando, grimacing. 'We'd better get him to hospital, or something. Should I call an ambulance?'

Roger lifted his head. His eyes were closed, his teeth clenched and chattering. Orlando did not think he had ever really heard anyone's teeth chatter before. 'Not an ambulance, if you don't mind, dears,' muttered Roger. A heavy sweat had broken out on his forehead. 'I've been having this on and off all day. It'll pass. Right as rain in a second.' He clasped himself again.

'Well, if he doesn't want an ambulance,' said Orlando, 'I'll go and get the car. It won't take more than ten minutes.' He half expected Jo to protest at being left with a sick junkie, but she didn't. She just hitched herself into a sitting position on the table and looked with concern at Roger, who seemed to be relaxing as his trembling fit passed.

'Well, you might at least introduce us, if we're to be left alone together in this way,' said Roger faintly, managing a smile, then scraping back the wisps of his faded blond hair with thin, shivering fingers.

'Oh . . .' Orlando hovered in impatience, then said, 'Jo, this is Roger, Roger, this is Jo. Look, I'm going.'

At a comfortable jog, Orlando made it back to the flat in seven minutes, and went inside to pick up the car keys. Dan was in the kitchen, making cheese on toast. 'What's up?' he asked.

'Roger's sitting in his flat with his temperature going through the roof,' said Orlando. 'He's got something that looks like a rotten golf ball growing out of the crook of his arm, and I think he's coming down with an infection. I'm taking him to hospital.'

Dan shook his head. 'Don't know why you bother, Paddy.' But Orlando had already closed the door and was gone.

When he got back to Roger's flat, he found Roger sitting with one foot propped up on the table, his chair tilted back, smoking a cigarette, while Jo was changing the record.

'Track one,' Roger was saying. 'Theme from *Love Story*. Delicious.' He closed his eyes and began to hum as the first strains of music drifted scratchily from the worn and well-loved LP, and then suddenly bent forwards again in another

216

paroxysm of uncontrollable shivering. Orlando moved forward to hold him, and Jo lifted the needle from the record and stood up.

'I didn't hear you come in,' she said, looking in alarm at Roger. 'He's been fine until now.'

'Come on,' said Orlando, 'let's get him into the car.'

They managed to help the shaking Roger into the back of the car, where he lay down on the seat, his limbs stiff in the foetal position, mumbling incoherently.

'God, he's delirious now,' said Jo, glancing at him over the back of the passenger seat as Orlando started the car.

'How was he?' asked Orlando, as they made their way in spasmodic bursts of speed through the evening traffic to Charing Cross Hospital.

Jo bit her thumbnail and gazed out at the pedestrians. 'Fine. Nice. Stoned.' She was silent for a moment. 'Like you said, all charm and clever lines.'

'What did you talk about?' asked Orlando curiously.

'Oh, who I was, whether I was your girlfriend, and so forth.'

'What did you say?'

'I told him the truth. That I was just a friend.' Her voice sounded empty.

Orlando smiled. 'Roger wouldn't like that. He's romantic as hell.'

He thought she was about to say something, but she merely looked out again at the traffic, and was silent for the rest of the journey.

By the time they reached the hospital, Roger was so bad, delirious and incapable of getting up, that a stretcher had to be brought out for him. As Orlando, by now genuinely alarmed, prepared to lock his car and follow the stretcher in, a porter said officiously, 'You can't leave that here.'

'Look, this is my cousin – I've got to see he's all right.'

The porter shook his head. 'Got to move it. Else you'll get clamped. Sorry.'

'You go and find a parking place,' said Jo. 'I'll go with him.'

His anxiety channelled into anger, Orlando drove off to circle the streets of Hammersmith for ten minutes before eventually finding somewhere to park. When he got back to the hospital, he found that Roger was still semi-conscious in casualty, waiting to be seen by a doctor. Jo sat in the waiting area with a plastic cup of coffee.

'Want one?' she asked. Orlando shook his head. He hoped they weren't going to have to wait for hours.

In the end, they did. It was ten to ten when the doctor who had examined Roger came to speak to them.

'Are you friends of Mr Stafford-Roper's?' the young house-man asked.

'I'm his cousin,' said Orlando. 'Is he all right?'

'He's comfortable now. He has a haematoma in his left arm which is badly infected, and it's resulted in septicaemia. That's a blood infection. We've given him high doses of antibiotic, which should sort it out, but his constitution is very weak, you know.' He looked levelly at Orlando. 'The kind of abuse to which your cousin has been subjecting his body has left him in very poor condition to fight this kind of thing.'

'You don't mean he could die?' Orlando felt his heart begin to thud.

The doctor jiggled his stethoscope. 'His temperature is extremely high. And a staphylococcus infection is potentially deadly, yes. But it's not an uncommon thing amongst drug-users, and he has every chance of recovering. It's just that I don't like to make any promises at this stage.'

Orlando nodded. 'Can I see him?' He realised that he very much did not want Roger to die.

'He's still delirious – you won't be able to talk to him. But you can see him, yes.'

'Do you want me to come with you?' Jo asked Orlando.

Orlando turned and stared at her, almost as though he had forgotten who she was. Then he said abruptly, 'No, I'd rather you didn't. Sorry about this evening.'

That was all. Then he turned and followed the doctor through a pair of swing doors, leaving her there. She stood for a moment, wondering whether to wait for him and get a lift home. But her pride wouldn't bear it. He hadn't even thanked her for helping, for waiting with him. He hadn't seen her in months and already he was treating her like some second-rate possession. He cared more about his bloody cousin than he did about her. She knew that she had already passed from his mind entirely, and that she might as well just go and wait for the bus.

Chapter Fifteen

After sitting by Roger's bedside for fifteen minutes, staring at the drips and tubes, at Roger's wasted, sunken face, at the dressing on the drained abscess above the black and ruined veins, listening to his cousin's occasional incoherent mumblings and shouts, Orlando realised that it was pointless staying. There was nothing he could do, and he might just as well go home. When he got back to the flat, it occurred to him that someone should tell Roger's family what had happened, but his only means of doing this were through his grandfather, and he was unable to get hold of him at his club. Finding he could not sleep, Orlando poured himself a beer and sat up until two watching a late film, wondering if Roger would make it through to the next day.

The following morning he rang the hospital at six, and was told that Roger was stable and in no danger. Still slightly groggy through lack of sleep, Orlando set off early for work and was at his desk by half-seven. At least this would earn him some points with the odious Barry.

After lunch, Barry announced that he was off to a seminar at Lloyd's for the rest of the day. 'Think you can get us all safely through the afternoon?' he asked Orlando.

'I'll try,' said Orlando, stifling a yawn.

The rest of the day went smoothly enough, and then at five Orlando remembered that there was still a half-million-dollar deal which Barry had asked him to conclude.

He rang a fellow dealer with whom he was friendly, bought the dollars at 1.65, spot, turned down an invitation to a drinks party that evening, and reminded himself that he really should visit Roger after work. Just as he put the phone down and was reaching for a confirmation slip to record his deal, the phone rang again.

'I have a Miss Lennox for you,' said the switchboard.

Orlando felt his insides turn over. 'Yes, put her through,' he said. The confirmation slip was forgotten. He had spent so many weeks wondering whether she might ring, that he had become convinced she never would.

'Hello?' He realised that his palms had begun to sweat and cursed inwardly, hating her for being able to have this effect on him.

'Orlando? It's Hannah.'

'I know. How are you?'

'Oh . . . fine.' There was a pause. 'I did say I would ring, didn't I?'

'You did.' Orlando was not quite sure how to go on. 'So, what's new?' he asked weakly.

'Oh, work's quite quiet. We have great lulls, you know, between fund-raising events.'

'Mmm.' There was another uneasy pause. If she wanted him to take the initiative, Orlando decided, she could forget it. He suddenly wondered, hopelessly, what was the point of this, anyway?

'I thought it might be nice,' she went on, 'if we – if we could see one another – have lunch together sometime.' Her voice sounded uncertain.

'Yes,' replied Orlando instantly. 'Yes, if you like.' He reached for his diary. 'When did you have in mind?'

'Any time this week, if you like. Friday?'

'Okay,' said Orlando, immediately crossing out a previous engagement. 'Where?'

'I'm afraid I don't really know the City well. Why don't I just meet you at your office?'

221

'All right,' said Orlando. 'You should find it quite easily. It's between Mincing Lane and Mark Lane. Amerco West. About twelve thirty?'

'Fine. I'll see you then. Bye.'

And she was gone. Orlando sat holding the receiver for a few seconds, realising that he had been gripping it fiercely. He relaxed and put it down, then sat back, wishing he could pretend that none of this mattered. She was engaged to someone else, after all. But of course it mattered – it mattered as much as it had done once before, only in a different way . . . He sat there for a good ten minutes, taking himself back over the events of six years ago, wondering what they would have to say to one another throughout an entire lunch. Then he sighed, put on his jacket, checked the screen and left the office.

Roger was considerably better than when Orlando had last seen him. When Orlando arrived he was sitting up, still pale and shaky, reading a copy of the *Evening Standard*.

'How are you?' asked Orlando, pulling up a chair.

'Fantastic,' said Roger, stretching the word out lazily. 'Did you know my hair's falling out?' He tugged at a clump, and several strands came away easily between his thin fingers.

'Don't do that!' said Orlando.

'Sorry,' said Roger, and looked contrite. Then he smiled his arch smile. 'So – Orlando to the rescue once again. You keep plucking me from the jaws of death.'

'I hardly think you were going to die,' said Orlando. 'You've just got an infection. What's that?' He pointed to the little tube bandaged into the vein on the back of Roger's hand.

Roger glanced at it. 'Darling, it's just what every junkie needs. It's where they pop my drugs in every hour or so. Handy, no? Antibiotics and methadone. That's the plus side of a hospital stay, I've always found. They pump you full of methadone so that you don't miss the heroin. Very convenient, but not very exciting.' He sighed and looked around

222

wearily. 'I'm so spastic I can't even go out to the lifts for a fag. For God's sake, cheer me up, Orlando. Tell me more about the pretty little blonde of last night. I can remember that much. Girlfriend?'

'She'd certainly like to be.' Orlando yawned and flipped over the pages of Roger's newspaper.

'God, you're an arrogant little sod, cousin,' said Roger, amused. 'Maybe it's a D'Ewes gene.' He closed his eyes, then remarked, 'I had a visit from the most deadly psychiatrist before you looked in.'

'Oh?'

'Just the usual routine. Anyway, I said I'd been thinking of trying to kick the habit . . .'

Orlando looked up just as Roger opened his eyes. 'And do you mean it?' he asked.

Roger smiled. 'Well, in so far as I ever mean anything – yes. I sat around at lunchtime thinking about things, and I reckon it's the least I can do for you. I've done it for everyone else, so why not you? Guaranteed to fail spectacularly, of course, but the gesture is everything, don't you think?'

'What will you do?'

'Oh, it's part and parcel of this hospital scene, anyway. They'll give me methadone prescriptions when they kick me out of here at the end of the week, but I'll have to attend one of their wretched rehab centres. Might as well give it a shot. You've been putting in all these hours, and it's only fair that you should get a reward for your efforts. Besides, you can't go on indefinitely snatching me from death's door.' His edgy glance hovered around the ward for a moment, then rested on Orlando's face.

'Well, excellent,' said Orlando. 'If you really want to do it, then maybe you can.'

'Si vita suppetit,' murmured Roger. He leaned back on his pillows. 'You look worse than I do,' he observed.

'Hardly,' replied Orlando. 'I'm whacked, actually. Early night tonight. By the way, I tried to get hold of your mother – '

'Don't,' said Roger. 'She's in New York, shopping. I wouldn't trouble her, if I were you. She's been through all this before. I think she finds it terribly boring.'

A nurse appeared, ready to give Roger his next dose of antibiotic, and Orlando rose. 'I'd better be off. I'll drop in tomorrow evening, all right?'

'Goodnight, sweet prince. Flights of angels ... all that kind of thing.' He raised his thin hand in benediction and farewell, watched Orlando until he had disappeared from the ward, and then closed his eyes.

'What do you think?' asked Sir Leonard, watching as Anne stepped from the hallway of the Belgravia flat into the sitting room. 'I had originally intended to buy, but then it all seemed too much trouble.' Anne gazed around at the elegant, formal interior, glancing at the expensive rugs on the polished floor, the chandeliers, the antique furniture, the view across the garden square.

'I like it,' she said, nodding. 'It's rather old-fashioned, but I like it. It's very ... you.' She turned as he came towards her, and put her arms round his neck. He kissed her softly for a long moment.

'I never felt less old-fashioned in my life,' he said. 'But I badly needed somewhere where I could be alone with you. A month at my club is more than flesh and blood can stand.' He unbuttoned the neck of her blouse and ran his fingers over the soft skin of her shoulders, and she bent her neck.

'Oh, just there ...' she murmured. 'My neck is so stiff ...' He rubbed gently at the nape of her neck with his fingers. 'God, you have the most wonderful hands ...' And she twisted her head up to kiss him again.

'I thought,' he said at last, 'that we could go out and shop for some food – ' He glanced at his watch, ' – cook for ourselves here, and – '

'And what?' She kissed him again, tugging his tie loose, unbuttoning his shirt and sliding her hands against his skin. He gave a slight groan, then smiled, realising that his carefully planned seduction was being overtaken by events, and that she had begun to undress him.

'I haven't . . .' he muttered, kissing her neck, '. . . made love to anyone for a long time, you know . . .'

'Oh, it's just like riding a bicycle,' murmured Anne. 'You never forget.'

'And you don't fall off the first time.'

She burst out laughing, then laid her head against his chest. 'I think we'd better find a bedroom . . .' She lifted her head. 'You do have one of those?'

'Oh, yes,' he replied, gazing down at her. 'Most certainly.'

Some time later, as she lay in his arms, stroking one grey eyebrow with her finger, she asked, 'Why have you never stayed at my flat? We could have been doing this weeks ago.'

He raised the eyebrow she was stroking. 'Because – you never asked me to.'

'Not directly. But you must have known you could. You're such a gentleman . . .' She kissed his mouth. 'Such a wonderful gentleman. Whenever things were getting – well, you know, to a certain point, you always said goodnight. Off you went. Incredibly frustrating for me.'

'Mmm. I can't say it did me a great deal of good, either.'

'But why? Why not there?'

'Because – well, now I *will* be old-fashioned. Because I didn't want it to be somewhere where you had had other lovers.' There was a brief silence, in which his gaze flickered over each feature of the face which he had recently begun to think the loveliest he had ever seen. 'This is . . . you are . . . remarkably special to me.' He kissed her. 'That is why. And I also think that certain things are worth waiting for. You young people tend to rush things so. Anticipation is half the fun.'

'Only half,' replied Anne. 'You old people know a thing or two, anyway.' She stroked his chest. 'I tell you what. Why don't you put on your shirt and trousers and shoes, and go out to the Chinese takeaway, get some food, and we can eat it in bed?'

'First, because that is a disgusting idea and puts you firmly in the category of persons below forty and, secondly, because I can think of much better things to do with the immediate moment.' He pulled her towards him. 'Thirdly,' he said, his voice growing slower, 'because I intend to take you to dinner shortly, and will then have the pleasure of bringing you back here, and knowing you will still be with me when I wake up.' She listened, smiling, as he added gently, 'I don't think you can imagine what that means to me.'

'Oh, yes, I can,' replied Anne, caressing him. 'We persons under forty aren't all hard-bitten cynics, you know. We have our romantic streak.'

He held her close against him, closing his eyes as she buried her face in his neck, and wondered why God had seen fit to bestow this happiness upon him, after all these years.

Orlando's Friday did not begin well. He cut himself shaving, then had a brief, but bitter, argument with Dan about the phone bill. He set off for work in a bad temper, wondering why, since he had more money than Dan, he begrudged paying Dan's share of the bill. Principle, he supposed. He tried to put the argument from his mind when he got to work, but it managed to put him on edge for the rest of the morning. He was nervous about seeing Hannah at lunchtime, too, and that annoyed him. He wanted to be cool and detached when he saw her, to show her that she didn't matter any more, and wished more than once that he possessed some of Roger's aplomb and general air of amused indifference to life. But she would have fallen for Roger straight away, he reminded himself – a whole and healthy Roger, that was. Anyone would.

It was ten past twelve, and Orlando was watching the clock, a growing feeling of apprehension in the pit of his stomach, when the bombshell came. He was sitting next to Barry, idly watching the Reuters screen, when Barry's phone rang. After speaking for a few moments, Barry put the phone down. He swivelled round in his chair, put his pencil between his teeth, took it out again, then sat tapping it against the palm of his hand.

'That was the settlement office,' he said. 'They've just been doing their reconcilations and they've got a transaction for half a million dollars that they can't match up.' Barry scratched his head with the end of the pencil. 'You can't remember doing a half-million deal with NatWest as the counterparty, by any chance?'

Orlando took his eyes from the screen and stared at Barry. He felt his heart sink like a stone. 'Oh, God,' he said.

'I thought as much,' said Barry, sighing. 'I leave you on your own for just one afternoon, and you start fucking up left, right and centre.'

'Oh, come on – I just forgot to fill in the confirmation slip! It was a mistake – I mean, I was going to write the slip out when the phone rang. Then I forgot . . .'

'Well, that's just the kind of stupid mistake you can't afford to make in this business, sunshine,' said Barry. 'Your university degrees won't help you here. That's a day's interest up the spout, isn't it?' He sighed again. 'I'm not going to tell tales on you like some bleeding schoolkid, Orlando –'

'Thanks,' said Orlando gratefully, cursing himself for his stupidity, but hoping it would go no further.

'So you'd better go and tell Mr Pfeiffer yourself. Better than him finding out later. Which he will.' He swivelled round in his chair. 'Off you go. No time like the present.'

Orlando made his way to Mr Pfeiffer's office and told him of his error of two days ago. 'It was a stupid mistake. I did intend to fill out the slip, but something came up, and I forgot.'

'Son, you can't afford to let these things slip your mind,' said Mr Pfeiffer, gazing at Orlando from behind his black-rimmed glasses, his lower lip pendulous with disapproval. 'You leave the bank exposed like that, it could cause us big problems.' He leaned forward, gave a little sigh. 'In this case, it's only twenty-five thousand – we can live with that. Hell, guys here are losing more than that every day. Point is, though – they're *making* ten times that much. They're experienced, they know what's what. Whereas you – still on probation – well, on you it just looks dumb. We can't afford dumb.' He shook his head. 'Well, it's not the biggest deal, I guess. We all make mistakes. But remember, this is your try-out, your chance to show you can do the job . . .'

Orlando had been trying hard to concentrate on what was being said to him, and on not reading Mr Pfeiffer's wrist watch upside down, but it was difficult. Twenty to one. Hannah would be waiting downstairs. Maybe they'd paged him. What if she didn't wait? Mr Pfeiffer's voice rumbled sadly on for a few more minutes, then he sat back in his chair.

'Okay, off you go. And try to keep your mind on your work from now on.' He waved Orlando out, and Orlando raced for the lift.

Hannah was waiting in reception, a tight little frown on her face, but she smiled when she saw him.

'God, I'm sorry,' said Orlando. 'I had to see my boss.'

'Promotion?'

'Ah – not quite,' replied Orlando, steering her towards the

revolving doors. 'I booked us a table. It's a new place. I haven't tried it out yet.'

They chatted as they walked to the restaurant, anxious to be at ease with one another, to look as though having lunch together was the most natural thing in the world. As they sat down at their table in the restaurant, Orlando made a joke about the little vase of flowers in the centre of the table, and he thought, anybody looking at us would think we were just another couple, laughing, talking. And yet it was nothing like that. The superficial small talk was merely a front, with nothing but uncertainty and strangeness behind it. What on earth was there to say to one another? he wondered, staring at the menu, silence falling between them.

He looked up and found that Hannah was looking at him. Nothing was said for a moment, then she asked suddenly, 'Are you finding this as difficult as I am?'

He smiled, then said, 'For the last ten minutes, it's been as though we've both been thinking that we must keep talking at all costs, in case – '

'In case what?'

'In case . . . in case we find that there's really nothing to say to one another.' He glanced at her, but could read nothing in her face. 'Let's order some wine,' he said abruptly. He had intended to drink only mineral water, with the afternoon's work ahead of him, but somehow he did not think he could get through this meal without alcohol.

She nodded, and glanced at the approaching waiter. When their orders had been taken, another silence fell.

'I don't think,' ventured Orlando, tracing a little series of grooves with his fork on the white linen of the tablecloth, 'that we can resume the small talk, can we?'

'But then, as you just pointed out, there might not be anything to say to one another.' She gave him a sad, challenging little smile.

'In which case, we're wasting each other's time,' said Orlando quietly. He looked up. 'I could tell you that that's a very pretty dress, that you look very lovely, ask you how your fiancé is – but it wouldn't take us very far, would it? Or I could bore you with a description of my job, and how the money markets work – but that's not really why you wanted us to meet, is it? Tell me why you wanted us to meet, Hannah. This lunch was your idea.'

'I didn't intend it to be like this,' she said softly. The waiter brought their wine, and there was another interval of silence as it was tasted and poured.

'Like what?' he asked, and drank off half his glass.

She forced a smile. 'I didn't expect you to be so – so angry,' she replied, trying to keep her voice light.

He stared at her, realising that she was absolutely right, that he *was* angry, had been so for six years, and probably always would be.

'I'm sorry,' he said. 'What did you expect?'

'I don't really know . . . Just to talk.'

'What about?'

'Oh, Orlando! I don't know!' she suddenly cried out, and a few heads turned. She lowered her voice. 'I just wanted to see you again, to – to – '

'To rake over the past? To talk about old times? All right, I'll give you old times,' said Orlando levelly. 'How about the time I came all the way to Scotland to see you, because I was in love with you, because you were the whole world to me, stupid schoolboy that I was, and found you with half your clothes off, being groped by your father's farmhand, or whatever he was? Is that what you came here to discuss? Or did you expect me to behave like a civilized adult, to pretend that all that never happened, to sit here and laugh and talk with you about the weather, or your wedding, or my morning at the office? Did you?'

230

She stared at him. 'Do you want me to go?' she asked quietly.

He sat back, anger draining from him. 'No,' he muttered, 'no, of course I don't want you to go. I just had to say it. I mean – yes, you're right, I am angry. I'm angry that I met you at the ball, you know? I'm angry that we're sitting here – that I didn't even have the strength of will to say "no" when you rang up . . .'

'Orlando,' she said earnestly, leaning across to gaze at him with her dark blue eyes, 'I didn't want to see you just to upset you. I hoped we could be friends again. We were once.'

The waiter set their plates before them, but Orlando just sat looking at her. No, she wasn't being trite – she really had meant what she'd said. She thought they had been friends. Maybe she did not remember a star-spun, shining, all-consuming love affair, something which had been the very beginning and end all at once, a transcending happiness and anguish . . . perhaps it had never been like that for her.

'Were we?' he murmured, watching her pick up her fork. 'I thought we were in love.' She glanced at him, then looked away. 'What's the difference?' he said wearily. 'If you want to be friends, let's be friends. Here's to us.' He lifted his glass and Hannah, slightly puzzled, raised hers. Orlando drank, then stared down at the cutlets which he had absent-mindedly ordered, and realised he was quite hungry.

They ate in silence for a moment or two, then Hannah said, 'You've changed, Orlando.'

'Well, that's hardly surprising,' he replied.

'I mean – there used to be something – something gentle and . . . oh, well . . .' She mused for a moment. 'Do you ever wonder,' she went on, 'how it would have been if you hadn't come up to Scotland that time?'

'Hmm. No. No, if I ever dwelt on that particular incident, I can't say that alternative scenarios have presented themselves. No.' She looked thoughtfully at her plate, her expression distant. Before she could speak, he added quickly, 'I imagine there would have been some other disillusionment eventually, don't you?'

She looked up at him speculatively and said, 'That's what it is. That's what's different. You used to be kind – you didn't say hard things.'

'I wonder what changed me?' he replied, then sighed. 'I'm sorry.' In an attempt to divert the conversation away from themselves, the past, he said, 'Let's change the subject. Tell me about your chap, Max. He seemed nice.'

She smiled. 'Oh, yes, he's nice. Max is nice. I had to tell him all about you . . . I don't quite think he understood. He wouldn't be very happy at the thought of my having lunch with you today, really.'

'I'll pretend you didn't say that. What does he do?'

'He's in the Foreign Office. You know, a diplomat.'

'Ah. Does he get posted abroad?'

'Yes. His last posting was in Colombia, and in a few months he's going to Paris. We'll probably be married there.' There was silence for a moment, then she said, 'Orlando?' He looked up as he refilled their glasses, waiting for whatever it was she was going to say. 'You know – ' She hesitated, toying with her glass, then drank quickly from it. 'You know, ever since that day – I mean, after that time, the last time I saw you in Scotland, I never . . . I never stopped loving you.' Her voice was low and nervous, and she did not look at him. 'I wanted . . . I just spent weeks wanting things to go back in time. Over and over. Wanting it all never to have happened.'

'But it did.' His voice was flat.

'Yes, it did,' she said sadly. 'The thing is . . . I wondered,

232

did you just stop loving me? In that very moment?' She looked up at him now, her expression open and curious; the wine had brought a light flush to her cheeks.

'In that very moment . . .' Orlando repeated, musing on this, gazing at his glass, stroking his chin. 'In that very moment? No, I didn't stop loving you. But I suppose I started hating you.'

'Do you still?'

'Hate you?' He smiled and leaned back. 'No, I don't hate you, because I don't love you. I hated you then for destroying something precious, for breaking my heart. But I didn't stop loving you. Not for a long time.'

'When?'

'When enough time had passed to turn me into the person I am now, and you into the person you are. Different people. Different from the way we were then.'

'Are we so very different?' Her voice was soft.

'Of course we are,' he replied. The waiter approached them again. 'Shall we just have coffee?' said Orlando. 'I'm afraid I can't be out of the office for too long.' She nodded. When the waiter had left, he went on, 'We were children then.' And how fresh, untouched, credulous and lucky, he thought. 'People change us. Events change us. We lose trust. We learn to hurt and be hurt.' He thought of Louisa, how she had worn away his capacity for affection until at the end he had wondered if there was anything left.

'I suppose you're right,' she replied. 'I thought I could come here today and rediscover – '

'What?'

'Whatever it was we had.'

'You have Max now.'

'I didn't quite mean it that way . . .' Her voice trailed away. She looked up at him. 'I can't describe . . . it's as though some small particle of you is embedded in my soul – as though some part of me has always been searching for you. Every day, in all those years.'

Her words touched him unbearably, but his face betrayed nothing.

'That's why I wasn't surprised to see you that evening,' she went on. 'I always knew I would, someday.'

'But whatever you've found,' said Orlando, 'is not what you're looking for. That's in the past. This is the way we are now.'

'Yes,' she said, and glanced down as the waiter put her coffee before her. 'You're right. Perhaps this lunch was a mistake.'

'I don't think so,' said Orlando. 'It will all get better. Despite what I said before, I am a civilized creature, and the next time we meet it will be much easier. One just builds up the layers. Social veneering.' He drank his coffee and motioned to the waiter for the bill. 'I'm sorry that this has had to be so rushed, but I made a bit of a cock-up at work this morning, so I'd better not stay out too long.'

'Well, it's been – I mean, I'm glad we had a chance to talk . . .' She suddenly put both hands on the table, and clenched her fists. 'Look – ' she began. Orlando glanced at her in surprise, taking his pen from his pocket as the bill was put in front of him. 'There's something I haven't said, and I've waited all this time to say it . . . You see, I just wanted to say that – that –' There was a catch in her voice, a trace of tears, '– that I'm sorry.'

He watched as she fought to hold back her tears, her knuckles white. She lifted her chin and met his eyes. For an instant he thought of reaching out, leaning across and kissing her, bugger what the people in the place might think, and bugger Max. But the instant passed. He could think of nothing to say.

Then at last he said slowly, 'I know you are,' and nodded.

234

They looked at one another, and Hannah thought, if he would just reach out, just touch her, then Max and everything else would be nothing. They could start all over again, find everything they once had. But he did not move.

'I have to go,' he said, the words sounding abrupt.

'Fine.'

He pocketed the receipt and his pen, and stood up. She remained seated, and he looked down uncertainly at her. 'I'll just stay here for a while,' she said, glancing up at him. 'I might have another coffee.'

'Right . . .' He touched her briefly on the shoulder. 'Bye, then.'

'Goodbye,' she said.

He took his hand away, and then he was gone.

That evening Sir Leonard returned to Stow Stocksley, as confused a man as he ever had been. All throughout the long drive he had thought about Anne, wondering what she would do that weekend. He imagined her going to dinner or clubs with friends, perhaps even with some man younger than himself. Well, what did he expect? She was young and lovely; what need had she of a decrepit sixty-two-year-old? He glanced at his reflection in the rear view mirror, at his own grim, stern face, and sighed. The whole thing had probably been utter folly, and he had most likely made a complete fool of himself. But then he remembered the evenings they had spent together, and the look on her face as she lay next to him after making love . . . Was he entirely out of his mind? Simply because he had become infatuated with a woman half his age, there was no reason to suppose that she felt anything for him.

He gripped the wheel, then tried consciously to relax, to concentrate on the road. How long would it be before he saw her again? What if she changed entirely in that time, no longer had any use for him? No, she was not like that . . . She was kind and sincere and affectionate. If only . . . He sighed again and reached out to switch on the car radio, and listened for a while to Mahler's Fourth Symphony on Radio 3. Damn, even a piece of music made him think of her.

He slowed the car and turned in through the gates of Stow Stocksley Hall, up the long driveway. The Hall was almost entirely dark except for a few lights in the west wing, on the ground floor. Annabel must be finishing some work, or possibly it was Mrs Cresswell. He let himself in and went through to the back of the house. He found Mr Cresswell about to switch off the lights in the kitchen.

'Oh, evening, Sir Leonard. Mrs C said you would be back tonight, but I didn't hear the car. She's left you something cold in the fridge. Did you need me to see to the car?'

'No, no, I've put it away, thank you, Geoff. Goodnight.'

Sir Leonard threw his overcoat on to a chair and opened the fridge. Mrs Cresswell had left him a plate of brown bread chicken sandwiches and some cherry tomatoes. Well, that would do, together with a glass of something. He poured himself a glass of white wine and decided to take his supper up to his study on a tray. It was his habit, living alone, to read with his meals, and during his absence Mrs Cresswell had efficiently tidied from the kitchen and dining room the clutter of books which had gradually made their way down from his library.

He mounted the large wooden staircase slowly with his tray and went into the study. There he switched on the red-shaded lamp by the fireplace and stood for a moment, glancing around, glad to be back. He lit the fire which Mrs Cresswell had laid, then went to his shelves and took down a copy of *Sense and Sensibility*, and sat down at his desk to eat his supper. Afterwards he sat with his glass of wine, still reading, but found his attention straying. He rose and went over to the window, where the curtains were still undrawn. There he stood looking out across the deep shadows of the park, conscious of the utter quiet of the house around him. He stood for a long time, thinking.

Then at last he went back to his desk, picked up the telephone and dialled Anne's number. The ringing tone went on for some time, and he was about to give up, his heart heavy with disappointment, when she answered.

'Hello?' Her voice sounded slightly breathless.

'Anne? It's – it's Leonard.' He paused uncertainly.

'Yes?' she said tentatively.

'This will sound absurd, I know, but –' He hesitated again. '– but I'm standing here in my study and I find – I find –' Again a pause ' – that I simply don't know how I can get through the weekend without you. It's extremely foolish, but I miss you already.'

Anne laughed, and then said, 'No, it's not foolish. I miss you, too.'

He suddenly wished very badly that she was here in this room with him. He closed his eyes. 'Do you think . . . Would you care to come down? I mean, there is a late train, and I could meet you . . .'

After a long, agonising moment, she said, 'Yes, if you'd like me to.'

'Yes, I would.' He paused. 'There is a train at nine thirty to Stow Stocksley Station. I can meet it.'

'All right. I'll be there.' Then she added. 'Don't worry.'

He put the phone down and stood there, aware of a sweet, calming relief filling his heart.

Chapter Sixteen

After his detoxification and three weeks of group therapy in the rehabilitation centre, Roger emerged cleansed and purified to face the happy prospect of a life without drugs. To Orlando it all seemed quite simple. Roger should just spend a few weeks adjusting to his new existence, trying to find rhythms and activities in the day to compensate for his lack of scoring and fixing and being generally spaced out, and then, when that had been achieved, he should set about finding something to do with his life. They discussed this one day when Orlando went round to visit Roger, and found him preparing a spaghetti bolognese. Roger had taken up rudimentary cooking as a way of filling his time.

'So, what kind of jobs have you ever done?' asked Orlando.

Roger picked up his cigarette from where it lay smoking on the rim of the sink, and took a couple of careful drags. Without heroin, he found he had to savour every tiny scrap of pleasurable activity, but the scraps seemed thin and few. He didn't even have the money to develop a full-blown drink problem which, during his days of recreational drug use, he had always earmarked as a possible sideline, if things got stale.

'I once worked for some Indian chaps, doing import and export work,' he remarked, then put down his cigarette and scooped the chopped onions into a frying pan.

'Really?' said Orlando, who thought this sounded promising.

Roger turned to smile at him. 'Heroin,' he said. 'I'd managed to blow my monthly income cheque from my trust fund in one weekend on coke, so I thought I'd get a job for a little while. The trouble is, you can't hold down a job when you're stoned all the time. The Indians gave me the boot.'

'Haven't you done *anything* else?'

Roger shook his head. 'Never had to work. Came into my trust fund when I was twenty, halfway through Oxford.' He popped a piece of green pepper into his mouth and chewed it. 'Mind you, I did help out behind the bar of the Admiral Cod for a few nights, when I had the house in Cadogan Square.' He sighed. 'Ah, happy days.'

'Well, I suppose you could always do something like that,' said Orlando. 'I mean, at least it would fill in the hours, give you a bit of money.'

'Be a barman? Get real, darling.'

'Well, maybe my grandfather could find something for you to do. I mean, it's in his interest – well, in the interest of the estate – for you to –'

'Lead a blameless and respectable existence?' interrupted Roger. 'My dear, you're on entirely the wrong tack. I'm unemployable. No, what my mother will do, once she's convinced that I'm all cleaned up, is to start hunting down some poor girl with a fortune, and try to marry me off to her.'

Orlando looked interested. 'Well, what about that?'

Roger shook his head. 'I've been married once. Don't remember a great deal about it, but I don't think I want to do it again.' He laid down his knife and turned round, resting his bony hips against the sink. 'In fact, there's not much that I ever want to do again. Can you imagine that? Can you possibly begin to imagine what that feels like?'

There was a silence. Roger's voice held such a note of quiet despair that Orlando was momentarily lost for words.

'Look, I'll come and see you at the end of the week,' he said, rising from the kitchen chair.

Roger smiled, his face tired. 'You do that. Come on Friday,

about eight. I'll take you for a drink. And I promise to be utterly scintillating and cheerfully optimistic about everything.'

When Orlando got home, he found Jo sitting in the kitchen with Dan over a half-empty bottle of wine. Orlando reached down and picked up the bottle.

'Dan, do you know what this is? It's a 1977 Chateau Calon that my grandfather gave me last birthday! I was saving it!' He felt truly angry at the sight of them both knocking back his good wine. 'Why can't you buy your own stuff, instead of guzzling mine?' He slammed the bottle back down and took off his jacket.

Dan set down his glass, his temper, as ever, on a short fuse. 'I didn't know it was so bloody precious!' he retorted. 'Why do you just leave it lying around, in that case?' He got up and put his glass by the sink. 'Anyway, all this Chateau 1977 stuff makes me sick. It's just part of a pose. Affectations about wine, your grandfather and his great estate. It's all part of your capitalist bullshit!'

'Yes, well, I notice you don't mind partaking of your fair share of it,' replied Orlando.

'Oh, come on,' said Jo. 'Dan was just entertaining me till you got back. We didn't know the wine was anything special.'

Orlando sighed. 'Well, since it's open, I might as well have a glass. Here, pass me yours as well, Dan. I'm sorry. I've had a bad day. And I've just been to see Roger.'

'What's up with him? I thought he was your pride and joy, now that he's all cleaned up,' said Jo.

Orlando sat down. 'I don't know. For some reason it's more depressing being with him now than when he was doing drugs. He can't see the point of anything. He doesn't seem to have any direction, any desire to do anything. I talked to him about trying to get a job, but he just treats it as a joke.'

'He should get himself a rich wife,' remarked Jo.

'That's what he said – at any rate, that's what he thinks his mother will want. Oh, I don't know . . .' He rubbed his hands over his face. 'In some ways I'd rather have nothing more to do with him, but I can't just leave him high and dry. Anyway,' he said, refilling Jo's glass, 'what brings you round here?'

'My night off. Thought I'd see if you fancied going for a drink.'

'Yes, why not,' said Orlando. He wasn't doing anything else. 'I'll just get changed. God, I wish Roger would get his phone reconnected, so that I could see how he is without having to go round there all the time.'

Later that evening he drove Jo back to her flat in Battersea. It was an old-fashioned block in a run-down street.

'So this is it?' said Orlando.

'Yeah. Not quite Smith Street, but it's not too bad. Most of the neighbours are old dears. Anyway, it's what I can afford. Do you want to come up for a coffee, or something?'

'No thanks. Busy day tomorrow.'

'Yeah, okay.'

He sat looking at her for a moment. The light from the street lamp made her blonde hair look silvery, and the tiny hairs on her cheek were like peach skin. Without thinking about it, almost as though she had willed it, he leaned across and kissed her. He remembered kissing her in the night club when he had first met her, had quite forgotten the pleasure of it, and wondered why this had never occurred before now. But when she put her hands up to his face, he remembered that he had no desire whatsoever to become involved with her. He drew back.

'Doesn't mean a thing,' he said, and smiled. She returned his look.

'I didn't say it did.'

For an instant, they knew one another's minds entirely. What she wanted, and what he was not prepared to offer.

241

She shrugged, and said, 'See you.' Then she got out of the car. He sat for a moment, watching her go into the building, then drove home.

Friday in the dealing room was hectic, and Orlando did not leave the office until six thirty. He had meant to go back to his flat to shower and change before going to see Roger, but when he looked at the clock he realised that he might as well go straight to Ladbroke Grove.

When he got there, he found the front door of the large, seedy house propped open to the early summer air, the usual clutter of unclaimed mail in the hallway. He knocked on Roger's door, and heard the crooning sounds of 'Home Loving Man' coming from Roger's stereo. It was a few moments before Roger opened the door, and then only by a few inches. He looked surprised to see Orlando, and said, 'You're early.' He hesitated, then opened the door properly, adding, 'Come right in, sweet thing.'

Orlando followed Roger through to the living room, where a tall, thickset man in a black tracksuit was standing by the fireplace. The man was bearded and wore a felt pork-pie hat on his close-cropped head. He glanced at Orlando and gave a quick nod of acknowledgement, but did not smile; he looked at Roger and began to tap his fingers on the mantelpiece.

'Okay, Leon,' said Roger to the bearded man in a bright, sighing tone of dismissal, 'we'll leave it there.' Roger swept his long fingers through his blond hair, which was shining and newly-washed.

The man glanced at Orlando, then back at Roger, pursed his lips and nodded. He eased himself away from the mantelpiece. 'Okay. Cool. I'll see you.' And he walked across to the door, his gait easy and swaggering, chopping the air with his hand in farewell. The door closed.

'Friend of mine,' murmured Roger. 'In the music business.

242

Sorry I didn't introduce you – shocking manners, I know, but he was just leaving.'

Orlando looked at Roger. 'How are you?' he asked.

'Oh . . . bloody bored, you know?' Roger's voice held a note of feverish impatience, but he tried to smile at his cousin. Then he bit the side of his finger and said, 'It's – it's finding things to do with one's time . . . Christ, when I had my trust fund it was easy. When I wasn't scoring I could go and spend money on having a good time, go off to Rome or New York, buy a new car . . .' He turned and leaned on the mantelpiece. 'I hate being fucking poor.' Then he laughed, reached out for his packet of cigarettes and lit one, glancing at Orlando. 'Maybe now that I'm all cleaned up, your grandfather might have the kindness to die. Hmm.' He turned away. 'Some hope.'

'What do you want to do this evening?' asked Orlando. 'We could go for a drink, see a film –'

'Christ, Orlando!' snapped Roger. 'You're like a bloody probation officer, or a childminder! Coming round and checking on me, taking me out to places where I can't get into trouble . . .' He sighed and ran his fingers nervously through his long hair again. 'I'm sorry, it's been a difficult week. Shit, it's been a difficult life . . .' There was a silence, then he looked across at Orlando and smiled his beautiful, disarming smile. 'Tell you what, I'm going to take you to dinner. Bugger the expense. Somewhere really good. The Savoy. You're decently dressed,' he said, glancing at Orlando's City suit, 'and I can change. Make yourself a drink. I won't be a moment.' He disappeared into his bedroom, calling as he went, 'Turn the record over.'

Dutifully Orlando flipped the LP over and let the stylus drop. He glanced round the room as he waited, saw the overfull ashtray, the pile of videos stacked next to the television. It must be a deadly dull existence, he reflected, and wondered what Roger could do to make better use of his time.

He couldn't be entirely useless; those dissipated good looks and that callous charm must be good for something. Only he couldn't think what.

'There – what do you think?' asked Roger, emerging ten minutes later from his bedroom. He was dressed in a cream-coloured linen suit over a white silk shirt, with a cerise cravat knotted at the neck. His blond hair was tied back, and the sleeves of his jacket were pushed to the elbow. He looked the epitome of the fashionable, rich young eighties man.

'Great,' said Orlando, faintly amused. 'I like the shirt.'

'Hand made,' said Roger. 'A friend and I blasted out to Hong Kong four years ago and had suits and shirts made up ... Ah, when the going was good.' He thrust wallet, keys and cigarettes into his pocket. 'Right, let's find a cab,' he said. 'American Bar first, plenty of whisky sours, then the River Room, yes? My treat. A reward for helping me.' He reached out and placed a rough, bony hand momentarily against Orlando's cheek. 'For being my good angel.' Then he swept Orlando out of the flat, down the steps and into the dusty, warm air of Ladbroke Grove.

'Don't we have to book?' asked Orlando, once they had found a taxi.

'I think my face and name will do the trick, darling,' replied Roger, lowering the taxi window and gazing across Hyde Park, at the green haze of the trees melting into the summer dusk. He turned to Orlando. 'The Savoy is one place where they haven't seen the darker side of me, fortunately, and where my regular custom and extravagant tipping will not have been forgotten.'

They had two drinks in the American Bar and then went down to the River Room. As Roger had predicted, he was greeted with smiles, and a table was found for them near the window. Orlando was aware of women glancing swiftly, discreetly, as Roger strolled to the table.

Roger was as scintillating that evening as he had promised to be. He monopolised the conversation completely, recounting his exploits from leaving university till the present day, making even the grisliest and darkest aspects of his life seem rakish and amusing, sketching portraits of lunatic and eccentric acquaintances, describing exotic locations, bizarre encounters and ghastly fates narrowly avoided.

'Maybe you should write about it,' said Orlando at the end of the meal. He was feeling rather drunk, seeing Roger in a different light, and was filled with a sense that he himself knew nothing of life, was callow and inexperienced compared to his worldly cousin. 'You manage to make drug-taking sound exciting, almost glamorous, and yet still utterly sordid.'

'A perfect description,' said Roger. 'It is all of those things. Can you wonder why I find my existence so completely tedious now?' He raised his cigarette to his lips, narrowing his eyes as he looked at Orlando.

'Come on,' said Orlando. 'You must be glad you've stopped. I mean, it wasn't what you would call living . . .'

'Wasn't it?' Roger leaned back, the enthusiasm which had burned so brilliantly within him for the past hour suddenly dying like a spent ember. He raised his glass of brandy, crushing out the stub of his cigarette. How could he explain to Orlando that life without drugs was simply a life of utter darkness, a darkness in which heroin had been the sudden, beautiful light, enabling him to see, to function, to exist without anguish? 'Don't you realise,' he said suddenly, 'that my way of life chose me? I thought that I was above addiction, that I was too clever and rich and extraordinary for drugs to claim me. I could have been anything. But I became what I deserved to become – a junkie.'

'But you're not one any more,' said Orlando, faintly puzzled and disquieted.

Roger frowned, stared at Orlando, then laughed. He threw back his head, the light falling on his blond hair, cutting shadows beneath his cheekbones, his long jawline. Then his laughter died away. 'No, dear cousin,' he said. 'Now – now I am nothing.' He sighed and then smiled. 'Forget all that,' he said, his eyes suddenly alight. 'Now we shall have another brandy and I shall tell you of the wonders of Mexican sunsets and amphetamine queens . . .'

It was after twelve when Roger got back to his flat. He paid off the taxi, which had dropped Orlando off ten minutes earlier, and went up the grimy stone steps to the house. As he fitted his key into the lock, Roger glanced at the peeling paintwork, conscious of the thump of reggae music from the house across the street. He entered his silent flat and closed the door, then stopped in the little hallway to light a cigarette. Clicking his lighter shut, he gazed around at the depressing squalor of the place, lit by the sickly pallor of a 40-watt bulb which he had never bothered to change. He went through to the kitchen, found himself a glass, rinsed it under the tap and splashed it full of neat vodka. He went back into the living room and sat down slowly on the battered green sofa, idly fingering the remnants of the gold braiding as his glance wandered round the room. He would be thirty next week, and this was as far as he had come in life. He had wasted his looks, his intelligence, and a trust fund of several hundred thousands. That very morning he had spent a good forty-five minutes with the manager of the branch at which he banked, and had been told that he had exactly £2,414.63 in his account, the remains of the proceeds of the sale of his great uncle's Seagos. After that was gone, no overdraft could be arranged for him without security of some kind. Roger had nothing he could offer by way of collateral. Quite the opposite. The flint-faced female bank manager had an inkling of Roger's personal history. And so Roger had withdrawn the entire balance from his account, given two thousand of it to Leon, the dealer, and had spent most of the remainder that evening at the Savoy and on taxi fares. He had a twenty-pound note and a handful of loose change in his pocket.

Roger stared at the dusty electric bar heater in the fireplace, at his battered portable colour television and the handful of videos, and then at the old Ferguson record player with the stack of treasured LPs next to it. He drank some of the vodka, then leaned forward, drew on his cigarette, and pressed the heel of his hand against his forehead and closed his eyes. The blond, shoulder-length hair had slipped free of the pony tail and fell around his shoulders. He sat thus for a long while, thinking.

He thought of the stash which he had brought from Leon and put away just as Orlando had arrived this evening. Enough heroin to last two weeks, at the outside – beyond that, he couldn't think. He had known from the very beginning, from the day in hospital when he had told Orlando that he would try to get clean, that this would happen. He could not cope without drugs. He had no life without them. What else was there to live for? This barren flat, the days dragging out their interminable length . . . As for Stow Stocksley, all the great wealth and wonders he was supposed to inherit some-day – what did any of that signify? His uncle could live for another twenty years, and Roger could not even envisage the next two months. And wasn't that the real point of Orlando's great mission to save him from himself – simply to protect and preserve that which Roger himself knew he would dissipate and destroy utterly, if he were to inherit it all tomorrow?

He drank off the remains of the vodka, then got up from the sofa and went over to the window. He pulled up the rickety sash and the night air blew in, fluttering the grimy net curtain. The music across the street had stopped, and only the distant sound of traffic, occasional footsteps in the street, broke the quiet of the London summer night. Roger thought of the heroin which he had bought from Leon that evening. A fix tonight, another tomorrow morning, then another . . . until it was all gone. Then what? When he was in that sordid spiral, anything could happen, desperation would spawn one squalid event after another. He remembered how in the past he had stolen from his mother, forged his sister's cheques, shoplifted, begged abjectly from weary and estranged friends. All without shame. That would begin again. And this time Orlando, too, would become a part of the lies and pleas, deceptions and false promises.

Roger turned to stare at his reflection, his own haunted eyes, his lined cheeks, in the mirror above the mantelpiece. He had lost his very soul, he thought; it had rotted and mouldered to dust long ago. He turned away, groping in his jacket pocket for his cigarettes, and lit another. Then he pulled off his jacket and flung it on the sofa, and stood in the middle of the room for a long moment, his arms at his sides, smoke trickling up against his yellowed fingers. He went across to the light switch by the kitchen door and ripped back the masking tape which held it in place against the wall. The plate dangled against the wall, and Roger put his hand carefully into the cavity of tangled wires and pulled out a cellophane bag filled with white powder. He dropped it into the palm of his other hand, feeling the familiar, slack weight of its slightness, its greatness. He pressed the switch plate clumsily back into place with the tape and, crossing to the table, dropped the bag on to it. Then he went into his bedroom and fished his bag of works from the chest of drawers, and brought it back through. He stood for a moment in the silence of the room, staring round.

'Some music, I think,' he murmured to himself, and went over to the stack of records. He fingered through them and eventually drew one out. Sliding the disc from its sleeve, he placed it carefully on the turntable, pressed the 'start' button and watched the LP revolve, the stylus jigger across and down, settling on the lightly scratched black vinyl. Then he straightened up, went over to the table, and drew up a wooden chair next to it and sat down. He unbuttoned the cuff of his silk shirt and rolled it to the top of his arm, staring down at the silky flesh of his inner arm, the healing veins, the purplish patch where the abscess had been. He set about cooking the heroin, retrieving his little platinum lighter from the mantelpiece for this purpose, watching the flame, feeling neither fear nor remorse in this intentional destruction of the work of the past few weeks, or anguish for himself. This was simply a ritual, these the motions of a professional – the musician tuning his intrument, the surgeon scrubbing up, the free-fall parachutist checking his harness. When that was done and the syringe filled, the tip of the needle pregnant with a shimmering drop of the drug, Roger pulled the silk scarf from his neck and wound it round his arm. He stared for a moment at the syringe, which contained more than enough for his purpose, and hummed a little as Andy sang, 'We're Almost There'. He smiled as the voice swooped and fell – oh, that lovely, tugging, yearning sound, those notes of anticipation and promise. '. . . Soon we'll share a paradise, a paradise, a dream come true . . .' he sang softly to himself as he flexed his arm over and over. And then the needle struck and the plunger went down, and the voluptuous tide swept through his body and carried him into oblivion for the last time, just as the curtain at the window lifted and billowed slightly in the night air, then fell slack.

It was two days later that Orlando found him, when he went round to visit late on Sunday evening. There followed a bizarre, nightmarish hour, in which Orlando rang for an ambulance, then sat outside on the front steps of Roger's house watching the trickle of human traffic on the night street, unable to bring himself to go back into the flat. It seemed grotesque that while he had been busy seeing friends, cooking, eating, reading, being, Roger had just lain there, the hours passing over him without meaning.

When the ambulance had come and gone he went back inside, feeling faintly nauseated by the presence of death still in the air. He glanced across at the record player, which had fallen silent at the end of the LP two days before, but whose red light still glowed. He went over and switched it off, then came back over to the table and stared down at the litter of Roger's drug paraphernalia. His foot crunched on the syringe which had slipped from Roger's fingers and lain on the floor since Friday night, giving him a small, unpleasant shock. He looked down and kicked at the shards with his foot, then noticed the open cellophane bag on the table, its white powdery contents. He stared at it for a moment or two. For some reason which he did not fully understand or explore, Orlando picked it up, wound the little wire tie around its neck, and slipped it into his pocket, then felt his heart begin to thud as he saw the revolving, flashing blue light of the police car in the dark street outside. He was debating whether or not to put the bag back when a policeman stepped into the room. And then it was too late.

The policeman nodded to Orlando and glanced round, his gaze resting briefly on the litter on the table, and the shards of glass on the floor.

'I take it you're Mr D'Ewes? You found the deceased's body?'

Orlando nodded. He saw through the open window that a small knot of passers-by had gathered at the front of the house, idly interested by the presence of the police. 'Yes. He was my cousin.'

'I see. Well, we'll be needing a statement from you, sir.'

'What, now?'

'Tomorrow morning will do.' The radio at the policeman's shoulder crackled, then fell silent. 'There's no hurry.'

Not any more, thought Orlando, and he rose and went out, down the steps to the pavement. He had an irrational half-expectation that the policeman would suddenly stop him, and search his pockets, but nothing of that kind happened. He wandered listlessly home, but when he reached the flat he did not go up. Thoughts were chasing through his brain, guilty, futile thoughts, and he realised that he badly needed to talk to someone. He stood irresolutely on the pavement for a few moments, then got into his car and drove round to Jo's.

It was a while before she opened the door. At first he thought that she might be out, that she had gone on somewhere after her stint at the wine bar. But she opened the door at last and looked round it sleepily. Her eyes widened in surprise when she saw Orlando, and without saying anything she slipped off the chain and let him in.

'Come through,' she said, aware from his face that something had happened, and led him into the living room, pulling her silky lemon-coloured wrap closer around her. The room was very small, and the kitchen no more than an alcove with a cooker, fridge and sink tucked behind a breakfast bar. But it was cosy, in an exotic, haphazard fashion, the floor covered with rugs, a heap of cushions and a couple of throws piled in one corner. She had hung large coloured silk scarves around the room, draped from the ceiling and over lamps, so that the atmosphere was muted and faintly mysterious. Wind chimes, wicker birds and Chinese paper ornaments hung from the ceiling.

'Come and sit down,' she said, 'and tell me what's up.'

He threw himself down on the heap of cushions and she sat near him, drawing her knees up and hugging them, gazing at him with her pale brown eyes. She yawned and rumpled her hair with one hand, waiting.

'It's Roger,' said Orlando flatly. 'He's dead. He must have taken an overdose. I went round to his flat this evening, and there he was. Shit . . .' He leaned his head on his arms, and Jo wondered if he was going to cry. She had felt an initial sense of shock, but was oddly not surprised by the news. She reached out and touched Orlando's arm, but when he looked up there were no tears. He simply sighed, then said, 'I was so convinced that he'd stopped, that eventually he would find something to do and would be all right.' Orlando stared into space, remembering the past few weeks, Roger's rage at his own futility, the despair he had spoken of. Even during those brilliant, amusing few hours at the Savoy, the dreariness of the future must all have seemed too much for him. It must have overwhelmed him. 'I was so complacent,' murmured Orlando. 'I was so naive. Maybe if I hadn't interfered, he wouldn't be dead now.'

'He was the one who went to the rehab centre,' said Jo. 'You didn't force him.'

'No,' said Orlando, 'but I didn't help – going round all the time, assuming that it would be easy for him, talking about finding things to do to fill his time. As though if he could just be like me, it would all be so easy. "Look, Roger, I'm happy, I'm straight – why can't you just be like me?" Jesus.' He laid his head on his arms again.

'You did a lot for him,' said Jo.

'I did nothing for him. Not really,' said Orlando, and looked up at her. Then he remembered, and dipped his hand into his pocket. 'I picked this up from the table in his flat just before the police came. Don't ask me why.' He held up the little bag of heroin. 'You take it. Get rid of it. Whatever.'

She took it from him thoughtfully, and carried it with her to the alcove. 'I'll make you some tea,' she said.

She sat back down next to him and handed him a mug of tea. He drank it silently, then turned to look at her. 'I'm sorry I

252

woke you up,' he said. 'I just needed to talk to someone. Dan didn't know Roger. You did – at least, a bit.' He felt weary, and suddenly filled with an overwhelming need to be touched, held. He thought of every resolution he had ever made about Jo, and discarded them in that instant. He needed someone too much, and there was no one else. He pushed back her hair from her face and looked at her. She did not take her eyes from his, sensing that this was her moment, that if she was to have what she had long wanted, she must take it now. He pulled her towards him and kissed her for a long moment and, when he lifted his head to push her back against the cushions, pulling down her robe from around her shoulders, she smiled to herself.

Chapter Seventeen

Orlando went to the funeral, which took place four days before Roger's thirtieth birthday, but nothing was said between him and Roger's immediate family. He had written to Roger's mother the previous week concerning the contents of the flat, which he had managed to salvage, but she had not replied. Nor did she attempt to speak to him at the funeral. Her thin, carefully made-up face looked out from behind the elegant mist of her black veil with eyes of tired indifference, as though she had dismissed her son from the ranks of the truly living years ago. Orlando gazed with curiosity at the tall, thickset figure of Barney Stafford-Roper, at the handsome, bloated features which echoed Roger's, and wondered whether all the disappointments he had felt in his son were already too great for his death to matter much. Sir Leonard approached Barney by the graveside afterwards, and although he could hear nothing of their brief exchange, Orlando saw the two men shake hands, and then part. Was his grandfather relieved by Roger's death, he wondered?

Sir Leonard walked across the turf to where Orlando stood, his manner grave but businesslike. He had murmured appropriate sentiments of regret regarding Roger when he and Orlando had first met at the church, and had nothing more to say about him.

'Are you busy this weekend?' he asked.

'Not very. I'm seeing some people on Friday evening, but that's all.'

'Good. I was wondering, in that case, whether you would

care to come down for the weekend. There is something I wish to discuss with you – now is not really the time or place.'

'Yes, fine,' replied Orlando, slightly bemused. 'I'll come down on Saturday in time for lunch.'

'Excellent.' Sir Leonard hesitated, then added. 'There will be someone else there. I should like it if you could stay over until Sunday, if you can.' Orlando nodded. 'Well – I shall expect you on Saturday, then.' And he left Orlando at Roger's graveside.

Orlando arrived at Stow Stocksley the following Saturday just before twelve. He parked his car in the shade of an ancient wisteria, and as he got out, he saw his grandfather coming up to the house across the park from the direction of the lake, Midas fat and wheezing at his heels. He stood and waited as his grandfather approached.

'Orlando – just in time for lunch. Good journey?'

'Not bad,' replied Orlando. 'Just under an hour. It's much better since they finished those roadworks near the by-pass.'

They walked together across the gravel towards the house. Sir Leonard squinted up at the sun, and Orlando glanced at him. His grandfather seemed nervous, as though collecting his thoughts in preparation to say something.

'How's work?' asked Sir Leonard.

'Fine,' said Orlando.

'And your aunts? Well?'

'Yes,' said Orlando, following his grandfather out of the summer sunshine and into the coolness of the flagged hall. 'Cicely was asking after you when I spoke to her last week. She said it was a long time since she'd seen you. Said something about a lecture you might like to attend. She'll probably call you.'

His grandfather murmured something in a distracted way, then as they reached the door leading into the drawing room, he stopped, laying a hand on Orlando's arm.

'I think I should tell you now why I asked you to come down this weekend. There is – ah – no easy way of giving you my news without it coming as something of a shock. I thought it would be better if I told you while you were here.' Sir Leonard hesitated, and Orlando looked at him questioningly. 'You were probably not aware that I had met Anne – your aunt?'

'No,' said Orlando. 'I didn't know that. When did you meet her?' he asked, wondering what all this was about.

'Well, I had received some slightly disturbing news from Cicely about your friendship with Roger, and since Anne was the source, I thought it better to speak to her before taking it up with you. So, when I came up to London a few months ago, I called on her. I have – we have seen a great deal of one another since then.' There was a silence. 'I have formed – well, a great attachment to her. I believe it is reciprocated.' Another silence. 'In fact, I have asked her to marry me, and she has consented. She is here at Stow Stocksley this weekend.'

Sir Leonard had avoided Orlando's gaze as he spoke, but now he looked directly at him and smiled. Orlando had not the faintest idea what to say. He was completely staggered by what his grandfather had just told him, and frankly a little embarrassed by its implications. His mind found it difficult to cope with the notion that Anne and his own grandfather must, he presumed, be lovers. He looked away, thrust his hands into his trouser pockets, and then laughed.

'Good grief . . .' he murmured, and ran a hand through his dark hair. He glanced up at his grandfather, and realised that Sir Leonard was regarding him with a faintly whimsical expression, anxious to gauge his reaction. 'Well . . . whew! You certainly know how to take the wind out of someone's sails . . . Anne . . .' He shook his head. 'You're really getting married?'

Sir Leonard nodded.

'Well –' Orlando took a hand from his pocket and held it out. 'Congratulations. I still can't quite . . .'

'Well, come and see Anne,' said Sir Leonard, opening the drawing room door. 'I know she's been as nervous about this as I.'

Anne was standing at the far end of the room, next to the large french windows, which were open to the garden. She turned as Orlando and Sir Leonard came in, and smiled hesitantly as Orlando approached her. They kissed, and then Orlando said, 'I can't tell you how astonished I am. But I'm very happy for you. Congratulations.'

'Thank you,' said Anne. Orlando looked at her, trying to assess her in this new light. Had she assumed some air of maturity, something more fitting to the future lady of Stow Stocksley Hall? She was wearing a dark blue, sleeveless linen dress, with a blue and cream silk scarf, and pearls. He had never seen her wear pearls before, and wondered if they were a gift from his grandfather. She seemed carefully dressed – in fact, the Anne he knew would not normally be dressed this way for the weekend. She would be wearing Armani jeans and a loose shirt, sandals.

'I would have rung you in London to tell you,' she said, 'but we thought it would be best if you came here and Leonard told you.'

It glanced lightly off his consciousness, the way in which she threw away his grandfather's name, lightly, proprietorially.

'I – I think it's wonderful,' said Orlando, not quite sure how to proceed from here. 'Have you told Cicely and Abigail?'

'No,' said Anne. 'I should have, I know. I just haven't got round to it.' She glanced at Sir Leonard. 'You can tell them, if you like.'

'Well, they'll be staggered,' said Orlando. Sir Leonard turned away.

'Shall we have a celebratory drink before lunch?' he said. 'I've asked Mrs Cresswell to bring it out to the terrace, since it's such a lovely day.'

The meal began rather awkwardly. It was the first time that Sir Leonard and Anne had shared themselves as a couple with an outsider – for Orlando, though close to them both, stood in that light – and it was taking Orlando time to adjust his perceptions of Anne and his grandfather in this novel and rather astonishing situation. He was still having trouble identifying his grandfather in his new role. Sir Leonard was no longer just an old man in charge of a country seat, pottering amongst his orchids and his genealogical studies, the widower of Lady Charlotte, one of the ranks of the incipient elderly. He was Anne's accepted lover, someone with whom she shared little secrets of affection and intimacy unknown to others, a rejuvenated being. And Anne – Anne was transformed from being his amusing, worldly young aunt, a sort of surrogate big sister, into a woman in whom his grandfather found depth and fascination.

As the meal progressed, things became easier. He noticed that Anne injected a new warmth into relations with his grandfather. Sir Leonard was more relaxed, laughed a good deal more than he ever had done, and treated Anne with a reserved and dignified affection which Orlando found faintly touching. He could not help wondering how they behaved together in private.

After lunch Sir Leonard went off to attend to estate business, and Orlando and Anne were left alone together.

'I still don't know Stow Stocksley very well, you know,' said Anne. 'I've only been here three times. Why don't you take me round?'

She was being kind to him, he knew, and wondered if she guessed at the sense of possessiveness he suddenly felt for the Hall and its contents. Throughout his life, she had never had anything to do with Stow Stocksley, and now she was about to become mistress of it all. The idea filled him with an irrational distaste.

He led her back through the house, through the drawing room and out into the large, stone-flagged hallway. They went together up the great wooden staircase and along the gallery, he telling her the names of the various ancestral portraits, explaining pieces of domestic social history.

'You know so much about it all,' said Anne.

'I should do,' said Orlando. 'I grew up here.'

Anne sat down on a carved oak settle at the end of the gallery and looked up at him, struck by the note in his voice.

'You don't resent this – I mean, me – do you?' she asked.

Orlando leaned back against the balustrade. 'Resent you? In what way?' He realised as soon as he had spoken that his voice had sounded unintentionally cold. He remembered that Roger had asked him this same question, once.

'I don't want you to feel supplanted. As though I'm intruding on your territory.' She was speaking carefully, anxious to secure his acceptance of the situation.

He said nothing, and then asked suddenly, 'Are you in love with him?'

She looked startled, then said, 'What a strange question. I love him, if that's what you mean. I've never met anyone like him. He's kind and – interesting, and he makes me feel safe. And he's in love with me.' Orlando said nothing. 'Look, Orlando, don't judge me,' went on Anne. 'I do love your grandfather. I know this may all be a little difficult for you. But this is what I want. I'm so very tired of the life I lead, the agency, the constant slog. I'm not so young, you know. The idea of slowing down, marrying, living somewhere as lovely as this, not having to worry... It's very appealing, you know.'

She has what she always wanted, thought Orlando. It's just as she used to say. Some splendid house in the country, someone to take care of her, enough money to do whatever she wants. He turned and gazed down from the gallery into the stone-flagged hall below. 'How do you think you'll like being the lady of the manor, hobnobbing with all the local worthies?' he asked.

'Oh, I shall conquer them all with my charm and wit,' said Anne, smiling.

Orlando wondered if she realised how slow, how dull and reserved most of the people around Stow Stocksley were. The County people. Had she met many? And what would they think of Sir Leonard's new young bride? He wondered if she intended to fill Stow Stocksley's annual garden party with her fashionable London friends, and how they would all fit in with Sir Leonard's long-established acquaintances. Had his grandfather thought about any of this, or did an old man in love not bother to consider such things?

He turned round. 'I hope you'll be very happy,' he said.

She glanced at him as if for reassurance, but his face was, as ever, quite impassive. 'I know everything you're thinking,' she said suddenly. 'You think that this may be some mercenary thing, that I simply want money and security. But I do love Leonard.'

'Good,' said Orlando, and suddenly realised that he could not face the claustrophobic prospect of remaining here with them both for the entire weekend.

He made plausible excuses and escaped the following morning. It wasn't until late on Sunday afternoon that he realised that Cicely and Abigail did not yet know the momentous tidings, and he called them. Abigail answered the phone, and Orlando relayed the news to her.

'No!' she said, clutching the phone to her ear. 'I don't believe it!' She turned away and gave a guilty glance in the direction of the kitchen, where Cicely was busy defrosting the freezer with the aid of a hair dryer.

'Takes a bit of getting used to, doesn't it?' said Orlando. 'I was at Stow Stocksley with them both this weekend. Very much the loving couple.'

'Well, how extraordinary,' said his aunt, busily revolving in her mind the most effective way of breaking this news to her sister. 'Very odd, to certain ways of thinking. One's grandfather marrying one's aunt. But, then, they're not exactly related, are they? Except through you . . . But he is twice her age. Do you think they're suited? I mean, he's not at all the kind of man I would have expected Anne . . . But, then, the ways of true love. Ah, well, I must go and tell Cicely.'

'You do that. I hope she's pleased.'

'Mmm.' Abigail suddenly realised that Orlando was probably unaware of the extent of Cicely's infatuation with Sir Leonard. 'Thank you for letting us know, dear. Bye.' As Abigail put the phone down, Cicely came through from the kitchen, an old scarf tied round her head, the hair dryer in one hand and a palette knife in the other.

'Who's twice whose age? What must you tell me?' she asked, her face red from the exertion of scraping ice from the freezer element. Abigail glanced at the palette knife.

'I think you'd better put those things down and come through here,' she said, disarming Cicely and leading her into the living room. Cicely sat down at the dining table opposite Abigail and said, 'Who was that on the phone? Why are you looking like that?'

Abigail looked at her sister's pink, plump face, the stray locks of hair escaping from the headscarf, and felt something almost like sympathy.

'That was Orlando. He had some news.'

'Oh?' As Cicely gazed at the expression on her sister's face, its badly-concealed mixture of triumph and pity, she felt suddenly afraid. It was the same look Abigail had worn when she announced that she was going to France with Michael, instead of to Frinton with Cicely.

Abigail spent a few seconds debating how best to put it. At last she simply said, 'Anne is getting married.'

'Oh,' said Cicely with relief. 'You had me thinking it was something dreadful for a moment. Oh, so that's who's twice someone's age? I see. Well, I always suspected her of hankering after a father figure.'

'You won't believe who the father figure is,' murmured Abigail.

'Somebody we know? Well, that's a change. She hasn't let us meet any of her boyfriends since she was fifteen.' Cicely pulled the scarf from her hair and ran a hand through her rumpled perm. 'Who is it?' An absurd, chilling suspicion struck her as soon as she had uttered the words. Her hand remained frozen in mid-air. She stared at her sister.

'Sir Leonard,' replied Abigail, and could look at her sister no longer.

Cicely's hand descended slowly to her lap. 'Sir Leonard?' She could hardly comprehend it. 'But when –?'

'I suppose,' said Abigail, 'that they must have met when Sir Leonard went to see her about Orlando. You remember – all that inflated nonsense about Roger? You gave him her address and telephone number.'

Cicely felt her mouth trembling. All that time – all that time spent hoping, imagining . . . God, what a fool she had been. She turned away from her sister, then rose. For a moment she stood there, remembering the visits to Stow Stocksley, the little trips to Vincent Square and Kew Gardens. The tête-à-tête meals. Then she thought of Anne – Anne with her brilliant smile and girlish figure, amusing, polished Anne, sophisticated and young. All the things she, Cicely, was not. She felt a dreadful bitterness rising within her. The man was a fool. An utter fool.

'I had better go and finish defrosting the freezer,' she said, and left the room.

Orlando reacted to his grandfather's impending marriage to Anne in two ways. On an adult level, he told himself that his grandfather had every right to conduct himself as he pleased and find happiness where he thought he could, and that he should be pleased for them both. But the childish, irrational part of his character, the one which had reacted with such a sense of betrayal to his grandmother's death, could not accept the matter in this way. There grew within him a jealous resentment of the fact that Anne was to become mistress of Stow Stocksley. It seemed to him that she had intervened between himself and his grandfather, that he would be pushed aside once the marriage had taken place, and might no longer be permitted to treat Stow Stocksley as his home.

Much of this was subconscious, but it manifested itself in a certain bitterness towards his grandfather. It seemed to Orlando that life, from the very beginning, had been a series of losses and betrayals, false promises and unfulfilled expectations. Now, by marrying Anne, his grandfather would be adding to this catalogue, excluding Orlando and destroying the illusion of his own pre-eminence in his grandfather's affections.

He was beginning to wish, too, that he had never allowed Jo to become his lover. He knew it was a mistake, and that they should simply have remained friends. He did not feel strongly enough about her for the thing to work, and the newly-developed sexual element in their relationship seemed somehow to be robbing it of the affection which had once characterised it. He was aware that his behaviour towards her was careless and sometimes selfish, but he found himself unable to end the affair entirely. He needed her, or someone, in whom to seek solace from the confusions and upsets in his life.

His growing sense of isolation was compounded by the discovery that Dan was moving out of the flat. Orlando came home late one evening and found Dan sitting up waiting for him, watching television. He switched off the set as soon as he heard Orlando come in.

'Hi,' said Orlando. 'Want a cup of coffee? I'm just going to make one.'

'No,' said Dan. 'I want to talk to you.' Orlando nodded slowly and took off his jacket. 'Jo rang. She said you were supposed to pick her up this evening.'

'Oh, God – was I? I forgot.' Orlando rubbed a hand across his face. It had completely slipped his mind. He would ring her tomorrow, make it up to her.

'Anyway, that's not what I waited up to talk to you about. I wanted to tell you that I've decided to move out.'

Orlando paused in the act of loosening his tie. 'Why?'

'Oh, come on, Paddy – you know why. It's not been working for a while now. If it ever did. The fact is, you've got money, a car, your grandfather gives you whatever you want, whereas I'm scraping along on what I get from the magazine, and being made to feel I'm not paying my way. Look at that argument we had the other day about the phone bill . . . The whole thing's just causing resentment.' He looked squarely at Orlando. 'Admit it.'

Orlando shrugged. 'If it's just about money, we can always sort something out.' Even as he said this, he knew it was untrue. They had had too many disagreements. It was the one serious flaw in the domestic arrangement.

'No, we can't. The fact is, I can't afford to live with you.'

There was silence for a moment, and then Orlando said, 'Is this something to do with Jo?'

'What are you getting at?'

'Come on. I know you've got a thing for her.' This was true, and Orlando had become increasingly aware of a certain tension in the flat when Jo was around. He knew that Dan thought that he behaved badly towards Jo, and felt guiltily resentful of Dan's implicit disapproval of him.

Dan broke in abruptly. 'That's got nothing to do with it.' He paused, then added, 'But, if you want to know, I think you're a complete bastard where she's concerned.'

'Oh?' Orlando stared at him coldly.

'You know you're out of her league and you just string her along. What is there for her in the long run? You can't exactly take her home to meet Grandpa at his stately home, can you? So why do you bother?'

'I hardly think it's any of your business, frankly,' replied Orlando.

Dan gave a sigh of exasperation. 'Anyway, she's beside the point. The point is you and me, Paddy. We don't have the same values. I don't like what you do and the way you do it. So I'm going before we lose a good friendship.'

'Fair enough,' said Orlando. His tone was casual, but he was far more upset and astonished by this defection than he wanted to admit. 'Where will you go?'

'There's a couple of guys at work who have a squat in Camden. It's pretty good, actually. I mean, nothing like this –' He smiled sardonically, glancing round at the snug, nicely furnished flat. '– but at least we'll be on an equal footing. I won't have to feel second-rate.'

'I didn't know you felt that,' said Orlando quietly.

'Aye, well in some ways I do, and in other ways –' His gaze met Orlando's and he paused. 'But I don't want us to part on a hard note.'

'We won't,' said Orlando. 'I'm just sorry you want to go.'

'I'll make us that coffee,' said Dan, and went through to the kitchen.

Orlando stood in the living room, slowly loosening his tie, conscious of a further sense of loneliness, a feeling that life was slipping in ways which he did not want it to, but which he was helpless to prevent.

Chapter Eighteen

Four weeks later, Orlando received his formal invitation to the wedding of Anne and Sir Leonard. It was to be held on the 17th of August at Stow Stocksley Parish Church, with a reception at the Hall afterwards. Orlando stared at the engraved invitation, and realised that he hadn't spoken to his grandfather for weeks, since the last time he had been to Stow Stocksley, when Anne had been there. Well, there was nothing to talk about. With an ever-present sense of resentment he placed the invitation on the mantelpiece, and was suddenly aware of a childish desire to do something to irritate or upset them both. It was as he stared at the invitation that it occurred to him to take Jo to the wedding. Why not? She was his girlfriend. And they could all think what they wanted.

He decided to mention it to Anne when he went round to her flat in Chelsea the following day. She had asked him to help her pack certain belongings away, to go into storage until she sold the place, in the hope that she could discover the cause of his recent lack of communication with his grandfather. She knew that Sir Leonard was disquieted by it.

'What I really want,' she said, as she piled books into boxes, 'is a house near the river. Cheyne Walk, somewhere like that. It's a question of talking your grandfather into it. He thinks the flat in Belgravia is good enough, but quite frankly, I don't like other people's furniture. I'd rather have somewhere larger, too, less stuffy. He says it's not worthwhile buying somewhere in London, that we won't spend enough time here to justify it, but he's wrong there. I don't intend to spend all my life at Stow Stocksley. I'm too fond of London for that . . . Now,' she said, getting to her feet, 'I think we both deserve a drink. By the way,' she added, as she went through to the kitchen, 'Leonard was wondering why he hadn't heard from you recently. He'd hoped you might come down last weekend.'

Orlando, packing bedding into a large polythene bag, merely said, 'I've been rather busy.'

It occurred to Anne, as she poured them both a glass of wine, to pursue the subject, to confront the resentment which she knew existed, and then she decided against it. He would come round eventually and, anyway, it was a matter for Orlando and Leonard to sort out between them. She brought the glasses through and handed one to Orlando. 'By the way,' she said, 'have you met the next baronet and future heir to the almighty estate of Stow Stocksley?'

'No,' said Orlando, genuinely surprised. 'Who is it? I honestly hadn't given it any thought.' This was true. Even at the time of Roger's death, the question had not occurred to him. He wondered now whether he had subconsciously shut it out.

'Well, you'll meet him at the wedding. He's a cousin of Leonard's, Nicholas D'Ewes. He's about forty, married, with a family, and he's something high and mighty at Sotheby's, or Phillip's, one of those places. He's a far more civilised prospect than Roger ever was, and he's a D'Ewes.'

Orlando felt an odd little pang at hearing this, and then reminded himself that at least Stow Stocksley would not suffer the ruinous fate of Capercailzie, that in the lottery of fortune its prosperity might be allowed to continue uninterrupted for a few more generations.

'Hmm. Well, he'll be able to give his future property the once-over when he comes to your wedding, won't he? Which reminds me – I wonder if you'd mind if I brought someone. To the wedding, I mean.'

268

Anne sipped her wine. 'Certainly. Who is it?'

'My girlfriend.'

'Well, I guessed that. Who is she?'

Orlando paused, then lifted his glass. 'It's Jo.' He took a swift drink of his wine.

'Jo? Who's Jo?' Anne looked away, frowning, then back at him. 'What – not that girl you met at the night club?' She looked shocked. 'The prostitute?'

'Yes,' said Orlando idly. 'As a matter of fact, it is. Not that she's one any more.'

'Oh, Orlando!' exclaimed Anne. 'I don't believe, out of all the women in London, that you're seeing her! What on earth are you thinking of? I thought she was just a friend – as though one wants friends of that type.'

'Well, she's become rather more than that now.'

'I can't believe you're being so stupid! I mean – do you think you can introduce her to people? That because she's not on the game any more that makes it all right? Have you got no taste, Orlando? What do you think your grandfather is going to say?'

'He can say what he likes,' replied Orlando. 'It's none of his business, after all.'

'How can you say that? He has a right to expect you to behave decently, not to take up with tarts and God knows who else!' Orlando watched her, aware that there was something perverse in his sense of satisfaction at her exasperation and disgust. But he was almost beginning to wish that he had not started this. What was he hoping to achieve? Then she added, 'Besides, he's hardly going to be very keen to establish your trust fund when he hears about this, is he?'

This hit home. Orlando's heart dropped. He had forgotten all about the business of his trust fund – it had been years since his grandfather had mentioned it, but he must have been talking to Anne about it recently, presumably with the intention of establishing it quite soon – maybe some vague sense of guilt at his own forthcoming marriage had prompted it. But what he had said about Jo could not now be unsaid. Something of this must have shown in his face, for Anne went on, 'Well, I can't dictate to you. It's your life. Ruin it your own way. I don't suppose I can stop you bringing whom you want to the wedding. But please don't expect me to speak to her.'

Orlando left the flat in a state of morose anger. The matter of Jo was neither here nor there. He was angry with himself for reacting with such trepidation to the threat that his grandfather might withdraw his benefaction if Orlando's behaviour did not meet required standards. He felt that this was a continuation of the same control which had been exerted over him by his grandfather throughout his life – first in the matter of the inheritance of Stow Stocksley, which had come to nothing, and now in the matter of his trust fund. Well, he earned a decent salary. He did not need to bow to the moral dictates of Sir Leonard. The more he dwelt on these things, the more Orlando resolved to behave exactly as he pleased, even if – particularly if – it incurred the displeasure of his grandfather.

In the event, he did not take Jo to the wedding, but his decision not to only confused and irritated him more. He felt that he was giving in in some way, compromising himself for the sake of his grandfather's money. But he was relieved to have been spared the ordeal of introducing her to his friends and family, which he suspected would have ruined his day entirely.

Cicely and Abigail were both there, the latter in a washed-out Laura Ashley number and canvas espadrilles, plus her father's panama, and the former in cherry silk, with shoes, bag and broad-brimmed hat to match. Cicely's original reaction had been to refuse the wedding invitation outright, but she eventually realised that this would not only look churlish, and be tantamount to an outright admission of her own disappointed hopes, but it might also have the effect of estranging her from Sir Leonard entirely. This was something she did not want. The pleasures of being the lady of Stow Stocksley might have been denied her (and she spent a good deal of time reassuring herself that she would have found the whole thing too much), but she still wished to maintain the association, as it was one which she felt gave her a certain amount of prestige amongst her Reigate circle.

It was at the end of the day, when most guests were departing, that Sir Leonard found an opportunity to speak to Orlando alone. He took his arm and led him across the bright and beautifully-mown grass to the shade of some trees. It was late in the afternoon, and a light summer wind billowed the canvas of the large marquee. Orlando, who had drunk more champagne than was good for him, still held a half-finished glass in his hand.

'Orlando, I hadn't expected to talk to you about something like this on my wedding day, but as Anne and I shall be away for some time, I find I must.' Orlando stiffened, preparing himself. 'Anne has told me about the young woman whom you are seeing. I can't tell you how deeply it disappoints me that you could form a relationship with such a person, but I do not intend to lecture you. Merely to advise you. You are a D'Ewes, and you have a name and a position to uphold. People will watch what you do, they will judge you. My advice to you is to end this relationship before it harms you and your reputation.'

Although he was aware of rising anger, Orlando managed to laugh. 'Grandfather, I don't care about my name! If it means that much to you, I'll happily go back to the one I was born with. What's the difference, after all? And I will do as I please with my own life, since that's exactly what you are doing with yours. For all you know, I may care very much for Jo, just as much as you do for Anne – do you honestly think that I would put a stop to it, just because you disapprove? You've got a pretty poor idea of me, in that case.'

Sir Leonard tried to keep his temper. He could see that Orlando was slightly drunk. He would try one more tactic. 'Anne tells me that she mentioned to you that I had intended to set up a trust fund on your behalf at the end of the year. I had supposed that you would have shown yourself sufficiently responsible and that your life might be moving in a sensible direction. That clearly is not the case –'

'I don't care about your money!' said Orlando furiously. 'You may think you're punishing me, but I don't need your help. I live my own life! I have a job, I can pay my own way, and I don't need to take your handouts just so that you can dictate what I do and who I see! All my life people have been telling me what to think, the right way to do things, turning me into the kind of person they want me to be. And have I ever once turned round and said "no"? Well, I wish I had! You can keep your money!' And he turned round and stalked away across the grass.

Sir Leonard sighed, and stood there for a few moments. He had not realised until now how deeply Orlando had been affected by his marriage to Anne. But he saw now that there were currents which ran deep within the young man, and which he did not understand. He supposed that Orlando had been given expectations throughout his life, and they had been, to an extent, disappointed. Well, if this was his revenge, let him play it out. He looked up at Orlando's retreating figure in the distance. He had enough faith to suppose that Orlando would see sense, and that the relationship with this girl would not last. Perhaps it would be best if he left the boy alone for a month or two, until life had become more settled. Sir Leonard's thoughts turned to the honeymoon cruise to Madeira which he and Anne had planned. They were to leave tomorrow. Glancing round the park, Sir Leonard realised that he would perhaps have been happy enough to stay here at Stow Stocksley, enjoying the mild early autumn and overseeing

272

preparations for the shooting season. But he was married now, and whatever made Anne happy, he was prepared to do.

Orlando took a lift back to London with friends, and returned home to his empty flat in the middle of the evening. The effects of the champagne were wearing off, and he felt morose and irritable. He vaguely regretted the fact of having quarrelled with his grandfather on his wedding day, but regretted none of the things which he had said. Nobody had any right to dictate to him, or try to bribe him into acting as they wished. That was what it came down to.

Nursing his anger, he wandered through to the kitchen, and wished for an instant that he had someone to come home to. He and Dan might have had their differences, but at least he was someone to talk to. He thought of Jo, who would be working in the wine bar right now. He wished that she was coming here afterwards, instead of to Battersea, that he could just sink into bed with her, and have the comfort of her warm, compliant body. The thought made the empty silence of the flat all the more stark. Well, why shouldn't he have her here if he wanted to? He had made his position clear to his grandfather. There was no way anyone was going to set up a trust fund for him now, anyway. He might as well do as he pleased. Yes, he decided, tomorrow he would ask her to move in with him. Then, for a while at least, he would feel less lonely, less isolated. And he would show them that he intended to lead his life exactly as he pleased.

By the time Sir Leonard had returned from the cruise, his resolve to leave Orlando alone for a month or so had weakened. He decided to invite Orlando to dine with him at his club, hoping that he might be able to heal the divisions created at their last meeting. He would prefer not to quarrel with his grandson, and had decided that he would try to treat the matter of Orlando's relationship with this eminently unsuitable young woman in a more diplomatic and less alarmist fashion. After all, young men of Orlando's age had relationships with girls of varying degrees of importance. This one might even be a thing of the past by the time he and Orlando met. He had reasoned to himself that Orlando's own innate sense of propriety would ensure the thing did not last long.

Orlando was therefore relieved to find his grandfather in pretty cordial humour when they met at his club. For the first hour or so they talked of Madeira, Sir Leonard confessing that, while he had been pleased that Anne had enjoyed the cruise, he had often wished himself back at Stow Stocksley.

'I'm afraid that Anne is much more energetic than I am. Really I am quite happy to spend my time pottering in the library. Anyway, I am going back down to Stow Stocksley tonight and she is staying on in town for a week or two. She is not, I'm afraid, very fond of the flat in Belgravia which I took last spring. She seems keen to find somewhere else . . .' He stared at the remains of his Beef Wellington, his expression thoughtful, and Orlando wondered how much thought his grandfather had ever given to the differences, both physical and mental, between himself and Anne. Perhaps he had had leisure to ponder these during the long weeks of their honeymoon cruise. Orlando suddenly felt sorry that he had ever harboured any ill-feeling concerning their marriage. 'In any event,' said Sir Leonard, changing the subject, 'tell me about yourself. How is your work in the City? Going well?' Before Orlando had a chance to answer, he added, 'I must confess that I was always a little disappointed that you didn't take that offer of a job with Morgan Grenfell. There is something – well, rather fly-by-night about the kind of work which you do. Dealers often strike me as being nothing more than glorified barrow-boys, really.'

Orlando gritted his teeth and replied politely, 'It's going

very well, actually. I finished my one year's probation three weeks ago, so I'm my own man these days.' Sir Leonard merely raised his eyebrows and nodded. 'It's important work, you know,' Orlando went on defensively. 'A lot of the deals I do are for enormous sums.' Feeling that this was a rather feeble justification, he added, 'And I'm earning far more than I would have at Morgan Grenfell.'

'Naturally, at your age that must seem a very important thing,' replied Sir Leonard, a touch sardonically. He could feel incipient indigestion coming on, and it made him feel ill-tempered. He had been having bouts of it ever since the cruise. Really he should have known better than to have the Beef Wellington; pastry always made it worse. 'But there's more to life than money. Isn't there a danger, in the kind of job you are doing, that you could find yourself burnt out in ten years or so, without any other resources? What then?'

'I think I can prove myself,' said Orlando quietly. 'I'm sorry you don't have more faith in my abilities.' He said this defensively, for he was by no means convinced of his own talents. He knew he would never possess Barry's streetwise edge, the hungry, market-sharp insincts of a really good dealer. At that moment he very much wanted to make his grandfather believe that he could succeed, and that he could do so on his own terms.

Sir Leonard could feel his indigestion growing worse, and knew he would have trouble sleeping tonight. Orlando's words made him feel even more irritable, and he began to forget his resolve to behave mildly and diplomatically. 'I find it hard to have faith, Orlando, in someone who has shown such significant lapses in taste and judgement in the past.'

'What do you mean?' asked Orlando.

'I am referring, of course, to your relationship with that streetwalker. I hope that you are not still seeing her?'

'As a matter of fact,' replied Orlando calmly, inwardly

incensed by his grandfather's high-handed tone, 'I'm living with her.'

Sir Leonard's faintly sour expression grew grim. His tone, when he spoke, was one of disgust. 'It seems you are as determined as your late cousin to drag yourself down. What must people think of you? Your behaviour is appalling, quite appalling! I am only glad your grandmother is not alive to witness it! I made it clear when we last met that I had reservations about the establishment of a trust fund for you, and what you tell me only confirms it. I will not provide you with funds to spend on this whore of yours –'

Orlando rose from the table. 'Grandfather,' he interrupted, 'you made the position perfectly clear when we last met. I don't think there's anything more to be said. Goodnight.' He flung down his napkin and stalked out, leaving Sir Leonard bewildered and furious.

Orlando drove moodily back to Kensington. It had been inevitable, once his grandfather had found out about Jo, that they would argue. There hadn't been any point in trying to defend his position where she was concerned. It was indefensible. He had grown to realise, over the past few weeks, that asking Jo to live with him had been a mistake. Everything to do with her was a mistake. The relationship which had survived successfully over three years through occasional platonic meetings now seemed to be disintegrating entirely. Sex was the only thing which held it together. He knew it had to come to an end, but he did not see any way in which to do it without being cruel to Jo.

When he got in, he found Jo curled up in an armchair after her stint at the wine bar, watching the late news. The increasingly familiar, grinning features of the Democratic candidate in the American presidential elections floated across the screen, and Orlando slumped on to the sofa, not bothering to take off his coat, and listened to the newsreader's account of

276

his recent triumphant bout of canvassing in the election run-up. He resolved to put his grandfather from his mind.

'I think he'll get in,' he remarked, biting the side of his finger, staring at the screen. 'I reckon the Americans have probably had enough of the Republicans by now. He's got every chance.'

Jo yawned and looked up from filing her nails. Her demeanour, since the small triumph of being asked by Orlando to live with him, had grown casual and domestic. 'Who is he, anyway?'

'He's the Democratic candidate running for the White House,' said Orlando with faint irritation, wondering why she even bothered watching the news. 'He could be in with a chance, after the way he performed in the primaries.'

'Oh, yeah? It's all above my head, politics and stuff. I don't even understand what's going on in this country, let alone over there.' She examined her nails. 'How was dinner with Grandad?'

Something in the phrasing of the question irked him, as did the sound of her nail file. 'Must you do that in here?' he asked.

She made a little face. 'Sorry.'

'It's just – I mean, that noise puts my teeth on edge.'

'Don't worry. Cup of tea?'

He nodded and took off his coat, and when she came back through with the tea, she curled up next to him on the sofa. 'So – how was it?' she asked again.

'Bloody awful,' said Orlando, rubbing his hands over his face. 'He doesn't like my job, he doesn't seem to think I'm ever going to make anything of it, and he doesn't like you.'

Jo felt a small gust of fear. 'He doesn't even know me.'

'He knows you used to be a call girl –'

'An escort.'

Again irritation swept Orlando. 'What difference does it make what you call it? Anyway, when I told him I was living

277

with you, all hell broke loose. He had been going to set up a trust fund for me, which would have been useful, but I'm certainly not going to see any of that money as long as I'm still seeing you.'

Jo was silent for a moment. 'Do you care about that? The money, I mean?'

Orlando, who had been considering whether this evening might not be the appropriate time to tell Jo that he wanted to end it, that she should move out, suddenly realised that, by saying what he had just said, he had lost the opportunity. He didn't want anyone, even Jo, thinking that he would allow his grandfather to buy him, dictate to him.

'No,' said Orlando carelessly. She had unbuttoned his shirt and slid her hand across his chest. He looked down at her and, smiling, she reached up to kiss him. 'I don't intend to be blackmailed by anyone,' he added, and kissed her back.

As she heard these words, Jo was suddenly filled with a cold realisation of what must lie ahead. He couldn't go against his family for ever. But she would cross that bridge when she came to it. She could do nothing more than make the best of the present. 'Come to bed,' she whispered.

Over the next week, to take his mind off his emotional problems, Orlando began to pay ever closer attention to the political situation across the Atlantic. He devoured profiles of the presidential candidates, read analyses of their various policies at home and abroad, absorbed the findings of the various polls, and even read the odd article about the fashion sense of the two possible First Ladies. He canvassed colleagues over lunch and discovered that the general view was ambivalent. Some thought the Democrats were damned by their candidate's pro-choice stance on abortion, others agreed with Orlando that the Americans were sick of the Republicans and ripe for change. He immersed himself in the elections, partly as a distraction, and partly because of a scheme which he had recently begun to dream up.

It seemed to him that people were mistaken in assuming that the Republicans would be returned to office, as they had been four years before. His own instincts told him that the Democrats would succeed, surprising everyone. He was sure he was reading the signs correctly. And if that happened, the dollar would fall. It had occurred to Orlando that if someone were to sell a huge amount of dollars before the event, then all they would have to do would be to buy them back at the new low rate straight after the election, when everyone was trying to get rid of them, and thus make a killing. And it occurred to him that he could be that someone.

It wasn't a stupid idea, he told himself – dealers took risks all the time, otherwise they would never make a profit. He became excited by his scheme, by the prospect of showing Mr Pfeiffer, Barry, his grandfather, that he could be a success in his own chosen field. That he could bring something like this off. It was his job, after all. It gave him tremors of nervousness, the thought of risking so much, but he had faith in his instinct. He studied the markets, calculated the rates, worked out just how much he would have to sell and when, and tried to judge just how far the dollar would fall in the event. He did not even stop to think what would happen if he were wrong. If one thought that way, one would never do anything.

For a week he hovered on the brink of putting his plan into action. But something, possibly the enormity of the sums involved, held him back. He would reach for the phone, and then lose his nerve. Every day he meant to go ahead, and every day something prevented him.

But when the US elections were only two weeks away, Orlando came into the dealing room one Monday morning and realised that unless he acted now, the chance would pass for ever. This was his moment. It was going to be his own personal piece of business, he wouldn't even write a confirmation slip, or check it out with the head dealer – things he would normally never think of failing to do. Nobody would know anything about it until he had bought the dollars back, and made his monumental profit.

He had thought he would feel nervous when he picked up the phone to make the transaction, but he didn't.

'I want to sell five hundred million at 1.61 and three-eighths, settlement in three months.' That was all he had to say, and when it was said, the thing was done. He put down the phone, glanced at his screen and, with a sense of unreality, got on with the rest of the morning's work. It wasn't until he was on his way home that evening that the thing actually hit him. He had sold a fortune in dollars, and had no real idea what their price might be when the time came to buy them back. For a split second a wave of panic hit him, and it even occurred to him to buy them back straight away. But it passed in an instant. He would be proved right. He was backing something with good odds – better than good, in fact – and he was going to make the bank a small fortune. Of that he was convinced.

Chapter Nineteen

On the eve of the election, Orlando spent a restless evening at home alone. Jo had gone out to her work at the wine bar, much to his relief. The business of his deal had been preoccupying him to the exclusion of everything else, and he had no desire for anyone's company, least of all hers. He had resolved that, as soon as this thing was over, he would find a way of telling her she must go. He sat watching television, not concentrating properly. Time seemed to be ticking by at a sickeningly slow rate. All across America, he realised, the polls were closing, and the outcome of his gamble had already been decided. He could think of nothing else, was plagued, hot and cold, by doubts and hopes. One moment he would feel supreme confidence, a happy anticipatory exultation at the probability that his prediction would be proved right, and in the next his heart would plummet, and a fear that all this had been a hideous mistake would begin to gnaw at him.

He watched the news, searching for clues but finding none, then went to bed early. Whatever was to happen, he had to be at his desk first thing in the morning. The results would start coming around 7 a.m. in London, when it was midnight in America and the first count had been finalised.

He slept badly, waking when Jo came in and unable to get back to sleep for a long time thereafter. He feigned sleep when she crept into bed next to him, and kissed him lightly. She knew nothing of what he was doing – would have understood even less – and he wanted to lie alone, containing his fears and hopes, until day came and he could learn the best, or the worst.

It was raw and unpleasantly chilly in the deserted City streets at 6.30 in the morning. No one else was in the trading room when he sat down at his desk, slung his jacket over the back of his chair, and flicked on his screen. Already his palms had begun to sweat. The Reuters screen, which stood at a height so that it could be seen by several dealers at once, trickled out news, but nothing yet of the election results. Orlando made himself a cup of coffee, but it grew cold and stale on his desk as he watched the screen and waited. He could not bring himself to swallow it.

A little after seven, the first of the results came on to the screen – Iowa, and it had gone to the Republicans. Orlando's heart dropped like a stone. He watched, clenching and unclenching his palms, as results from the Eastern Seaboard states began to come in. The dealing room was filling up now, people were watching the screen, murmuring conversationally to one another, drinking coffee. Their voices sounded like a roaring river in Orlando's ears. He watched in disbelief as the declarations came in – New Jersey, Delaware, Rhode Island, Maine. He held on pointlessly, he knew, to one last shred of hope until, at 8.40, one of the really big ones came in. California. The Republicans had walked it, the Democrats were nowhere. He sat numbly, staring into space, and then he glanced at his screen. The markets were in action all over the world, and the dollar was rising like a rocket.

Christ, thought Orlando, it was bad, but it could only get worse. He realised that he had no option but to close out his position as fast as possible, to start buying back now, before the rate went any higher and his losses soared. The next ten minutes were spent in frantic activity, and he had no time to think about himself, about the personal repercussions of his actions. The best he could get was a rate of 1.54 – two weeks before, he had confidently and happily anticipated that he would be buying back at between 1.75 and 1.80. Even as he talked on the phone, a part of his mind felt detached, lost in incredulity at his own enormous folly. When it was over, and he had salvaged what he could of his blown and blasted deal, Orlando sat stupefied, staring at his own pencilled calculations, which he had made automatically, in a trancelike state. Far from achieving a triumphant profit, he had lost Amerco West over twenty million dollars. He thought back to the time when he had inadvertently made that simple error which had cost the bank a day's interest. That had seemed bad at the time. Compared to what he had just done, it was nothing. Nothing.

He looked up, gazing around the dealing room, aware of people coming and going, of phones ringing, Barry thrusting a piece of paper in front of him and then hurrying off. What was he to do now? Not only had he taken a position which had risked half a billion of the bank's money, he had exposed them to huge losses. He had signed no slip, deliberately failed to consult his head dealer, and had in every way compounded his folly. His actions might even be seen as verging on the criminal. And in that instant he realised that his job at Amerco West was finished. As of this moment, he knew that he was no longer a dealer. Everything he had done showed that. He thought of all he had hoped to prove to his grandfather, and wondered what possible future there could be for him after this. But worst of all, possibly, were the immediate consequences – he had no option but to go now to his head dealer and tell all. The thought made his blood run cold. And then the interview with Mr Pfeiffer, the knowledge of his astonishing folly trickling back through to the dealing room, his colleagues whispering behind his back, Barry's gratified and cynical reaction . . . Orlando put his head in his hands and almost wept. It was ten past nine on a November morning, and his brief career in the City was at an end.

There followed the nightmare of his interview with Mr Pfeiffer. If anything, Pfeiffer's disappointment was worse than his anger at what Orlando had perpetrated. But when he added, at the end of the chilly discussion, conducted in the presence of two other senior members of the bank's staff, that Orlando's dealings might require an external investigation, Orlando felt his insides turn cold. It was clearly a hint at the possibility that the police might have to become involved. Yet he had never intended to do anything criminal – his sole intention had been to make a profit for the bank, and, like a spoilt, vain young man, to draw credit and attention to himself. Now all that his folly had earned him was opprobrium, the threat of criminal action, and the disgrace of immediate dismissal from Amerco West.

He was escorted from Mr Pfeiffer's office and was forced to suffer the ignominy of clearing his desk under the glances of curious and embarrassed colleagues, while the rest of the dealing room rattled on with the day's work. By eleven o'clock he was back in Kensington. His life had taken a sudden, drastic turning, and the future yawned before him, empty and meaningless. His fatuous arrogance had brought him to this. Who would employ him now? How was he going to keep up the mortgage payments, meet the bills?

Parking his car, gazing up at the windows of the flat, Orlando realised that he could no longer afford to antagonise his grandfather. He needed his money, needed the promised trust fund that suddenly seemed so precious. He was going to have to do some work to recover the ground lost by this morning's débâcle, but at least he could start by getting rid of Jo. He was sick of the whole thing, anyway. He had been a fool to let the relationship change, had really only allowed it to drift on to spite his grandfather. It had been selfish and pointless.

He mounted the stairs to the flat slowly, knowing Jo would be in, not wanting to have to face her questions, her commiserations, the sympathy and cup of tea which she would offer him. He smiled cynically to himself as he inserted his key in the lock. Perhaps he was wrong about this. If Jo was still the girl he had met long ago in a West End club, she probably wouldn't want to know him once she learned that he was penniless. He had no illusions about her.

Jo came out of the bedroom, still in her robe, looking startled.

'What are you doing home at this time?' she asked. For a moment, Orlando found himself wondering if she had someone in the bedroom. It would spare him an excuse for getting rid of her, at any rate. But no guilty lover emerged. He sighed and dumped his possessions on the sofa.

'I've lost my job,' he said.

She bit her thumbnail, then, frowning, moved towards him to embrace him, but he put up his hands. 'And there's more than that.' He sat down, and then, aware that she was waiting, said, 'I think maybe it would be best if you moved out.' He could think of no preamble, and simply said it bluntly. She said nothing, so, glancing up, meeting her gaze briefly, guiltily, he added, 'It's not working out. Nothing is. I don't know where I go from here, but I don't think it's fair to carry this thing on.'

'Fair to whom?' Her voice was clear, cold. He hoped that this was not the prelude to a row. After this morning, he did not feel he had the emotional capability.

'To either of us,' he replied. 'Look –' He reached up and took her hand, which rested unresponsively between his fingers and thumb. ' – I'd like it to go back to the way it was a year ago. When we were just friends. It was better then. You know that.'

She pulled her hand away, then shrugged. He wondered why she didn't say anything; he had expected tears, histrionics, but she was merely gazing out of the window, arms folded.

'Why aren't you angry?' he asked. 'You should be.'

She turned to look at him. 'What's the point? I suppose I've seen it coming. In fact, I don't know why I ever thought it would work out.' Again she shrugged. It was as though she felt suddenly tired. She added, 'I've always been just an idle amusement for you, haven't I, Orlando? Nothing to be taken too seriously.' Then, lifting her chin slightly and pushing her hair from her forehead, she asked, 'When do you want me to go? Today?'

'Christ, no . . .' Relieved that the thing seemed to have been so easily accomplished, he pulled her down next to him. He suddenly wanted, after the past few hours of rejection and humiliation, both to be comforted and to ease the burden of his own guilt. He held her for a moment, but she pushed him gently away, her face expressionless. 'Please . . .' he murmured, drawing her back against him. 'I want us to stay friends . . .'

She supposed, as he pushed back her robe and began to kiss her shoulder, sliding his hands over her body, that she should not be in the least surprised. He had been taught to behave in this way, to take what he wanted and leave it when he pleased, as he pleased. And she was too weak, too consumed by love and hatred, to know how to prevail against him and everything that had made him.

Later Jo left for work, and when she came home after midnight, Orlando was out. When she woke the next morning, around ten, it was to the sound of his key in the front door. She turned her head on the pillow and watched him as he came into the bedroom. Her first thought, as the edges of sleep drifted from her mind, was to ask where he had been, but she did not. It occurred to her for a brief moment that perhaps he had thought better of what he had said the day before, that maybe he wanted her to stay, after all. But as she looked at him, standing at the edge of the bed, his face drawn and tired, his hair lank and uncombed, threading the car keys between his fingers, gazing at her, she knew that that was the last thing he wanted. It was there in his eyes. She was suddenly horribly conscious of the distance between them, and knew that, where once Orlando had been a good friend, he was now a stranger.

It was a cold, sad moment as they looked at one another. There was nothing that needed to be said. Orlando turned and left the room, and Jo lay there staring at the space where he had stood, before getting up slowly and putting on her robe.

While she dressed and began to pack, she could hear him showering. When he came back through in his bathrobe she could see that he had shaved, but his manner and movements were slow, desultory, those of a man with nothing to do for the rest of the day. 'Do you want a coffee?' he asked. 'I'm making some.'

She straightened up from zipping the last of her bags. 'Yes, fine,' she said, her voice blunt, matter-of-fact.

He glanced at her luggage, then added, 'I'll give you a lift once I've dressed – to wherever it is you're going.' She thought he sounded faintly embarrassed.

She shrugged, but before she could respond the phone began to ring, and he went back into the kitchen to answer it. After a few seconds he closed the kitchen door.

He lifted the receiver and spoke, and then recognised Hannah's voice. His sense of inertia left him instantly.

'Orlando, I'm sorry to call you like this. But I had to talk to you.'

'Where are you?' he asked.

'I'm in Paris. We've been here for a month. I tried to call you at work, but they said you'd left . . . Orlando . . .' Her voice, close and clear as though she were in the next room, trailed away miserably.

'What is it? Tell me.'

287

'Oh, Orlando, I've been so unhappy since I saw you. I can't make it work with Max. Not now. We've just had row after row since we've been here. He knows it's to do with you. I told him this morning that I can't marry him . . .' Her voice was on the brink of tears. She gave a gasp, like a sigh, trying to contain a rising sob.

He said nothing for a moment. Although she had not said so, it was obvious why she had called. 'What are you going to do?' he asked.

'I don't know,' she said. 'I don't even know why I rang you . . .'

He hesitated, wondering if this was what he wanted, whether he could bear to surrender himself to the possibility of loving her all over again, of risking himself. At that moment, after recent events, he was unsure if he would ever be worth anything to anyone again. But then he knew instantly that if she wanted him, he had no alternative. And if they had argued about him, then she must want him, she must still love him.

'I'll come and get you,' he said abruptly. Whatever decision there was to be made, he realised that it had been made for him six years ago, irrevocably.

'Oh – no, Orlando, you don't have to –' Her voice was shaky.

'Shut up. It's what I'm going to do.' He scribbled down her address in Paris, reassured her, told her he loved her, and that he would be with her before the evening. After he had put the phone down, he stood staring out of the kitchen window, the realisation growing upon him that life, which had seemed so pointless yesterday, still had its possibilities. He had no idea what direction things would take, but he decided he would let the future take care of that. He would have Hannah, at any rate. He suddenly felt filled with a sense of hope.

He went back into the bedroom, his movements now swift and purposeful, and randomly selected a dark blue suit, a shirt and a tie. The first thing to do was to secure a flight to Paris as soon as possible. Jo, who had wandered into the living room during Hannah's phone call, now reappeared in the bedroom doorway.

'I'll take my things down to the car, if you give me the keys,' she said.

'What?' He looked up at her absently as he tucked his shirt into the waistband of his trousers, his face preoccupied, and then realised what she was saying. 'Oh, look,' he said, only the vaguest note of apology in his voice, 'I'm afraid I'm not going to be able to give you a lift, actually. Something's come up. I've got to fly to France today. It's a friend who's in a spot of bother. You should find the number of that mini-cab firm in the kitchen somewhere . . . oh, where the bloody hell is my other shoe . . . ?'

'To France?' She echoed his words thoughtfully. He glanced at her, and for the fraction of a second in which their eyes met, she knew. It was some other woman, someone important to him. She felt the little burning nugget of hatred within her cool and harden.

'Yes – just to help this friend . . .' His voice was light, his happiness unmistakable. As he retrieved his shoe and slipped it on, the doorbell rang. 'God, what now?' He left the bedroom, brushing past Jo in the doorway.

She stood motionless for a few seconds, thinking, then suddenly she crossed the room to where her belongings lay, ready for her departure. She unzipped one of the bags, and, after fishing intently for a few seconds, brought out a small cellophane bag with white powder in it, the same bag which Orlando had given to her on the night he had found Roger dead in his flat. Without thinking twice, she walked over to where Orlando's jacket lay on the bed, and slipped the little packet into the inside breast pocket. She patted it lightly, flattening it. It seemed only right that Orlando should have it back, now that she was leaving.

Three hours later Orlando was standing anxiously at the British Airways ticket sales desk, watching as the girl tapped methodically and with maddening serenity on her keyboard. At last she looked up. 'There is availability on the 15.50, or the 17.50.'

'Fine. I'll take the 15.50.' Only an hour and ten minutes to wait. He would be with Hannah by the early evening.

The girl began to tap her keyboard again. 'And how would you like to pay, sir?'

Two and a half hours later, the plane touched down at Orly. Orlando closed the copy of *The Economist*, which he had been trying without success to read, his mind too full of the events of the morning, and those still to come. It occurred to him, as he left the plane with the other passengers, that he hadn't checked the availability of return flights that evening, and hadn't brought even hand luggage. He would just have to hope for the best. He headed for the green customs channel, thinking about Hannah, of being with her in just half an hour, if he got the stations right, and felt only a slight gust of irritation when one of the douaniers making random searches stepped up to him and touched him lightly on the shoulder.

In her hotel room Hannah lay in the darkness, listening to the sounds from the corridor, the distant hum of Paris traffic. She had stopped expecting the phone to ring some time ago. If he was coming, he would have been here by now. She had called the airport and found out the last flight from London had arrived at six thirty. Even allowing for traffic, it could not possibly take him five hours to get here. She glanced at the travel clock on her bedside table and saw that it was a quarter past twelve. She closed her eyes and felt a cold despair settle on her. Orlando had changed his mind. He would not be coming. Why should he? Just because she had decided that she did not love Max enough to marry him, was that any reason why he should come to her? Clearly, after he had spoken to her this morning, he had asked himself this question, and this was the answer. She turned over and pressed her face against the brocaded pattern of the bedspread. Maybe this was his revenge. Maybe he had waited six years for the chance to betray her trust, as she had once betrayed his, to let her taste the loneliness and pain.

Just as she was wondering what on earth she was going to do now, the phone by the bed rang, its sudden shrillness shocking her, setting her nerve ends tingling. She swung her legs off the bed and sat there letting it ring twice more, calming herself before picking up the receiver.

When she heard Orlando's voice she felt a wave of relief flooding her, weakening her.

'Where are you?' she gasped. 'I was beginning to think something had happened . . .'

In the inner offices of Orly customs hall, Orlando leaned against the grimy grey wall and tried to ignore the fixed stare of the customs policeman who was watching him. He closed his eyes and wondered where to begin.

Hannah listened incredulously as he told her what had happened.

'But what were you doing with it?' she asked, when he told her about the heroin.

'I wasn't doing *anything* with it.' He sighed. 'I didn't know it was there. Someone put it there.' He thought briefly, venomously of Jo. 'The point is, it's a common and not very credible explanation, and I'm going to be charged. I'm going to be taken to a police station in Paris tonight, and they'll charge me tomorrow. They're letting me make this one phone call so that I can get a lawyer. Only I don't know any lawyers in Paris.' He glanced at the customs officer, who was beginning to look impatient.

By this time Hannah, as she listened, had switched on the bedside light. She picked up a pen and said, 'Tell me which police station they're taking you to. I don't know any lawyers either, but I'm quite sure Max does.'

Orlando groaned. 'Look, I'm sorry. I'm sure Max is the last person you want to ask a favour of right now, especially on my behalf –'

'True,' interrupted Hannah, 'but it's not something we have much choice about. Tell me which police station they're taking you to.'

Orlando covered the mouthpiece and tried his O-level French on the customs officer, and eventually discovered his destination that night. He told Hannah, who scribbled it down.

'Right. Now, don't worry. I'll be there first thing tomorrow, and we'll have you a lawyer by then.' She sounded crisp and reassuring, and as he put the phone down, Orlando thought bitterly how suddenly their roles had been reversed in just a few hours. But she believed him, and had offered help unhesitatingly, and for that he was grateful. As the customs officer led him off, Orlando wondered how much worse his life could possibly get, and whether his grandfather would ever speak to him again.

At Plumtree Villa the following morning, happily unaware of the calamitous events which had befallen their nephew, Cicely and Abigail were making preparations for the arrival of Abigail's new home computer. The assault on the contents of the attic was under way, and while Cicely sorted out the spare room, Abigail was foraging in the attic. It seemed that junk had been accumulating up here for decades. She dragged out a bulging cardboard box and knelt to examine its contents. Old knitting patterns of their mother's, sheaves of Anne's school exercise books, and a broken fan heater. Behind it were several ancient tennis racquets with broken gut stringing, and a sagging mock-crocodile hat box. She sighed as she stared around at the jumble of discarded objects. There seemed to be countless cardboard boxes filled with old clothing and shoes.

'These should have gone to the jumble long ago,' muttered Abigail, struggling through to the back to rummage around. Then she paused, recognised the heel of a white patent sling-back shoe, and realised that these were Melissa's things. She and Cicely had stored them up here after her death, unable then to give them straight to charity. God knows what they had ever intended to do with them. Abigail sighed. Well, that time was well in the past. They must be thrown out now. She dragged them one by one to the lip of the trapdoor, then stood there, uncertain as to how best to manoeuvre them and herself down the ladder. As she was standing there, she glanced down at one of the boxes and noticed a flowered soap box tucked in amongst some papers and books. The flowers were pink and purple and orange, a psychedelic sixties pattern that reminded Abigail vividly, just as the sling-back shoe had, of Melissa. She knelt down and pulled out the box and felt the rattle of objects, papers, within. She eased off the lid, and a faded breath of moss rose soap touched the air. Laying the lid aside, she began to go through the objects in the box. On top was a little chocolate mouse in tinfoil, which over the years had disintegrated, seeping and staining the photographs which lay underneath. There were three of these, all of Melissa and Alec. Abigail stared at them with sad curiosity. She had quite forgotten what Alec had looked like. She had only seen him four or five times in her life. He was like Orlando, yet not; his face was longer, his colouring lighter. She put the pictures aside and fished around at the other items in the box. They seemed to be various little sentimental souvenirs, presumably of things Melissa and Alec had done together. A faded programme from some concert, a tarnished bell on a chain, a cheap cigarette lighter inset with mother-of-pearl, a few more photographs of Alec on his own, even one of him astride his beloved Harley-Davidson. Abigail was about to replace the lid when she noticed the folded paper right at the bottom. She hadn't noticed it at first because it was almost exactly the same size as the box. With irresistible curiosity she pulled it out and unfolded it.

She stared at it for several long seconds before she properly comprehended its contents. It was headed 'Certified Copy of an Entry of Marriage', registration district Kensington and Chelsea, and dated June the 15th, 1965. And there were the names. Alec Leonard Bathurst D'Ewes, bachelor, and Melissa Mary Patrick, spinster. Abigail breathed very hard and raised her eyes. Then she looked down again and read the entire document, taking in every detail, even the name of the registrar. She was aware that her heart had begun to hammer. Trembling, almost missing her footing on the ladder, Abigail made her way precariously down to show the document to her sister.

'Cicely,' she called, though her voice came out as a strangulated croak. Cicely emerged from the spare room.

'What?' she demanded. 'If you think I'm going to try to move this knitting machine up to the attic on my own, you're very much mistaken. There's plenty of room for it to stay down here with your –' She stared at her sister, who was looking at her in a spectral fashion, a piece of paper clasped to her bony chest. 'What on earth is it?' she asked.

Abigail held out the paper. 'Look,' she murmured.

Cicely looked. She leaned back against the landing wall. She read it again. 'Good God,' she said, and looked up at Abigail.

'Absolutely,' said Abigail. 'Orlando isn't illegitimate, after all.'

Cicely stared disbelievingly at the marriage certificate, all kinds of doubts and wonders darting through her mind.

'But why on earth did she never tell us?' Her voice was almost a whisper. 'Why would she ever keep it a secret? She must have realised what was at stake for Orlando!'

Abigail took the paper from Cicely's hand and looked at it again, turning it over. She shook her head. 'You remember how things were at the time of Alec's death. How Sir Leonard and Lady Charlotte behaved.' It seemed so long ago, and at a very far remove from present relations between the two families. But Abigail had not forgotten the vituperation, then the coldness, the refusal of the D'Ewes to take any interest in the existence or welfare of their infant grandson. 'They didn't want to know about Orlando, remember, or about Melissa. She had her pride, too. It was we who thought they should do something for her. She was the one who utterly refused to make any approach to them. She had as little time for them as they for her. This would be the last thing she would care about.'

'But at the end? I mean, surely, when she was dying, she must have realised . . .'

'Why should she? None of us did. Even Sir Leonard assumed that things could be set right. We didn't know. Why should she?'

And now things would be set entirely right, thought Cicely. The disappointed dream had had substance all along. There had never been any doubt about it, if only they had all known.

'Then Orlando will inherit everything,' she said, looking at her sister. 'Stow Stocksley, everything.'

There was a silence. Abigail, tired of standing, sat down on the stairs. 'Well, what do we do now? We have to tell someone.'

'I suppose so,' replied Cicely. 'I think we'd better start with Leonard.'

Chapter Twenty

In a small room in the Paris police station to which he had been brought the previous night, and where he had passed an extremely miserable nine hours, Orlando was recounting his story for the seventh time to three French policemen and the lawyer whom Hannah, through Max, had managed to procure for him. He did not think even the lawyer believed his story, and he wished that the bloody French didn't have to smoke all the time. His head was aching, and he badly needed a shower and a shave.

At the end of the interview, while his laywer conferred in an unintelligible undertone with the police officers, Orlando had an opportunity to talk to Hannah.

'The point is, this girl, Jo, put the stuff in my pocket. I'd given it to her ages ago, after I found it at Roger's place, and she must have put it in my pocket –'

'When?' asked Hannah.

'Well, yesterday, just before I left to catch the flight here –'

'Why?' Her blue eyes scrutinised his face intently.

Orlando sighed heavily and wished he didn't have to concentrate on explaining more than one thing to one person in a day. 'Look, we'd had – well, we had been having some sort of an affair, and I'd finished it, and so I suppose –'

'She was living with you?'

'Well, I suppose, if you put it like that –'

'And if she would tell everyone all this, then we could possibly clear the whole thing up.'

'Ha,' said Orlando. 'I find that very unlikely. Very.'

'Tell me where I can get hold of her,' said Hannah. 'Just tell me, Orlando.' Orlando gave her the name of the wine bar in Ebury Street.

While Orlando languished in the police cells for the second night in the third arondissement, Hannah, who had caught a flight the same day for London, finally found Jo in Cuff's wine bar. She had been so intent on finding the place, and the girl, that, she realised, as she walked up to where the pretty blonde was serving a customer, she had no idea what she was going to say to her. So she asked for a glass of house white wine, and while Jo was pouring it, she said, 'You don't know me, but my name's Hannah. I'm a friend of Orlando's.' Jo looked up at her. 'And right now, he's in a police station in Paris.'

Jo stared at her for a moment, and put down the bottle. Then she smiled slowly, leaned across and said, 'Guess what? I couldn't care sodding less. That'll be one eighty.'

Hannah fished for the money. 'Come on,' she said, as Jo held out her hand. 'You don't want to do this to him.' She put the coins in Jo's outstretched palm, and Jo raised her gaze to meet Hannah's. 'They could send him to prison. And it's not a joke, you know. Maybe putting the stuff in his pocket was a joke, maybe getting him arrested at the airport and having him spend a couple of nights in the cells was, too – but that should be as far as it goes – don't you think?' Her voice was quiet, her tone level and reasonable.

Jo hesitated, then closed her fingers over the coins. 'I didn't honestly think anyone would find it. I just did it – well, in case . . . Anyway, why have you come looking for me? Why are you bothering?'

'Because I love Orlando. And because if you tell the police what you did, it'll sort the whole thing out. Please.'

Jo drew in a deep breath. 'If you ask me, far too many bloody women love Orlando.' She glanced at Hannah again, taking in

298

the cloud of soft, dark hair, the lovely face and eyes. 'Anyway, why should I go and bail him out, and land myself in it with the police?'

'You won't! If you explain everything, how you got it, where Orlando got it, that you did it just – well, just to be bloody-minded – then no one's going to do anything!'

'Oh, yeah, sure. Listen, I've got customers –'

'I swear! I talked to Orlando's lawyer. And I have a – a friend at the embassy there who's willing to pull a few strings. They'll just drop the whole thing. All you have to do is go and tell them.'

'Go and tell them! Hop on a flight to Paris and just tell them? Maybe you can afford plane fares, but I can't.'

'I'll pay,' said Hannah shortly. Jo said nothing, but moved further down the bar to serve another customer. Hannah sat sipping her wine, waiting, and after a few moments Jo came back.

'Yeah, all right,' she sighed. 'He's a bastard and I hate him, but he was a good friend once, and I don't really want him to get into trouble.'

'Thanks,' said Hannah. 'Look, I'm staying at his flat tonight, so give me your address and I'll pick you up in the morning once I've got our flights arranged.'

Jo wrote down the address of the girlfriend she was staying with and handed it to Hannah. 'I'll have to go and see my boss about getting the day off,' she said.

'All right. I'll see you in the morning.'

Hannah took a taxi to Orlando's flat. She had never been there before, and glanced around with curiosity as she took off her coat. It struck her that she really knew very little about Orlando, the kind of person he had become in the years since they had first met. She would not have supposed that Jo would be the kind of girl he would have an affair with. And that conversation they had had in the restaurant had not revealed

299

much more about him, except that he had become a more contained person, more defensive. But he was still Orlando, and because of him she had thrown over the man she had once intended to marry. She was prepared to alter her whole life on the chance that he might still love her. Too tired to think about it any more, she crept into Orlando's unmade bed and slept.

At lunchtime the next day, while Jo and Orlando were closeted in the Paris police station with three very weary French police officers, Cicely eventually managed to reach Sir Leonard at Stow Stocksley. When he answered the phone, she felt a brief flicker of the old excitement at the sound of his voice, but it was gone in an instant.

'Oh, Leonard,' she said. 'At last! I've been trying to get hold of you since Monday.'

Sir Leonard crossed the drawing room at Stow Stocksley, telephone in hand, and sat down. 'I've been in London with Anne. She's still up there, attending to a few things. I had to come back down today to deal with some problems regarding the estate.' He let out an involuntary sigh, passing a hand briefly over his forehead. He felt fatigued after his early start this morning, and his back ached with driving. It sometimes seemed to him that his new life demanded more than he possessed, in terms of energy and enthusiasm. He never stayed still for long. He had not spoken to Cicely for some time, except in the passing throng of the wedding, and the sound of her plump, capable voice recalled quieter, less stressful times, when it seemed he had been beset by fewer anxieties, and the pace of life had been more suited to his capabilities. But there was no point in dwelling on that now. Some movement at the window caught his eye, and he glanced out at the workmen, remembering the plans which Anne had set in train for the installation of a swimming pool. Damn. He wondered how long he would have to put up with the thumping and clattering and whistling and the sound of Radio 1. And the expense was going to be considerable. Cicely was saying something, and his wandering attention returned.

'I'm sorry, what were you saying, Cicely?'

'I rang to tell you that Abigail and I have made a most extraordinary discovery,' Cicely repeated. 'In the attic. When we were clearing out. Amongst Melissa's things.' Her voice was weak with nervous excitement.

'Melissa?' said Sir Leonard, totally mystified. Who on earth was she talking about? And then, from the dim recesses of long ago, came a recollection. 'Melissa,' he repeated, 'Orlando's mother?'

'That's right. And we have found –' Cicely hesitated, '– we have found Melissa's marriage certificate. Hers and Alec's.' She waited, listening. The silence was profound. She turned to glance at Abigail, who was standing next to her, anxiously shredding the edges of the Yellow Pages and making a questioning face. Then she looked away again and added, 'It's dated June the fifteenth, five months before Orlando was born.'

'Good God,' said Sir Leonard. He said it again. 'Good God. Are you . . . ? Now, look, Cicely – are you absolutely sure about this? I mean, that it is a genuine document?'

'Of course I am,' replied Cicely, faintly annoyed. 'I have checked with the registry office in Chelsea, and it is perfectly genuine. I mean, such a document isn't likely to be anything but, is it?' Silly man, she thought. This marriage business must be affecting his faculties.

'I don't know what to say,' said Sir Leonard, slowly. 'I simply do not know . . .'

'Well, naturally you must be pleased,' said Cicely. She turned to her sister and rolled her eyes heavenwards.

'Yes . . .' said Sir Leonard. 'Of course I am. I'm simply

301

rather – rather shocked.' He paused. 'Does Orlando know?'

'Well, we decided we should tell you first,' said Cicely, who had anticipated a rather more delirious response from Sir Leonard and was mildly disgruntled. 'And, in the circumstances, we thought you might like to tell Orlando. It does rather more concern your family than ours, if you see what I mean.'

'Yes. Yes, I do see,' replied Sir Leonard. 'What I suggest, then . . . what I suggest is that I have a word with my lawyer today, and then perhaps I could come over and see the document. Not,' he added hastily, 'that I doubt its veracity. I should just like to see it. Then we can see about telling Orlando.'

'Very well,' said Cicely. She thought Sir Leonard sounded a trifle distracted, as though he wasn't taking it all in properly. Still, one had to make allowances for his age.

'I will call you later today,' said Sir Leonard. 'And thank you for letting me know, Cicely. Yes. Thank you.'

He put the phone down and sat staring at the carpet. Then he looked up at the workmen passing backwards and forwards outside the window. Time had rolled back twenty-three years, and a simple scrap of paper had changed everything. All the bitterness and estrangement, the reconciliation, then the anxieties and legal consultations, the adoption, the disappointment, Orlando's disaffection . . . It had all been quite unnecessary. Why, he wondered, had Melissa never told anyone? She must have had her reasons. He recalled his own behaviour at the time of Alec's death, and then when Orlando had been born. Pride was not his personal prerogative, he supposed. And Alec – well, Alec had probably just decided to keep it quiet for a while. Only the while had turned into eternity, and silence.

He rose and walked over to the window. It seemed as though all the loose and untidy ends of Orlando's existence had, after all this time and in an instant, been ravelled up and pulled tight. It was extraordinary. Sir Leonard felt tired and perplexed, uncertain what his emotions were. He looked back over the months and years and tried to establish how things would have been if the fact of Melissa and Alec's marriage had been known from the outset. There would have been none of the nonsense which, through his own fault, had kept Orlando apart from the family for eight years. Everything would have been different. Roger would have had no expectations, no prospect of another fortune to squander. Orlando would have grown up in the certain knowledge of his future, and might have been a very different young man from the one he was today, possibly not behaving in his present foolish fashion. And himself . . . how would it have been for him? His gaze travelled round the room, and he thought for a sad, brief instant of his first wife. Well, there was no point in dwelling on all of that. The present was what was important. Cicely and Abigail had verified the marriage certificate, so he could take it that it was genuine – all that was left, after he had gone to see them both later today, was to tell Orlando. He would call him tomorrow. He felt a relief in the knowledge the momentous nature of this news would be sufficient to sweep away all the recent rancour between them.

Jo, Hannah and Orlando emerged into the rainy Paris street at the end of a very long day and stood together uncertainly on the pavement.

'Christ, what a nightmare,' muttered Orlando, blinking and rubbing a hand across his stubbly jaw. He looked at Jo. 'What on earth – what on *earth* possessed you to do something like that to me?'

'Don't you start, Orlando,' she said in a warning voice. 'Just don't bloody well start . . .'

'Come on,' interrupted Hannah. 'It's over. Whatever she got you into, Jo got you out of it.'

Orlando sighed and looked at Hannah. All his romantic notions of coming to Paris to reclaim his lost love, of being alone with her, of starting now as he meant to go on, had been completely shattered. He felt awful, he looked awful, and the effect of being lectured to by the French police had been debilitating to his ego. Still, at least she was here. Unfortunately, so was Jo.

'So, what happens now?' asked Jo nonchalantly. She was quite enjoying this situation. It was a pleasure to see Orlando at a loss.

Hannah intervened. 'Look, I'm going back to my hotel. I think you two have some things to sort out between you. I'll see you back there, Orlando. You still have the address?'

Orlando looked at Hannah blankly, then nodded. Jo stared at her as she walked away. Hannah's composure was absolute, she realised; she felt so sure of Orlando, in a way that Jo had never done.

She looked back at Orlando warily. 'Well?'

'Well, what?' Orlando shivered, glancing up and down the street, then he sighed and said, 'I think we're back to square one, Jo, and I also think that is where we should be. Where we should have stayed in the first place.' She shrugged, smiled her crooked little smile, and her eyes slid away from his. 'Don't you think so, too?'

She looked back at him, thinking about the first time that she had seen him in the night club. 'Sure. Just good friends.' She shook her head slowly. 'You haven't half got a bloody nerve, Orlando.'

'I came close to losing it not long ago, thanks to you,' said Orlando. He sighed. 'God, I need a drink. Come on, let's go and find one, then we'll see about putting you on a flight back to London.'

That night, Orlando crawled into bed and slept the sleep of

304

one utterly exhausted. He and Hannah, out of some odd, unspoken reticence, took separate rooms, and the same atmosphere of uncertainty between them lasted throughout their flight back the next day, and until they arrived at Orlando's Kensington flat late in the afternoon.

Orlando still felt weary and disorientated by recent events, and in the flat he flung himself on to the sofa and lay there in supine depression, thinking about his lost job at Amerco West, and where he would go from here. Hannah set down her small bag of possessions and took off her coat. Outside, the late November light was oppressive and leaden.

'Where are the rest of your things?' asked Orlando suddenly.

'In storage, for the present. I was going to send for everything once Max and I had got an apartment sorted out.' She shrugged.

They were both conscious of the sudden stillness in the flat, after the day's bustle of terminals and flights and taxis and traffic. In the silence of the room the space between them seemed to contract, charged with memories and present uncertainties. Hannah stood looking across at Orlando, hardly able to discern his features in the grey twilight. He raised his hand and stretched it towards her, and she went to him, sitting down slowly next to him in the crook of his knees.

'Do you realise,' he said, stroking a hand across her dark curls, 'that I haven't kissed you for nearly seven years?' She bent her head towards him, and the touch of her lips took him back in time, back to the happiness of recollected days, and for a few moments the bleakness left him utterly, and he felt peacefully certain of one thing in his life. 'You know,' he said, looking up at her, 'that I'm a completely useless human being, don't you? I haven't told you, but I lost my job the other day. I was no good at it. In fact, worse than no good at it. And I haven't a clue what I'm going to do now. My grandfather and I

305

aren't speaking, I've got no money, no prospects . . . The only thing I've got is a mortgage that I can't pay.'

'And me,' Hannah added. 'You have me.' But even as she sat regarding his features, marvelling at how much she could still love him, how lucky they were to have found one another, she could not help reflecting that life with Orlando now was not going to be quite so easy as life with Orlando the schoolboy. There were considerations beyond their mutual affection, and she realised that she had no idea how they would cope with them.

'Have I?' he asked, and kissed her again. They lay together for a time in the dimness of the room, saying nothing, each thinking their separate thoughts, the dull afternoon light settling a certain melancholy on their spirits. When the telephone rang, Orlando, filled with a sense of inertia, felt inclined to let it ring. Eventually, however, he got up and went through to the kitchen to answer it. Hannah lay back on the cushions, gazing after him, thinking.

Orlando picked up the receiver, and said, 'Hello?', his voice tired.

'Orlando – I was just about to give up!' said his grandfather's voice. Orlando's spirits sank. 'I have been calling for the last two days. Your firm tells me that you have left them –' Orlando was summoning his powers of diplomacy to explain matters to his grandfather, but Sir Leonard's voice hurried on. 'However, we can come to that another time. I have something to tell you . . .'

Orlando stood, listening as his grandfather explained about the marriage certificate, how his aunts had found it. He stared unseeingly at the branches of the plane trees etched against the grey sky, hardly daring to believe what he was being told. He asked some questions, listening attentively to the answers, marvelling at this news, that it should come like this, now, after all this time.

306

Aware that it might take Orlando a little time to absorb all that he had just been told, Sir Leonard hesitated and then added, 'I know that relations have not been good between us of late, Orlando. I have not been happy with the way you have conducted yourself, and for some reason you seem to have – well, grown angry with me.' He paused, but Orlando, listening, said nothing. 'I hope that this news means we can make a fresh start.'

He waited, and Orlando said, 'Yes, yes . . . I mean, I'm sorry for the way I've been. I think it's all going to change, though.' He thought briefly of his ignominious departure from his job, but the enormity of his grandfather's news blotted it out. 'The thing is, I can't quite believe all this . . .'

'Well, you take some time to digest it, and then perhaps you could come down to Stow Stocksley for a weekend. I think there are things we should talk about.'

'All right. Yes, I'd like to.' Orlando paused. 'What does Anne say about it all?'

'Oh, she's still in London at the moment. I haven't told her yet.'

'I see . . . Grandfather?'

'Mmm?'

Orlando hesitated, then said, 'Are you pleased – about this, I mean?'

At the other end Sir Leonard smiled. 'Yes. Yes, I'm very pleased.'

'Good,' said Orlando. 'So am I. Well, you can imagine . . .' There was a moment's charged silence, then each said goodbye, and Orlando hung up. He was still standing by the telephone when Hannah came into the kitchen. She switched on the kettle and glanced curiously at Orlando's face, which seemed to have lost its despondent look. His expression was happy and speculative. Her presence broke his thoughts and he turned to her, smiling.

307

'That was my grandfather,' he said. 'They've found my mother and father's marriage certificate.' She stared at him in disbelief. 'Do you know what that means?' She nodded, comprehension slowly dawning, and he put his arms around her and buried his head in her shoulder. 'It's all I ever really wanted, and one day it's all going to be mine. Do you realise?' He let out a great sigh of relief, then drew away from her. 'I don't have to worry any more. Oh, thank God. I can't believe it. I can't.' He kissed her lightly, the happiness within him almost uncontainable.

Hannah studied his face uncertainly. 'Are you sure about all this?'

'Of course! It's all been verified – they wouldn't have told me otherwise. Now, look, the first thing we must do is go down to Oddbins and get a bottle of champagne, and tonight I'll take you out to celebrate.' And he kissed her, thinking, as he had thought so often before, how perfect life was going to be from now on. As for his job, why worry about that? His grandfather was bound to go ahead with the trust fund now, so money wouldn't be a problem. Besides, there were plenty of jobs out there – it would just be something to fill in the time, anyway, until he became the ninth baronet of Stow Stocksley.

Later that same afternoon, Anne sat in the little curtained cubicle in the Harley Street consulting rooms, buttoning up her blouse. She slipped on her shoes and pushed back the curtain around the bed, then went to sit attentively at Mr Lampard's desk. She watched as he scribbled on her notes in his impressively erratic hand.

'"Elderly primagravida",' she murmured aloud, reading her notes upside down. She laughed and made a little face. 'That sounds pretty awful,' she added.

'It sounds worse than it is,' said Mr Lampard, smiling and capping his pen. 'It simply means that you are over thirty and that this is your first baby. Now, let us see . . .' He sat back in his chair and made some calculations with a little plastic disc. 'Yes.' He raised his eyebrows and smiled at Anne. 'Some time in June – the fifteenth, according to this little wheel of fortune.'

'It seems like a long time away,' said Anne. 'I don't frankly think I can bear another seven months of feeling like this. It's like having perpetual flu.'

'Oh, that will pass in a couple of weeks. A year from now you'll have forgotten all about morning sickness and will be raring to go again.'

'I doubt that,' said Anne, rising and slipping on her coat. 'I can assure you that this is definitely the first and last.'

Mr Lampard leaned forward and closed her notes. 'I'll be in touch with you in a week or so about the scan, and we can discuss whether you want to have any further tests.' He rose and shook Anne's hand. 'And I'd like to see you in four weeks' time, in any event. You can make an appointment with my secretary on the way out, if you wish.'

'I'd better check my diary first, and call,' said Anne. 'Goodbye.'

She left the consulting rooms and went slowly down the carpeted staircase, through the doors and out on to the street. She stood for a moment on the pavement, looking round for a taxi, and wishing she could quell the faintly bilious feeling in her throat. Well, this was going to be something of a surprise for Leonard. It certainly wasn't something either of them had planned. Perhaps they should have been a bit more careful. Still, there it was. A taxi appeared, its yellow light on, and she flagged it down. She gave the driver directions to the Belgravia flat and sat back against the seat, deliberating whether to ring Leonard from there, or let the news wait until she got back to Surrey. She gazed out at the traffic, wondering vaguely whether it would be a boy or a girl. A little girl would be nice, but how delighted Leonard would be to have a new heir to Stow Stocksley.

If you have enjoyed *An Inheritance*
here is a taste of Caro Fraser's latest book

AN IMMORAL CODE

Available soon from Orion Books
ISBN: 0 75281 169 X
Price: £16.99

Chapter 1

Charles Beecham could see the postman from where he sat at his desk, next to the stone-framed window. He knew that he himself was screened from the postman's gaze by the tumble of fading jasmine and honeysuckle leaves which partly obscured the window, and for this he felt both secretly relieved and ashamed. He was reminded of early days in his marriage to Hetty, when his heart had contracted at the sound of letters flipping on to the doormat, and at the awful sight of those cheap brown envelopes containing bills and reminders and letters from his bank manager. Even worse were the ones which Hetty had concealed, or mislaid under a jumble of overdue library books and children's belongings on the hall table. Hetty was gone. Those days were gone. But, twenty years on, the guilt and dread of financial indebtedness had returned with a vengeance.

The envelopes were no longer cheap little brown things. They were long and white, franked in the City of London, and the paper on which the demands for money were written was thick and expensive, the demands themselves elegantly phrased and gentlemanly. Just as a struggling young polytechnic lecturer in a terraced house in Maida Vale had deserved nothing more than scrappy, terse final demands for mean little sums in double figures, so it befitted a middle-aged man of independent means, living in intellectual tranquillity in his snug eighteenth-century house in the Wiltshire countryside, to receive demands from Lloyd's of London for sums that ran into tens of thousands.

He heard the flap and clink of the letter box, and watched the postman as he made his way down the long, stone-flagged path, brushing past the clumps of lavender that grew beneath the mulberry tree. It was irrational, of course, to live in the fearful assumption that each delivery of post might contain yet another reminder from his members' agents that there were overdue calls for which they had yet to receive settlement. However, when one owed money, when the yearly demands from Lloyd's were relentless and overwhelming, one lived in a perpetual state of anxiety and guilt. Gone were the days when he would stroll carelessly into the hall and stoop to pick up the mail, confident perhaps of another royalty cheque, or a letter from his agent confirming the sale of television rights to his latest work. Those might still come, Charles Beecham might still be a familiar name to the elite who cared to watch his documentaries, or buy his books, but the comfortable living which his occupation as a historian and academic had once provided him had long since been eclipsed, obscured by the fiasco of Lloyd's.

Joining Lloyd's had seemed the right thing to do at the time, back in the mid-eighties, when his finances had taken that wonderful upward swing. He no longer needed to pay money to Hetty, who had remarried some stockbroker, and the children were both past school age. His elder brother, a childless bachelor, had recently died, so that he had inherited the modest country house in which he now lived, together with a tidy little fortune tied up in gilts and treasury bonds. He had been able to give up lecturing, and to use his new-found leisure to write a series of books, which were well received. He had become established as a popular historian, and his boyish good looks, his blond curling hair, had made him a natural for television. His first BBC 2 series, on the history of the Mogul empire, had been a success. The familiarity of his face ensured that his subsequent book on the history of Assyria sold widely,

2

and a further television series followed. Successful and reasonably wealthy, he had every reason to believe that membership of Lloyd's would bring advantages in terms of both money and status. He remembered all the enticements which had been spelt out to him – making one's capital work twice, setting off losses against taxed income, an unbroken seven-year record of profits – and how he had been told that an investment of £100,000 could net him yearly returns of £15,000 or £20,000. Now, seven years later, his boyish good looks were fading slightly, and the golden hair was greying, but he was still attractive, his books still sold well, and his latest documentary attracted a healthy audience. The nice amount of additional annual income which he had been told Lloyd's would bring him had, however, never manifested. Disaster after disaster had hit the market, and now he was the embittered recipient of regular demands for money which he could no longer pay. It had never been meant to work that way. Lloyd's should have brought him in money, instead of draining him of it. And there was no way out. He glanced round at the comfortable room in which he now sat, at the carefully collected pieces of furniture, the shelves of books, and then out at the rambling garden surrounded by warm, worn brick walls, and wondered how soon he would manage to sell the house. It had been on the market for five months now.

The sound of the telephone interrupted his meditations and he reached out to pick it up. When he heard Freddie Hendry's voice, he sighed inwardly. At least, he thought, whatever bitteness he might feel about the Lloyd's business, it hadn't sent him barmy, like poor old Freddie.

'Beecham?' barked the voice.

'Freddie,' sighed Charles. 'How are you?'

But Freddie did not bother with preliminary pleasantries. 'Look, Charles, we're going to have to rally the troops over this time bar point. That ass Cochrane has been writing letters to

3

everybody, and I can see we're going to have canvass support against the rest of the committee. Now, what I propose . . .'

But Charles did not listen to the rest. He just sat, the receiver against his ear, waiting for Freddie to finish. He wished, oh, how he wished, that he had never been talked into going on this committee. Charles and Freddie, along with a couple of thousand other unfortunates, were on the Capstall syndicate, number 1766, one of the worst-hit syndicates at Lloyd's. Alan Capstall, a flamboyant Lloyd's underwriter whose successes in the seventies were legendary, had managed to underwrite a series of run-off policies involving asbestos and pollution risks which exposed his Names to liabilities of horrific, undreamt-of proportions, and had triggered the beginning of Charles Beecham's financial disaster. Of course, the Capstall syndicate was not the only Lloyd's syndicate to be adversely affected by the negligent underwriting of spectacularly bad risks. Other syndicates – Outhwaite, Pherrett, Gooda Walker – had all suffered calamitous losses. The Capstall syndicate Names had banded together to form an action group with the aim of taking legal proceedings against Alan Capstall and the members' agents. With all the enthusiasm of grievously wronged litigants, they formed a committee to oversee the matter of the litigation, and Charles Beecham, as a prominent figure, had seemed an obvious choice as a committee member. People liked the idea of having someone on the committee who was something of a celebrity. Besides, at forty-two, Charles was relatively youthful, compared to many of the Names, and it was felt he might inject a certain amount of enthusiasm and energy into the project.

Now, as he listened to Freddie Hendry's dotty ramblings, Charles felt anything but enthusiastic. When they had launched the case a year ago, his energies had been fuelled by outrage at the disaster which had befallen him, by a bitter sense of complete betrayal by an institution which he had

4

regarded as impregnable. However, the warmth of those feelings had gradually been cooled by tedious months of painstakingly slow litigation, and by the increasingly apparent eccentricities and fixations of his fellow committee members. He was still keen to pursue the litigation – anything to avert the financial nightmare which threatened to ruin his life – but he wished now that he did not have to be in any way involved in the co-ordination of the thing. It seemed that all the energies of the committee were taken up with internal wranglings and petty vendettas against their chairman, a harmless and well-meaning man by the name of Snodgrass. Freddie Hendry was one of the worst of the lot, forever ringing Charles and other members of the committee, and sending endless faxes to Nichols & Co, the solicitors, and even to Godfrey Ellwood and Anthony Cross, the counsel retained by the action group to fight their case.

'. . . did you see that article in the *Sunday Telegraph*? Perfectly obvious that Capstall is a complete crook, and worse besides. I rather think they're bugging my phone now, Charles. That happened a lot in 1981. And another odd thing. Chap came up to me three times in Wimpole Street the other day and asked me the way to Grosvenor Square. Three times! Same chap! It reminded me of the time when I was in Regent's Street, couple of years after the war, actually on my way to Garrard's . . .'

'Freddie,' interrupted Charles, 'I'm afraid there's someone at the door . . . I'll have to go . . . Yes, yes – I understood all of it. Perfectly. Well, maybe we should just leave all that to counsel. They are the experts, after all . . . No, I don't imagine that Godfrey Ellwood is related to the Ellwood whom your cousin knew in MI6 . . . You get those letters out. Super. Bye.'

He heaved a sigh of relief as he put the phone down, then sat motionless in his chair, wondering if he should go out and look at the mail lying on the mat in the hall.

*

In the living room of his small Bloomsbury flat, Freddie Hendry put the phone down and rubbed his chin. He sometimes wondered if Beecham appreciated the urgency of this whole thing. All very well for him to sit there in the country with his history books, doing his bit towards co-ordinating and so forth, but what they needed at a time like this was spirit, people prepared to fight their corner.

Freddie rose slowly and went through to the kitchen. It was small and spartan, with just the few basics – pots and pans, some crockery, a kettle, tea in a caddy, powdered milk, a packet of cereal, some tins and packets of food. He hadn't really cooked much for himself since Dorothy died. Just the odd bit of spaghetti on toast, cold tuna . . . he rather liked those Batchelor's Cup-a-Soups, particularly the pea and ham. Poor Dorothy – what would she think if she could see how he lived now? Of course, it had been the Lloyd's business which had finished her. She had never got over losing the house in Hampshire, seeing everything sold, leaving all their friends. When they had been forced to move into this poky little flat, that had been the end for her. Freddie muttered to himself, baring his teeth and jerking up his salt-and-pepper moustache as he did so, as he engaged yet again in one of his imaginary diatribes against Capstall. Capstall the smooth-talking charlatan, the crook, the swindler who had abused the trust of his syndicate members, who had cynically underwritten those asbestos risks when the evidence of mounting asbestos claims was there for all to see.

With a hand that trembled faintly, Freddie poured boiling water on to his powdered soup and stirred it carefully. He took it back through to the living room, which was sparsely furnished with a few handsome remnants of furniture from the Hampshire house. Silver-framed pictures of his two grown-up children and their families adorned the mantelpiece, and in the grate stood an old, inefficient gas heater.

From the landing outside, beyond the faceless front doors of countless apartments whose inhabitants Freddie did not know, came the distant sound of the lift doors opening and closing, then the whine of the mechanism. It was a bleak sound. On days like this, with the autumn melancholy setting in and long hours to fill, Freddie had to try hard to stave off the loneliness. At least this litigation gave him a sense of purpose. This was probably the last fight he would fight in his life and, by God, he was determined to win it. He sat down beside the telephone and fax machine and set his mug of soup carefully next to it. Freddie had got the fax machine from a second-hand office equipment shop, and he regarded it as indispensable to his work as a committee member. It seemed to him vital that he should be able to transmit his thoughts as quickly as possible to those in charge of the case. Ideas often came to him in the middle of the night, and at a time when phones would have rung unanswered, Freddie could sit in his dressing-gown, feeding in hand-written pages.

He sipped his soup and wiped his moustache, staring at the pale October sky through the window. What should his next line of campaign be? He must muster more support for his views over this time bar point. Cochrane and his quislings mustn't be allowed to get away with what they were doing. Basher Snodgrass was far too weak to be the committee chairman. Freddie had sent three faxes to Godfrey Ellwood on the subject of the time bar in the past two days, and he had the feeling Ellwood hadn't paid them much attention. Freddie suspected him of approaching this case too cynically. Well, he would try that junior of Ellwood's, Anthony Cross. The boy looked far too young to be handling such important litigation, let alone to be a barrister, but everyone assured Freddie he was tremendously good. Maybe he would pay more attention. Freddie took another sip of his soup, picked up his pen and pad of A4 paper, and began to write in his steady, sloping hand, marking the first page for the *urgent* attention of Anthony Cross, 5 Caper Court, the Temple, London.

In the buildings of 5 Caper Court, all was not as tranquil as it should normally have been on a Friday morning. True, to the eye of the idle clerk passing by on his way from Fleet Street to King's Bench Walk, or to any barrister glancing in at the windows as they hurried through Serjeant's Inn to Middle Temple Lane, the picture was ostensibly that of one of the most select of barristers' chambers in the Temple going diligently about its work. Shirt-sleeved barristers toiled over briefs and books, computers and word processors hummed and winked reassuringly, figures came and went, and all seemed testimony to a composed little world where the fees were fat and the opinions eminently learned. Among the figures which came and went, however, one moved with greater rapidity and fluster than was normal within those sedate walls.

Felicity Waller thought she would burst into tears if she couldn't have either a fag or a good swear – right now. Why couldn't Anthony look after his own effing files? She was a clerk now, not a bleeding secretary, and this stupid Lloyd's Names case of his was driving her demented. If she had to find yet another frigging Capstall file for him again – and there were 208 of the bleeding things, and more to come, apparently – she'd scream.

She tapped up the wooden stairs of chambers at furious speed in her heels, swearing under her breath, and knocked briefly on Anthony Cross's door before entering in a flurry of lycra and bad temper. Anthony Cross, one of the more junior barristers in 5 Caper Court, but presently made self-important and irritable by the cares and complexities of the case in which he was involved, was in a state of temper fit to match his clerk's.

8

'Well?' he demanded, straightening up from a swamp of documents. 'Have you found it?'

'No,' replied Felicity shortly. 'Wherever you think that file is, Mr Cross, it is certainly not downstairs.' She marched over to a stack of lever arch files that had come to resemble a small stockade.

'Don't touch those!'

Felicity ignored him and began unbuilding the stockade. Halfway down, she reached in behind and triumphantly pulled out a dog-eared blue cardboard wallet, thick with papers. She held it out to Anthony without a word, but the ominous tilt of that formidable bust and the set of those pursed lips told him that he had better search his own room thoroughly another time before setting Felicity off to scour the building for his files. Although she had started as a lowly typist at 5 Caper Court a year ago, Felicity possessed all the streetwise talents necessary for a good barrister's clerk. Henry, the chief clerk, had recognised this and made her his protégée a few months ago. Felicity was determined that the members of chambers should appreciate her new status, and not carry on treating her like a complete dogsbody. Clerks generally received respect, and Felicity wanted some of it.

'Thanks,' muttered Anthony, his hauteur somewhat dented by this incident. Then he added, 'Sorry,' and shot a look of such charming apology from those great dark eyes of his that Felicity, as she usually did after getting into a temper with Anthony, melted. Only inwardly, however, and only slightly. She still had plenty of work to do and not much of the morning left to do it in. Leaving Anthony's room and turning to go downstairs, she bumped into Leo Davies returning from a conference with counsel in Hare Court, overcoat on and papers tucked beneath his arm. He smiled as he saw Felicity's face.

'Our young Mr Cross been giving you grief, then?' he asked,

9

adopting Felicity's idiom, which was something he enjoyed doing, in a middle-aged way. He felt a sort of paternal responsibility for her since he had got her the job here. She had been his wife's secretary once but had lost that job through no fault of her own. He was glad Henry had made her a clerk, was pleased to see her doing well. He enjoyed, too, the way that her micro-skirts and generous expanse of cleavage enlivened the sombre atmosphere of chambers.

She gave him a look, thinking that you could forget Anthony's dark, pretty good looks, and give her Leo any day. His voice had a light Welsh lilt, which Felicity thought very sexy. And that chiselled face, the silver hair, the blue of his eyes, reminded her of Terence Stamp. She could die for Leo. 'Don't, Mr Davies,' she sighed. 'You'd think this Capstall case of his was the only one in the world.'

'You are seeing an up-and-coming junior in the heady throes of his first really big case. It's like a love affair. You have to make allowances.' Leo fished in his pocket for the key to his room. 'By the way, have we got a date for that Driscoll hearing yet?'

'Yeah, we did. I can't remember it off-hand, but it's in the book. I'll look it up.'

'Thanks.' She clattered off downstairs, and Leo, about to go up to his room on the next landing, paused, glancing at Anthony's door. They hadn't really had much to do with one another over the past few months. Just the odd snatch of conversation over tea, and whatever exchanges their work might necessitate. But apart from that Anthony had been careful to avoid Leo unless there were other people around. Leo could understand it. There was no real resolution to that whole sorry mess, which had begun with Anthony falling in love with Rachel, and had ended with Leo marrying her. Surely by this time he must have grown to accept the situation – whatever he imagined the situation to be. Leo wished that he could take him out, explain it to him over a drink. He didn't really understand it all himself, though. And Rachel? What did Rachel, alone in her big, beautiful house with her baby, think was going on?

Leo hesitated, then raised his hand, knocked on Anthony's door, and went in. Anthony was sitting at his desk, flicking through the file which Felicity had found for him. He had loosened his tie and unfastened his collar, and his dark hair was rumpled from where he had been running his fingers through it in concentration. As always, the sight of Anthony's vulnerable, frowning face, caught unawares at his work, had a powerful effect on Leo. He wished that he could study Anthony in that pose, gaze at his youthfulness for a long moment. But the moment passed. Anthony cleared his throat and said, 'Yes?' His voice was distant, preoccupied, as though the intrusion was slightly unwelcome. Leo could remember times when it would not have been so.

'I just wondered whether you fancied lunch round the corner. If you're nearly finished, that is.' Anthony looked back at his papers, saying nothing, and Leo added, in a slightly gentler tone, 'We don't seem to have talked to one another properly in a long time.'

Anthony looked up. 'I'm afraid I've still got rather a lot of work to do,' he said. It was true. Next Wednesday they were in the House of Lords, and there were still documents which he had not read. 'Sorry,' he added stiffly.

Leo paused, his hand on the doorknob, then nodded. 'Right,' he said. 'Some other time.' He closed the door, and Anthony sat listening to the sound of his feet on the stairs as Leo made his way to his room. He did not resume his work. He sat staring at the far corner of his room, at the stacks of documents. He remembered how he had sat in this room five years ago, when he had been Michael Gibbon's pupil and new to 5 Caper Court, and had listened out for Leo's tread on the stairs, hoping that he would stop and look in. He had always

11

been able to tell Leo's footsteps; they were more rapid than the others. His heart used to beat painfully if the footsteps passed the room and went on upstairs. He could feel his heartbeat beginning to slow now. The sight of Leo always affected him in this way. Nothing about him ever grew stale or too familiar. His presence was always electrifying. But then Leo seemed to have that effect upon most people. Look at Rachel.

Anthony swivelled round in his chair and stared out at the grey autumn sky above the roofs of the Caper Court buildings. Of course, it was nothing to do with Rachel. Anthony had been in love more than a few times, and he couldn't pretend that he hadn't got over it by now. Naturally he had. Well, he assumed he had – he hadn't seen her since just before she and Leo got married, and that was nearly a year ago. Admittedly, he had been steering clear of women since then, but that was largely to do with the burden of this Lloyd's case, and the amount of work he had to put in. No, it was not Rachel. It was not even the fact that she had married Leo. Rather, it was that Leo had married her. That he had married anyone. Anthony thought back to the times that he and Leo had spent together, times when his friendship with the older man had seemed the most passionately important thing in the world. That was where he felt betrayed. He rubbed his hands over his tired face and turned back to his work, gazing unseeingly down at the papers before him. So why hadn't he said yes just now? Why hadn't he just gone for lunch with Leo, let him work his old magic, maybe make things as they had once been? God knows, he missed his company. Anthony sighed. It was because, he told himself, that now Leo was married all that was over. It should stay that way. What was the point of resuming a friendship which seemed to produce nothing but pain? He put his elbows on the desk and propped his head between his fists, and stared down at the page in front of him:

12

. . .a line slip is a device whereby a broker places 100% of a maximum limit for pre-defined classes of business, and is then able to cede risks to this line slip upon the approval of the rate and terms by the first two subscribing underwriters without having to see the remainder of the underwriters subscribing to the line slip.

He read this sentence over and over until it made sense, and Leo's visit had faded from his mind. Five minutes later, Felicity came in with a few pages of paper.

'This fax just came in for you. It says it's urgent, so I thought I'd bring it up.'

'Thanks,' said Anthony. He picked up the first page and recognised the name of the sender. It was the daft old geezer who had been deluging Godfrey Ellwood with missives. Anthony groaned. Now it was obviously his turn. With a sigh, he began patiently to read Freddie's fax.

In his own room, Leo chucked his papers on to the bare surface of his desk and sat down, still in his overcoat. He sighed and leaned back wearily in his chair. There had been a time, on Fridays such as this with the weekend ahead of him, when his life had been his own, the next two days an expanse of time in which he could do as he pleased. He made a wry face as he thought of all the things which it had once pleased him to do. It had been those very things – the lovers, the rent boys, the occasional enjoyable ménage à trois in his country home, the pleasurable, careless dissipation of his private life – which had threatened a mere twelve months ago, to wreck his career, to blight his prospects of taking silk, of moving on in his profession as a barrister. In this most proper of worlds image was all. At the time, salvaging his respectability in the face of growing rumours had seemed like the most important task in the world. Yet how might it have been if he had not married Rachel? Leo often wondered this. But it was too late for wondering now. He had not intended to marry her. Not at first. She had been just a good-looking young woman, a solicitor from one of the big City firms, and he had hoped that the fact of having her as his girlfriend would be enough to scotch the rumours which might have wrecked his prospects of becoming a QC. The fact that Anthony had been in love with her had not mattered. Of what significance was that, compared to his own career? Then Rachel had got pregnant, and the rest was history. He had married her, and there she was at home now, waiting for him, with their child, a weight in his heart and in his life.

Leo sighed and looked up across the room at the familiar, warm rectangular shapes in the Patrick Heron painting which hung on the wall opposite. He remembered purchasing the picture at the Redfern Gallery eight years ago, as well as the two Tabner drawing which hung next to the bookcase, with some of the money he had earned from a large case. It was his habit, if a case was particularly lucrative, to buy himself a painting, or a piece of sculpture, by way of reward. It harked back to his time as a boy in Wales, when he would reward himself with extra sweets, or a comic, if the money from his gardening jobs exceeded the amount designated for his savings account. Gazing at the picture, then at the drawings, it occurred to Leo that this room in chambers was now the only place in the world which was utterly, absolutely his own.

His mind returned to Rachel. She was going to say something to him soon, he knew. He could see it in her eyes. It was merely extraordinary that she had not said anything before. Where did she think he went on those nights when he did not come home? She never asked. Her silence was astonishing, unsettling. In many way, he had hoped that there would be some sort of confrontation before now, that the issue might be resolved. The issue of their respective lives, and of where they went from here. He thought of his infant son, Oliver, and a certain guilt touched his heart momentarily. He did not want

14

to be like his own father, did not want to desert his son and leave a painful space in his life for ever.

He sat motionless for a moment, toying with the crimson ribbon tied round the papers on his desk, then picked up the telephone and rang Rachel to tell her to book a babysitter, that they would dine out that night.

All Orion/Phoenix titles are available at your local bookshop or from the following address:

Littlehampton Book Services
Cash Sales Department L
14 Eldon Way, Lineside Industrial Estate
Littlehampton
West Sussex BN17 7HE
telephone 01903 721596, *facsimile* 01903 730914

Payment can either be made by credit card (Visa and Mastercard accepted) or by sending a cheque or postal order made payable to *Littlehampton Book Services.*

DO NOT SEND CASH OR CURRENCY.

Please add the following to cover postage and packing

UK and BFPO:
£1.50 for the first book, and 50p for each additional book to a maximum of £3.50

Overseas and Eire:
£2.50 for the first book plus £1.00 for the second book and 50p for each additional book ordered

---

BLOCK CAPITALS PLEASE

name of cardholder .... *delivery address*
.... *(if different from cardholder)*

address of cardholder ....
....
....
....
postcode .... *postcode* ....

☐ I enclose my remittance for £...............................

☐ please debit my Mastercard/Visa (delete as appropriate)

card number ☐☐☐☐☐☐☐☐☐☐☐☐☐☐☐☐

expiry date ☐☐☐☐

signature ....

prices and availability are subject to change without notice